NO MATTER, NO GRAVITY

By

Martin E. Goodman

DEDICATION

For Maggie.

To my dearest friends
Thank you, for
everything.

Martin x.

CONTENTS

ACKNOWLEDGMENTS

My thanks to Alex White for her advice on the structure of the
book together with literary guidance.

Also my thanks to Lynne Pearson who provided drama and life to
the dialogue.

CHAPTER 1

An Unstable Future

S tuart Ashley sat at his desk looking over the Thames through the large sliding window, twilight transformed the scene and hundreds of lights appeared, reminding him of the office industry across the water that would continue well into the evening. It was a smart modern desk of wild oak and chrome that was designed to incorporate tomorrow's technology, so the lady in the posh designer shop said. Stuart wasn't really sure he liked it, but Rose was enthusiastic which was good enough for him.

They had decided to live together just three months ago and jointly agreed that the apartment should have none of the past. It had meant that they both kept some sentimental stuff in store; for Stuart it was just a couple of cardboard boxes with photos and mementos of his past life. That's it, he thought, my whole life condensed into a couple of boxes whereas Rose needed a container for all her things. He smiled to himself; he was known across the globe for his discovery; a discovery that has changed the world but not necessarily for the good, it amounted to two boxes of his past.

He rearranged the desktop for the nth time that day. His reading papers were in three piles by size, all neatly arranged against the back of the desk, equidistant apart. The telephone was in the opposite corner with his mobile alongside it. The screen and keyboard were angled at forty-five degrees to the length of the desk and there was a miscellany of desk trivia like a stapler and penholder that were hidden behind it. It still felt wrong; and unconsciously he began to consider a new layout. Against all this neatness in the centre of the desk rested a large A1 paper pad that was covered in notes, doodles and diagrams. This was where Stuart dumped his thoughts. He looked at his watch, it was late afternoon and Rose wouldn't be back until about eight that evening. It was a perfectly good Rolex that he wore most of the time since he couldn't bear to use the beautiful Patek Philippe that he stored in the safe, old memories and sad memories.

Rose had a very senior job in the Cabinet Office. She played it down as a mundane civil servant but those who knew her understood the power of her intellect and her ability to provide outstanding counsel on the political world stage. She worked with Sir Peter Dawson, an immensely powerful individual who had the ear and respect of senior government ministers as well as their shadow counterparts. Their department had a wide brief that was guided by the inner Cabinet, usually providing support and advice to departments that were floundering on some issue or, most importantly, taking ownership on behalf of the Prime Minister when big cross-departmental issues arose. Sir Peter had been head of various secure services and naturally became the PM's unofficial coordinator of the UK SIS. When Stuart had first come into contact with Sir Peter he thought that he was a friend and supporter, only to be shafted by him; that betrayal nearly cost Stuart his life. They had be reconciled about a year ago with a certain degree of forgiveness on Stuart's behalf but never to be forgotten caution in dealing with him. The reconciliation had been in Canada in surreal circumstances and that was when he became reacquainted with Rose.

Rose's office in Whitehall was a convenient journey from their penthouse on the south bank at Battersea. Their choice of penthouse had been carefully vetted by MI5 given the previous kidnap attempts on Stuart. It was a new building and was at a stage where the builder had been advised on changes to accommodate the security that Stuart needed. Those changes included secure parking, a protected entrance as well as premises for security personnel alongside various monitoring equipment. Of course, Stuart and Rose knew about the arrangements, but security was now a way of life to both of them and together they ignored its implications.

His discovery demonstrated that gravity was not a single force; indeed, it was still unclear how many components it did contain.

Stuart had found a way to harness one of those components into something he termed LeviProp which provided completely new drives for use in transport. The discovery went viral about 18 months ago rendering all previous power drives from the internal combustion engine to jet engines completely obsolete. Stuart had anticipated the global impact of the discovery but naively thought he could use it to create a universal benefit to all: and so the turmoil started.

The application of LeviProp did grow quickly but not in ways that Stuart expected, he had anticipated a completely new class of vehicles designed around the drive. Instead it was used as replacement engines into existing vehicles, with the likes of Mercedes and Boeing capitalising on the opportunity.

OPEC saw the end to their economic prosperity and so reduced their production alongside an ultimatum through the UN that they needed funding guarantees for the next 20 years to help them to adapt to a time without the need for oil. It was plain old blackmail and it caused a protectionist backlash with sovereign funds being frozen and, in some instances, seized. The global economy, fragile at best, became unstable. All of that happened over six months ago and the world limped along with the poorest countries being disadvantaged the most.

Like the rest of Europe, the UK Government had implemented emergency powers around that time. Imports were quickly impacted with some food becoming rationed, there were always long queues for fuel and random electricity outages became a way of life. Only time would rebalance the global economy but how long would people put up with the hardship? The UK had a LeviProp manufacturing plant, which was a joint enterprise between the government and Stuart's Company. The plant was running at maximum capacity with two new plants about two months away from commissioning. Very few countries had the facilities to make LeviProp units, but the UK government had created a fast-track license programme to support manufacturing overseas.

It's pointless to speculate which countries were hit hardest by the crisis; the US seemed to maintain a strong position and Stuart knew why: at the outset of his discovery the US had set up a clandestine facility to exploit LeviProp. He knew through Peter Dawson that

Russia, India and China weren't far behind. If this situation wasn't bad enough, the discovery kicked off a new military race where missiles were outdated by the speed and power of LeviProp. Military planes, ships and land vehicles were all affected leaving existing forces with massive weaknesses; the resulting destabilisation was so frightening that people tried to put it out of their minds.

Against this backdrop Stuart's security was increased since there had been numerous threats against him. There was also speculation that he had some knowledge, some insight that he was withholding that could resolve things. In truth Stuart did have some further research around the discovery but it would enhance and extend the power. Stuart felt helpless; he had created this chimera but couldn't control it. It didn't matter how often he suppressed the feeling of regret he still couldn't think of another way that would have avoided the issues facing the world today. Naively, he had looked on the discovery through a lens of the benefits to mankind rather than the cynic's lens of who has the most to lose… or gain.

Rose had been closely involved in the UK Government's exploitation of LeviProp but had asked to be detached from her role as her relationship with Stuart grew. It was a good move since they could share their thoughts and Stuart's emotional burden without influence.

Normally Stuart would commute to the LeviProp Research Centre in Farnborough, but that day he needed some space to further refine his current thinking. The Research Centre had two units; one was based on pure research, and the other was on applied work. At the moment much of the emphasis was on the applied area with a particular focus on getting safe drive engines out the door as soon as possible. Stuart was an engineer at heart and mostly enjoyed the applied research, especially the work on new engines for space travel, but much of that work was on the back burner given the economic priorities.

His 'paired gravitational model' worked; the mathematics worked, and scientists across the globe had supported his proof; it had become accepted theory in a matter of months. Although only a few people had heard him voice concerns, he had a nagging feeling that there was more to his theory; yes, the mathematics worked, but supposing he had bounded his ideas unnecessarily. Initially he had

4

focused on finding more paired forces but more recently, for some inexplicable reason, he widened his thinking to something he termed a 'paired lattice model'. Fortunately, there was enough talent at Farnborough to help him, although they kept their ideas to a few trusted colleagues.

He was deep in thought trying to think of ways to create an experiment to prove his idea when he heard the buzz of the electronic entrance system and Rose came into the room. She wore her government uniform, a black sexless trouser suit with her long hair scragged back as an afterthought. Stuart could see the real person behind the disguise; he always thought of her as a ballerina with a supple frame that brought a natural grace. He face almost held a smile with her wide lips and her twinkling yet piercing grey-blue eyes. She put down two heavy black briefcases.

"You're home early, got a lot of work?" he said looking at the cases.

"Only one of them is mine, the other's for you," she replied, looking a bit more serious.

"Beware of public servants bringing gifts?"

"Believe me, you really don't want this gift; the PM asked me to deliver it to you before you see her tomorrow."

Intrigued, Stuart took the case and scanned his left thumbprint, then entered his security code. Inside was a red numbered file with security coding.

"Enjoy your reading," Rose went to the bedroom to change out of her uniform.

From the bedroom she heard Stuart yell, "I just don't fucking believe it! Fucking madness. Talk about history repeating itself." She went back to the sitting room to see Stuart standing by the window nodding his head in disbelief. Rose had knowledge of the documents' contents but had not been involved in its production. He had just read the letter from the PM requesting him to attend a meeting at the MOD the following day to endorse a submission to the UN limiting weapons development using LeviProp.

It wasn't a long report, perhaps 20 pages at most, with half of it containing various satellite photos and prints from various image detection and analysis devices. Stuart reviewed the report distribution list; apart from the PM, it included a number of key Cabinet members, various heads of security services, as well as Chiefs of the Defence Staff and key members of the scientific community including Stuart; its authorship was unknown. Interesting, Stuart thought, this is a UK only report.

The Contents page was simple and stark.

Section 1) Russian Drone – findings

Section 2) Strategic implications

Section 3) Possible scenarios

Section 4) UK Options

Section 5) Supporting Evidence

Over the last year most countries had been busy applying LeviProp for commercial reasons, Russia however had been applying its efforts to military use and very successfully. The report clarified the historic sophistication of drone development in Russia in terms of guidance systems, defensive capability, and weapons payload. It had now developed a number of small LeviProp drives, which made global multi-drone warfare possible. The report showed that Russia already had more than a thousand of these devices; they fly at extraordinary speeds, much faster than conventional missiles and at extreme low level, just a few feet off the ground: the concept of missile warfare was completely redundant, as was ground based warfare.

Stuart skipped to the back of the document, to look at the various images; sure enough, they showed drones of various sizes with smallest being scaled at just 400 millimetres. They were sited in at least six separate locations, although the analysis was careful to say that they believed that there were a lot more sites under construction. He could barely take it all in. In such a brief time, the Russians had fundamentally shifted the nature of warfare; moreover, the report showed that the UK defence people hadn't predicted it either.

Although GCHQ had constructed the report, a lot of the intelligence had come from China with additional information from India, Stuart couldn't figure out why this alliance had arisen. Why were the UK, India and China collaborating? Moreover, it was disconcerting that no mention was made of traditional allies. There were no surprises in the Strategic implications section; Stuart knew the potential of LeviProp and the idea of a miniature drive carrying a small explosive or nuclear device made his blood run cold. Imagine, thousands of drones tightly targeted arriving in seconds without any defensive mechanism to stop them.

It was worrying that the Scenarios section was lightweight and yet, because of the very power that the Russians now held, they had almost limitless options for their global ambitions. The UK options section was designed to stimulate the debate since it posed a series of questions and possible answers. Stuart found himself mentally asking questions behind the questions posed. Why wasn't Uncle Sam involved? What about Europe? What was Russia's agenda or for that matter China and India? As he read on he found the document combining one option with another; it was a complex piece of analysis. As he expected, one component of the options was to find a way to neutralise LeviProp.

"The UN approach is useless, and I am going to tell them so; they should know anyway after the last fiasco."

"Easy, Stuart, the circumstances are different from the last time, it has to be worth a try."

"The Russians didn't attend last time, I expect they were busy miniaturising LeviProp already. The Chinese were obstructive and the US fucked me over. Why should I care?"

"Come on, Stuart, I know you have some new ideas on LeviProp, perhaps it can help?"

"What I don't understand is there is no reference to the US. It as if they have been excluded."

"I don't have any inside knowledge, our relationship with our counterparts is as strong as ever. Perhaps it was a precondition from the Chinese?"

"You know we would ignore it, even if it was."

"The only way to get some answers is to go tomorrow."

"I have no choice, you know I will."

He recalled the previous time the UN had tried to get some

global harmony into the application of LeviProp; it was called the Tangent Programme. The discovery was in its infancy and had only really been public for about six months. He was held prisoner in a safe house in the US for his own protection and the UK had done nothing, no support, and no contact. Various countries were dubious of his discovery or quietly working to gain advantage of it. There was no trust at the meetings and the hostility towards Stuart, the creator of this global dissonance, was evident.

"Rose, this time I'm better prepared."

Where was Edmund Burke when we needed him?

CHAPTER 2

Tangent

(Roughly 18 months before)

S tuart took a lift from the basement car park to an unmarked
floor. His escorts took him through a long corridor and ushered
him into a large conference room. As he entered, all
conversations stopped, and he became the focus of attention; I feel
like a condemned man, he thought, sensing the surrounding hostility.
He was escorted to a seat at the smart oak conference table and
surveyed the delegates seated around. They are the great and good of
the world, or perhaps just the great and powerful, I doubt many of
them are good. Not one of them showed any emotion as each group
returned to their previous discussion.

All told, there were ten representatives of the UN Emergency
Taskforce that had gathered together, with a Chairman. These people
in theory represented all member countries of the UN, it was bit like
the Security Council where all the big players dominate, however it
was fair to say that there had been a full UN vote in favour of this
group managing all the interests. Over the last two months the UN
delegates had held many meetings - some public, mostly private - to
determine their positions on the Tangent Programme. Originally, I
had named the project 'Levelling Mankind', it was a silly name, but it
was exactly the outcome I wanted; in hindsight it seemed naive. I
wanted my discovery to benefit all mankind, but I forgot about

politics, power, economics, nationalism and every other aspect of behaviour that gets in the way of universal progress; nevertheless, I was here to uphold that position.

Stuart took some time to look at his surroundings. Each of the ten delegates had two people immediately behind them and in close contact, presumably advisors. Stuart thought and noted that there was significant space between each delegate as if they each wanted to avoid being overheard in their deliberations. On the outskirts of the room there were a few notetakers and a couple of people who looked as if they came from some security service. There were glass-panelled sections in the two long walls behind which sat even more people in subdued lighting; Stuart could only guess that they were more observers or translators. I bet there is no press here though!

Stuart's seat was positioned on the left of the Chairman, Lawrence Banard, the previous Prime Minister of Canada. He was around the mid-fifties, overweight and thinning, although his marvellous sideburns more than compensated for lack of hair on top. His eyes never remained still for long, which made you feel that he was uncomfortable and insecure. I couldn't help but notice his small feminine hands that just didn't fit with his swarthy complexion. Lawrence's English had a hint of French in it.

"How are you feeling my friend?" he enquired.

"Like I am being set up," Stuart replied, "I haven't seen my colleagues or friends or family for months, despite Uncle Sam telling me it's for my own good."

"We will be starting soon," he said, ignoring Stuart's comment. He hadn't had any freedom for weeks, of course he was a prisoner, and everyone seemed complicit in his confinement – perhaps he was becoming paranoid, he thought. Following the kidnap incident, this was the first time he had been 'allowed' out of the house, which had been his cell for the last fifty odd days. He says cell, but actually it was a pretty fantastic mansion with every possible facility somewhere north of New York City near a place called Glens Falls, wherever that is; his 3-hour journey by black limo started at 6am this morning and followed the I87 to New Jersey when he lost his bearings completely. Anyway, since he had some serious minders around him all the time, who cares about the journey? Indeed, it was more interesting to see how smoothly they negotiated the rush-hour traffic, finally turning into a fairly innocuous underground carpark.

At least by sitting next to Lawrence Stuart didn't quite feel in the dock, although he was trying hard not to look nervous. His problem is that whenever he is nervous his mouth goes dry and he has to keep swallowing, so his Adam's apple is doing some sort of public dance. Then he adds his red-hot ears and sweating brow and it's a dead giveaway to his current condition; if only he had some papers like everyone else then he could pretend to read them!

"I feel like I should I have a lawyer here to represent me," Stuart said to Lawrence. He was sure he saw the delegate to his left smile at this request.

"Your work, your discoveries, has to be viewed in an international context. The potential impact on the world economy and political stability not to mention security, means we need to find a solution that meets the national interests of all the major powers."

"But the genie is out of the bottle," Stuart said, "and anyway there is now enough information on the web that you can't control it."

"That's the purpose of this meeting," he said, "to do just that — control it."

"You are just delaying the inevitable, do you think that each of the countries around the table is going to sit tight and twiddle their thumbs?"

"Ladies and Gentlemen, I call this meeting to order," he said, to no-one in particular. Lawrence read from a prepared script. "Firstly, I would like to thank ALL those member countries for agreeing that this nominated group, this Taskforce, would represent all their interests over this critical matter. All the minutes of this meeting will be available for secure access to all participating members. As you all know there are a few member countries that have chosen not to support this initiative and our handling of their position is also part of our agenda."

"Can we start with the assumption that everyone is in agreement with the 'Implications Paper' that followed on from the meeting last Friday?"

There was general nodding of agreement around the table.

"Can I see this document?" Stuart asked.

"Did you not get a copy?" said Lawrence, clearly annoyed that someone had dropped a ball. "Give him your copy," he said to the person on his right who must have been his secretary, "and find out why a copy was not given to Mr Ashley". Stuart was handed a thin beige folder entitled 'TANGENT Programme – Implications'. It was clearly a UN headed document with 'Confidential' emblazoned all over it. Stuart noted that it was numbered copy with some sort of optical marking to ensure it could not be reproduced. This copy belonged to a Colonel G. Banham – the secretary, he presumed.

"Mr Ashley, I don't intend to delay this meeting, but I will ensure that we have an extra one hour at lunchtime to enable you to catch up. Essentially this document represents the guiding principles that will be put in place through the UN to ensure that your discovery does not destabilise the world economy."

Stuart glanced over the document to see if he could pick up any salient points that he needed to know over the next couple of hours before lunch. He noted that Colonel Banham had highlighted several sections himself in bright pink; the Colonel obviously had another role as well as secretary since his highlighting particularity focused on Oil-based Infrastructures as well as National Security.

The UN Taskforce had concentrated on five operating principles; Knowledge Transfer, Commonality, Sustainability, Economics, and Operational Rules. There was also a Section on International Rules as well as a final Section on Transition. Many months ago, Stuart had given input to the first two sections.

"Mr Bruckner, you want to say something?" Lawrence has seen the light flashing on Edward Bruckner's desk. Bruckner was the US delegate and Stuart remembered him from the recent past. Before that he had been the US National Security Advisor although he didn't know his exact role now.

"Mr Chairman, I know many people have spent a lot of time developing this document and a very worthy one it is too." Stuart was waiting for the BUT…

"But… it's all about trust. There is no way anyone or any country can police this stuff and in a free market every person or country is going to do their best to ensure they are not disadvantaged by these new discoveries."

What he really means, Stuart thought, is that the US want to be advantaged and is not going to be hidebound by a set of rules. Bruckner had all the signs of a tough negotiator. His dress sense was conservative with an expensive grey suit, white shirt and striped tie. His tailor did deserve an award for disguising his overweight frame but couldn't disguise his chubby face, which looked grey to match his suit. Perhaps it was the combination of the tightly cut grey hair together with the steel glasses that enhanced his steely grey eyes?

His advisors were a matter of inches from him; Stuart did recognise Professor Leo Catani from MIT, as one of the original academic team he had hoped would support his ideas on ensuring everyone benefitted from the discovery. The other person alongside Bruckner looked like the very caricature of a Pentagon Officer although one sensed that he was there for a very clear purpose.

"The US Government supports the need for technical inter-operability as well as a need to ensure any future developments do not cause an environmental catastrophe, after all we don't know what we have got on our hand yet, do we?"

"The Operational Transport Rules should be common where possible, but we will continue with our own national rules like driving on the right for example, and International Rules must apply absolutely, it would be chaos without flight lanes. The rest, Gentlemen, we will not endorse, and don't believe it is in world interests to try and create such rules."

Stuart was thinking over this position when Lawrence invited the Chinese delegate to speak; he tried to read his name card, it looked like Táng Hu. He was a sharp, angular man who one imagined always had order in everything he did. His papers were laid out in a structured way, almost symmetrical, defining his ownership of that part of the table, his boundary.

His English was good with a slight US twang, maybe time spent at Harvard? He clearly had prepared notes in front of him but Stuart's eyes were drawn to the woman on his left. She was perhaps around 40 with typical business dress giving nothing of her personality away, her hair was tied back tightly as if it were the only way to get rid of an encumbrance but it was her face that entranced Stuart. She was just beautiful, not pretty, not perfect, but somehow her nose, her mouth, her eyes, her bone structure and complexion were in such harmony that you could not fail to admire her. Stuart's mind returned to Táng Hu, who had been talking through each of operating principles.

"In summary, Chairman, the team from China have done their best to participate and contribute to the TANGENT programme and we too feel that we cannot underwrite such stringent controls on our country. Mr Ashley's discoveries re-define so many fundamental parts of our lives that the People's Republic must ensure that they protect their own interests. Where there are common international issues then we will support and participate in such initiatives."

As Táng Hu was speaking, the woman was pointing to the papers in front of him with her pen. Táng Hu was trying to show his leadership and authority but kept glancing down at her pen, which suddenly burst into action. Táng Hu paused, as if to reflect. "In fact, at this time we will need to focus on internal developments and I should say that any international issues such as Sustainability and Interoperability will be subject to normal evaluation before we can commit any further. We will of course wish to be fully involved in future UN developments." Táng Hu and the woman exchanged looks of agreement.

So, a very beautiful and powerful lady, thought Stuart, with a few strokes of a pen, the Chinese Government had completely disassociated themselves from the TANGENT recommendations and yet remained at the table... just in case.

It was now just before 11am and two of the major world powers had essentially taken the same line, that their own self-interest was the most important policy which, sort of, explains why there will never be world peace, thought Stuart rather cynically. At this rate I won't need that extra hour to read the TANDEM report, I wonder who will go next? Stuart had to admire Lawrence, he was trying to ensure a full and balanced discussion but it looked like it was just turning into a series of defensive protectionist speeches. Where was all this going? The rest of the delegates seemed more relaxed at speaking next; perhaps they had been waiting to get a clear steer from the USA and China before committing their positions.

"Who would like to speak next?" Lawrence asked, the UAE delegate put his hand up and pressed the indicator light as well.

The UAE Delegate, Rahul bin Moussa, had been elected to

represent the major Arab oil-producing countries as well as most members of OPEC. This should be a worried man, thought Stuart, he is trying to represent a group of countries that have very different agendas but are linked through one common interest; keeping the oil income rolling in. Likewise, to ensure there is no bias to any of the countries he seemed pretty low-level for such a gathering.

Rahul spent a significant time going through the principles in detail. It was a painful process since he was reading it from a prepared text, which he had not rehearsed. There were quite a few questions at the end of his statement mainly around clarifying the exact meaning that he had failed to make. Lawrence felt compelled to sum up for Rahul.

"So, can I just check that you fully support the recommended action behind the following TANDEM principles? One, that all members should pool their knowledge in a transparent way and without reservation. Two, we will devise a set of standards to ensure interoperability of developments country by country. Three, that we will initiate a programme to investigate the Sustainability implications of Mr Ashley's discovery." It's got to be better for the planet than oil, thought Lawrence. "Four, that there will need to be a careful transition period of at least 20 years to enable the financial markets to absorb the change. In addition all sovereign funds based on oil futures will need guarantees over that same period."

"Excuse me, Chairman, but who in hell is going to pay for that?" A heated interruption at last, Edward Bruckner was making his point clear.

"For the last sixty-odd years we have lived with an economic stranglehold based on oil, if you think Uncle Sam is going to put his hands in his pockets to the tune of trillions of dollars to protect the economies of those countries that have benefited, then think again."

Rahul had been conferring in a rapid discussion with his two sidekicks who were seriously animated over Bruckner's outburst. Rahul said, "On behalf of the countries I represent, we know that you will need our oil for a least another decade but if you are not prepared to support us in this transition we may have no choice but to reduce our production."

Everyone in that large room suddenly sensed the sheer scale of the issues and the consequent tensions were starting to show. It was difficult to see whether the contagion in that room had spread to the people behind the glass panels but Stuart would bet it had.

"Ladies and Gentlemen, this fourth point is a potential problem to all of us," said Lawrence, retaking control. "Can I ask that we hold the overall discussion on transition until everyone has had their say?" Lawrence didn't wait for consent, instead he moved on, not a bad Chairman after all, thought Stuart. Bruckner waved his hands in exasperation.

"Moving to point five, you support the work needed to put common national operating rules together as well as ensuring that there is a clear protocol surrounding the international operation. Can we record this formally as your position?"

"You can, and thank you, Chairman," confirmed Rahul.

As Lawrence was conferring with Colonel Banham over some admin, Mark Briand, the French delegate requested to speak.

"Monsieur Briand, we have a few minutes before we break for lunch, can you make the French position clear by then?"

"You seem very keen to have lunch, Lawrence," Stuart quipped as an aside.

Lawrence leaned over and in a lower voice said, "I am giving you as much time to consider your position as I can." Stuart was concerned... what position, he thought? Was he expected to defend his work or were they all looking to ways of managing his future. Stuart's paranoia returned, as did the sweats. I must grab some time with Lawrence and maybe the British delegates could help, although thus far Sir Peter Dawson had been very quiet.

Stuart had worked with Sir Peter when the UK supported the project many months ago before his incarceration in Glens Falls and he had liked him immediately. He was a man who somehow managed to give you a feeling of friendliness, even kindness, and when he spoke it was often interlaced with tinges of humour. It wasn't that he took things lightly, and for those who thought his levity was shallow, they missed the point; Sir Peter just had an extraordinary gift of being sharp and to the point, but in such a disarming way that barriers relaxed, and dialogue flourished. A true politician, thought Stuart, a friend to everyone but you couldn't help but wonder when the smiling crocodile was going to bite your leg off, and yet Stuart still liked the man and had trusted his support over the last year.

Stuart's concentration returned to Mark Briand, he spoke English with a very heavy accent not typical of so many of his countrymen but harder and guttural. Perhaps it's to ensure nothing is lost in communication that so many French avoid using English or perhaps it's French pride in the diplomatic legacy of their language. Still, Mark Briand was making the French position very clear. He was a small and wiry man with tight black curly hair and a sallow skin, which made his impeccably white shirt, seem so very white he could have been in a commercial for washing powder. His exquisite blue suit and expensive striped tie made him top in Stuart's award for best-dressed man around the table, and Monsieur Briand knew it. Shame it can't make up for his overlarge nose and wide nostrils thought Stuart rather bitchily.

"...and so, we have no hesitation in supporting the TANGENT recommendations," said Briand. Did I just hear that someone around this table is supportive of ensuring every nation benefits from the discovery? I must have misheard.

"Indeed, we do not believe that the recommendations go far enough," continued Briand, "we have a unique opportunity here to ensure that these developments are only used for peaceful means. Some of you know that we have put some ideas together in a discussion document that extends the TANGENT document to incorporate a Treaty of Use covering national security. Chairman, I request that we table this document for consideration and incorporation into TANGENT."

Stuart looked around the room. If he read it right the German and the EU Delegates were aware of this amendment although he wasn't so sure whether Peter Dawson knew of it. Certainly, by the way he was shaking his head Ed Bruckner didn't like it, meanwhile most of the other delegates were in deep discussion within their own groups.

Briand was definitely an aspiring President of France and if he could pull this off would show his authority on the world's stage. Lawrence was in deep discussion with his team.

"Ladies and Gentlemen," he said, "I am frankly surprised at this request from France, there was every opportunity to put forward this proposal for discussion during the last six weeks, why is it that you have chosen this time to table this amendment?"

Yes, why is it that you have chosen this time, thought Stuart, there were many possible reasons but one thing for sure, it wasn't that France had forgotten to include it… timing is everything. If the discussion stalled now then France could be seen to want to support TANGENT, indeed to improve upon it and yet it failed because other nations did not have such high ambitions.

"Ladies and Gentlemen, we are facing intense time pressure in getting consensus. However, that time pressure should not deter us from omitting the opportunity to exclude military exploitation of this new technology. France will not sign up to TANGENT without such assurances."

The German and EU delegates remained impassive as the stakes increased. It was hard to read the delegates from Japan, Brazil and India but the Chinese and US teams were looking frustrated and exasperated; it seemed like a bit of show. Lawrence knew that an impasse had been reached and delegates needed to consider their position.

"Ladies and Gentlemen, I suggest the following way forward. Can I ask Monsieur Briand to circulate the amendment paper today for discussion tomorrow at 10am? Monsieur, please do not take this as an endorsement of the paper to the Taskforce. We must have a clear overall position by the end of today, so I will ask Brazil, UK, Germany, India, Africa and Japan to present their position in that order this afternoon starting at 1400. Is everyone in agreement?" There was a nodding of heads around the table. Stuart could see lots of the people behind the glass panels already leaving their viewing point.

"May I remind everyone about the terms of this Taskforce? We will not be leaving this building, it is a secure site and you all have a suite allocated with telecommunication access to your colleagues under your specified encrypted standards and equipment. As agreed there will be verification monitoring by your nominated security staff. This is a UN building and it operates as a neutral territory for every nation. Food is available in various assigned areas. If you need any help contact the secretariat opposite the exit of this conference centre; see you again at 1400."

The delegates carefully filed their papers and started to leave the room making sure that the very act of leaving did not betray a position to other delegates.

"What a bloody mess," said Stuart to no-one in particular.

"It's of your making," said Lawrence, "if you hadn't created this matter alignment device the world would be happily progressing as it has for centuries."

"Progressing? Is that what you call it? Wars, poverty, bribery corruption violence, religious intolerance, not to mention the destruction on the planet… that's progress? Anyway, it's not a matter alignment device."

"You know what I mean, of course it's imperfect but slowly, sometimes painfully slowly, mankind is improving the overall welfare of all nations. Anyway, who gives you the right to be so fucking pompous?"

Dangerous ground, thought Stuart. "The problem is that someone, sometime would have figured out that large parts of our science is built on sand. It just happens to be me that found it out."

"And now we have a meeting like the one that just happened, the wires will be buzzing with advice and positions. Frankly I am not optimistic about chairing a positive outcome."

"Well I am impressed that you have kept the agenda moving although as you say, the real national positions are just starting to show. Ever since I stumbled on the discovery I knew it was disruptive."

"Disruptive is an understatement, you have created a grenade and pulled out the pin; how fucking naïve are you?"

"What I meant is that, well, if you look at the past then most technical developments have been a step on from that which went before. Admittedly some of those steps were quite big, steam power, electricity and the transistors being good examples. Nevertheless, mankind has always adapted and adopted with relative ease. In this instance we have to undo conventional thinking, we have taken several wrong scientific paths that have compounded us to a cul-de-sac."

Lawrence was irritated at the lecture from Stuart. "Thanks for the speech; I suggest you get some food now."

"I will, I'm starving, by the way do I have a suite or just a cell?"

"You're beginning to bore me Ashley; yes, you do have a suite and it will be easier to stay there for the next couple of days rather that head back to wherever you are being kept."

"Held actually; remember I am a prisoner."

"Look, let's be absolutely clear. Everyone, and I mean fucking everyone wants what's inside your brain, your discovery and if they can't have you, then no-one will. The attempted kidnap should have proved that to you. So, my friend, your discovery will be determined at this meeting as well, best read the Implications Report quickly." With that he mumbled something about spanners and left.

Interesting how his language had become more florid when out of earshot... well I don't give a flying fuck for you either... my friend! It was then that I noticed the room was empty apart from two of my minders who had accompanied me that morning, and a woman who looked like she would rather be somewhere else.

As I headed for the exit I asked all of them where I should be heading, the minders didn't know but the woman said, "If you follow me, sir, I will show you to your quarters." I hate that use of "sir" it meant, I have to call you that, but I would rather call you something else like dog turd or something equally derogatory. Why keep up the pretence of courtesy here, I can't go anywhere?

Outside the conference room was an open area with black leather pouffes adjacent to stainless steel and glass coffee tables. I figured out that we were in the UN Conference Centre but not the usual areas open to the public. There were a few people sitting around but I didn't recognise anyone, they all looked like they were suffering from telecoms withdrawal symptoms...

The woman was led the way down the corridors to a lift lobby. She then used some sort of device to override the lift system and we got into a waiting lift... interesting, was it just for me? Even more interesting, there were no floor numbers in the lift itself and I couldn't see which floor we were on when we got out either. The corridor was just like those in so many mainstream hotels, it was functional although eerily empty of people.

As we swung through the second door on the left I noticed that the window at the end of the corridor was opaque. This place had been purposely designed such that residents couldn't see out and prying eyes couldn't see in.

The suite followed the same personality as the corridor. It was neutral and clinical with a large L-shaped settee dominating the main sitting room. It had a TV on the wall and Stuart hoped that he would have more access to news outside, but suspected that it would have a channel filter, as did the Glens Falls place. There was a well-stocked fridge disguised as a cupboard in one corner; a desk with a workstation on top plus a tiny printer embedded to the side sat in the other corner just beside a large opaque window. The lighting was the only aspect of the room that reduced the antiseptic nature of the place. There were several table lamps, a reading lamp beside the desk and an array of spotlights in the ceiling that had been dimmed to reduce the glare of the whites and creams. The bedroom was very functional with a sliding-door wardrobe and a large double bed with a chest of drawers either side. Stuart saw his case and backpack on a large bench just under the opaque window.

Stuart's inspection of the stainless steel and white tile bathroom completed the tour. This really was a grim place to spend the next couple of days; at least there was a bookcase in the sitting room with hopefully some books to divert his mind from things. Interestingly, someone had arranged them in order of size like Stuart would. I can't believe they are letting me have internet access or use of a phone, thought Stuart, when the anonymous woman spoke.

"The phone is for housekeeping and room service," she said, "it will not allow outside calls. Oh… and the PC is disabled, I'm afraid."

"Am I able to leave the suite?"

"Sorry, we will come and collect you in time for the restart at 1400 and I have taken the liberty of getting a light lunch delivered, you know, just sandwiches and fruit, help yourself from the bar if you want and as you saw, your bags are in the bedroom." As she left Stuart noticed the two men outside who had found some seats and were settling down in the corridor.

"You're welcome to join me for lunch if you like?" he said, they didn't even respond.

Stuart sat down and picked up the beige folder marked 'TANGENT' from the coffee table and started to read. What on earth was it that Lawrence wanted him to read? Stuart skipped the preamble stressing the importance of the TANGENT programme and its confidentiality, he also skipped the section thanking the various contributors although made a marker to come back to it. The Section on knowledge transfer was good in as far as it went. It laid out the principles of sharing information and transparency as well as mechanisms for policing member states that signed up. He identified a lot of his own text had been woven into the section.

Stuart had a gift of speed reading, well it wasn't so much reading quickly but over the years he could identify the key points embedded in a lot of superfluous text. It was as if the important information glowed on the pages just waiting to be read. That was how Stuart digested the section on Commonality in ten minutes. He had found a pencil and pen on the desk and was using the pen to highlight areas of concern with comments, and the pencil to mark those things he knew to be wrong. Stuart applied his own code so that it would be difficult to figure out what his writings meant, he avoided literal comments and instead he used reference phrases that he would understand from his own life events. In fact, the commonality section like its predecessor wasn't bad and again he recognised much of his own text. A lot of serious thought had gone into these two sections and as Stuart knew it was the devil in the detail that mattered.

The next section on Sustainability in contrast, was very weak. I'm not surprised, thought Stuart. About six months ago Stuart's research team numbered about 20 of the brightest young scientists and mathematicians from around the globe. One of the team, I think it was Harry Franks, had said that we were playing with energy forces that had their genesis from somewhere and for some reason, consequently we need to figure out what would happen if we disturbed that equilibrium. We had all been so excited with the potential of what we were doing; we hadn't focused on the Sustainability issues. That discussion kicked off a workstream to look at Sustainability, but it had only been going for about a month before I was invited to meet with the UN and the priority was lost. The only outcome of that one-month's work was that the magnitude of misusing or misapplying our work might have a disastrous impact on the world environment and so the team had agreed that all future work would only proceed with sustainability consequences being of equal importance in further research and development.

The Economic section was a very complex report and Stuart decided that this was not a speed-read and needed time to figure out the meaning of the various scenarios. Although it needed more time to understand it was clear that there were very few winners. The application of his discovery to make transport easy and affordable had such far-reaching impact, even the economic experts couldn't agree on the outcomes.

The arrival of some beautifully constructed sandwiches, dips and fruit broke his concentration. Stuart took out a cold beer from the fridge and helped himself to a selection of sandwiches, he suddenly realised he was famished. After eating far too many carbs, he picked up an apple and turned to the TANGENT report again. The rules surrounding international operations actually made sense and were to some degree an extension of the Commonality section. It was clear that the team that wrote it had used the original work from Farnborough and therefore recognised some of the big pitfalls, such as nations trying to apply their own standards and consequently dragging a whole bunch of legacy issues into the future.

Stuart automatically went to check his watch only to remember it was never returned to him when he was transferred from the UK to the US. He hadn't exactly lost a sense of time over the last two months but since time was punctuated by events and he had no events it was just a void, a continuum of nothing except eating and sleeping. He had no meetings, problems, fun, food, things to plan; he had nothing, Stuart always looked forward to weekends for no particular reason but now it seemed meaningless. Once he realised that a whole bunch of false promises about the way the UN would support his work started to dissolve and that he was not allowed contact with anyone who remotely was a part of his life; he had settled into a period of self-pity. That was the first month at Glens Falls. He somehow knew he was in this state and so he started setting himself mental challenges to force himself to see this period as something he could exploit.

It was a fantastic watch, a Patek Gondolo in white gold. Stuart always admired quality engineering, and this was one of the finest examples. It was true that he often forgot to wind it up and was constantly worried about it being stolen but it was one of his few prised possessions. Zoe had given it to him on their 20th wedding anniversary and it really was a genuine surprise, He had taken her to Rick Stein's restaurant in Padstow as a special treat; he had booked it months in advance as well as a small boutique hotel for a couple of days away; real romance after 20 years. He recalled the time.

"Is it real?" he said, wishing the words had not come out.

"No, it's a cheap copy from Taiwan," she snapped. "Look they have even forged the box and papers."

"I'm sorry, darling; it's just that I know how much these things cost."

"I know you always wanted one and I had a bit put by."

"A bit?... darling I don't know which bank you robbed but thank you from the bottom of my heart." He kissed her hand tenderly.

"I wonder how many people here are celebrating something?"

"The majority I should think, it's that sort of *plaice.*," he said.

"Very droll, I am not going to rise to the *bait.*"

"You know I am really *hooked* on you... even after 20 years."

"Enough, enough let's get off the fish talk, you do know it's not new, I got it from a posh watch shop in Mayfair."

Good memories, somehow he never sensed Zoe's recent frustration with him. I am going to demand that watch back determined Stuart as he returned to the Report. The last Section entitled Transition carried a disturbing introduction: -

"This Section is aimed at developing solutions that will enable all member nations to successfully exploit this new discovery both collectively and individually. Its focus is based around agreeing the baseline of the technical developments so far, and ensuring all nations have the opportunity to share in the position. This covers equipment, computer and paper records and people, such that there is a 'wrapper' incorporating all the Intellectual Property that will avoid any nation being disadvantaged. It is hoped that from this baseline we can all move forward under a new UN Transition Committee that would take the agreed principles arising from the other supporting sections.

The Economic issues will be particularly complex, and it is recommended that there is a separate committee to deal with issues in this area."

How the hell do you put a wrapper around the people, thought Stuart, and specifically what does it mean to me? Stuart started paging forward to the subsection on People. He knew he should read this whole thing properly after all he had just bypassed the subsections on Internet Controls and National Exclusions.

The people section was headed 'Talent Map', there was a table of people's names, probably about forty or so, Stuart knew about half of them. Alongside each name was five columns headed Skills, Contribution, Ability, Team, Alignment and Placement. These columns were codified for everyone except Stuart's name at the top; he just had blanks in each column and TBA in the last one.

What the fuck is this, do they think they can decide on all these people's lives...? Now Stuart understood what Lawrence was getting at.

"The meeting is restarting, we have to get back," it was the faceless woman.

CHAPTER 3

Restoration Man

(The beginning)

Stuart was a hoarder and everyone who knew him teased him relentlessly about it. In fact, it wasn't that Stuart really did hoard things he just looked at them in a different way. If something might be useful, then depending on what it was, it would go into one of the many boxes ordered around his workshop. Very often if Stuart was about to throw something away he would take it apart first just in case there were a few bits that could come in handy.

Strangely without any real methodology, Stuart could always lay his hands on the exact thing he needed from the thousands of bits.

If there was one talent that everyone agreed upon it was Stuart's ability to fix things. Even Stuart thought he was pretty good; he wasn't sure what he would call himself, an engineer, a technician or just a very practical person. It really didn't matter what needed repairing or restoring; Stuart would tackle it. Most of the time he had a supreme confidence in his ability even, as was often the case; he knew nothing about the topic. So, Stuart plunged into repairing vacuum cleaners, radios, ceramics, engines, antiques and even restoring oil paintings. Hence the need to hoard things since he could always find something useful in one of his boxes to help in his passion to make all things right.

Stuart knew that he was obsessed with order in the workshop and if someone had been in there moving things he would know immediately. In fact, Stuart ran his whole life in an organised way, sometimes he faced up to the reality that he has some sort of Obsessive-Compulsive Personality Disorder and then dismissed it as his way of managing things.

Zoe, of course, was the biggest beneficiary of this talent since as soon as something went wrong in the house it was mended, it also drove her mad, living with such a perfectionist. In truth she knew that when Stuart spent a few hours in his workshop the self-satisfaction and order was good for him. He wasn't so passionate in his quest that he became a bore or indeed would not replace things when they really were at their end of life. Zoe did find two things really irritating though. The first was that everyone took advantage of him so there was always a conveyer belt full of promises to repair or restore, the second was when Stuart didn't understand how something worked or was having trouble repairing it then he became completely single-minded until was sorted.

Typical of Stuart, he had rigged a communications system to his workshop, after all it was at least a hundred metres from the house, and it was a hands-free device so if Stuart was covered in oil he could still answer Zoe.

"Time to stop Stuart; remember we have the Hensons coming round tonight."

"Nearly finished, I will stop in five… shit, that was your fault."

"What was?"

"I nearly lost my finger on the mortice; you distracted me."

"Please Stuart don't be long."

"OK I will leave it for today, I'm on my way."

Zoe had enough experience to know that Stuart would be another twenty-odd minutes and then he would need to clean up, so she built this delay into her first call. Stuart knew that Zoe was anticipating his delay and sometimes he forced a second call from her. The second call was usually in a tone and language that would make fishmonger blush.

Stuart chuckled to himself; how he loved that woman. She seemed to be more cross and impatient with him recently, so he made a note to be more loving. He ran to the house just as the heavens opened and reached the back door, thoroughly wet through.

"I'm soaked, still I have to strip off anyway, I need a good wash," he said to no-one in particular.

"If you strip off here then you will have to clean up my vomit," said Marc, Stuart and Zoe's youngest son. Marc was 17 with a humour to match.

"Well vomit on my dirty shirt," said Stuart as he threw it across the room, missing Marc and nearly breaking a vase.

"Stuart, behave," yelled Zoe from the pantry, Stuart went for the trousers.

"Stop Dad, you really are mad, you know."

A ritual play fight ensued for half a minute, with Stuart giving in with great drama.

"What are you reading, my little bookworm?" Marc always seemed to have his nose in a book and was desperate for an e-book.

"It's about the early history of the French Revolution, what an amazing time."

"I'm sure Louis XIII didn't think so!!!"

Stuart was very proud of his son, although he was biased; Marc truly was dark and handsome in a Mediterranean way. He didn't have Stuart's height or physique but was rather slight which seemed to make a lot of the local girls want to mother him. Not that he had much to do with girls, he always seemed so very shy as soon as there were any females around, and he didn't regard his older sister Lucy as female anyway.

"Henry phoned an hour ago'," Zoe mentioned as she hid a basket of dirty washing in the utility room.

"And?" said Stuart.

"He is coming down from uni this weekend for someone's 21st party. He should be around late Friday; can you pick him up from the station?"

"Does he ever study?' said Stuart. "He is always out somewhere on the razzle." He leapt up the stairs knowing the Hensons were always on time and he probably had ten minutes to look respectable.

"Is anyone else coming for supper?" he yelled from the landing.

"Rob and Sue, I told you that they might be late, Rob had something on at school."

The Hensons were on time and Nigel Henson true to form said all the same old things again.

"You really should go on your own, Stuart; your firm doesn't deserve you."

"Why?" I said, "I am happy with what I am doing, the kids and Zoe don't want for anything; do you, darling?"

Zoe pouted in an indecent way and said, "Well there is always room for improvement."

"You know what I mean, you vulgar woman, you wait 'til later." How he wished the banter would yield something.

"How's the new Jag?" said Stuart changing the subject and wondering why Nigel Henson was so obsessed about his future.

"It's great, 0-60mph in 6.3 seconds, not much gets past me!"

"That's true," sneered Wendy, his long-suffering wife. In truth Wendy wasn't long-suffering, somewhere in their married lives they had gone their separate ways with Nigel concentrating on his business success to the exclusion of anything else. Indeed, apart from a superficial interest I don't think he knew what his wife and teenage children were doing with their lives.

"It would be nice for you to drive with some consideration for your passengers," she continued. Wendy and Zoe had met on an Art History course at the local college and found they had a common passion for early Byzantine paintings.

"It's Rob's temper that I can't stand," said Sue, "he becomes another person when he is behind the wheel." Sue was Rob's partner of nearly two years and they were well matched. Sue tried to dominate Rob who was so laid back he really didn't care, although he did confide to Stuart that his relationship was fantastic with Sue, especially his sex life. Stuart always looked at Sue with different eyes after that confession.

It was a good evening once Nigel was back in his box, with the discussion ranging across the world economy, through recently read books to TV and latest news.

"You teach physics, Rob, what's this Higgs boson all about then?" said Nigel.

"After several great bottles of Bordeaux, you want me to clear my head and talk about Higgs boson? It's a bit of a party killer you know." Zoe, Wendy and Sue were already engaged in a discussion on the latest exhibition at the Tate.

"Well," drawled Rob trying to buy time to get his brain in order. "You must understand that this stuff is very specialised and although I do teach the theory of Standard Model of physics as part of the curriculum, it's not my strong point."

"You don't really know, do you?" teased Stuart.

"The trouble is that unless you are immersed in the topic with a good grasp of math and physics, it's hard to explain."

"Well that's your test, make it simple for Nigel and me." Nigel was pouring himself another glass of wine; I do hope you are letting Wendy drive tonight he thought.

"OK here goes, the simple guide to the God Particle as it's known. The boson essentially enables other particles to gain mass and in so doing decays immediately, so it's difficult to find. That's what all this work on the Large Hadron Colliders is all about, trying to identify the Higgs particle at the event of mass creation. By the way, they claim that they have found it."

"I think I understand what you said but why don't the particles have mass in the first place?"

"That's the problem with this discussion because it can't take place in a vacuum; you need to understand quantum science on a sub-atomic scale and topics such as string theory."

"Fine, so if after spending all this money, they actually prove the Higgs boson exists, then what?"

"I guess it will reinforce the Standard Model for sub-atomic particles."

"Frankly, Rob, I worry that science is becoming so complicated that it no longer has the elegance of nature. All this Standard Model stuff just feels wrong."

"Excuse me, but I make a living from this stuff and talking of living, I have an early meeting of the science society at school tomorrow, so we should be going."

"Me too," said Nigel, "I have to make an honest shilling tomorrow, well a shilling anyway!" he said with a chuckle. Many a true word, thought Stuart.

It was late evening, Stuart was still washing up the supper things.

"We need a bigger dishwasher, I always seem to be washing up and the dishwasher is always full, it's useless. If you used fewer saucepans my life would be easier!"

"So, you didn't enjoy the meal then?" said Zoe.

"No, I didn't say that, the whole meal was fabulous, but it is mid-week and it could have been more modest."

"Sorry, mate, that's the way it is, if you don't like it, find another woman who enjoys packet meals!"

That was always the way with Zoe, she always painted a picture of two extremes.

"OK I choose the pans," he said in his usual defeated way.

"I'm up to bed, my skivvy, see you later," and with that she raced up the stairs, just in case Stuart was going to take retribution for his lowly status in the Ashley household.

Later when both were in bed Zoe said, "And why in the hell did you promise to repair Nigel's strimmer? The cheek of it, he even had it wrapped carefully in the back of his fucking Jag. It's not as if he can't afford a new one, if it had been Rob then I would understand but Rob could have mended it himself anyway!"

"It's hard to say no," said Stuart in his semi-sleep state.

"I'm surprised you didn't bore them to death with all your discussion on atoms. You know your problem... you think too much."

Yes, I do think too much; yes, I do.

It was Friday the next day, and as usual the engine of the Ashley household was in gear and running fairly smoothly.

"Don't forget to pick up Henry love, he will text you when he is at the station, and Marc are you doing sports at school tomorrow?" Zoe said through a mouthful of toast.

"Got to go, babe, see you around seven." And Stuart disappeared through the back door to the garage. He got into his Range Rover and left for Southampton. Stuart had a love-hate relationship with the car; it was a diesel and was well engineered as well as meeting his needs of speed and comfort. Most importantly it had lots of space for the numerous times he transported some mechanical objects around. He hated it because in Smythfield they were a sort of badge of who you were; a country person, possibly with a few acres, some horses, dogs and the daughter called Annabel, in fact Stuart could imagine everyone in Hampshire lusted after Range Rovers.

I wonder why it is that people like to brand themselves? It's near impossible to buy clothes without some logo or name on it; perhaps it's a need for conformity, I probably am the same in some ways, he mused.

It was a good 20 minutes later that Stuart arrived at the factory on an industrial estate on the outskirts of Southampton. He worked for a division of GE Power Systems that made large generators. As operations manager Stuart was responsible for the manufacturing and assembly of a range of standard generator products but also some specialist custom designed work. The factory was not working to capacity, which meant that Stuart had weekends free but it also worried him since he would have to put the factory on short-time unless some new orders turned up.

It was a frustrating day, with much of the work proceeding as normal with the exception of one custom job where the specification seemed wrong. It wasn't until late afternoon that they had figured out that some of the pipework was the problem and that it needed re-calculating. It was agreed that to catch up on the job, the designers would work late such that the factory could machine the new pipes the following day. So much for a free Saturday, still at least he had a job, which was more than some could say.

Henry had texted to say he would be at Smythfield station at 1915 and Stuart duly collected him from work.

"So, how are you, Dad?" said Henry as he got into the car.

"Not bad, no real highs or lows, all pretty boring really. Not like your life, I am amazed you aren't burnt out yet. Do you think you'll make the third year?"

"No probs, my tutor thinks I'm doing pretty well and this term's rugby has been brilliant." Henry was reading Physics at Birmingham and was one of those people who could balance the world of study, sport and play with ease. Over the last two years at uni Henry had filled out and now looked like a seriously strong lad. The beer will be his undoing, thought Stuart, although he seemed to have an amazing metabolism and was able to keep going when others simply folded.

"Fancy coming out for a curry tonight?"

"Sorry Dad, Steve is picking me up in an hour and I may stay over at his place tonight." That's another thing, how is it that Henry's generation use their mobile phones almost as an extension of their senses? Here was Henry having a perfectly good conversation with me and at the same time communicating with others... never mind.

Stuart and Zoe did go out for a curry that night, with Marc and his best friend Peter joining them. Everyone turned in early that night; Stuart planned to get to work around 9am.

The Saturday turned out to be less productive than Stuart had hoped; the modified pipework wasn't good enough and they would have to wait until Monday for the engineers and designers to go through the calculations again. Stuart should have conceded to the nagging doubt he felt on the Friday. Somehow his practical nature often gave him a sixth sense of what would work. Too much haste. Still it might have worked, he thought, as he headed for home at midday.

CHAPTER 4

Positioning

Stuart pulled the papers together and had a quick visit to the toilet; you never know how long this session is going to go on.

His entourage retraced their steps back to the lift, with Stuart trying to see as much as possible of his surroundings just in case. Just in case what? Are you going to try and escape, thought Stuart, well that would be stupid; this place is like a fortress. Anyway, it's better to fight from within, or is it... why are these people determining his future? His mind was spinning with the options. Just calm down, he thought, everyone will have their say during the afternoon. I don't think that any decision will be made for a while, so a step at a time, Stuart... a step at a time.

There was the usual background noise of a meeting that had yet to start as Stuart was led to the Conference room. As he made his way towards his appointed seat he decided to try and speak to Peter Dawson.

"When are you speaking, Peter?' He wasn't the sort of person to get flustered, but he was definitely uncomfortable with me being around him. "I figured out that you knew I was going to be detained when I accepted the UN invitation, didn't you?'

"Actually no; following the kidnap attempt we were worried for your safety. I really was surprised at the US action, but I don't expect you to believe me."

"Well did anyone in the British Government have an inkling of what was going on and indeed support it?"" he shifted uncomfortably. "I can only assume that the PM and others did know, or that they are working their socks off to get me back to the UK." Silence.

"Just so you know, I really trusted you and valued your support, I am such a shitty judge of character."

"Time to sit down, Stuart" said Lawrence Banard guiding me over towards the top of the table. He had obviously decided to rescue Dawson.

"I am trying to be inclusive my friend, but your position here is well… difficult"

"One, I am not your friend and two if I can't say anything then why do you want me here? Is it some sort of veneer that this is a democratic process?"

"Listen, you arsehole," he said in his best whisper "this is as democratic as things can be, this really is unchartered territory for everyone and we all know, that is, everyone round this table knows that we are on the precipice of destabilising just about everything, and I really mean world order!! Just shut the fuck up, I will let you have your day, I promise you."

I really did feel he was sincere and decided to try and be a little more circumspect. "Ok, I apologise, but if you were in my position…"

"Apology accepted, and yes you are not my friend."

"Ladies and Gentlemen, this meeting is now formally in session. Can I remind every speaker to confine his or her comments to the TANGENT report? Just to remind everyone, this afternoon's session will include comments from Brazil, United Kingdom, India, Africa and Japan. Mr Santos Almeida are you ready?"

Henrique Santos Almeida opened his file and looked around the table. He was in his late forties and had almost an aristocratic air that this meeting was beneath him. He was very tall with sandy hair and a sharp face with a pointed chin and a pointed nose and pointed ears. He obviously wasn't aware that his half-moon reading glasses accentuated all these features.

"Delegates, may I remind you that I am speaking on behalf of my country Brazil as well as the Latin American Integration Association representing the whole continent of South America." Talk about pompous, thought Stuart, he probably owns a large part of Brazil.

Henrique then went on about the emerging economic power of South America and that it would no longer be regarded as a secondary economic region but rather as an emerging economic powerhouse. He spent considerable time giving the views of various countries that made up LAIA.

"In summary, our position is very clear, we plan to create unified standards for South America that we would hope meets the UN criteria. We are unresolved about sharing our developments but would expect to be part of the UN initiative on sustainability. We have unfortunately not been able to agree a unified position on the Transition aspect of the TANGENT Report since many countries rely heavily on importing their energy needs."

"Can I assume from your comments that you will not support any International operation standards?" said Lawrence Banard.

"On the contrary, Chairman, it is our wish to support any international standards for interoperability but only if it is not in conflict with the interest of the LAIA."

A very protectionist position, thought Stuart, and I bet there is no harmony or agreement in the South American team.

"Thank you, Mr Santos Almeida, just so everyone is aware we are compiling each delegate's comments against the relevant sections in the TANGENT report and we plan to get your confirmation that your position has been correctly understood in the summary session tomorrow. Now, Sir Peter Dawson please can we have your comments?"

Sir Peter cleared his throat as he did every time he had to make a public speech.

"Ladies and Gentlemen, the United Kingdom is in a rather different position to the other delegates," he began. "Mr Ashley, as you know, is a UK citizen and we have been absolutely supportive in ensuring that no nation will be disadvantaged from his work and associated developments. It is for that reason that the UK Government agreed to second Mr Ashley to what is now known as the TANGENT programme."

Stuart could not believe what he was hearing; he looked hard at Sir Peter who would not look up from his papers. Stuart turned to Lawrence Banard who slightly nodded his head side to side as if to say… don't say a word! Stuart's mind was racing, if he challenged Sir Peter, he would alienate him, but on the other hand it looked like Sir Peter didn't want anything to do with him anyway. Calm Stuart, calm… let's hear all the lies first before challenging them, if I make a big scene now I could get thrown out. So, Stuart started making notes.

"In addition, as all the delegates are aware the International Patents on all the Intellectual Property associated with Mr Ashley's discoveries has been registered to the UK Government. This is clearly laid out in the first section of the TANGENT report." Damn I must have missed it, thought Stuart, I know I had the patents nailed; here I am being double crossed and stitched up by a fellow countryman! "So, assuming we all believe in, and adhere to, international law then the United Kingdom has the right to define all of the five main principles defined in TANGENT."

That really brought the house down, in the space of five seconds every delegate was objecting loudly, some in their native language, some in coarser tones with people standing and waving. The woman next to Táng Hu was standing and signalling him to leave the meeting. Ed Bruckner was pointing to Lawrence Banard in a very threatening way, who, as Chairman, was desperately trying to restore some sort of order. Stuart could see lots of activity in the glass booths around the room and wondered what would happen next. At least I kept my powder dry he thought smugly, but what if they thought this was set piece between Sir Peter and himself?

Lawrence Banard quickly got up and rushed to the exit to bar the way from the delegates leaving.

"Gentlemen, Gentlemen PLEASE can you wait. I am as surprised by Sir Peter's comments as you are, but I beg of you to stay to ensure we are all absolutely clear on the UK position."

"Sir Peter in the next few minutes your words will determine whether we will have some international harmony in exploiting Mr Ashley's discoveries or a complete breakdown in world order. Let's be clear this discovery means that mankind will have unlimited energy for our homes, our factories, our transport indeed the whole world has the opportunity to be transformed."

No-one moved or returned to their seats, the glass booths were lined with people standing, headphones still attached. All eyes were on Sir Peter who continued to look at his notes. What a professional, Stuart thought, cool as a cucumber; he then saw a slight tremor in Sir Peter's left hand and it was clear that he was sweating heavily. Finally, he stood up and looked around the room.

"Ladies and Gentlemen, I am sorry, but for me this meeting has been a proof point. Indeed, not just for me but for my government. I agree with the Chairman; the substance of Stuart Ashley's discoveries is so fundamental that unless we can somehow work together… well… I hate to think what the future will bring if we don't."

There was total silence.

"I know you recognise the opportunities we have here right now, and I know that you have similar feelings of foreboding if we cannot conclude something sensible here."

"I could easily argue the UK rights to enforce our patents but why bother, would you agree to them?"

"No fucking way," said Ed Bruckner having lost any veneer of diplomacy.

"Exactly, but you didn't hear me out, did you?"

"The United Kingdom Government has led this fabulous work and is open and transparent in wanting to ensure that all countries can gain the benefits."

"Levelling Mankind," yelled Stuart beaming.

"Shut up, Ashley, you just don't understand the complexities we are dealing with here."

"We, that is our government wanted to use TANGENT to see if we could work together internationally. When Russia, North Korea and South Africa would not join this programme, it was a major setback and all the more reason that we need to come together and agree operating principles. We are less than halfway through this debate and it's already clear that each country has irreconcilable self-interest. I for one, am willing to stay here until we do get it solved.

Many of you will need to go back to your countries to agree the scope of your negotiations but we need to do it quickly. The UK government is very unhappy that Russia and South Africa have aggressive plans underway already."

Back to total silence, but then some low guarded chatter started. Lawrence Banard spoke from the door.

"Ladies and Gentlemen, can I ask that you don't go but that I ask for a vote to reconvene is one weeks' time to resolve the universal principle of… what should we call it?" All turned to Stuart.

"Inertia Conversion, IC for short, its harnessing and directing gravity although strictly speaking it's not gravity."

"Fine, fine, that's better than all the stuff in the TANGENT Appendix, "OK so can I ask the voting delegates if they support the resolution to reconvene in one week to agree a baseline of operating principles?"

"I am happy to put a brief outline of base principles together with the original TANGENT team," said Sir Peter. "After all, that means you will all have representatives involved, but it will not be a 200-page document this time, 10 pages at the most."

"Everyone in favour please raise your hands," said Lawrence. "Banham, can you confirm and record the vote?" Several hands went up including that of Sir Peter, however Ed Bruckner and Táng Hu's arms remain resolutely by their side.

"Can I take it that we have a majority, but that China and the USA are not prepared to continue?"

"Absolutely," said Bruckner.

"We will not continue," said Táng Hu.

"That means that your representatives will not participate in the new TANGENT workstream. I do hope you will reconsider when you have reflected upon your position to your governments. All that is left for me is to thank you for your participation, and we will have a new document ready for discussion in one week's time. I suggest we use the same facilities here."

There was almost a release of air as the tension in the room relaxed. The delegates picked up their papers and without much further discussion left smartly. Lawrence Banard slumped back in his chair and for the first time showed signs of exhaustion at trying to hold the meeting together. Colonel Banham remained beside him making some final notes together with the other secretary.

Sir Peter and his staff had remained as well, and they were busy chatting together.

"You bastard, you fucking bastard… why did you ambush the meeting? Couldn't you have told me your concerns? Now we are well and truly screwed… no China… no US… and Russia up to God knows what… not forgetting North Korea… and what the hell South Africa think they are doing I don't know."

"I hadn't expected such a reaction," Sir Peter said lamely. "It's clear that we need to get some serious discussion moving between respective leaders if we are to pull something back."

"Well the UN will need to find a new Chairman, I can't make it happen."

"Lawrence hang in there, I think you did a fantastic job," said Sir Peter.

"So do I," said Stuart.

"Sod off, you are just a pain in my arse my friend."

"Seriously Lawrence, it has to be you, there isn't anyone with your qualities and knowledge that can pick up the pieces."

"I will think about it."

"I don't suppose there is any chance of my release?" I said.

"What does he know?" said the man on Sir Peter's left. It was Nigel Jones; Stuart had spent a lot of time with him on the early days of the project, he hadn't really noticed him before. Perhaps that was how he liked it. Nigel was ordinary, he had a plain round face, was thinning on top with grey at the sides, he needed to cut his eyebrows and had the sort of beard that always looked as if he hadn't shaved. Medium height, medium build a slight double chin with pursed lips, poorly fitting suit, what more was there to say?

The other member of Sir Peter's staff was a woman, probably late thirties and dark. She had almost black hair, cut short with a gorgeous sallow complexion, perhaps an Indian background with the most piercing dark eyes that seemed to penetrate your mind. She wasn't skinny but had that supple physique of someone who does yoga every day.

"Absolutely nothing," said Sir Peter, breaking into Stuart's thoughts. The three of them started a whispered conversation.

"Ok, back to my cell, see you Lawrence." Stuart got up and headed for the door, his minders moved into position and escorted him to the lift.

"What time is it?" he asked.

"Nearly 1800, sir," the woman replied.

"How do I get my wristwatch back? You people took it and it has sentimental value."

"I don't know anything about a wristwatch, sir."

"So how do I get my possessions back?"

"I would ask the officers at Glens Falls, sir."

"Thanks for the help ma'am," I replied cynically as I entered the cell again. A large beer I think and where is tonight's menu? Well what a day; full of high drama, I have to admit it, the politics are really beyond me. Did anyone in that meeting really mean what they said, and what a surprise about Russia and South Africa. I should have spotted that Russia didn't have a delegate. North Korea is a rogue state so no surprise there, but what was South Africa up to?

I rang 22 which was the room service number and ordered a Salad Niçoise with a bottle of Beaujolais, let's see if it's as good as Glens Falls.

I was listening to some old Bob Dylan on the digital player when the door opened.

"Don't you guys ever knock, no fucking manners that's the problem." I looked up to see Sir Peter Dawson with his staff retinue and that minder woman.

"Can we chat?" he said.

"Aren't you meant to say, can I come in?"

"Cut that shit, Stuart, you need some friends."

"That's what I thought you were Peter, remember when we were working on the project in Farnborough?"

"I owe you an explanation I think. This hasn't gone the way we expected, we have been in detailed discussion and agreement so despite their feigned surprise, the US, France and Germany all supported our TANGENT initiative to try and get the basics hammered out, so we could discuss what to do with the non-participating nations. I don't know whether the US is playing a new game and I will get the PM to talk to the President as soon as I can. Frankly I was amazed that China agreed to join TANGENT originally, now I think they were just waiting for a reason to pull out."

"If the US doesn't re-join then there really isn't enough world representation to get anything done," I said

"Even if they do, it's far too one-sided, the old European and transatlantic players together again."

"I don't know why I feel quite disillusioned after today, as you know I naively tried to get countries to participate when I kicked off the meeting for academia last year and I know it was a stupid thing to do... now... but this. TANGENT thing is far worse... I still don't know why I have to attend."

"You were the er... the magnet to attract people, we gave them the impression that you have more to give on your discovery."

"Great, well funnily enough I do have more but I'm not sharing it with anyone."

"Well let's discuss that when we meet, and away from this zoo."

"It's OK we don't need to meet, I am just taking care of number one in future."

"Do either of you speak or is my minder cramping your style?" said Stuart.

"Forgive me, Stuart, you know Rose Hammond and Nigel Jones, both are special advisors in the Cabinet Office, but then you've met Nigel many times before."

"What did you think of today's events then?" Stuart said.

Nigel was the first to answer. "Stuart, as Sir Peter said we are surprised at the turn of events, I think we need to have a further chat once we are back at the embassy on the next move."

Sir Peter nodded agreement, but Rose didn't say a word and just looked around the room in a disinterested way.

"Well since I have been the guest of the UN and hosted by the USA who want no further part in this fiasco am I free to go, do you know?" The minder shifted in the background.

"Do you know?" Stuart asked her.

"I am sorry, sir, I have no information at present," she said.

"What of Zoe, have you heard from her, is she OK?" said Stuart to Sir Peter.

"Afraid not, I will do some digging and let you know, well we will get back to the office, but I promise to keep contact."

"You said that once before, the difference is I believed you then!"

"Look, this isn't right, I need help, I shouldn't go back to Glens Falls if the US is out of it."

"You're right but there is not much I can do now, is there? Maybe it's best to stay here, after all it is a UN office, I will talk with Ed Bruckner."

Stuart noticed someone outside the room, it was Bruckner's Pentagon man, he nodded to my minder on his way into the room.

"I am sorry, Sir Peter, I just caught the tail end of your conversation, you want to talk with Ed, and by the way the name's Rick Marsh, I am on Ed's Staff."

"He left in a bit of a hurry and asked me to say that he was sure we could sort things out and in the meantime the best thing was for me to take Mr Ashley back to Glens Falls for the next week, it's got to be better than this room. He asked me to remind you of the original agreement."

"OK, Rick, I get the message, but let Ed know that I expect to hear from him soonest. Stuart go back to Glens Falls, I will come and see you there, I will be able to see him, won't I Rick?"

"I'm sure, Sir Peter."

"Anyway, as Rick says, it's better than here and you owe me a tennis re-match after that rubbish game at Smythfield. Nigel, when can I be there?"

"Next Wednesday would be good, Sir Peter," said Nigel.

"I would make it Thursday," said Rose, "we have a lot to do before then."

So, she speaks, thought Stuart and what's all this about tennis, I have never played with Sir Peter?

"You should be OK to get there by 1530," she continued.

"Hold fire," said Rick, "I will have to clear this first."

"Well let's go for it and if things change, so be it," said Sir Peter. "Come on team we have lots to do. See you then Stuart."

"I certainly hope so," I said, still confused by the turn of the conversation.

As they left, Rose looked at Stuart and said, "Don't worry, we will find your watch."

The food and wine came in as they left, but Rick still remained. "It's best we leave tomorrow around seven to be ahead of the traffic."

"Are you joining me then?" I said.

"I don't know yet, things are pretty fluid!"

"What I don't understand is that as a British citizen I am somehow under your jurisdiction?"

"As I reminded Sir Peter, there is an agreement between our respective governments on your stay with us."

"You do put things well. Can I at least have some privacy now? Maybe I will see you tomorrow."

Rick Marsh hovered around, he wasn't used to being dismissed, still he turned and went in his own time.

Stuart drank a large glass of the Beaujolais and started the salad, musing over the conversation. It was stilted, so Peter Dawson and his merry team were being cautious, on the assumption that they felt the room was bugged... or were they just incompetent.

What was today's date? I've lost all sense of time, he found the remote and turned on the TV, getting to the news channel... it was Friday. Yet another evening to kill, Stuart thought, as he flicked through the channels, just the usual array of programmes, it's all so boring, he stopped on one of the movie channels and refilled his glass.

Stuart awoke to the ringing or rather buzzing of the phone, he picked up the receiver to hear,

"Good morning, sir, your breakfast will arrive in 15 minutes, please can you pack since you will be travelling back to Glens Falls in an hour?"

Stuart dragged himself to the bathroom to wash and shave; he heard someone in his room presumably delivering breakfast? When he came out of the bathroom, the room was empty save for a tray with a standard healthy US-style breakfast. Stuart had long-since learned to avoid American coffee but downed the glass of orange and proceeded to eat the scrambled eggs. I'm putting on weight, he thought, it's all this inactivity, I will start to use the facilities at Glens Falls and get fit again.

Rick Marsh didn't show up, instead Stuart was accompanied by the two men who had originally brought him down to the UN offices. The journey back was uneventful and being Saturday there was less traffic, so they made good time getting back to the mansion late morning. This time, though, Stuart spent more time looking at his surroundings. His first arrival had been in the middle of the night in an ambulance, and so he didn't really notice that there were two sets of robust electric gates to pass through. The gravel drive swung left through a small wood and thus obscured the main house from the entrance. There were overhead cameras everywhere, reinforcing a substantial level of security.

The limo pulled up outside the main entrance where Marion Homer was waiting for Stuart. Marion seemed to be in charge of the smooth running of the mansion. Stuart wasn't in any doubt that she had security credentials but still he had found her a pretty genuine person who had befriended him at a pretty low time.

"Hi Marion, did you miss me?"

"Oh Stuart, you don't know how much I have pined for you," she said with a mischievous grin that belied her age. She must be in her fifties, Stuart thought, but he could still see the girl in her and she cut a fine figure since she made much use of the sports facilities in the grounds.

"Is my suite ready?" Stuart said in mock tone.

"Indeed, it is sir, but your old suite is taken I'm afraid. However, I am sure you will approve of the new one we can offer," she countered in the same mock tone. "Let me escort you," and with that, she went into the house.

The new suite, and it really was a suite, was on the first floor unlike the last one, which had been on the ground floor.

"Who has taken my old rooms?" said Stuart as he inspected the large lounge/sitting room.

"No-one actually, it just having some work done on it."

"The windows don't seem to open properly."

"Sorry Stuart, they will only open a couple of inches, they are special security windows; obviously the chiefs think you need protection."

"Or I need locking in?"

"Sorry Stu, I know something's up and I was told that we had to put you here."

Stuart hated being called Stu but somehow it was OK with Marion. "I know you are only obeying orders, have supper with me, I could do with some sane conversation."

"Love to, can I organise the food with chef, it's great to stretch his talent."

"Fine, around seven, remember that nice Californian red we had last time?"

"It will be done, sir," she said, "by the way, I have put all your clothes in the bedroom and your papers have been put on desk, I may have muddled them up."

"It's OK, Marion, I am sure they will have been copied!"

"What? How could you think that? See you later," she said as she flounced out of the room.

Stuart examined the suite, he couldn't complain, it was even more luxurious that the last, the only difference being this really was a cell. He had no doubt now that it was bugged and indeed there were probably hidden cameras around too.

The bedroom was large, with enough room for the very large bed, wardrobes and two settees, although Stuart never did understand why one would want to sit in the bedroom; however, unlike the last suite this bedroom had a massive TV on the wall. The bathroom was very modern yet expensively furnished with a fantastic double power shower that had various jets rendering every part of the body being blasted into submission. If I were renting a place, this would be pretty high on the list, thought Stuart, as he entered the main sitting room again, it had the very latest in technology for entertainment with major audio and video facilities. I will have some fun with that, he thought, you never know I might get some decent programmes. He spent some time moving furniture around until it felt right in his mind. The desk did have a phone and a workstation on it, which he reorganised; it would be a challenge to see if he could find internet access. He looked at his papers, yes they were in a muddle and did they have any idea of their meaning.

During his last stay at Glens Falls Stuart had become depressed and yet somehow he had managed to pull himself out of it by concentrating on a problem that had been on his mind before he was spirited out the Farnborough site to the USA.

It was all very well harnessing the forces of inertia conversion as Stuart had proved and demonstrated, but the team he assembled had indeed focused too much on that outcome without true understanding of the balance of inertia that existed in the Universe. The creation and sources of the energy need to be known and understood if any damage to the Universe's equilibrium is to be avoided.

I suppose it's only natural that we all got caught up with the prospect of unlimited energy for all. Indeed, it was probably Stuart as the discoverer who was most responsible for driving things forward without properly understanding the whole equation.

It's classic, Stuart thought, as he tried to put order back into his notes, I am an engineer and a damn good one, I can make things work and I have some good science, but I don't have the discipline of good scientific analysis and, worse still, the level of mathematics needed was beyond me. Getting Jerry Housden on the team was a real coup, what Jerry didn't understand mathematically wasn't worth knowing he thought. What was especially good about Jerry is he didn't bring any baggage with him. Stuart has encountered so much prejudice to his ideas that he felt sure that Jerry would have them too, but the man was gifted, probably a genius and he understood and articulated Stuart's ideas and made sense of them.

I am the lucky (or unlucky) bastard that happened to discover this strange force and through some crude mathematics, how to harness it. What was always clear to me is that many super clever people had developed theoretical physics to such a point of sophistication that my discovery had to be a part of the jigsaw, it had to fit in somehow; perhaps it still does.

Anyway, to the matter at hand, Stuart was concentrating on the theory and supporting lemma, he had developed with Jerry and the team. The theory was based on the equilibrium of inertia, it recognised Einstein's theory that the Universe is expanding, but specifically in a holistic way and all the energy is counterbalanced, and that the dark matter was fundamental to the equilibrium. So, if that energy was used to redirect itself, could that event disturb the equilibrium and have consequence in space and time somewhere else in the cosmos?

Stuart was engrossed in trying to see whether the theory that enabled energy to be harnessed could be extended and reversed to see what counter effect it would have. The next thing Stuart noticed was hunger, it was mid-afternoon and he was frustrated he wasn't getting anywhere. If he had the intellectual horsepower of his Farnborough team he was sure they would have made some progress. However, he knew that his notes were being analysed to death in some US lab. He also knew that he had some developments in the work that had never been made public and was worried that the information would be misused, so his workings carefully avoided such information, the analysts would think him mad and never get to the bottom of it, unless one of the team had divulged it.

Food… now… he thought, and opened the door to the landing, a uniformed officer immediate stood up from a chair that he had positioned between his door and the staircase.

"Can I help you, sir?" Here we go again, thought Stuart.

"I was going down to the kitchen area to see if can get some food."

"I am happy to get it for you if you wish," he said as he reached for a phone on the wall beside him.

"Well I wanted to go down and stretch my legs. Look, officer is this going to be a problem?"

"No, sir, just trying to be helpful, please follow me down to the kitchen," so I was to be chaperoned. I noticed that his uniform wasn't that of the Police but was Military.

"Are you Army?" Stuart said trying to start a conversation.

"In a way, sir," the man responded.

"That looks a like a pretty powerful handgun?" I ventured.

"Yes, sir it's Glock 22, fourth generation," he said as if I should have known.

"Is it standard US Army issue?"

"Sometimes, sir," he said evasively. I thought, I wouldn't want to cross this man on a dark night. We went down to the kitchen; whereas before I would just raid the fridge and make something up, now there were two men there working on some dish or other.

"You must be Stuart Ashley," the taller of the two men said.

"I am Harry the new chef, and this is Jonny my sous-chef," he said with a big smile pointing to the smaller, man who was equally thin, Jonny nodded an acknowledgement.

"I am not a sous-chef whatever that is, I have been seconded here to help out in the kitchen; at no notice I may add," he said somewhat resentfully.

"Well, that may be so," said Harry, "but Stuart here is a pretty important man, even I have seen his pictures on TV."

"So how do I get some food here?" Stuart asked.

"Just say what you want and I will fix it," replied Harry. "Although Marion has already discussed tonight's menu with me."

"A cheese or ham sandwich?"

"Sure, consider it done."

"Can I go outside to the grounds while I'm waiting?" Stuart said to the soldier. "Sorry I don't know your name."

"Call me Nat, sir, and sure let's get some air."

They went through the double door in the nearby corridor that led out to a large terrace area, which had a series of grand steps going down to various levels with formal gardens stretching down to a lake. On the right there was a large dome-like building which housed a 50-metre pool. Further on behind the dome there were four tennis courts and behind that there was a large enclosed area that was used for various sports.

To the left of the lake was a large wooded area which had a series of paths. Along each path there were a number of exercise stations each demanding a different skill. In the entrance foyer of the main house there were maps showing various training routes, their difficulty and target times to complete. Stuart had used the beginners' path from the day he arrived; it was good fun on the balancing beams and ropes, things he hadn't done since he was a kid, moreover he was starting to feel a little fitter.

There was a lot to explore; Stuart didn't know how far the grounds extended or what was housed in the various small bungalows around the place. It must be some sort of training ground, thought Stuart, but at the moment it's empty and it's all mine!

"I was starting to use the training paths before, can I use them again, Nat?"

"Sure, no problem, I could do with the exercise too," Nat looked like the last thing he needed was more exercise.

"I would like to head out around eight for about an hour tomorrow."

"Great I will see you there," said Nat, "now let's get that sandwich."

"I think I will eat it out here," Stuart didn't want to have this false conversation which really was a way of asking permission for everything or letting his minders know what he was up to, he would just have to earn their trust. At least Marion doesn't make any pretence, and has a sense of humour, I can relax with her.

Sitting out on the patio in the warm sunshine Stuart consumed the sandwich followed by an ice-cold beer. He wasn't going anywhere and decided to try and make sense of recent events. The trouble is that I only have a few pieces of the jigsaw and there are some very large gaps that could easily be misinterpreted. However, the bits I do have may fit together.

My invitation to the UN happened as a result of an agreement between the UK and US governments. It was dressed up as an opportunity for me to put my case to all the UN members and to ensure they all shared in the value of my discovery. The US was to be my host and facilitator to the UN. Stuart had participated with the US and UK as they embarked on project TANGENT that clearly had a political agenda and the report was used as a way of drawing out the political and economic position of countries across the globe. Certainly, it was clear that Peter Dawson and Ed Bruckner had cooked this up, and then it had backfired on them both but in different ways. They hadn't expected the attempted kidnap, or was that part of a plot? Even more worrying was that Russia, North Korea and South Africa were all up to something; Peter and Ed's concern was real, and they had lost the support of China as well.

So what sort of race is this, thought Stuart, his discovery was so revolutionary that it impacted everything, but he and the team had tried to focus its value on specific areas such as transport. The team had already developed prototypes of utility vehicles that needed no fuel and could handle seemingly unlimited loads; at least we haven't found the limit so far, thought Stuart. There had been some fun work on a replacement for the car as well, plus the development of a craft for the air and indeed space. One step at a time we all agreed, or did we? I hope the UK team is holding up otherwise we will have anarchy or at least the chaos that the UN threw up. God what a mess, I wonder if there is a way through.

Marion came onto the terrace. "You're deep in thought," she said. Stuart looked around and sure enough Nat was over by the main steps talking to someone, another security man I suspect.

"I assume you have been briefed about the fiasco at the UN?"

"Yes, I have, or I have been told as much as I need to know," she replied. "It seems that everyone has fallen out with your country."

"Not my country or I thought it was, once. I don't belong anywhere now."

"Well I am sure Uncle Sam would want you."

"Please Marion; this stuff is too big for any country, that's the problem."

"You are being melodramatic now."

"No Marion, I wish I was, but even the team is nervous about what we have found out."

"Well I am serious; I know we would want you to help improve things for everyone."

"Now who's being naïve?"

"Anyway, I was just thinking what a mess this is, I've lost my family and I have created a monster that everyone wants. I only hope the team are staying together and holding the line, that's all that is left."

"What's happened, Marion?" he continued.

"What do you mean?"

"I saw the look on your face, what's happened to the people on the team?"

"Stu, I don't know, I really don't but…"

"You do know something, for God's sake Marion fucking tell me."

"And I'm meant to be a professional, never giving anything away."

"Marion?"

"Ok, I really don't know, but I overheard some discussion about someone called Gary coming here and that you would know him."

"It must be Gary Marshall, I have been working with him for nearly a year before he was repatriated. When is he coming?"

"I really don't know anything more, Stu, I promise."

"When Marion?"

"Tomorrow sometime, thank God we are on the terrace, I just hope the cameras can't read my lips," she said looking into the middle distance.

"It's OK, I know the place is bugged and there are cameras."

"You don't know the level of sophistication, Stu, they see everything."

"I know this is old-fashioned, Marion, but trust me, I will be really surprised to see Gary tomorrow, but I know the team is broken up which means it's all over and there is nothing to control."

"Can we enjoy the meal now, Stu?"

"Of course we can, but there is one taboo subject, and then I will whip you."

The old Marion returned, "I like a good whipping," there was a twinkle in her eye.

"At backgammon Marion.... backgammon," although his mind was on a lower plane.

They had wanted to sleep together, there was real attraction there, but neither could forsake the idea of the microphones and cameras, as well as the liability to have it on record, as it were!

Stuart awoke at 0730 and apart from a brief scrub of his teeth, he dressed in his sports gear that had magically appeared in his room. By the time he reached the terrace Nat was there with another fit-looking man.

"This is Paul, he is on the security staff here," Paul nodded in my direction and proceeded to finish off his warm-up routine.

"Look guys, I know you have to keep an eye on me, though God knows why? This place is like a fortress, but if you want to exercise at your pace not mine, just do it, I'm not going anywhere."

"You know we can't do that, Mr Ashley."

"Please, it's Stuart."

"Well if you or Nat take it in turns to do your own thing, I am not going to keep up with you."

"OK we will do that," replied Nat looking at Paul.

"I'm happy to take the first 15 minutes," ventured Paul. "Then we can swap over."

"Great," yelled Nat as he sprinted off.

Paul and I dropped to a steady jog on the beginner circuit. In fact, it was good fun and a real distraction. Paul had been a PE trainer in the Army some time ago and he really enjoyed helping me on and through the various obstacles. We arrived back on the terrace 90 minutes later and I thought I would die of exhaustion; neither Nat nor Paul looked as if they had really been straining themselves. I had a great shower and returned to the terrace for breakfast. Paul and Nat were there already, they could beat me at everything. Still at least their stiffness had gone, and we could talk like normal humans.

"Do either of you guys play tennis?" I asked.

"Not really," Paul ventured.

"Not my game," said Nat.

"Right, then maybe we should play, and I will be able to beat you guys at something."

They both smiled at each other and then at me.

"Oh shit, I bet you are both Davis cup level," Paul just chucked, "that means you are. Still let's have a game about mid-afternoon."

They both agreed and Nat said, "There is one of those ball serving machines somewhere if you want some early practice."

"It sounds like a bit of practice may be a good idea," I said, thinking that I was in for a real drubbing.

I went back to my room and tried to concentrate on the nagging problem with the theory we have developed. The trouble is the theory was just too clean; it fitted too well. It's ironic, Stuart thought, that our work has undone so much of modern scientific theory and yet in the same way, the Inertia Conversion Theory only exposed how much we still don't know about the forces in the Universe. Perhaps it's always like this he reflected, you make a step forward and it fits with the past and the present knowledge and shines a light on the scientific future and its possibilities, the next steps as it were.

This train of thought didn't fit with the IC discovery though, science had gone down a cul-de-sac, and we had taken a wrong turning in the past. It's a bit like the London smog arising from the massive use of coal, cause and effect; cause and effect. There is no such thing as a free lunch as they say; this abundance of free energy, if used, will cause damage somewhere, or should we care. We destroyed much of the South American rain forest before we observed the changes in climate. These comparisons are too trite, Stuart mused; we could do something about the smog and indeed about the climate change. These were in the hands of mankind to repair, but we are dealing with the Cosmos, God alone knows about the cause and effect here... perhaps God does know, he thought with a smile. I am becoming a philosopher and a bad one too.

Marion knocking on the door interrupted his thoughts.

"Gary Marshall is here. Will you come down?"

"Yup, can we have a cuppa on the terrace?"

"Your wish, master," her voice trailing off as she went downstairs.

Stuart went to bathroom and freshened up, he shook his head, I mustn't let this thing eat any more of me than it has, he reflected. He was excited to see Gary and get some news.

Gary was one of the first members to join the joint UK/US IC team last year. The UK Government had decided that it would fund a small international development team which would provide input to the UN science committee. Stuart knew it was political and that there was some judicious pruning of the candidates to join the team before he even got to interview them. Nevertheless, the long list of candidates was pretty good despite any pre-vetting. Gary's CV was impeccable; Columbia, MIT and some time in Cambridge, we all agreed that he was a big asset for the team.

Gary was amazing, life was so unfair when God was handing out attributes…

"Gary," he/she said in a booming voice, "I give you intelligence (both intellectual and emotional), outstanding physique, beauty and oh I nearly forgot, kindness!"

How does one deal with people like that who seem to find everything easy and yet you just like them anyway? He was in his mid-twenties about six-feet high and muscular. He reminded me of Robert Redford in that he had a twinkle in his blue eyes. He was a little vain about his hair, which was long wavy and dark except for the dyed streaks of blond. I never did find out what the tattooed writing on the side of his neck meant and he never mentioned it.

The thing for me was that like all the team, he did not come with any preconceptions but with an outstanding understanding of natural science with strong mathematical analysis. He was first to bring order from the work I had done and then break it down into manageable units for further analysis. Perhaps his analytical skills limited him in the numerous brainstorming sessions but without doubt his contribution had been extraordinary.

"Gary, how the devil are you?" Gary was sitting at one of the tables on the veranda talking with Marion. It looked like I had interrupted a private conversation. Gary got up and gave Stuart a warm hug.

"How are you, Chief, apart from carrying a bit of weight?"

"That was below the belt, I am getting fit here, it's my new health farm."

"I will leave you two to chat," said Marion as she got up to leave. "Jonny will bring some tea."

"Marion, I assume our conversation will be heard? I say this so that Gary knows that I know."

"Thanks, Chief, nothing changes, we have been living in a goldfish bowl for a long time."

"So, tell me, Gary, what's been happening to the old team, to you, have you seen Zoe?"

"In reverse order I did see Zoe but only for a moment when I was at the government's Victoria Street place for a progress review. She was leaving as I arrived; she was ushered out to a waiting car and briefly nodded to me en-route."

"How was she, it's been ages and I still miss her."

"Honestly... she looked thin and tired, really not at all well."

"I must get to see her," Stuart said.

"Chief, she won't be able to see you."

"OK let's change the subject," Stuart said in a resigned voice. "I can't do anything while I am imprisoned here anyway."

"A comfortable prison, though, Chief."

"Yeah but a prison nevertheless, so the team has been disbanded?"

"Almost immediately you were shipped off to the TANGENT thing."

"Well as you know I didn't really get a chance to participate after the kidnap, so I wasn't part of TANGENT unless you count my presence at its disintegration."

"I had heard that it had not gone well but that it was expected to be restructured?"

"Very unlikely, there aren't enough major players now."

"I have my own sort of prison as well."

"Explain?"

"Well I was sent back to the US and had a weird debriefing, as if we had been doing something secret and keeping it back from all the heads. Anyway, after that I was asked, at least I think I was asked, to join a US-only team to continue developments."

"How many in the team, do I know them?"

"Sorry, Chief, I was told not to say anything about the new team, it's somewhere on the West Coast and well-funded so I can't complain, although we are restricted to the application of IC now."

"So, what brings you here?"

"Just to see how you were, as a friend."

"Gary, I appreciate that, and I do see you as a real friend. We did some fantastic things and had some fun on the way. Do you remember that daft skateboard thing you designed?"

"Hell, Harry Franks said he was a good skier, so I assumed he could handle the board at height."

"Sure, but at 20 feet, he got himself into a real mess, I am just glad he wasn't hurt."

"His pride was though," said Gary with that wicked twinkle in his eyes.

"Good times, anyway I'm glad it worked out for you."

"Come and work with us Stuart, it could be like the old team. I said I would ask so it gave me the chance of knowing you were OK."

"No thanks, Gary; I am spending my time thinking about that equilibrium issue and whether we should progress at all."

"It's out of our hands, Chief, now it's a race to see who gets the lead on IC."

"Just like the arms race of the sixties and seventies except with more players…"

"And the trouble is they don't know the end game."

"Can you say what area you are working on?"

"Would it entice you, if I told you?"

"It might," said Stuart without much sincerity.

"Hell, I can tell you some of the basics, it was agreed that I could release sufficient info to interest you."

"Approved by who, Gary? I tell you I don't know who is running the show but there seems to be so many people with fingers in this pie."

"The Project Director is a guy called Leo Catani, do you know him, he was at MIT for the last five or six years?"

"Sure, I had hoped to get him onboard before our original team was formed. He seemed keen to engage and then went cold on the whole thing."

"I don't think he did go cold, it's clear that he has been building his team for some time, long before this TANGENT thing imploded. He works for Ed Bruckner who as you know reports to the President."

"Oh yes, I have met Mr Bruckner, he's as untrustworthy as they get… I hope that's recorded on video!!"

"You don't change do you, Stuart? As soon as you smell authority, you get all bolshie. Anyway, they are all well past my pay-grade and to be frank if this is the only way to pursue IC then I will do it, it's like a drug, I can't leave it alone."

"I know how that feels, that's why this equilibrium issue is bugging me."

"Chief, we all know that the energy has to come from somewhere and we will figure that out eventually. In the meantime I reckon there is enough power in the whole cosmos to keep this little planet ticking along."

"Maybe, you are right, but I will keep it in my mind. So, what are you working on?"

"Well it's primarily air travel. We have all the basics sorted so it's about design and function. We are doing some interesting things on friction by using the IC technology to create a 'pull layer' around the craft so that we shield it from all the obvious inhibitors that a conventional aircraft has to endure."

"It sounds like some sort of force field right?"

"Yup, you could really call it that. It's my baby, I figured out how we extend the IC power unit to the surface of the craft."

"Gary, I can see why you are so enthusiastic, I bet it's all military craft, though?"

"Yes and no, the programme is funded through the DoD but there are secondees from Lockheed and Boeing there, looking at civilian travel."

"Amazing, you know this TANGENT project was flawed in so many ways but one thing that was worth sorting out was the new rules of the air, it's going to be chaos otherwise. I tell you what, Gary, let's get a couple of beers and I will walk you round my country club. We will have escorts of course and maybe you can stay to dinner?"

"Already agreed with Marion, although I will have to leave around ten tonight. I am giving a briefing at the Pentagon Monday afternoon."

"Lucky you, I promise not to talk work anymore. How's your love life going? Have you seen Jerry Housden?"

It was a great afternoon and evening for Stuart, for the first time in recent memory he wasn't relentlessly on guard. In fact, both he and Gary sparked off each other. Gary remembered some of the boozy evenings where Stuart, Jerry and Harry Franks had argued for hours about how to take known current science and translate it into new theory. It was tough to try and align The Standard Model for example, since dark energy changed the way fundamental particles should be considered.

There was heavy rainfall that Monday and Stuart really didn't feel like attempting the fitness trail. Nevertheless, he needed something to while away the time and getting fit seemed like a good plan and, perhaps, getting into bed with Marion. He duly arrived at the terrace to be greeted by Paul and Nat who suspected he was only a fair-weather man. Stuart did his best but was still in awe of Nat and Paul, they were just so incredibly fit and good at every sport.

In the afternoon Stuart had that game of tennis, he had been a pretty good player a few years back, so he knew he could give a reasonable game. There were four courts in pristine condition just behind the dome; the courts were surrounded by a large yew hedge on three sides with the fourth side facing over a lawn to the lake. Behind the rear hedge there was some sort of rifle range that Stuart had seen when on the fitness trail.

He should have beaten Nat on skill, but his fitness let him down. Paul on the other hand was a seriously good player and Stuart barely managed to win a point; Nat fared little better. They uncovered the automatic ball server and set it up so that Stuart could get some practice in. He didn't want to be rusty should Peter Dawson turn up on Thursday.

Tuesday and Wednesday followed a similar routine except that Stuart also did some swimming; it was clear he was beginning to get some stamina back. Parts of day were spent with Stuart playing around with ideas to create Gary's force field as well as some other ideas on IC application he had been toying with. There was no doubt that he and Marion were getting as close as they could without the event; backgammon can be a poor substitute for sex.

Paul and Nat were more relaxed, leaving Stuart alone from time to time albeit only briefly. They suddenly became sharper and more remote and Stuart knew something was up. Sure enough Rick Marsh appeared at the door of the old library that Stuart had adopted as his reading room; it had no clear exit apart from the door and was considered a safe place to leave Stuart to his thoughts. If there were hidden cameras in the room, Stuart couldn't discover them despite his best effort. Indeed it had been one of those silly personal challenges he had set himself to identify all the hidden cameras at the location.

"Stuart, it's good to see you, I hear you are on a fitness regime?"

"Hello, Rick, what brings you here?" Stuart asked coldly, whatever brought him here is not in my best interests, he thought.

"I promised to come here and give you an update; quite a lot has been happening you know, or rather you don't know," he said chuckling at his wit.

"I don't remember you promising to do that?"

"So you don't want an update and I've wasted my time coming up here?" he said cynically.

"It's like Foucault's Pendulum, you know there is one at the UN building?"

"I'm confused," said Rick. "What's Foucault's Pendulum got to do with anything?"

"Do you know what is?" I said.

"Of course I know what it fucking is. Do you think I am sort of thick prick, well think again?"

My God you are a prickly SoB, a definite chip on the shoulder, thought Stuart.

"When I was a kid I was fascinated by it, I just couldn't understand that the pendulum didn't change its path but that the earth did. It sort of set me thinking that we are such a tiny fraction of all the forces that surround us."

"I still don't get what you are saying."

"Well, at the TANGENT meeting there were so many agendas and there we were trying to find a constant, some common ground to unite our interests and ironically all those interests amount to nothing in the bigger scheme of things."

"Well I believe in the here and now and I am not going to see my country disadvantaged."

"I understand," Stuart said resignedly, "the trouble is I am not a political animal and cannot see all the variables at play. I am just a pawn on the sidelines."

"I wish you were," he said, "and where is that coffee I asked for?" He got up and went to the doorway and yelled for coffee.

Jonny turned up almost immediately. "Sorry for the delay, sir," he said bringing a jug of coffee on a tray. "Anything for you, Stuart?" he asked.

"Thanks Jonny, I will have my usual beer."

"I'll have one of those as well," Rick said, "and make it snappy this time." Jonny retired quickly to the kitchens.

"So, you were about to give me an update?"

"Sure, let me explain why. Firstly because there was this agreement between our two counties to try and lead a programme on how we best use this invention of yours. You were a major part of that linkage to show the world that we weren't trying to keep our cards to ourselves so to speak. Frankly, both the US and the UK are very nervous that China and Russia may misuse the technology for their own interests; indeed we have concerns about India too. That's why we tried to use the UN to drive some agreement."

"So your motives were genuine? I am not so naïve that the US and UK don't have their own self-interest."

"Of course, and the way I see it we are already protecting our interests, imagine the whole of the US Defence capability being compromised. What we were trying to do was just get some harmonisation across the globe rather than anarchy. The world has never faced such a dilemma, it's new ground for all of us."

Stuart was intrigued, was this guy for real? "Please go on."

"Well you have had plenty of time to think about it. Your invention changes everything, the world order is based on some basic stable principles and they are no longer valid. Every country's trade and economy is affected with consequent political pressures. The world has become more fragile and unstable thanks to you."

"Oh great, you think I didn't see this coming. You talk about stable principles; well the world order is based on wealth, power and corruption. That's why I published as much as I could on the net to make sure no country was disadvantaged; it's like resetting the global economy."

"Who the fuck do you think you are...? GOD...? If only you had thought about what you were doing. Listen, no-one in their right mind would be against making sure the whole world was a better place over time, but not immediately, it needs transition, anyway you have unlocked the box and it's all theory now. You already see every country trying to get further ahead in applying IC technology and the poorer countries will inevitably be disadvantaged. And yes Uncle Sam will be OK. So your fucking idealism has backfired."

"And, by the way, this isn't Rick Marsh speaking, you can check it out with every influential leader in both our countries. Hell, just about every democracy for that matter!"

"So tell me why you and Dawson didn't engage with me, I could have helped TANGENT?"

"Come on, you thought it was all conspiracy and with your brand of naïve idealism? I bet you still don't see the mess we are in?"

Stuart was numb; Marsh had told him what he knew deep down. His motives had been right at the time but yes everything had backfired. If only people had believed in his discovery, but just about every scientist, and every politician did their best to ignore or disprove his findings.

"Ok, but you didn't come here just to tell me it's a mess?"

"No, but it seems that you needed some straight-talking and a reality check. We are looking at trying to restart TANGENT and wanted to put out a new UN-led manifesto, so we need some input from you."

"What do you need?"

"Something that shows you have more new input on IC that you want to share."

"A sort of incentive to come?"

"Exactly."

"Well, I don't think I have anything new to add, but I do have a concern that there may be a knock-on effect from using IC."

"Such as?"

"Well, there's no free lunch here, using dark matter energy must alter things."

"Forget that, it needs to be something positive."

"Then I can't help."

"Ok I thought I would ask, they said it was unlikely, so we will put out something anyway."

"Really, like what?"

"We already have some new developments we could partially share."

"From Catani's labs?"

"How did you know? Of course, you spoke with Gary."

"It will go out in your name and, by the way, we don't expect to reconvene for another three weeks so enjoy yourself here."

"Do you know if Peter Dawson is coming here, he mentioned

something about Thursday?"

"Not if Ed Bruckner has anything to do with it, Dawson wrecked the last meeting and Ed hasn't forgiven him."

"Must go back to the bear pit, I will be back sometime next week to update you and get some time with Marion!" he said with a pretend leer.

"You're OK, Marsh," I said.

"I wish you were OK, Stuart. See you."

Stuart saw Rick Marsh through the library window talking with Marion and Nat on the veranda area. It was an animated discussion with Marsh waving his arms about to express something! Stuart reflected on things, he was a prisoner in a US secure location and a previous plan (or plot) between the UK and the US had broken down and he was now being used as bait for a restart of TANGENT. What was TANGENT all about really? He felt powerless to do anything, he didn't have the skill to escape and then even if he did where would he go? The UK had abandoned him, and he didn't know why, so the only thing to do was play along.

Later that Wednesday night Stuart asked Marion if there was any news about Peter Dawson coming the following day. Marion didn't know if his visit had been arranged which would have been strange since she is responsible for all visitors and residents. She went off to check and said there wasn't a planned visit and added that she wasn't surprised given the relationship Peter Dawson now had with Ed Bruckner.

On Thursday there was no sign of Dawson, so Stuart resigned himself to a routine. A few weeks later, after the fitness trail and a swim, Stuart said to Nat and Paul that he would have a tennis practice. They all went down to the courts, Paul and Nat sat chatting while Stuart proved that he could at least beat a ball-serving machine.

It was close to lunchtime and Stuart was tiring, he hadn't had so much exercise for a long time. He noticed that Paul was talking urgently into his phone, and Nat was alert. Paul relayed some words to Nat and then took off at a run to the main house.

"What's the matter?" said Stuart with tennis balls landing all around him.

"Security alert, probably nothing but an alarm has been breached near the front entrance. Paul and some of the others are checking it out. Meanwhile we stay here." Stuart stopped the serving machine and sat next to a very different Nat, all his senses on high alert holding a Glock 22 which he had taken from his sports bag. His phone, clearly a sophisticated comms device, was pinned to his ear.

"Relax, Stuart, if something happens just follow my instructions," said Nat. Stuart felt very vulnerable. Suddenly there was a loud bang which seemed to come from the front of the house; Stuart heard more unintelligible chatter coming franticly from the comms. Then there was a strange swishing sound behind the yew hedge close to the court.

Nat yelled, "Follow me, stay close," and within seconds they were both immersed in dense choking smoke followed by several large explosions. Stuart dropped to his knees coughing and wheezing, his ears were ringing, and he felt completely numb; he couldn't see Nat anywhere. Suddenly strong arms held him, he yelled out for Nat and then everything went dark; a bag had been put over his head. Stuart was about 180 pounds but was being carried by someone with immense strength, they went through some trees and a bush or was it the yew hedge? He tried to yell for help, but it just emerged as muffled grunts. He was then being carried by two or was it three people at a pace? It felt like several people taking turns to carry him,; the pace never slowing.

Suddenly he was hoisted onto a seat and his arms were clamped down by straps onto some tubular frame, his legs too were strapped onto the frame; finally another strap was bound across his chest, he was completely immobile. What existed of Stuart's conscious mind was in turmoil, he had never been involved in any violence whatsoever, he felt his bladder going. All he could think was help me, someone please help me.

A motor fired up and Stuart felt the vibrations through his body, it's a motorbike, I am strapped to a bloody motorbike. Just then the bike took off with a deep roar and Stuart was forced back into the frame. They were going very fast, firstly up a hill then a quick right into a dip and out again almost taking off, then a bit of flat bumpy surface followed by a plunge down. All Stuart could do was follow the flow of the powerful machine since he was physically part of its structure. He lost consciousness momentarily and realised he was vomiting into the bag and gagging, fighting for breath. The machine did not slow for what seemed hours, over one hill into a dip, left right and on again. Finally, it eventually slowed and went through some undergrowth, Stuart could feel branches whipping him but then he was on a flat surface accelerating again, this time even faster then just as suddenly braking and stopping.

"Get the bag off," someone yelled, "he's bloody choking." With that the hood was roughly pulled off and Stuart saw several people all dressed differently but with faces covered. He felt the straps being undone and was hauled up again and put into the rear of some sort of truck onto soft bedding; there was another man already in the rear of the van. As the back doors were closing there was a prick in Stuart's arm and he felt some force flowing through him, closing him down; he gave up and passed out.

CHAPTER 5

Genesis

It was Friday, a strange week, Stuart thought, work was going OK but there had been a delegation from one of the HQ divisions. Ostensibly the visit was to provide an internal audit but somehow there was more to it than that.

There were four people in the team, a chap called Sawyer who was a finance man from HQ that Stuart had met before, plus three external consultants. The consultants were the usual mix of one senior partner or associate leading things and two younger trainees recently recruited from university and doing all the real work. Their main focus was on the plant and the production staff. As Operation Manager, Stuart was quizzed on the manufacturing equipment and its utilisation as well as the workforce shift arrangements. None of this was much of a surprise to Stuart and he was able to handle the visit and provide all the necessary information. Sadly though the order book was low, and the figures did not look good.

"Are you looking at consolidating our capacity with other plants to optimise overheads?" Stuart asked. This was code for 'are you closing us down?'

"Not at all," replied Sawyer sharply, "but you are obviously aware that the production is under capacity and we have to look at ways to keep costs down."

The team would not be drawn on the objective and so Stuart surmised wearily that their findings would not be good for the site. Their communication continued to be limited, even abrupt, which added to the general rumour that the plant was for the chop. This sort of thing feeds off itself, mused Stuart, moral is now low, and so production and quality are likely to fall, making the situation worse. I am not trusted enough to know the truth and so most of the workforce think I know what's going on but will not share it. What's worse is, at fifty-two, this is the not a good age to be made redundant.

Stuart got into the Range Rover, cleared his mind and started the drive home. He always looked forward to Friday evenings; it was a special part of the week especially after the shitty week he had just finished. He was looking forward to a family evening; it was a rare event but somehow Lucy, Henry and Mark were all home this weekend. Admittedly it was Zoe's birthday, but you couldn't rely on the kids even then. Stuart looked at the sky, yes the weather would hold, and we can have the BBQ outdoors.

When he got home, it was chaos as usual. Lucy and Henry had argued and were not talking although Marc seemed to be the liaison officer.

"They had a row, Dad, why are they always arguing?" said Marc.

"I give up, Marc, why are they always arguing?" said Stuart.

"Stop it, Dad, it's true, they must hate each other."

"It's the way of families, Marc, they would do anything for each other and for that matter for you too. It's just that since leaving home they have gone separate ways and have developed strong personalities. At least that's my view."

"Great view," said Zoe rather cynically. "You two," she yelled, "make it up NOW or leave. I will not have my birthday weekend spoilt by bickering!"

"Diplomacy always wins out, Marc," Stuart said.

It was a good evening and indeed a good weekend, everyone in the family re-bonded (well sort of!).

As he drove into work on the Monday, Stuart mused on his fortunes. The most important thing to him was his family and although both he and Zoe were at the point where the fledglings leave the nest, it was a good feeling inside that they were all well-prepared for their future lives.

As he arrived at the car park he noticed that Sawyer and his merry men had arrived before him. Very impressive, he thought, since it was only 730. Indeed the Sawyer team had been there all weekend.

"Good morning guys," he said with as much enthusiasm he could muster, "have you been working all weekend?"

There was a look of disdain from Sawyer. "If only the factory was working all weekend then we wouldn't be here," he said.

"Point taken," said Stuart, as he went into his small glass office to ensure the week's work schedule was in place, also avoiding more of Sawyer's looks.

Stuart was on his second coffee of the day when Sawyer opened the office door. "Are you free to chat now?"

That feels like an order thought Stuart repressing his natural dislike for the man.

"We have to move quickly," he said "every day that the factory operates at its current capacity is costing the company £165k. So I have spoken to Earl Newton with my recommendations and he wants them in place as of today."

"And what are the recommendations?" asked Stuart, knowing that it was going to be painful.

Sawyer looked at the paper he had in front of him.

"Number one. It's a three-day week for everyone, so the plant will close this Thursday and everything is to be powered down. There will be a two-shift system covering fourteen hours each day."

"Number two. All subcontractors are to be removed unless absolutely necessary."

"Number three. All future purchasing will be authorised by me. The rest is detail," he concluded. "It's all listed here, please action it urgently."

"The workforce won't like it any more than I do," said Stuart.

"I know it's unpalatable, but there really aren't any other options," Sawyer replied. Stuart did sense some sympathy from Sawyer.

"If you guys made the plan, why don't you execute it?" Stuart said, rather more sharply than he intended.

"This is an instruction, Ashley, just get on with it."

"And by the way, your job is formally on the 'at risk' register, here is the confirmation," Sawyer passed him a letter confirming that he could have his job terminated with immediate effect.

"We have a new HR lady joining us later today, her name is Elise Ripley, she will handle all the people issues, and we will be around over coming weeks just to make sure it's all happening," and with that, he left the office.

Stuart was frozen for a minute. This is daft, he thought, I knew something was coming and in fact I probably would have done the same as them. So why am I surprised? I guess it's the reality of things plus the fact that they want me to be Mr Nasty and their clean little hands will never have the dirt of their actions under their fingernails. It's easy to make decisions if you don't take responsibility for your actions. Oh well here goes.

Stuart called his production team together and gave them the news. Their reaction was predictable.

"Look guys, this is not a conspiracy, we all know that things couldn't go on without a better order book."

"Why didn't you confide in us, Stu, we knew Sawyer was a hatchet man, but you could have involved us, maybe we could have produced a better solution," said Dick Chivers, one the production managers.

"Dick, I am not being sloped-shouldered but they really didn't involve me in their thinking, or lack of it," Stuart said irritably.

"Well I bet you are ok," he retorted.

"That's strange, this 'at risk' letter doesn't say that," said Stuart waving the paper around. I really shouldn't have done that, he thought. "Guys we are in the same boat so let's make it happen, if things improve, we may still have jobs. There may be some union problems, let me know if there are and please involve Elise Ripley, our HR expert, who has lots of experience in handling short working."

Stuart called the meeting to an end; there really were no words he could use to give them a sense of optimism. Still, they were a good and loyal team and he knew that would do their best. He noticed that the Sawyer team was huddled together having some sort of whispered conversation. Stuart went over to them.

"The deed is done," he said and walked out. As he walked across the car park he took several deep breaths. God I feel stifled, he thought. He tried to phone Zoe but without success. Tonight is soon enough to tell her the news; best keep things going.

It was around seven in the evening that Stuart got home. He had stopped for a beer with a few of his team for mutual consolation and frustration.

"Hi Zoe, I'm home."

"So I hear. I'm in the kitchen," came a response.

"Good day, love?" she said.

"Bad day... no... very bad day," Stuart sagged, it had been a very shitty day. He really didn't want to discuss it with anyone but nevertheless went through his narrative of the day's events, Zoe asking questions, the answers to which Stuart thought were blindingly obvious.

"So the good news is you will have me around more," he said.

"And the bad news is we won't have enough money to survive very long," she replied. "Well it's done, let's go out and have a celebratory steak."

"I do love you Zoe, we will find a way through this, I promise."

"I know," she said finding her jacket. It was strange, but Stuart felt Zoe was somewhat distracted by something else. "Oh well."

The rest of that short week was spent smoothing things over and getting some order into the new way of operating at the factory. In fact it had gone better than expected. Many local businesses had folded over recent months and it wasn't exactly a surprise to anyone. It was strange not to go to work that Thursday and Stuart took the liberty of staying in bed for an hour longer, until Zoe roused him with a diatribe of obscenities all to do with Stuart being a lazy bastard who had better sort himself out.

"What are you doing today?" Zoe asked when Stuart finally appeared in the kitchen.

"I thought I would start to sort out the garage and workshop," he replied.

"Well before you do, why don't you start exploring other jobs?

Let's face it your current one is tenuous at best and doesn't really offer much of a future."

"OK, Zoe," he said rather resignedly, "but there aren't too many firms looking for a fifty-two-year-old operation executive, not around Smythfield anyway."

"I know Stuart, but Portsmouth is not that far, if you spread your net a bit wider I am sure something will emerge."

"Yup, you're right, as ever, I will get on the web this morning and initiate some contacts. I will make it a daily discipline."

"And it would be good if you got rid of the junk in the garage and workshop, maybe I could put my car away for a change."

"Will do, my little pet," he replied as he made a swift exit to the study with a plate of toast in one hand.

It hadn't been a particularly productive morning, but Stuart knew he had started the process and was sure that if he kept at it then something would turn up. Meanwhile they would learn to live on three quarters of their previous income. Stuart remembered the advice he had got from a local estate agent who said that good handymen were in short supply and that their large number of rented properties always had something going wrong, from a leaking roof to a broken dishwasher. Maybe I could do something for two days a week, he mused.

Zoe was out again, attending some exhibition at a local college, so Stuart made a sandwich and took it out to his workshop. It was an impressive building, its space measuring around nine metres by six. It was located behind two large garages and was originally built by a previous owner as part of his business. Stuart had immediately wanted to buy the house once he had seen the workshop. Previously he had stored all his machinery in a couple of old wooden sheds, so the place was like a palace to him.

His palace, however, was rather tarnished since he had accumulated so much 'stuff' over the years. I am going to be robust this time, if I haven't used something in the last five years then it goes, Stuart decided, unless of course it might be useful!

Where to start, that was the problem. The Morgan was taking up a lot of space in the second garage but there were lots of parts in the workshop. The solution was to finish what had become a five-year project. Stuart knew that one of the easiest decisions was to get rid of those three power generators that the company had been throwing out a couple of years ago. They were massive units and all from the late '40s early '50s Two of them were the same model, but one was much larger. It was known that none of them worked but Stuart was sure he could cannibalise enough from all three to get one working, but why? Well it had just been something in his psyche, he hated quality things not working and put to use.

He had thought that he could rig some sort of wind contraption to drive the generator, but it had only been a whim and not really thought through. The problem now was weight. The company had only been too pleased to let the generators go, they were large and heavy and taking up space, which is exactly what they were doing to Stuart. If I don't do anything else, getting rid of these is absolutely necessary. They may be worth something for scrap; after all they each had a series of massive magnets and plenty of copper. Stuart had stored the larger of the generators against the side of the workshop and the other two on the opposite side. He had managed to squeeze his main workbench between them, so he knew that moving them was major task and he would have to find someone with a mobile block and a crane.

Stuart had arranged some home comforts in his workshop, he had installed a homemade music system to give him mega-watts of surround sound, an old American fridge storing an abundant supply of beer and cokes and, most recently, a communications system to give him broadband. Using the web, he tracked down someone who was interested in the generators and even seemed to know the model. They were able to come down from Newcastle in a couple of weeks and if they could agree a price then he would take them. That's it, thought Stuart, if I have to pay to get rid of them then I will.

He decided the next job in his tidying task was to get rid of the backlog of repairs that he had accepted especially Nigel's bloody strimmer. Wendy had contacted Zoe several times on behalf of Nigel to see if was repaired. Stuart put the strimmer on his bench and span the blade; it ran freely. He decided to power it up, plugged it in, held it down near the floor and pulled the operation switch. The strimmer went wild and Stuart nearly dropped it. The motor was turning but the blade was idle, the shaft must be broken or disconnected. Diagnostic complete, that's not a big problem, thought Stuart, I will take it apart and see what needs repairing. But why did the strimmer go berserk when he powered it up; Stuart repeated the exercise this time with a firmer grip on the strimmer, the same thing happened again, the unit pulling wildly left to right and reversing. The power generators of course, it was those massive magnets that interfered with the small electric motor causing some sort of forces, Stuart didn't know much about magnetism but did know that some powerful flux had caused the strimmer to be out of control. He vaguely recalled something about gauss from his school days.

He decided to strip the strimmer on the mechanics bench at the other end of the workshop; the sound system was blasting *Rebel Rebel* by Bowie so he never heard the gentle hum coming from two of the generators. It was about seven in the evening when he heard Zoe on the intercom.

"This is base to workshop, come in."

"Yes, Zoe, workshop to base come back little buddy."

"Don't give me any shit, your supper is on the table or in the bin, your choice."

"Whoa, Mrs Grumpy, I am coming in, workshop out."

Stuart turned off all the power and opened the back door, it was heavy rain, he sprinted up the garden to the house. Meanwhile the low hum from the generators continued. He joined Zoe and Marc for supper; Zoe was cross at the waste of talent at the local college because of inadequate funding and was determined to rectify it. To be fair Zoe had a long list of causes that she was passionate about and she always seemed to improve things. Stuart was proud of her, she had a set of values that were uncompromising, and moreover if she felt someone or something wasn't right she would put all her energy into making it right.

"So what's your plan?" Stuart asked.

"A number of us are getting together to lobby the Arts Council, I'll keep you posted."

"And what about you, Marc, did your day go well?"

"OKish, I didn't get a real part in the play." He couldn't hide the disappointment in his voice.

"What was the play?" asked Stuart.

"Stuart, don't you ever listen, you know Marc has been in the dramatic society for a while and they are putting on a production of *Hamlet*, Marc was hoping for the part of Horatio."

"So what happened, Marc, did you have an audition?"

"Yeh, but I screwed up and all I have now is a part as a palace guard."

"Anyway, one of the other boys is a better actor so I didn't expect it." Stuart made a mental note to talk to Marc about it when the disappointment had worn off. He decided to change the subject.

"Well I have made three commitments today," Stuart said proudly.

"Oh really," said Zoe, "like what?"

"To get the Morgan restored by summer, to get all the repairs completed and to get rid of those generators."

"What about the fourth commitment?"

"The fourth, Zoe?"

"Yes, finding another job?"

"Absolutely it's four commitments," conceded Stuart.

Marc laughed. "I'll help you with the Morgan, Dad," Stuart was pleased that at least one of his offspring had a passion for repairing things.

It was Friday and that morning Stuart had continued his hunt for another job. He had not made much progress but was starting to assemble ideas and opportunities in his head. There was a chance of working for one of the large defence suppliers down in Portsmouth; it was slightly less pay but worth a punt. He had re-written his CV and asked for an application form online.

Just after a snack lunch Stuart returned to his workshop. Nigel's strimmer was in pieces on the bench, the drive shaft was broken, and the easiest repair was to turn a new shaft in the metal lathe. Stuart found the right grade steel and rigged up the lathe. He didn't have any music on and he vaguely heard a soft hum with a definite frequency to it. He thought it was coming from the fluorescent lights; they often made some humming noises, so he put it out of his mind and concentrated on turning the new spindle and then cutting new threads at either end. When he had re-fixed the shaft and reassembled the trimmer he plugged it in and tested it. It worked as good as new, Stuart was smug, he couldn't share it with anyone, but he knew that his work was better than the original manufacturer. Just for fun, he took the running strimmer to the far end of the workshop to watch the magnetic effect. Sure enough the strimmer did its little dance. Stuart observed that it was the same dance each time, at least magnetic forces are consistent.

He left the strimmer by the door; later he would take it back to the house for Nigel to collect. No, Nigel probably expected Stuart to deliver it to him and thank him for the opportunity to repair it. In practice he knew that Zoe would phone Wendy who would collect it.

What is my next repair job, thought Stuart, as he rummaged around one of the machine benches? Of course it had to be that door on a wood-burning stove. Stuart couldn't even remember who had asked him to repair it and then recalled that it was of Zoe's friends. Well it just needed some re-welding once the large decorative handle had been removed. However, it was a very stubborn handle and being cast iron Stuart had to be careful not to break it even further. Stuart knew that welding cast iron was difficult, so he decided to provide studded reinforcements behind the break. The job looked simple but it was much harder than the strimmer. If only the bloody bolts would give and release the handle. Eventually one of the bolts moved and Stuart started on the second. The spanner slipped and Stuart dropped it, but instead of hitting the floor the spanner hovered. It was about a foot off the floor and was rising and falling gently about once a second. Stuart was intrigued, it must be those magnets, he thought, and reached for the spanner. As he did so the spanner continued in motion and Stuart was surprised that no matter how hard he pulled, he could not break it out of its defined path. This is seriously weird, he thought, I must figure out what's going on.

The practical part of Stuart's brain kicked in; let's get a video going so I can check out all the factors that may be influencing the effect. He went back to the house and grabbed a video recorder, once back in the workshop he rigged up the video on a tripod with the focus on an area around the spanner that was still happily performing its gravity-defying dance.

Stuart made a list of all the things that he thought might be causing the effect. He decided to be absolutely methodical in creating the list since the spanner may fall to the floor any time. Let's get the obvious things out the way first, he decided; so he noted the lighting, the day and time, and the workshop temperature, the sound and heat coming from the generators. What else was there? The humidity? The PC is powered on, the arc welder is ready but in standby mode, what other machinery was on? He had his mobile phone with him. Was there anything in the vicinity of the workshop that could have an impact?

When he had exhausted his recording of all the things he could observe, the spanner remained oscillating. The video was still running so Stuart decided to record a few tests on the spanner. Firstly he put a hoop around the spanner a few times to prove (to himself) that it was truly floating, and he wasn't dreaming, then he decided to try and pull the spanner from its place; it really was held strongly by some forces and despite applying all his power, it would not change its path. Stuart remembered that he had a block and tackle that he used for removing engines and decided to see if he could move the spanner using its mechanical advantage. He collected the equipment from the garage and rigged it on a roof beam that was slightly offset above the spanner. Stuart attached the lifting chain to the spanner and took up the slack on the block as the spanner rose to its height. As the spanner descended, the strain on the big wooden beam was evident. He could hear the beam beginning to crack so he hit the quick release ratchet. Well, he thought, how in the hell do I measure the force that is controlling all of this?

Stuart had unconsciously moved to trying to remove the forces that were acting on the spanner and so he turned off all the electricity in the workshop with the mains fuse; it had no effect on the magical spanner! It reminded him of an experiment in super-conductivity that he saw many years ago whereby a metal disc floated in mid-air due to a low temperature super-conductor. Well this effect wasn't based on temperature, or was it? He needed to keep an open mind on what was happening.

It was close to five in the afternoon when he phoned Rob Willard.

"Hi, is that Sue? It's Stuart here; is Rob around by any chance?"

"Stuart, hello, yes he is, he just got in from school five minutes ago."

"Rob," she yelled, "it's Stuart on the phone."

"Hi, Stuart, how's it going?"

"Rob, any chance you could come over, I have something to show you."

"Well I am just finishing a cup of tea, and I have some marking to do, how about six-thirty?"

"It's urgent, Rob, can you come now?"

"What's so urgent it can't wait an hour?" Rob said with some irritation.

"Trust me, Rob; it's really important you come now."

"Is it you and Zoe?" Rob asked.

"What? No... I just have something strange going on and it may be over any minute!"

"Now I am intrigued, OK see you in ten minutes."

"I will be in the workshop... bye."

Stuart heard Rob coming up the path in less than ten minutes.

"OK, I'm here, what's so urgent... shit... what is that?"

"Now you see, Rob... the spanner slipped off the bolt and instead of hitting the floor it just sat in mid-air oscillating."

"Ok, there must be a reasonable explanation... let's have a look," Rob did most of the things that Stuart had done including the powering off all things electrical.

"You must have put a few tonnes on it with the block, and it didn't budge?"

"No, the power holding it is serious stuff. As you can see I have recorded all the variables that I can think of plus a video."

"It's got to be something do with those industrial generators," said Rob.

"Well they are warm and making a humming noise, so I agree," said Stuart. "Also the strimmer went mad when I brought it near them."

"Show me," said Rob. Stuart brought the spinning strimmer within the similar area to the spanner, again it became uncontrollable. Rob took the strimmer from Stuart. "It's following a very definite path; can you record it?" Stuart took the video and spent some time ensuring he had the tracking of the strimmer.

"So what do you think?" said Stuart.

"No idea, mate, no idea, has Zoe seen it?"

"She is picking Marc up and should be in soon. Come on, you are the bloody scientist, you must have a clue?"

"Seriously, Stu, I really have no idea, I am torn between dismantling everything to stop it and then seeing whether we can re-start it. Or… leaving it alone and getting some more intellectual horsepower in to examine it."

"Yes, we should leave it, I think," Rob finally concluded. "What an amazing phenomenon, I have never heard of anything like it."

Zoe and Marc came into the workshop just then.

"I wondered what you two were doing here?"

"I asked Rob over since I can't figure out why this spanner is floating in mid-air."

Zoe did a double take on the spanner whist Marc just said, "Cool," and tried to hold the spanner still, only to find that it was stronger than him!

"Neither of us have a clue, so Rob suggests we get someone in who may have more knowledge about its cause."

"Good idea," said Zoe, "there will be a rational explanation, just because the intellect of Smythfield can't solve it."

"I bet it will all be over by tomorrow," she concluded, "anyway let's check it out then," and with that, she headed back to the house.

"Well, I can't turn it off anyway," Stuart said. "If it is still going tomorrow, perhaps you could give me some names of people who may be interested."

"I will think on," said Rob, "although I am not sure who has the specialist knowledge. Let's speak tomorrow," and he left.

"Dad, this is really weird, you know, I do hope it's still going tomorrow, I had better get in; I have a lot of homework tonight."

Stuart was left alone, he tried to free his thinking from all the obvious explanations, was the spanner defying gravity and if so what forces were at play and why were they so powerful? He put a marker at the highest and the lowest point of the oscillation to see if it changed overnight. Stuart closed the workshop door and headed for the house.

It didn't surprise Stuart that his night sleep was deeply disturbed. There have been many times when he had a problem on his mind and somehow he always seemed to think through a solution in his semi-conscious state. Only this time, the solution was not to be found, and yet for some daft reason he wanted it solved immediately, he always found a solution to everything and now was in a desert of ideas.

He awoke about 6am, or rather he capitulated to consciousness and made a cup of tea. It was Saturday; I wonder if Rob can get someone on the case, he thought. He couldn't resist going to the workshop, albeit in the dark and pouring rain, to check on his spanner; his spanner, that sounded so stupid!

Still there it was, waiting for him, doing its motion in a well-behaved way. He took the tea up to Zoe. "It's still going," he said.

"What is?" she blearily replied.

"My bloody spanner dear, my bloody spanner!"

"Why don't you give it a name?" she said cynically.

"I will," he said, "in future I shall call it the floater."

"That's a bit vulgar," she giggled, "but it's your floater."

It was frustrating. Stuart kept looking at the floater; its oscillation hadn't changed at all over night. I must find the answer, he thought, but knowing there were folk who could probably resolve things very quickly.

Rob phoned at ten. "I have spoken with an old mate of mine who teaches Natural Sciences at Southampton. She has agreed to come over this afternoon and have a look." Great, thought Stuart, a solution at last. He returned to the workshop and tried to move the spanner again, he also dropped several other spanners from the same set around the same point and they just fell as normal. Whatever force this is it's the spanner that's key, all around it normal gravitation applies.

About three that afternoon, Rob arrived with a lady in her late forties called Ruth Jones. She was stout, running to fat and clearly didn't care much about her appearance. Her lank hair was a mix of mousy and grey and was scragged back to get out of the way. She wore no makeup and yet had a strangely young complexion. She wore tatty blue track bottoms with a sort of blue smock to hide her being overweight.

"Stu, this is the prof I was talking about, Ruthie and I go back to Uni days together."

"Rob, I hated being called Ruthie then and it hasn't improved with the fucking years," she snarled.

"Sorry Ruth, just being playful," said Rob with slight embarrassment.

This is a great start, thought Stuart; she doesn't look old enough to be a professor, but she is a feisty lady for sure.

"Ruth, I'm Stuart, thanks for coming."

"Well I wouldn't be here if it wasn't the weekend; I am seeing my dear old mum who lives about five miles away."

"Well thanks to your mum then, please come and explain the unexplained," he escorted her down the path to the workshop.

"Interesting," she said as she took in the dancing spanner and some of its surroundings.

"I decided to call it the floater; it was slightly vulgar yet descriptive," Stuart explained.

"A bit like you," chipped in Rob.

"Give me some background," said Ruth "like when and how did it start?"

Stuart went through the background as well as showing her the recorded detail and the video.

"It's clearly some sort of magnetic induction," she said to herself. "I'm just going back to the car to get a gauss meter."

"Is that the same thing as a magnetometer?" said Stuart.

"Yup," said Rob, "only I expect her kit is pretty sophisticated."

Ruth came back in carrying her equipment. "Thanks Rob, you were right this is interesting. Once I have got some measurements then things will be clearer."

"I hope so," said Stuart as he watched Ruth open a large black case. There were instruments and dials, switches and knobs; it all looked the business. Ruth hooked the instrument to her laptop.

"I just have to calibrate the system and then we can put some probes around the room to figure out the forces at play."

About ten minutes later Ruth was ready, she firstly did a test to ensure that the kit was working properly.

"I'm not sure where to set the measurements, though," she said.

"I don't understand?" said Stuart.

"Well it's clear that there are some very powerful forces here, this device can measure in gauss or tesla depending on the strength of magnetic density. I think I will stick to a Gauss measurement though, after all an MRI magnet is pretty powerful at around 1500 gauss."

"You're the expert," said Stuart trying to remember what a tesla was.

"Rob can you take this first probe and stand at the other end of the room." The probe was encased in some blue synthetic rubberised material with a concave metal end, two red lights and small meter. It was on a sort of tripod and was attached by lead to the main meter.

"Stuart, you take the other meter to the opposite end of the workshop." It was a similar device except it was coloured red. "What I want to do is measure the magnetic topology of the building, so we will need to ensure that both probes are correctly positioned, the metres on the devices will let us know when the position is right."

After a couple of false starts, the three of them got going and started recording a grid of reading at various points of the workshop.

"Ok everything normal so far, so we know that the forces at play are inside the horizontal plane of this building." Good thinking and analysis, though Stuart. Ruth had a good methodology, as they approached the generators they started getting strange inconsistent readings. It took a while to see that the magnetic density was pulsing with a similar frequency to the oscillations of the spanner. As they approached the area between the generators in the vicinity of the spanner then the readings started to escalate.

"Stop!" yelled Ruth. "If it goes on like this we will need to switch to a larger measurement. Hold on I am going to rejig the gear to higher tesla measurements, then we will go back to our last recoding position and start from there."

Stuart and Rob did as they were told. The room was very quiet as all three of them knew that they were in unchartered territory. As they approached the spanner they started to receive mad oscillations in the density from negative to positive.

"I'm not sure how much further we can go," said Ruth. "I thought this kit was built for large density recordings, but we are way out of our league here. Let's just try one more position and then stop." Rob and Stuart positioned the tripods about a meter away from the spanner then it happened. Simultaneously the spanner just dropped to the ground and the gauss meter disintegrated into smoke.

"Oh shit," cried Ruth, "the fucking thing is completely fried." There was an unpleasant smell of melting circuitry.

"What about the laptop, is it OK?" yelled Stuart, Rob was strangely quiet.

"I have no idea what we have just experienced," said Ruth, "but this is not science we understand, the metres were off the register before it fried."

"I agree," said Rob; "it felt really strange as we got closer. Didn't you feel it, Stu?"

"I just felt, well, tense but then I think we were all expecting something to happen."

"Sod it," said Ruth to no-one in particular. "I should have recorded this, now all we have is the historic data on the laptop. All I can say is the forces that we encountered were like no other I have seen or read about."

Stuart picked up the spanner and examined it; it was just an ordinary spanner… what the hell had happened. "Well unless you want to write up what we have now, I suggest we go inside and have a cuppa." As they sat around the table, all three were very quiet. They all knew that they had a shared experience of something not normal.

"The laptop seems OK, so I will see what I can analyse from the results, it may take me a week or so. I'd better go and see my mum, I am late."

"Thanks, Ruth, please keep me and Rob posted. I will contact you if anything develops."

Zoe had been making tea and listening in to the discussion for the last twenty minutes. "Why so glum? You never know you might be able to replicate it, I don't think either of you are quitters, if you found something, figure it out. I have to go out for couple of hours or so. Rob, you and Sue are welcome to supper."

"Not tonight thanks, Zoe, I must be off, Stu, I will phone you tomorrow, Zoe's right, perhaps we can replicate it."

That evening Zoe and Stuart discussed the afternoon's events and future course of action.

"You're right, love, I must try and replicate it. I'm not being obsessive and just want a conclusion."

"Stuart you have always been obsessive, you know it's getting worse, but I don't expect anything else. Just don't let it interfere with us or the family." She sighed, as she knew it would. "After all you were obsessed with me once."

"Darling, I still am, let's take our mind off it upstairs."

"As ever, a one-track mind," she smiled. He hoped he saw a knowing wink.

Stuart's mind was not focused on the event in the workshop for some of the night; Zoe had been true to her word.

After a swift breakfast, Stuart returned to the workshop. Let's list what we know, he thought. One, the spanner and its composition seem to be key to the phenomenon. Two, nothing laterally in the workshop was likely to be a cause, assuming Ruth's analysis held true. Three, normal gravity surrounded the spanner. Four, the forces on the spanner were immense but broadly in equilibrium. Five, the oscillation was predictable. Six, some electromagnetic force catalysed the event. This last one was less conclusive but the finding on Ruth's measurements definitely showed something strange going on. Seven, the measuring process broke the equilibrium. Not a bad start, he thought.

Stuart started to replicate the original event, even down to trying the remove the handle bolt from the cast iron door. Unfortunately he could not replicate the spanner slipping from the bolt; he would just have to do his best. No matter what he tried he couldn't reproduce the effect, he was becoming very frustrated. He then remembered to follow his original activities when he went into the workshop. He couldn't repair the strimmer again, but he could run it by the big generators and immediately he heard the soft hum start up from the two generators opposite one another as the strimmer went into its wild movement. Bingo, he thought, well at least I have got one of the components going. Stuart couldn't remember how long it had been after the strimmer episode when he dropped the spanner. He had recorded so much information around the floater but not the activities leading up to it. It must have taken a couple of hours to remake the strimmer shaft so let's leave the generators cooking, he decided.

He phoned Rob from the speakerphone in the workshop to give him an update.

"Damn, damn, damn," said Stuart as Rob answered.

"What the hell have I done wrong now?" said Rob.

"Sorry Rob, it's not you, I am trying to simulate the same conditions that caused the floater and by phoning you I have broken the events. The trouble is I can't exactly recall all that I was doing in the workshop prior to the event and that may have a bearing on things. I'm normally so good at ordering things; it could be that Nigel's bloody strimmer is important."

"Stuart, what the hell are you talking about?"

"Sorry, mate, it's just I'm not very good at this replication work."

"Relax, more haste, less speed, I will come over after lunch and help out."

85

Stuart decided to do some work on the Morgan to take his mind off things although he did put a timer in place to remind him when to retry the spanner episode. Rob arrived at about the time that Stuart was restarting the spanner dropping… it was a complete anticlimax. The spanner just fell to the ground as expected.

"Is it the same spanner?" asked Rob.

"Of course it fucking is," snapped Stuart. "Sorry… sorry Rob, it's just so frustrating."

Dismissing Stuart's anger, Rob said, "Look, let's figure out what we know and also what we don't know and then have a process to resolve each item until we find an answer. The trick is to ensure we have thought of absolutely everything before we kick off."

"You sound like Donald Rumsfeld," said Stuart with a grin. "The trouble is that if there are unknown unknowns then we will never get an answer."

"True but let's give it a shot."

"OK, let's get to it."

They worked most of that afternoon building a list of variables, no matter how insignificant that they were, they were still factored in, until they reached a point of complete emptiness. They jointly agreed that they couldn't weight any of the variables since they were in Rumsfeld territory, but they did make an attempt at any obvious links between the variables.

"OK let's stop," said Rob. "I have to go anyway. I think that Ruth will give us a lot of information on the magnetics, my gut instinct is that we should examine the composition of the spanner."

"I had the same idea," said Stuart. "I will get onto it. It's one of a set of chrome vanadium ring spanners that I got when Smythfield Hardware closed last year."

"Keep me posted, Stuart," said Rob as he left.

Stuart tidied up the workshop and went into the house.

"Any progress?" asked Zoe.

"Nothing, absolutely nothing," said Stuart. "This thing is going to eat away at me, you know that, don't you?"

"Stu, nothing changes, that's the man you are. I am sure you will find an answer. In the meantime, I will get on with my life. How's the job search?"

Back to reality, what does she mean get on with her life, thought Stuart? "Well it has been a distraction, Zoe."

"Yes and a welcome one if I'm not mistaken."

"You know me far too well... I will get back on the conveyer belt!!"

"See that you do; I am serious, treat this 'float thing' of yours as a project but don't get obsessive about it." She was angry since she had seen this relentless compulsive behaviour in him so often.

"I will try, but it does go against everything I know about."

"Well you said yourself you're not all knowledgeable."

"True, but this thing just doesn't make sense."

"OK but make sense of laying the table so we can eat." Somehow the household got back into routine and Stuart was able to clear his mind, especially when Marc asked him for some career advice since he had to make some subject choices for next school year.

It was a good reality check when Stuart arrived at work the following day. Somehow there was a feeling from his team that they were damned if they would let the short working week get in the way of producing quality products. It was good for Stuart since it was so easy to slip into 'sod it' mode as he was beginning to do himself. There was a small piece of test work from a new client that if successful could start to rebuild the order book and that certainly was a stimulus to the tentative optimism. Stuart was still keen to explore other job options, though, this recent episode from Head Office showed how little he is valued.

On the way home, Stuart's mind returned to the enigma of the spanner. The trouble is, he thought, there were too many variables in the way. No point in speculating, he mused. Perhaps the clue will come from an analysis of the spanner's composition plus input from Ruth Jones.

That evening, Stuart had time and space to research the best sources for analysing the composition of the spanner since Zoe was out seeing friends and Marc was out somewhere. He had just jotted down some potential analysis companies from the net when the phone rang.

"Hi Stuart, it's Ruth Jones here, just to update you that I am looking at the results, but I am not sure it's going to help."

"Why is that Ruth, surely you got some good data?"

"Yes, but it's inconsistent with any knowledge of EMS that we have, plus and it's a big plus, the forces were outside of anything that has ever been recorded before. I should qualify that; certainly there are mega forces in the Cosmos but not on Earth particularly. It goes against all my scientific thinking, but you seem to have stumbled onto a phenomenon that doesn't seem to have been found before. I have some PhD helpers that are trying to see if there is anything similar that has been recorded elsewhere but so far it's a blank."

"Ok, well thanks for trying," said Stuart, "it's all a bit frustrating."

"Stuart, I am staying on the case, it's just that it's going to take some time and serious research. I want to stay involved and as I said I have assigned some of my department to help. I am away for the next six weeks at a conference in Cleveland and I am taking some time off to visit some old mates in the US, but I will be keeping an eye on things through email. Fortunately Rob is involved too, he has a really good brain and can refine the thinking, but don't tell him I said that!"

"Thanks, Ruth, your help is really appreciated, and I won't tell Rob, promise."

"Oh and before I forget," Ruth continued, "I have asked Dr Mike Lester at our metallurgy department to do an analysis on the spanner, I hope that's OK?"

Stuart was really pleased. "Thanks, Ruth, I was just investigating metallurgy analysis sources."

"Well Mike is one of the best in the business, and he owes me a favour," she said. "He is expecting you at Southampton; I will send an email to link you together, OK?"

"Thanks, Ruth, and I will keep you posted, have fun in the States."

Stuart mulled things over, it's got to be the composition of the spanner. He would have time on Wednesday to drop it off at the Uni.

It was late afternoon that Wednesday when Stuart arrived at the University campus and it took some time to find the metallurgy department, having asked direction several times, it amazed Stuart to think that many of the students didn't even know there was one.

In hindsight it wasn't surprising given the small sign above some very tired double doors with cracked windows that should have replaced years ago. Inside, the department was basically a very large room with an office positioned in the middle of the left side and a cluster of various benches around all the other sides. The room was badly lit and only had a metal window running high on the right. Most of the benches carried some form of electronic device together with a host of screens from various eras of computing. At the far end there was another pair of glass double doors that led onto an area that held some very heavy equipment; Stuart recognised an old tension meter that would have gone quite well in an industrial museum. Apart from a couple who were engrossed in some information on a screen, the place was empty.

Stuart decided to interrupt the couple. "I am trying to find Mike Lester, is this the right place?" For a moment it seemed that he wasn't going to get any response, then without even moving his head from the screen one of the couple said,

"He has just popped out and should be back soon, take a seat in his office," and with that restored his concentration back to the screen.

It wasn't really an office, just some partitioning built many years ago, it didn't even go up to the ceiling, so it offered no privacy. The place was a mess, the walls were covered in posters that had been around for years supposedly to brighten it up. There were papers everywhere, but they did look like there was some order to them. The only new and impressive thing in the room was the large computer screen that was displaying a complex picture of something that looked like a bit of an airplane. Just then Mike Lester came in chewing on a sandwich.

"Late lunch," he mumbled through the sandwich. "And you are?"

He was in his mid-thirties with tight black curly hair that had a few grey wisps, a bit thin, middle height with a long neck which unfortunately accentuated a large Adam's apple which otherwise detracted from his handsome face.

"Stuart Ashley, Ruth Jones said you might be able to help me?"

"Ah yes, the man who destroyed some of her equipment, I saw some of the readings she had, and I did say that there was an error somewhere." Lester sounded grumpy.

"Well I don't know about that," Stuart replied and was interrupted by Lester.

"Well, leave the sample with me and we will see what we can do."

"Any idea when you will be able to look at it?" said Stuart, depositing the spanner in the only space on his desk.

"I will get to it in the next couple of weeks," said Lester consuming more sandwiches.

"But that's too late," said Stuart, clearly exasperated.

"Too late for what? Why the urgency?" said Lester.

"Sorry Mike, it's me; Ruth may have told you that I stumbled onto something really strange, believe it or not, this spanner just floated in mid-air for over a day. I just want to get to the bottom of it urgently and put my mind at rest. It's really bugging me."

"Wow, it is getting to you! Look, I can get the two lab technicians outside to run some basic tests on it but if it needs further analysis then it will take a few weeks. That the best I can offer, sorry."

"That's fine, Mike, I really appreciate it, and you have my email and phone number?"

"Yes, I will let you know what we find. By the way, your spanner is going to be sliced up, is that OK?"

"Of course, sorry I must go; I should be back at work."

"Fine," said Lester, "and you must learn to chill out," and with that he returned to his sandwich.

Later that same day, Stuart recounted his meeting with Lester to Zoe.

"You really have become more obsessive with this thing than anything I have seen before, you are going to have to sort this out because I am tired of it and the kids are tired of it."

"I haven't made much of it to you," said Stuart defensively.

"Good God, how can you say that? We have had nothing but that fucking spanner morning, noon and night."

"It so happens that Maddie is not well, and I promised to see her, so I am going tomorrow morning for a couple of days and during that time sort yourself out, Stuart."

"I didn't know your sister wasn't well," he said lamely.

"Well she has suspected breast cancer and I did tell you but you're so focused on this fucking spanner you didn't hear."

"I'm sorry love, please send her my love."

"Just think on, Stuart, I am serious."

Stuart did think on, he didn't go into the workshop and busied himself with the new client work at the office. It was there that he got a call from Mike Lester saying could he come down to the department to see the preliminary results. Stuart wasn't doing anything, so they agreed to meet about 1900. It was closer to 1930 when Stuart finally got to the department.

"Hi, Mike. Sorry I'm late, bloody rush hour traffic."

Mike had been in discussion with the two technicians, which he now introduced as Gareth and Steve. "Come and join us at this bench, Stuart and we can show you the preliminary analysis," said Mike Lester who was altogether friendlier that the last encounter. As he joined the other three, Mike asked Gareth to take the lead on the findings.

"So how much do you know about materials science?" he said.

"Not a lot, but I have a pretty good understanding of basics and can grasp things pretty quickly," replied Stuart.

"Well I could go through all the tests we have done so far or just go to the findings."

"Let's go the findings and go back to the testing process to clarify things if necessary."

"Fine by me," said Gareth as he scrolled through rows of results and loaded a pie chart of the composition of the spanner.

"As you can see, this chart shows the various alloys, impurities etc in the spanner. In fact it's pretty good quality with even consistency of vanadium in the steel. The vanadium makes the steel much stronger, even at high temperatures."

He scrolled to the next diagram. "This one really shows us that there is quite a lot of small gas bubbles in the metal, which very unusual since the casting process is designed to avoid gas porosity as it is termed. We had to analyse the structure to see if it was caused by gas being in the alloy itself of whether it happened through micro shrinkage. If we look at the next chart it shows the actual structure, OK so far?"

"I'm hanging in there," Stuart replied.

"The idea of any casting process is to minimise turbulence in the casting flow otherwise you get gas embedded in the casting. In this instance there seems to have been a lot of turbulence and most interestingly that it's produced a very even distribution of gas. Even more interesting is that all the tests we have done so far show the bubbles are made up of Argon and nothing else."

"Is that unusual?" said Stuart.

"Bloody right it is," said Steve, who had been quiet up to now.

"Steve is our resident expert on casting techniques," clarified Mike. "Sorry to interrupt, Steve, please go on," Steve was obviously a prickly character that Mike had to handle carefully.

"As I was saying," said Steve, "I have never seen anything like it, and I have checked it out on the web and can't find anything that compares."

"Any idea how it happened?" said Stuart.

"My guess is that it was caused by a glitch in the casting process. You see there are some processes like induction furnaces that use argon to purge oxygen and water vapour from the molten metal."

"Is it a bit like argon welding?" Stuart asked.

"Exactly," said Mike. "Being inert it can provide a shield from oxygen for instance."

"Got it," said Stuart.

"Anyway," Steve continued, "I would suspect that the molten

metal was superheated and that would increase the velocity of pouring which combined with argon which, incidentally, allows a reduction in temperature for pouring, means the casting happened at breakneck speed. Frankly I'm surprised there wasn't an accident with some sort of blowback."

"Well maybe there was an accident, but we won't know, the manufacturer won't make it public that they were making dangerous mistakes in their casting. Anyway, how are we to track down a spanner from China for God's sake?" said Gareth.

"So, it was made in China then?"

"Can't you read," said Steve, "it's written on the damn thing? Anyway everything is made in China nowadays."

Why is he so grumpy, thought Stuart to himself, and then ignoring Steve, he asked Mike, "So is it possible to replicate the structure of the casting?"

"Probably," said Mike, "we would need to find a good casting shop and experiment with the process."

"I can do it," piped up Steve. "Gareth and I were thinking about it and there is a small foundry near Basingstoke that has some pretty good superheating capability. We would need to get their agreement to do it since, in theory; it could bugger up their kit. I don't know whether they do much vanadium work or whether they are able to contain the argon in the pour. We would like to do it, Mike, if you're OK, of course, we will need to cover the costs."

"Understood," said Stuart. "I guess you will need to figure that out with the factory in Basingstoke?"

"I'm OK about this, but it can't interfere with your workload guys and Stuart, you will need to agree to the University costs, these guys aren't free!"

"Good stuff, let's plan on going ahead, we will need to spec out the cast size and shape."

"Gareth and me will check it out, it may be that they have limited size and scope on the casting anyway. This a bit of fun, but what's your interest?"

"Ruth Jones said that you had some sort of levitation experience with the spanner; she had some unbelievable readings on her kit before it blew up," said Mike to the two technicians.

"Cool!" said Gareth. "Well perhaps we have the start of an explanation."

"Guys, I don't know what to say but a big thanks, I was beginning to think I imagined all this stuff; you have put some solid facts together which goes towards an explanation."

"Premature thanks, Stuart, we have to replicate this metal structure yet," Steve replied. Somehow, Stuart felt confident that Steve would make it happen despite his gruff exterior.

"We will email all this stuff to you, Stuart, and copy Ruth as well," said Mike. "I have to get back to Uni life now as do you two," he continued.

"Thanks again, guys, I hope to hear from you soon, sorry to take so much of your time," and with that left.

As he opened his car, Stuart took a deep breath, there really is something going on here and we are making progress. It wasn't excitement but rather almost a feeling of butterflies in his stomach that he was in unchartered territory. He tried phoning Zoe but only got a recording. When he got home he found Marc was making supper, well, heating pizzas isn't too hard for him.

"Shall I put one in for you as well, Dad?"

"Yes please, where's Mum?"

"Over at Aunt Marion's."

"Oh shit, I forgot, has she phoned?"

"About an hour ago, she said to let you know that Auntie needs more tests and Mum won't be back this coming weekend. She said it was OK for me to stay over with Pete, his parents have said it's alright so you're on your own with your spanner." The irony wasn't lost on Stuart, clearly the whole family is getting bored about it, he thought, still it's close to getting solved, I hope.

"Seriously Dad, how is it with the floater?"

"Are you really interested?"

"Of course I am."

Stuart gave him an account of the findings so far, and Marc was genuinely interested.

"Anyway, Dad, you have to keep it in perspective cos Mum is really pissed off."

"I know, I know, come on let's watch some tele, anything on?"

"Catch up of the Ireland Wales game?"

"Let's do it," Stuart felt a bit like old times with Marc, they both turned in early with Stuart thinking he must sort it out with Zoe asap.

CHAPTER 6

Trust

Stuart regained consciousness, no that's wrong, he had several episodes where some of his senses faded in and then they would stop abruptly. So it was with his vision, he could see shapes moving above his head but then the blur would move to blackness. He heard a continuous rumble mixed in with what might have been voices, the volume oscillating between loud and soft but always indistinguishable. The smell of shit and vomit and something sweet was always there and was the relentless pounding in his head, the king of all hangovers.

At some time all of the senses became sharper together with introduction of pain in his whole body. He wanted to move but just didn't have the strength.

"Relax, old son, you will feel a lot worse for a while, but you will slowly start to recover."

Stuart tried to say something; he thought his lips were moving and heard his weird efforts at speaking with dribble gargling in the background, he went back to the simple process of breathing. Lying there, he began to focus on a window, no not a window; it was a skylight. Over time it became evident he was in some sort of van and as his sight slowly returned, he recognised it was a motorhome and the continuous rumble was the engine that never seemed to alter its revs as if on some sort of motorway.

Apart from the occupants of the driving cab there were two people in the main part of the van. A man, perhaps early forties, who has the kind face that had the wrinkles of many smiles in his life. His sandy hair was grey at the sides. His eyes were nondescript, colourless, his eyebrows needed trimming and he had a gap between his front teeth, which perhaps made him seem friendlier than he was.

"Still feeling like shit?" he enquired.

Stuart tried to reply but still couldn't.

"Don't try to speak yet, here have a sip of water from this straw."

Stuart tried to drink but that failed too.

"It's ok, you are on a drip, so you can't dehydrate. By the way, you are strapped down so don't try to move. It's for your own good."

"Let me talk and you can listen, perhaps there will be some answers for you."

"Firstly, we extracted you from Glens Falls where you were held prisoner by the US security folk. It may have been comfortable, but they knew your every move. It's a pretty swish operation; Uncle Sam wasn't going to let you go. In fact given the sophistication of the location I think we did a pretty good extraction although there will be some sore heads, a lot of embarrassment together with a dash of recrimination." The man continued, "We are not in the States anymore, we're in Canada and heading for Halifax, more of that later. Sorry, I forgot to introduce myself, please call me Larry and this young lady here is Ali." Ali did a pretend salute but didn't say anything. "We are sort of British army."

Of course you are, thought Stuart, between the throbs in his head. This is mad, the stuff of Ian Fleming, it doesn't happen in real life. Still the two of them look much fitter than me and I feel like shit anyway so just go with it Stuart and see what happens.

"I don't suppose you think we are good guys on your side," continued Larry, "but Peter Dawson did ask me to say sorry he couldn't make the tennis, if that's any help." Stuart nodded his head and wished he hadn't. Who are these people, he thought? Ali came over and took his pulse, shone light onto his eyes and checked a screen that Stuart hadn't noticed before.

"He is recovering more quickly that I thought," she said to Larry.

"That's good; I had a vision of having to hold up somewhere to let him recover which is risky since I'm sure our friends looking hard for him."

Ali was interesting; she had short grey hair, which went well with her sallow complexion. She was pretty but now just sufficiently overweight that it distorted her face. Stuart's guess was that she was a military doctor who had been dragged into the extraction to keep him alive.

"I'm going to give you something that will accelerate your recovery, but it will knock you out in four or five hours. It's necessary since we need to use a small boat to get us to our ship."

Would Stuart have protested? It really didn't matter; a needle was in his arm and he was starting to feel very strange. He felt his heart racing and began to sweat.

"Just relax, sweetheart, we have at least another hour before you have to get up, so make the most of it." She proceeded to sort out the medical equipment that was attached to him.

The van rumbled on, the engine strained at some hills and Stuart knew he was going over some large bridges. He had no idea where Halifax was and frankly didn't care, but what was his destination, back to the UK, if so why? Peter Dawson was unpredictable; the UK government had turned their backs on him as had Zoe. Maybe they weren't Brits but were working for someone else? Perhaps it would have been better to take up Gary Marshall's offer.

Eventually the van slowed and went over a series of bumps, maybe a port railway? It then turned sharp right for about another five minutes, finally stopping. The side door eventually opened allowing some grey evening light into the van. There was a strong smell of sea, of fish, of oil in fact Stuart realised his senses were much stronger than they were usually, a result of whatever they had injected him with, no doubt.

Ali and Larry helped him to sit up and release his straps. Stuart felt very faint and light-headed.

"I want you to stand but not move," said Ali.

"Your blood pressure needs to adjust, it will take a minute." Stuart stood up; there were aches everywhere. At some time when he was unconscious he had been cleaned up and dressed. I don't remember a bloody thing, thought Stuart, as he wobbled and then begun to steady himself. There were two other men who emerged from the driver's cab and stood by the doorway, initially looking at Stuart and then checking on the surrounding area. These must be the extraction squad, he thought.

He was helped to get out of the van; thank god it had steps. They were on the quayside and alongside a fishing trawler that looked like it had seen better days. It was quite large, he guessed about thirty metres with a central wheelhouse that sat on an extended structure with portholes, at the stern there was another structure with various cranes nearby together with a large space for landing the nets and getting the fish into store There were winches everywhere all of them covered in a layer of thick black grease.

Before Stuart could take it all in he was helped onto the steel ramp that led down to the deck. He realised that the engines were already running and that the boat was rigged to let go. He was helped to an iron door and once through, carefully went down some corroded iron stairs into the heart of the boat. He was surprised by the size of general living area, it obviously served as a sitting and eating area when not sleeping or working. He was amazed that there was a large new flat TV fixed to one of the side walls. The place was divided up by a number of fixed benches together with tables, the back and seat of the benches was padded with a leatherette material that was worn and ripped and showed signs of being tan in colour once. Apart from Larry and Ali the place was empty; the two other men were nowhere to be seen.

"We have chartered the boat," said Larry, "it's our crew and the plan is to transfer you to another vessel in the next couple of days, then the team will return it to Halifax. No need for any witnesses to know what we are up to," he said with a wink. Stuart just slumped onto a bench. He felt bile in his mouth, but nothing came up. Ali passed him a water bottle and he took a slug then lay back onto the bench.

"Bugger, bugger," Dawson said in exasperation. "Now we're fucked... does the PM know?

"Unfortunately, he and the US President have had a real falling out over it. To quote, 'so a special relationship means aggressive tactics on US fucking soil!'" replied Nigel Jones.

"Oh shit, we are really fucked. So where is Ashley now?"

"Somewhere off the Atlantic," said Jones.

"We have to assume that they have been tracking him?"

"How?" said Dawson, "didn't our team scan for a tracker?"

"Yes, but obviously not well enough."

"Any ideas?" said Dawson.

"Ideas? On what?"

"What we say to the fucking PM and the US President."

Jones said, "Well the PM was aware, and the Cabinet Office initiated the idea anyway."

"Well they will deny that!! So the shit's on us."

"We all knew the risks," defended Jones.

"I know we all knew the risks, I just thought we were more fucking competent; we have two choices," Dawson continued, "come clean and fall on our sword or invent something that avoids any loss of face."

Jones thought for a moment. "We can't fall on our sword, the yanks won't believe we did this without the PM knowing, so we have to find something that we can play out."

"Agree," said Dawson, "but we need every security agency onside, north, south, the lot."

"They all had their noses put out when you created this unit, so they will want us to take it all, and be destroyed."

"Yes they will, but this is so big that they can't score points, not now anyway."

"Cabinet Office on the phone, PM wants to see you at 1400," Rose Hammond said as she entered the room. It was rare to see someone like Dawson really phased but this was the day!

OK, he thought, let's decouple ourselves from this now, we will need to clear up loose ends but that comes second.

"Alert the Navy and tell them to get that fucking frigate as far away from the rendezvous now. Send a code to the trawlerman to abort, get back to Canada, dump the boat, and drop Ashley off with local police, reduce headcount, confirm and vanish. And… make sure it's properly coded."

"Done deal before the PM then?" said Rose.

"Yup, done deal," said Dawson with a big sigh. "OK team we have a few hours to ensure our actions are watertight."

Stuart was roused by Ali. "Wake up, Stuart, change of plan; we are heading back to Canada." Stuart didn't even ask why, he didn't trust anyone and didn't have a choice anyway. "Get into these fresh clothes; it's going to be cold. Across the room he saw Larry busy on a small ruggedized laptop.

"I'm going to check out the rib on deck," he said, "we can't go back to the main harbour." He finished putting on some filthy foul weather gear that was orange once but now had a covering of years of work.

In the main navigation area Larry got an update from the two other men.

"We're heading west towards Halifax and should be in sight of land in the next hour. It's a tricky place, lots of small islands so we will get as close as possible and then drop you off, we plan to head north along the coast to one of the small ports."

"Let me know when we are close enough." Larry knew that the other two hired crew were no more, as instructed. Larry then checked out the rib, it was in good order with an inboard motor that he would have to hope worked when he got into the sea. He went back up to the steering area to join the other two who were discussing their course.

Eventually one of them said, "I'm pretty sure that's McNab's Island and if so, then we can drop you off in about 10 minutes. We came out on the western side, but you will find it easier if you head up the eastern passage into Halifax."

"OK, one of you help me lower the rib and I will get Ali and our man."

As Stuart arrived on deck he could see the heavy swell with whitecaps that were accentuated in the cold twilight mist. He then saw the rib alongside the trawler rising and falling by several metres.

"This is going to be tricky," said Larry. "I'm going first and will wave for you to follow. Ali you come once Stuart is in the rib." With that he released a retaining rail and started down a rope ladder that was swinging wildly towards the sea. The swell meant he couldn't get the rib close to the ladder and had to time a jump onto the reeling rib. He then looked up and waved.

"I can't do this," said Stuart. "I feel like shit and I won't make it."

"You have to, Stuart," Ali said, "you don't have a choice."

"I'm not going," he repeated.

Ali looked at one of the men to help. The man signalled to Larry to hold and went to one of the deck boxes and pulled out a long rope, which he tied to one of the cranes used for lifting the nets. Despite weak resistance from Stuart he then tied the rope beneath Stuart's arms and started pushing him over the edge of the deck. Stuart fell and hit the side of the boat before swinging, pendulum-like towards the water. Stuart passed out and yet somehow Larry managed to manoeuvre the dead weight into the rib. They used the same technique for Ali except she used the rope ladder as a guide and avoided smashing into the side of the boat. Larry cast off and began the task of riding the waves to the eastern side of the island. The mist seemed to be even thicker and Larry took a wide berth to avoid any rocks. The swell receded as they entered the eastern channel and Larry could see a bridge about a mile away. Ali was clinging to a side rope of the rib and looked awful, Stuart was still unconscious.

"Don't just stay there, make sure Stuart's breathing OK," he yelled.

Ali moved cautiously towards Stuart and briefly examined him; his breath was very shallow, and his lips had a bluish tint. "He doesn't look good," she yelled.

They got closer and left McNab's Island behind them, it was possible to see a jetty on the western shore of the channel. It was a concrete affair, quite large, with a few sodium lamps easing through the mist. It looked deserted but Larry thought he saw some light from a building towards the road that led from the jetty to the bridge. There were a couple of medium-sized yachts moored up plus a large cabin cruiser. Larry aimed the rib towards a space between one of the yachts and the cruiser only to realise that they would have to climb a ladder up to the jetty. So far every move presented a new obstacle however Larry knew that there had to be a way of getting Stuart and Ali to land, he manoeuvred the rib along the side of the cruiser to see if there was a way on board but then noticed a ramp that was obviously used to launch small craft. At last my first bit of luck, he thought, as he grounded the rib onto the ramp. Ali was able to get out but looked done in. Larry too didn't have the energy to get Stuart onto land but knew he would have to move fast. He saw some launch trolleys nearby some small trainer yachts and used one to pull Stuart up the ramp. Eventually all three of them were resting on a step outside of a grey building that was used for some sort of storage.

It was cold, with an icy wind being funnelled up the channel; it was dark although early evening. Larry had no plan and no help. He had taken the precaution to secure a wallet with money and credit cards but no passports, anyway he had been told to disappear and already had some ideas developing, and he could get back to the US pretty easily where he had good contacts. Ali might be a liability, well he would cross that bridge when it was necessary, right now, he had to get rid of Stuart.

Hell, where am I going to get transport, he thought? The only obvious place was the road that led down from the bridge; Larry could see the headlights of passing traffic up there. It wasn't far, but it was a hell of a long way when you had an unconscious man as baggage. Larry decided that the launch trolley was the only way to haul Stuart up the road. Larry used some discarded rope to make a sort of cradle for Stuart and after a lot of exertion, finally managed to rig Stuart onto the trolley. Together, they pulled the trolley up the road until they reached the main road. They looked a sorry sight. Larry wondered whether he should leave Ali behind but had second thoughts, he didn't know how resourceful she was and potentially could be a bigger liability on her own, anyway her presence might make it easier to flag down a car.

All the cars and trucks were moving at a pace that made it difficult to get them to stop, it was clear that stopping someone was going to be difficult. Larry made an instant decision and ran out in front of a small truck, waving his arms. The truck slowed, and Larry ran towards it as it pulled to the side of the road. The driver, a balding man in his mid-fifties did not lower the window and Larry tried the door, but it was locked. Cautious man, he thought. Larry waved for the man to bring the window down which he did but only a little.

"You nearly got yourself fucking killed," he shouted.

"We found a man unconscious by the side of the road, he needs help urgently," Larry screamed.

"Where?" the man demanded, "I don't see anyone?"

Ali was bending over Stuart to protect him from the icy wind; she waved at the truck driver who saw Stuart.

The driver lowered the window sufficiently to talk to Larry. "I will phone 911," he said, "but I won't let you in, there have been too many muggings around here." He picked up his phone and within a few seconds was talking to someone. This is better, thought Larry, since I haven't a clue about the name of the road and he thinks I just discovered the body.

"Appreciate it," said Larry, wondering how he was going to extract himself. It seemed longer than the five minutes it took, before they saw a flashing light coming from the other side of the bridge.

The truck driver saw the lights too and with a wave accelerated heading east. It was a large multi-purpose emergency vehicle that pulled up near Ali. A uniformed man and woman came over to where Stuart was slumped. They carried a flashlight as well as a powerful lantern. In the light, Stuart looked awful and the team quickly got their emergency routine underway. They wrapped him in a blanket and then tested his vital signs; the man said,

"Do you know who he is?"

"No," said Larry, "we were just dropping off some sailing gear by the jetty, and saw him beside the road, our car is down there," he said pointing down the road.

"It's a good job you found him," said the woman, "in this wind he would have died overnight."

"Was he hit by a car?" said Larry with obvious concern.

"It doesn't look like it!" she said. "We will know better when we have got him to hospital. We will need your details," she continued.

In a practiced movement they got Stuart onto a wheeled stretcher and into the back of the ambulance.

"Our ID is in the car down by the jetty," said Larry. "Can you wait while I get it, I will only be five minutes?" Larry knew they couldn't wait.

"Sorry," the woman said and passed Larry a form, which she had written a few details.

"You are required to take this to the Police to confirm who you are."

"Sure," said Larry taking the paper, "just to let you know anyway, my name is Paul Winterton, and this is my sister, Sue."

"Well thanks, Paul. You two have probably saved this guy's life." You just don't know how right you are, thought Larry, as the ambulance moved off.

"God you are a smooth bastard," said Ali "your lies sound so real." Larry took time to smile; he was tired.

"Come on Sue, let's find a way back to civilisation."

CHAPTER 7

Getting Closer and Losing

"Is there anything I can do, love?"

"Keep an eye on Marc rather than that bloody spanner," Zoe responded. "And any progress on the job front?"

"No, nothing," lied Stuart.

"I am so sorry about Marion, how is she taking things?"

"Resolutely, in fact the whole family is bearing up well, even Arthur has been supportive." Arthur separated from Marion a few years back, but the relationship held up well for their family.

"Are you OK?" said Stuart.

"Fine, and I am pleased to be away from your obsession for a while."

Stuart was getting fed up with all the digs; it wasn't like Zoe.

"Talk to you sometime," said Stuart hanging up. He then felt guilty but not so guilty to phone back. In a brief period Zoe had become quite angry with him and he couldn't figure out why. In the past she had put up with his projects, but this time is seemed so different. Perhaps it was her age, anyway it couldn't be sorted over the phone that's for sure.

He checked his email and there was a note from Steve Smith from Southampton saying he was making good progress and was confident he could do vanadium recast but needed more information on shapes and size. Stuart didn't know and decided to chat over the point with

Rob. He phoned Rob and they agreed to meet over a pint to discuss progress; there was no doubt that Rob was as intrigued as Stuart and keen to find a solution, indeed he was getting a lot of flak from Sue about his involvement.

Stuart updated Rob on all the findings at the metallurgy analysis. "So it was probably a casting error that produced even bubbles of argon."

"The Southampton folk think so, since it was not a good outcome of casting and should have been rejected on a quality basis, moreover they think it was positively dangerous. They want us to advise them on the shape of a recast if they can do it," Stuart continued. "Any ideas?"

"I know we shouldn't be assumptive, but I can't believe it's the shape of a spanner that induced the effect. I would suggest a small bar, perhaps of a similar weight if possible. That way future analysis will be easier and if we can't reproduce the effect then maybe we go to the spanner shape."

"That makes sense to me," said Stuart, "I will let them know tomorrow."

"I must say that Zoe is giving me a hard time over all this and it's not like her."

"Well Sue isn't too happy either," said Rob, "shall we cry in our beer?"

"It's watery enough, Rob. Anyway I can't give this up, I just can't, especially when your Ruthie couldn't figure it out, are you keeping her posted on events?"

"Not so far," said Rob. "I will email an update tomorrow, anyway Liverpool is playing Arsenal tonight so I am off home."

"OK, mate, see you soon. When I get the new sample I would like to try and simulate things. Will you help out?"

"You bet," said Rob. "See you," and he left.

Stuart felt lost and maybe a bit lonely; he went home and watched a movie with another pizza on his lap.

The three-day week was hitting everyone at work and it was hard to be enthused. Stuart felt there was inevitability in the plant closing and given no new orders this was the death throe of the business. He remembered fondly how well things had been and tried to avoid being too down in front of his team.

He realised that he had put his best years into the job and this was his reward. It was Thursday the following day, so he decided that he should follow up on some of the job opportunities rather than lie to Zoe. In truth his heart wasn't in it, he restrained himself from phoning Gareth and Steve that day but contacted them early on Friday.

"You must have a sixth sense," said Steve. "We have got a casting slot over this weekend. Apparently the foundry is going through a rebuild starting on Monday so they have some spare capacity."

"I called in some favours," Gareth yelled in the background.

"So if all goes well we will have you a sample by Monday." Again Gareth yelled that they were going to try and create a few samples with differing sizes and argon intensities.

Stuart held back from asking how they were going to do it but thanked them with the promise of beer and hung up. He phoned Zoe for the third time that day but all he got was voicemail, which he knew she wouldn't listen to. He found Marc in his bedroom with his friend Alec. They were busy on their tablets and stopped as Stuart entered, they had guilty looks on their faces.

"What is it, guys? Cyberporn or what?"

"Dad, as if we would?" Marc protested.

"Just don't get into cyber bullying, I hate that."

"So porn is OK then?" said Marc with an impish grin.

Stuart suddenly remembered that Marc was off on a school rugby tour to New Zealand on the Monday.

"Sorry Marc, are you all ready for the trip?"

"All sorted, Dad. Mum helped me put everything together before she went to Aunt Marion's."

"Money, passport?"

"Done," said Marc patting his backpack, "and we are both staying over at Pete's; his dad is taking us to school on Monday afternoon."

Stuart gave his son a hug, he felt like a useless dad. "I will miss you and just phone if you have any problems."

"Relax Dad, focus on Mum, she been strange lately."

"Tell me about it… ok let me know when you go."

"Will do."

Stuart went downstairs, it's not me, he thought, and something is going on with Zoe. Anyway we will have the place to ourselves for nearly three weeks, so we can get it sorted.

Zoe did phone later that day. "Did Marc get everything sorted for the trip?" No reference to me, thought Stuart.

"Fine," said Stuart, "he said he would email us when he arrived, and he promised to take lots of piccies."

"I will miss him," she said, "I hope he doesn't get hurt."

"The teachers are pretty good but it's a rough game," Stuart replied. "So when are you coming home?"

"Not sure, Stu, it's good here, even in the circumstances, home has been getting me down."

"Is it me, love, or the fucking thing in the workshop? If so I will drop it?"

"No, Stu, you haven't changed, it's me, and somehow I want something more, something different."

Stuart felt a twinge in the pit in his stomach; he wanted this talk to be face-to-face. "I will be down to you in a couple of hours, let's talk then."

"No please don't, Stu. I want time and space, I get it here and I don't want to face into anything yet. I can't explain it, but I just need to sort out my feelings. Seriously I really want you to give me a week or so."

The phone went dead, what should I do? The emotional thing was to go there anyway, but if she wanted time then I should allow her that. Stuart began to wonder if there was someone else. He had taken Zoe for granted for so long. They had rubbed along really well and even when the kids were less of a bonding focus they had still got time for one another. He had always been loving in his own way and she had always put up with his mini obsessions with a good heart. This time it was different.

He resolved to see Zoe the following day and set off after breakfast, the satnav leading him towards Somerset. He arrived at Marion's house just before midday. It was a classic fifties box with various extensions that didn't fit. Marion saw him through the window and opened the door.

"Stu, how are you? Zoe said you would come."

"Marion, how are you, what's the status?"

"Not good, Stu. I start chemo next week," Stuart had never been close to Marion, they had been at various family events over the years and indeed Zoe had never been really attached either despite less than two years between them. Marion had that dark sallow skin, that said all was not well, her eyes were sunken too.

Stuart decided to get straight to the point. "You probably know that Zoe is off me for some reason, hence my timely arrival."

"Frankly, Stu, I don't understand my sister. She turned up and has been really kind to me and then suddenly decided to leave, so it's not timely. Do you want a cup of something?"

"She isn't here... really?"

"Stu, why would I lie? Do you want to search the place? She said that something had come up and that she thought you would come. She left this note for you."

"Sorry, Marion, I don't doubt you, but ALL this is so strange and so unlike Zoe." He opened the note.

Stu, I knew you would come. I said I want some space to think things through. I will phone. Zoe

No kisses or love, just an abrupt note. He showed it to Marion. "What the hell do I do, what's going on, she must have found someone else."

"Stu, she didn't confide in me, she never has, but she spent a lot of time on the phone talking to people. If it's any help she spoke a lot to someone called Liz."

"Was it Liz French?"

"I don't know."

"I'm so sorry, Marion. You have enough to worry about, I am heading home."

"Stu, I can't help but keep me posted and if she comes here I will let you know... promise."

The empty pit in his stomach was mixed with a weird form of butterflies as if something unexpected was about to happen. In fact it had happened. Stuart only had a view that he could always see it coming when he heard of someone's marriage breakdown. They were either playing around or had grown tired and bored of one another. Yet here he was, completely surprised that he hadn't spotted that his wife of twenty-nine years was disenchanted with him. Maybe he had become so obsessed with the phenomenon that he didn't spot the changes in Zoe. Stuart felt sick; he hated himself for failing her. He decided to call Lucy then Henry to find out if they knew anything. He also decided against talking it over with Marc, he was 17 and away on Rugby tour on the other side of the world. Stuart figured out that when Marc returned in three weeks' time that things would be clearer.

"Hi, Dad," said Lucy, "you never phone, so what's up?"

"Hi love, it's your mother, I think she has left me."

There was a long silence.

"Lucy, Lucy are you there?"

"Yes, Dad," more silence.

"Lucy, you knew, didn't you?"

"No, Dad... honestly. But now it all fits together."

"What does... Lucy please fucking explain?"

"Calm down, Dad, I didn't know anything, until you said she has gone. As you know, we speak every few days, but it's been daily just recently. Strangely, she always spoke about you and how she still thinks she loves you. She also confided that she wanted more but didn't know why. She has such a passion for art that she can't share with you. Something is eating away at her."

"Or someone?"

"I don't know, Dad; I didn't sense that she was looking for someone else. I promise to keep you posted, the next time she phones."

"Thanks love… it's… I just don't know what to do."

"Go home, Dad. I can come down to Smythfield this weekend, if you want?"

"Let's speak before then? Love you."

"Love you, Dad, I am so sorry."

The call to Henry was very similar except, as a party animal, he just thought it was one of those phases that marriages go through. He didn't know any more than Lucy but wasn't surprised at her behaviour.

"Frankly, Dad, I always thought that Mum wanted more out of life."

Stuart reflected that both his older children had reached the same conclusion, that Zoe wanted more out of life. Well I didn't spot that, thought Stuart.

The house seemed emptier than it had before. Stuart contemplated getting blind drunk but couldn't really see the point; he did have several glasses of wine though. Zoe was still in the house somehow, everything around him was part of them together. He couldn't face staying in and went to the local curry house with yesterday's newspaper feeling like Norman-no-mates.

As expected he slept badly with things going round and round in his head. He didn't want to speak to anyone that weekend but did call Lucy and Henry again to see if they had any news. There was none. He spent most of the weekend tinkering with the Morgan, but his heart was not in it. He did however decide that he couldn't face work anymore and was going to chuck it in on Monday.

As Stuart arrived at the factory car park, he felt assured that he had made the right decision. He watched people arriving, and they all had the same look, an acceptance of the inevitable. He couldn't see joy on any of the faces, just a spirit that had been sapped of its strength. Stuart reflected on what the factory closure would mean to these people; a blessed relief from something they hated doing, or passive acceptance that the drudgery would be over, or the fear of making ends meet or indeed, all of these things. I wonder how they see me, he thought, if they knew that my life had collapsed.

He went over to the HR department and arranged some time with Elise Ripley for later that morning. It gave Stuart some time to think how he should handle the meeting. He favoured the 'stuff your job' approach but knew he had too much to lose, so maybe a 'stuff your job' once he had cut a contractual deal. I may be in a mess at home, but I am not going to jeopardise my fucking pension as well, he thought. He decided to see what the thinking was on redundancies and then negotiate a separation.

"Elise, good to see you, how's everything going?" said Stuart.

Elise looked up and over her black reading glasses. Stuart realised that she was all in black.

"Sorry, have you had a bereavement" he blurted out, wishing he could retract the words.

"Why?" she said "Oh... the black, it's my favourite colour. Actually I always go to funerals in white," she said with a grin. She was slim, mid-forties and had a pretty face that she disguised with the glasses and the severe way she pulled back her hair. Stuart suspected that this image protected her a little from the unpleasant nature of her job.

"You may recall that I was formally advised that my job was at risk a while ago, we haven't seen any new orders coming through, so I wondered what's the thinking."

"I can't give you a formal answer yet, but decisions have been made and you, alongside others, will be advised soon."

"Any idea when, it's just that I have to plan my finances, my son is 17 and I want to help him get to University," Stuart said smoothly.

"I know it's tough, look give me five minutes and I will see if I can give you more detail."

"Thanks Elise, I appreciate it. I have to pop over to the workshop to see if we have some insulation material in stock, so I will come back in half an hour."

Stuart came back at the due time and Elise waved him in.

"Ok Stuart, I have agreement to release your position since you have been key to getting us onto short working. I think it's a good offer given your age and time in position." Stuart remained impassive. "The offer is that we bring your time in position to the point of 53 years of age. This enables you to take early retirement plus a lump sum. As you know the corporate pension is particularity favourable for your level of management. It works out at 65 percent of current salary with an inflation linkage. The lump sum is 12 months' salary and the offer is based on you leaving today."

Stuart was surprised at the package; it was pretty good. They obviously thought he was expensive and they wanted him off their books as fast as possible. He also knew that there was always some negotiating flexibility.

"What's the notice period?"

"One month," Elise replied.

"Come on Elise, three is the minimum."

"OK three it is," she said rather quickly.

Stuart felt that he had under called it. "Elise it's a good offer but the lump sum is just not enough to cover my needs. Is there any flex?"

"Try me."

"Twenty-four months?"

"Sorry, too rich."

"Twenty-two?"

"Still too rich, I will go to 18," Elise said.

"Come on Elise, let's settle at 20?"

Elise feigned deep thought. "Ok," she said at last, "but payable in two phases six months apart. It helps with cashflow," she remarked.

"How about it all being paid in the next tax year?" added Stuart.

"Done deal," she said, "you will have the offer to sign in the next hour."

"Thanks Elise, can I have the lump sum paid into a nominated account?"

"Wherever you like, just give me the details." Stuart felt bad, but if Zoe was leaving him, then maybe he could shield it from her.

He went back to his office, it was sad that it was ending like this. Although Stuart wasn't sentimental, there were bits of his life in this office including a photo of Zoe and the kids in happier times. He found a cardboard box and started putting his few possessions into it plus a few mementos of his working life. Natalie, his secretary came in.

"So you're off, when were you going to tell me?"

"Natalie, I only knew a few minutes ago, I am instructed to leave today, so it's all a bit sudden." Her face showed she didn't believe him. She had been his secretary for the last eight months and whilst she was competent, she had not had his interests at heart, unlike her predecessor, Amy.

"I expect they will be getting rid of me then," she said.

Stuart knew the obvious answer but ducked it. "I don't know Natalie, there is still a lot of work to do."

Judging by his email, there were several of his colleagues who were leaving too so he agreed to participate in a farewell party. He said, "See you soon and let's keep contact," to many people as he left, knowing that it was most unlikely.

Stuart didn't fancy going home and to what? Instead he phoned the University to see how things were going. Gareth answered the phone.

"The cast went really well considering," he said.

"It was a fucking nightmare," Steve said from another extension phone.

"We were getting some really dangerous pouring to start; I thought we were going to get a blowback."

Gareth said, "Steve's right, I was all for giving up by mid-morning but he found a way to control the pour and we then had several goes at it. The trouble is that we had to analyse the metal after each cast to see what effect we were having."

"Well I got it right on the third go," piped up Steve.

"We did, Steve, it was a team effort remember," Gareth testily retorted.

"OK... OK, it was a team effort. Anyway point is we have created several bars of different sizes and thicknesses that have the same structure and form as your spanner. Not bad for a couple of academics."

"Fantastic stuff, can I come down to collect them today?" said Stuart.

"Sure," said Steve, "but be here before five, the campus is really busy then."

"And you can buy us that beer," said Gareth in the background.

"Done deal, see you later."

Stuart headed the car to Southampton and began thinking about replicating the experiment. It was the first time that Zoe had not been at the forefront of his thoughts... no that was wrong, he remembered not thinking much about Zoe when he was negotiating his separation package. They were right, the traffic was heavy, and Stuart didn't arrive until gone five when he entered the department.

"Stuck in traffic?" said Steve. "Told you."

"Hi guys, thanks again for doing this."

Mike Lester came out from his office to say hello. "Hi Stuart, it looks like these two have produced the goods." Steve and Gareth carried two heavy wooden boxes and placed them on a bench. There were about twenty different bars of various sizes in each box.

"Well they look pretty ordinary."

"What do you want, pink stripes?!" said Gareth in his customary cynical tone.

"We have kept a few bars back for our own use since we have never seen anything like it before, so we are going to experiment with its properties," said Mike.

"Well, beer apart, how much do I owe you?"

Steve said, "You don't know how much beer we can drink!! But if you give us two fifty quid each as expenses that will be fine."

"What about the department cost, Mike?"

"Beer will do, Stuart, but we would like to be part of your experimental work, from a metallurgy standpoint, if it's ok with you?"

"I would be delighted; if I am onto something then I need all the horsepower I can get."

"Ok let's go and get a drink," said Gareth "and we can discuss your plans for the experiment."

"I haven't really got any," Stuart said lamely.

"Well, we have some pretty good knowledge on experimental planning, so we can discuss it over the beer," said Mike.

It turned out that they were serious about the beer, and the plans. Despite the harsh banter they were indeed very good friends. Stuart was happy to be included in this team; it felt good to be with them. He left the curry house later that night by taxi and managed to check into a local hotel, knowing he would feel like shit the next day. It was an ordinary hotel but it did have a few complementary basics, including toothbrush and razor, both of which went some way to making him feel human that morning. The breakfast was substantial and a vital ingredient to help him dive home with the boxes of test metal bars. They had gone through the experimental planning process with him whilst Stuart was still sober, and they had made some notes on various scraps of paper. Steve had promised to send an email with more detail.

Stuart checked the voice messages when he got home, nothing from Zoe. There was post though, and in particular a formal letter confirming his redundancy. He was eager to try and replicate the floater effect but knew that experimental discipline was important to avoid wasting his effort. There was a copy of an outline experimental plan from Steve, which Stuart printed. He started to populate the plan with variable forms of measurement, much of which he had gained from the last time he tried to figure things out.

The first thing to occupy his mind was the need to control the fall of the metal bars. He needed a device that would enable him to vary all ways that the bar could fall, as well as the velocity. This was just the stimulus Stuart needed as he sketched out ways to drop the metal bar using a series of guides. He was pleased that he had a range of different sized bars, but it did cause him more problems in building the launch guide, as he termed it. He decided that the framework would be a wooden structure with various plastic runners and chokes to slow the bar down on its descent. There couldn't be any metal in the structure for obvious reasons. It was mid-day when Stuart completed his sketches. He had already developed and discarded five versions, but his latest drawing showed promise. He thought about phoning Rob but remembered he was probably at school teaching, and anyway Rob's engineering skills probably wouldn't help.

He went into the workshop to see if he had materials to fabricate the launch guide he had. His Aladdin's cave didn't let him down. He was confident that he had the wood, it was the plastic runners that would be a problem and he couldn't find anything that would suffice. He decided to go the local DIY store and found some angle edging and some electrical trunking, which would make excellent runners.

It was late afternoon when he went into the workshop; he suddenly remembered he hadn't eaten so he went back to the house to dig something out of the freezer. He noticed the answer phone flashing and pressed the play button, it was Zoe's voice.

"Hi Stuart, she said, "just to let you know that I have picked up a few things, but I expect you noticed. I will contact you sometime in the next week or so. My life is getting sorted. Speak soon."

Her fucking life is getting sorted, thought Stuart, well what about mine? I really thought I knew you Zoe, but how wrong I was. He still ached for her and wished he didn't. He realised he had been keeping her departure to himself apart from the kids who seemed pretty relaxed about things… perhaps they had been given a different story. He thought about calling Joe, his elder brother but in the end he didn't. Until he could speak with Zoe he had no answers, he still held a vague hope that things would come right. Instead of going back to the workshop he devoured some sort of frozen pie and downed it with a bottle of wine.

Zoe had been to the house as she said; I wish I had been here, thought Stuart. He decided to see what she had taken… some toiletries were missing from a shelf in the bathroom, there was a gap in the wardrobe where her clothes had been, and all her undies had gone. It was then he noticed that all her jewellery had gone; if anything said I am gone for good that did. None of the cases were gone so she must have brought empty ones with her, in truth she had left the things that she didn't care about.

The next day he rose early and started work building the launch guide. He had decided the draw a detailed grid on the floor around the area where the floater had happened. He could then use this to record each individual experiment. Stuart made the base frame that would prove the slope of the drop; he calibrated it in degrees. He was worried that it may not be accurate enough and was deep in thought when Rob arrived.

"Hello, maestro, I haven't seen you for while," he said.

"Sorry, Rob, lots of things have been going on."

"Care to share anything; how's the experiment?"

"In no particular order, I've lost my job, Zoe's left me, and I am trying to reproduce the floater effect... so it's a fuck of a time." Stuart hadn't meant to say anything, it just all came out. Rob looked stunned, not sure what to say. "Sorry Rob, I didn't mean to dump on you, please... please keep this to yourself."

"Zoe left... what happened?" Stuart told him all he knew. He felt better for sharing it, but it still left him with butterflies in his stomach and he didn't know why. "I don't know what I can do to help, Stu. It not like Zoe... I always had you two down as the perfect pair."

"So did I, Rob, maybe that was the problem, everything was too stable, too comfortable and maybe she was thirsting for something more. Anyway, until she contacts me I can't do anything, hence my focus on this," he said pointing at the launch guide.

"OK, Stu, please let me know if I can help... what the fuck is it? A clothes horse?" Stuart knew Rob was changing the subject.

"This, mate, is what's going to keep me sane. It's part of my design to enable me to control the drop of a metal bar. There are lots of spacial dimensions as well as velocity so it's a bit of a nightmare!"

"Explain how it works then."

Stuart went through his design and the early construction, Rob put in some good ideas. They were both considering how to ensure that any other factors could influence the experiment. The magnetics should be the same and they both agreed that it was practical to go ahead but it could be a waste of time if there was something beyond their understanding that was causing the effect. Even now the number of variables in the experiment was very high.

"It would be so much easier if I could eliminate some of the variables through computer simulation," said Rob. "The trouble is I can't see how we could do it."

"Remember I was here when it happened, and I did take some photos, so that will narrow the grid considerably. I also plan to limit the height to that of my vice where I was using the spanner and we know the floating height of the spanner, so it reduces the number of variables quite a lot."

"Good plan, do you want a hand with the definition of scope, so we can record the outcomes? I probably can't really help with the construction."

"Thanks Rob. Can you build it on my laptop?"

"Consider it done," said Rob. "I should be able to get it ready for tomorrow afternoon. Meanwhile you and Heath-Robinson better get on with the launch pad."

"Launch Guide," said Stuart.

"Whatever," said Rob as he closed the workshop door.

Stuart started the second part of the guide that provided rotation. He would have to rework the first section to include Rob's ideas but that could wait until tomorrow. It was slow work since its accuracy was crucial to the experiment, but this was Stuart's pleasure. He got much of it complete before turning in about two in the morning. He was up early again the next day and had a big breakfast to make up for not eating the day before. Stuart had a sense of urgency with the project, but he didn't know why. Perhaps he wanted to get it out of the way, leaving him clear to fix things with Zoe… no that wasn't it, it was just sheer excitement that he might be on the verge of discovering something important.

It was mid-morning when Stuart stopped for a cup of coffee. He had finished the rotation platform and was rather pleased with it, having made some improvement as he went. He finished the modifications to the base frame by lunchtime. The final task was the runner assembly. It had to be adjustable to take the various sizes of bar and, at the same time, needed to allow for an offset in fall angle. He had already created a choke mechanism to slow down the speed of the falling bar, but it was crudely calibrated. The key to this was that the calibration would allow him to reproduce the fall if he needed to.

Stuart had nearly finished the runner when Rob arrived. "Stuart, I am really impressed, the launch guide should simulate the spanner drop. If of course it works."

"Pessimist," said Stuart with a smile. "How have you got on?"

"Well following our discussion I have put a simple table together to take five recordings... height obviously, drop angle, rotation point in degrees, bar angle and bar speed, how are you recording bar speed?"

"Well I've made calibrations based on various choke points on the runners, but I am beginning to wonder if it's necessary since we will be varying the height anyway."

"Leave it in, Stuart, the one aspect we haven't covered is spin, it's highly likely that the spanner was turning as it fell."

"Agree," said Stuart. "I don't know how to deal with spin and whether it's important. If the float event happened at a single point in time then the spanner would be in a position that we can replicate; if the spin is important then we are buggered."

"True, when do you want to start the experiment?"

"Well I think it needs two of us, so I was hoping to start this Saturday then we have the whole weekend."

"Careful, sunshine, I don't think Susie will let me off that amount of time."

"Sorry Rob, whatever time you can give." Maybe my single-mindedness was the reason Zoe left... "I will finish off the launch guide and test it so we are ready."

"Come to supper on Friday and we can persuade Susie then."

"Shouldn't you ask her if I can come, she will wonder about Zoe?"

"It's up to you, Stu, I have to go, more bloody marking from school."

Stuart spent the next day finishing off the guide and testing various bars on the device. It all seemed to work really well although Stuart had doubts on the choke mechanism. He assembled it all in the workshop where the event took place. He had already used the various images of the floater to create a 'sweet spot' on the grid and positioned it accordingly. He then arranged various cameras around the workshop, positioned in such a way that they could be easily focused on the drop.

Stuart was still concerned that he wasn't recording any of the magnetics but since Ruth's equipment had been so badly damaged he decided to concentrate on reproducing the effect. If he could replicate it then that would be the time to get more information.

So, the stage is set; Stuart couldn't suppress his excitement and it stayed with him as he went round to Rob's place.

Sue answered the door. "Hi Stuart, no Zoe?"

"Sorry, Sue, she's away," as he lightly kissed her cheek. Rob appeared, and Stuart gave him a bottle of wine. "Come on in," he said.

They had a kitchen-diner and the table was laid. "I am trying a new dish on you," Sue said as Rob waved him to a chair. It was a fun evening, but Stuart was sure Rob had told Sue abut Zoe since it was so carefully avoided. There was a lot of discussion about the experiment and it was obvious that Sue was excited about it. If only Zoe had been the same, thought Stuart. At midnight, he said his farewell and walked home in the cold night air, musing on things. There had been so much change in his life and somewhere inside him was a sense of self-pity. Get over it, he said to himself, you can only control your own actions, so be positive, Stuart, throw yourself into the experiment.

It was early morning and Stuart had just had breakfast when Rob arrived. "Come on, Stu, let's get to the bottom of this fucking thing."

They went into the workshop. "Great stuff; it's all set up and ready."

"Not quite, I haven't been able to figure out what to do with the magnetics. All I have is the original video and my memory that the two generators were humming quietly and were warm to touch."

"I agree," said Rob, "we should have got Ruth to calibrate their magnetics before anything else."

"I'm not sure that would have been possible given all the forces that were in play anyway. We do have a bit of luck though, despite Nigel wanting that strimmer repaired urgently, Wendy still hasn't picked it up. Remember that I wondered whether it initialised the magnetic effect on the generators. It's in the garage." Stuart returned with the strimmer and plugged it in. He positioned the strimmer between the generators and pressed the trigger. Sure enough the strimmer swayed violently as before, as if it didn't want to be in that place. Stuart turned it off and they both heard the gentle hum from both generators, something had clearly been excited, but whether it was the same as before, they couldn't know.

They had already made a plan on the sequence of trials and Rob's table of results laid out that plan. They both agreed to start with a bar that was similar in size to the spanner. Stuart placed the bar on the guide and let go; the bar fell to the floor. Both Rob and Stuart laughed at the anti-climax.

"Nothing happened," said Rob. "By my calculations we only have about a thousand more trials to go before we expand it to the larger area."

"We are going to get slicker as time goes on," said Stuart readying the next drop. In fairness, they were doing well and by lunchtime had completed over 80 readings. They ploughed on throughout the afternoon and by the evening their tally was just over 300 observations. In one instance the bar had vibrated a bit, but they ignored it.

"OK, Stu I must go, I'm already late and in Sue's bad books. I don't want her leaving me," Rob wished his brain took more control of his mouth. "Sorry Stu, I didn't mean that."

"Don't get sensitive, Rob, any time you can help is great, I might keep going for a while albeit a bit slower."

"Ok, I can definitely do three hours tomorrow afternoon."

"See you then," and he left.

Stuart kept going; in fact he streamlined the process for one person and found he was nearly going at the same speed as before.

Just before midnight he had completed nearly 500 readings overall. Again one of the observations had produced a vibration or more of a shiver and Stuart noted that he would re-look at the reading the next day.

In the morning Stuart decided that needed to speak to Lucy and Henry to see how things were going and if they had any news from Zoe. He had been exchanging emails with Marc who was clearly having a great time in New Zealand. He spoke with Lucy straight away, she had no more news but was hurt that she hadn't been able to speak with Zoe either.

"Dad you will just have to wait it out. I know it's frustrating, but none of know what we are dealing with, keep the faith."

His call to Henry a little later went the same way. Both he and Zoe made sure that all the kids were independent and although the family bonds were strong, they didn't live in each other's lives, hence they both felt that time was needed, and things would become clearer. Neither of them was taking sides and Stuart was sure there would never be any schism there.

Before his pub lunch Stuart had completed nearly 60 additional observations. The old generators were humming nicely and were warm to the touch. He had sat in the pub on his own, his mind wandered from the newspaper back to the experiment and making notes on things he might have missed. It wasn't that Stuart was antisocial, but he was comfortable with his own company. This was in contrast to Zoe who loved a strong social life. It was funny that the two of them got on so well, Stuart mused, they were so different in many ways. Maybe she wanted a more vibrant life. True, Stuart enjoyed the social life that Zoe brought to the household but equally he welcomed solitude and time to ponder over things.

He arrived back at the workshop a few minutes before Rob. They discussed the various shortcuts that Stuart had employed and got down to the experiment straight away. It was halfway through the afternoon when the bar shivered before it hit the floor.

"Did you see that?" yelled Rob.

Stuart had been looking at the observation screen, wondering if the precision could be tightened up.

"No sorry Rob, what was it?"

"Stu we both need to keep our concentration on the drops."

"Agreed, sorry, what did you see?"

"Well the last bar sort of shivered before it hit the floor."

"Let's have a look at the recording then," and Stuart repositioned the video to playback the last observation. It certainly looked like the bar shivered. He replayed the drop again but this time in a slower timeframe.

"You see, that doesn't look natural, something is interfering in its fall."

Stuart remembered that he had seen a sort of shiver earlier that day and eventually found the observation. It was similar in nature but not quite so pronounced.

"Maybe that observation yesterday was more important than we thought, we should have noted it."

"Ok, well let's re-run this one anyway."

It was disappointing, the bar just fell naturally.

"Let's give it another try," said Stuart; this time the bar shivered again. "I bet it's the lack of accuracy in the launch guide that gives different outcomes. Let's do another 20 drops to confirm it." They carried out another twenty drops, the tension and concentration were palpable as it become clear that 14 of the drops produced the shiver effect.

"We are onto something, Rob; how can we tighten up the accuracy of the drop?"

"I'm not sure we can unless we redesign the guide assembly. Anyway, what would it prove? We have enough observation to say something weird is happening."

"Let's stop for a moment and take stock, coffee?"

"I didn't think we would find anything, you know, but here we are two days into the experiment and something has happened." As Rob was talking, Stuart correlated the two separate incidents, they both happened in an area quite close to each other.

"My guess is that we are covering more area on the grid than we need to."

"Guess?" said Rob. "That's not very scientific."

"What I mean, Rob, is that if we narrow down the observations to this area here," Stuart pointed to an area about a metre square on the grid, "then we may have a higher chance of discovering something. At the moment we are following a linear pattern across the grid, I'm just suggesting this may be a 'sweet spot' for results. If it's not then we revert to the original plan."

Rob was clearly unhappy at this approach, but Stuart couldn't figure out why. Anyway Rob spent some time redefining the 'sweet spot' on the computer and they restarted.

After about 30 drops they got the effect again although it was more pronounced, it was a vibration now, less of a shiver. The two tried to add the coordinates of this observation into the correlation but couldn't establish any relationship. They both knew they were getting closer to something which causes increased amplitude. The experiments continued until early evening without further developments. As they were wrapping up they both decided to setup the launch at the last location that produced results. They got the vibrations straight away; it was a form of reassurance before closing that day.

They both left the workshop on a high. The construct of the experiment they knew held inaccuracies as well as assumptions and yet their hunches had been right, and they were on track to find something... even if they didn't know what!

Stuart decided he would spend some time trying to see if there was some mathematical fit between the three results, it was clearly non-linear, and he knew he needed more results to flesh out any conclusion. He was really doing the exercise to learn a little about ways he could understand the variables and their influence on each other. He had decided to leave it when the phone rang.

"Hi Stuart, it's me, I am sorry I am mucking you around," Stuart froze; he didn't know what to say. He had prepared various questions in his head but they all disappeared.

"But why, love, what have I done?" he finally mumbled.

"We can't discuss this on the phone, can we meet tomorrow at the Green Man pub for coffee at eleven?"

She obviously had this all prepared, thought Stuart. "The Green Man?"

"Yes, it's off the Reading Road."

"I know where it is, I will be there."

"Good, see you then. Bye."

That was it, short and sharp, Stuart suddenly realised his hands were shaking and he was sweating. Get control, he said to himself. At least I will get some answers. That was the end of sleep; his mind was oscillating around the meeting with Zoe interspersed by thoughts on the experiment. He vaguely submitted to sleep or emotional exhaustion, whichever.

Despite his best efforts he knew the bad night showed on his face, nevertheless he decided to dress well, not too well, just in case she still missed him. Somehow he wasn't optimistic about the day. He was sure she had met a man who had swept her off her feet. He hated him already and would hurt him if he could. No, what's the point; if she wants to go then fine, but she isn't changing me, and my life here... sod them both. He oscillated between vindictiveness and forgiveness; how can this be, its irrational... come on, Stuart, what do you want? No it's not me, it's what she wants and the fact that she has left gives you a clue. So assume the worst and forget vindictiveness. He was compelled to check on things in the workshop before leaving. Everything was as it should be the generators still doing their thing. The sparkle had gone; he viewed the experiment through a different lens, it wasn't bright and new and exciting, but rather grey and uninspiring.

It was a short drive to the pub, short enough for 9,000 butterflies to enter his gut. He practiced lots of options in his head... if she says this, I will say that... until he arrived in the car park, no sign of Zoe's car and he entered. It was one of those pubs that was built in the thirties and had undergone various facelifts... it needed another one, the place was tired and wore the scars of use from the last ten years. Stuart was pleased that it was quiet; one man in the corner enjoying his newspaper, two women chatting animatedly over their coffee but no Zoe. He found a table that was away from the others and ordered coffee. He felt conspicuous and wished he had some reading material. At that moment Zoe came in and Stuart stood. She was with someone who Stuart vaguely recalled having met at some time, moral support, he thought. Stuart tried to remember where he had met her; she was tall, very tall, maybe six feet and slim in an athletic way, probably jogs every day he thought. She had a strange beauty with a defined bone structure that you might see in a ballerina. Strangely she was very like a taller version of Zoe, although her long blonde hair with purple highlights distinguished her.

"Hello Stuart, thanks for coming."

"Why wouldn't I want to see you, to understand why my wife has left me?" he said in a bitter voice that he regretted.

"Stuart, I'm really sorry… we have had a good life together and I had to be sure in myself why I wouldn't want it to continue," she said enigmatically.

"I'm sorry, I just don't understand," he noticed that the woman was holding Zoe's hand, more moral support..

"Do we have to discuss this in public?"

"Stuart, this is Diana, Diana Slater do you recall she works at the college? No matter, Diana is part of this Stuart."

"Ok, so I'm listening."

"There's not much to say but that Diana and I love each other very much." Stuart saw Diana squeeze her hand. "We have both been in turmoil wondering how to deal with such emotions, it's new to both of us." Stuart didn't know what to say he just nodded and let Zoe talk. "I feel selfish and have been wrestling with what I should do, I am still very fond of you, Stuart, but these emotions are so strong, I can't deceive you."

"Has it been going on long?"

Zoe shrugged. "A few months."

"You disguised it well," he said bitterly.

"You wouldn't have noticed," she snapped back.

This wasn't going anywhere, he thought. "So what do you want?"

"A new life."

"Well you've certainly got that, batting for the other side."

"Let's leave," said Diana, "this is going nowhere."

"Stuart I thought you might have understood just a little."

"So what do we do about the kids, especially Marc?"

"I've given it some thought, I think Lucy and Henry know and are ok."

"Well if they know, they didn't tell me."

"Well they wouldn't, would they?"

"I didn't know I was an ogre!"

"Look Stuart, I do worry about Marc given that it's exam time and hopefully Uni."

"We will have to offer him the choice of living with you or me and then having freedom to see each of us."

"Well we don't really have the space, so I was wondering?"

"Stop… don't wonder, I am not moving out and… before you say it I am not having you two moving in."

"I think he would be better with you then," she said. Stuart was really surprised, Marc was still her baby and here she was sacrificing her support of him in favour of Diana. She really was completely besotted with her.

"You should know, I have left the job, so there is no more money coming in. I assume your savings will cover you until the solicitor have sorted things out and had their cut." Stuart was already planning to get to the bank that day and close the joint accounts and shared cards.

"Well it will give you time to play in your workshop," she said sarcastically.

"I am so sorry, Zoe, you are a different person to the one who married me, I still love that woman, but she is no longer there, so I might as well go. I will need your new address and phone number."

She gave him an envelope. "It's all in there including my solicitor's details."

This was so well planned "Ok, so all we will to do is figure out the meeting arrangement with Marc. Shall I tell him?"

"I don't think you should do it, you are too emotional."

"Well so are you… I am happy to hold off until he is back and then the two of us can speak to him together."

"Fine by me," she said, "by the way, we are off to India for three weeks, so I won't really be contactable."

"I will hold off discussing anything with Marc until your return. I hope Lucy and Henry don't say something."

"They won't," she said.

"True, they didn't," he said cynically, "well goodbye, and I hope you find the happiness you are looking for." He knew he was breaking down and was fucked that Diana would see it, so he stood up and left. Out of the corner of his eye he thought he saw Zoe breaking down with fucking Diana comforting her.

He wiped his eyes when he was in the car. Did he screw it all up… he didn't know… he wasn't ready for a woman to steal his wife's love for him? He drove badly, too fast and realised he was taking his anger out on the road. He settled back and started planning the important and urgent parts of separation. He went to the town and found that he couldn't close the shared account, but he transferred all the funds to a new account in a new bank. He closed all shared cards and cut them up having reapplied for new ones. At home, he reassigned insurance and pension policies to exclude Zoe so that by the end of the day he had created a financial separation that stopped her getting to any monies. He wasn't being vindictive and would readily ensure she got an equitable settlement, but he didn't trust Diana. Where were they getting all the money for three weeks in India for example?

He had hard conversations with Henry and Lucy asking them why they wanted to lie to him. "Because Mum asked us to say nothing," was the weak reply from both of them. Stuart didn't hold out any olive branches, they had clearly conspired with their mother. He confirmed that things wouldn't change in terms of his support for them especially on the money side they should be ok, although he no longer had a job. He did sense in Henry that he felt to have been too remote from Stuart, sadly Lucy had always been remote from him and things wouldn't change. He didn't arrange to see them, leaving that initiative to come from them; he felt betrayed but didn't know why.

Life is strange, he thought, a few months ago we seemed like a family with its normal ups and downs, and now the Ashley family had just imploded. Well I am 52 and have a lot of horsepower left in me… so let's move on and restart my life… maybe it was meant to be.

He got up early the next morning and strangely he felt a spring in his step. At last, he knew where he stood, the unknowns had gone, and somehow his wife giving up her heterosexual life was more acceptable to him, perhaps because he couldn't compete. He had resolved to start a new life and was already fed up with thinking what might have been, and where did it all go wrong, and was it my entire fault.

He took a coffee into the workshop and with the refined plan restarted the experiment around the sweet spot. He had hoped that something might happen quite quickly but laboured on throughout the day with no unusual results. He knew that he needed to get on with his social life, so he went down to the tennis club for a light supper.

"Hello stranger," said Bob the club manager from behind the bar. "What have you been up to, it's been a while?"

"It has, Bob; I've decided I need to get playing again."

"Well get your name down, there are lots of players who will take you on." Stuart had been a reasonably good player and as his age progressed found that he did pretty well in the senior league. He chatted with a few people and had supper with a couple who he and Zoe used to play. It was the first time he had to say that he was separated, and it did produce an uncomfortable silence. He knew he needed to practice how he dealt with other people on the issue. Nevertheless he felt that started the healing process and enjoyed being away from the house.

Stuart had stacked up nearly 200 observations the previous day and restarted the experiment having checked the generators. Within an hour the bar received a violent movement, it was difficult to analyse so Stuart reviewed the video a few times in slow motion; it was definitely an elliptical movement. He repeated the drop again to confirm the results. This was the first observation which had shown considerable force, and it didn't add up to the original floating spanner, which was relatively benign, although he did recall the sheer forces that were in play when he tried to move it. Some while later he got a similar result perhaps a little stronger, and then it happened.

In fact it was three drops later that the bar shot across the grid area and sliced through part of the launch guide before swinging back across the workshop in an arc to the floor. It all happened so fast; that all Stuart could see was the collapse of the launch frame. He had to slow the video replay down much more than before in order to see the bar and its trajectory.

Obviously, time to stop, Stuart thought, as he examined the launch frame. One side of it had been shattered, admittedly it was only softwood, but the speed and force had been considerable. The humming from the generators also seemed louder. He left a message on Rob's mobile, he needed Rob's mathematical help to analyse the results.

Rob arrived later that day; Stuart was in the workshop making a new frame for the launch guide. It gave him the opportunity to make some alterations, which would make it more stable.

"So, you've had some new results?"

"Just a bit, Rob, I am making this new launch frame because the bar smashed the original into pieces."

"Amazing… let's see the video."

Rob and Stuart replayed the video in ultra-slow motion; the bar was still moving at speed. "You've got some other results as well," said Rob after some time.

"Yes, but I need your help to see if we can find out any relationship."

"Ok, so let's look at the height and speed of the active results first." After a few minutes on the computer he declared that he didn't think these two variables were complicit in the behaviour. The rotation point seemed to have some influence, but it was the drop angle and the bar angle which held the most promise. There was no doubt that Stuart's 'sweet point' theory was also a contributing factor.

"So, my conclusion is that we are nearing a point of maximum influence from something, maybe from the generators. The angle that the bar hits that point of influence is also important, the rest we disregard, except for the drop angle which, of course, will influence the angle at the point of influence."

"Ok, agreed, so we narrow the experiment even more?"

"Yes and given the amplitude of the POI is growing, I suspect that this area on the grid is most fertile." He marked an area on the grid.

"I will spend some more time on these results, when will you have the guide ready to restart?"

Stuart gave it some thought. "Let's give it a couple of days," he said. "I heard from Zoe, so I have some things I need to sort out."

"Do you want to talk about it?"

"Nothing to say, Rob, she is in love with another woman and won't be coming back."

"I am staggered, Stu, I never had Zoe down as a closet lesser."

"Careful, Rob, I don't want to talk about it," snapped Stuart. Rob changed the subject. "Fine shall we restart in two days' time? We are getting close to something and I think it will need both of us."

"What about school? Can you get the time off?

"No probs, it's exam time and I can schedule it."

The next two days were uneventful; Stuart finished the improved base for the launch guide. He phoned an old friend who was a solicitor to get some advice on separation. He made it sound quite complex, largely because the separations were usually acrimonious. Stuart was determined that the separation with Zoe should be on good terms. Why? Well maybe he still loved her?

Stuart and Rob had spoken on the phone and agreed to start about ten that day. They were both excited but also a little tense given the force of the last result. They were unusually precise in setting up the first drop. They decided to focus around the centre of the area that Rob had outlined and then keeping the height constant, vary the angles. It was an anticlimax as the bar dropped and nothing happened. They decided to focus on the bar angle and increased it by ten degrees, still nothing. Two further increases produced no result.

"Well we know that the bar angle was around 75 degrees on the last 2 results so let's increase it to that."

"No Rob, come on... you are the scientist! As with all the experiments so far we have covered the full spectrum of settings. Let's stick to that discipline," and so they progressed, but it was fair so say that their expectations grew as the angle grew. The setting was at 70 degrees as the bar dropped and disappeared with an almighty bang. The noise and the feeling of a powerful force stunned both Rob and Stuart.

Stuart was the first to speak. "Fuck me, what happened, any idea?"

Rob was already reaching for the video replay. The camera closest to the experiment was not working. "Whatever that was, it's buggered this camera," said Rob shakily.

"Let's look at the others," said Stuart and he released the one furthest from the experiment, hoping that it may not have been damaged, sadly it was.

"OK something happened, and we have no visual record of it… oh shit, the computer's fucked too."

"Don't worry," said Rob, I backed it up yesterday and I have a hard record of today's few results.

"So where's the bar and what else has been damaged?" They both noticed the hole in the brick wall adjacent to the garage around the same time. It was about half a metre wide.

"Well we know where it went and unlike the other it hasn't returned." They went into the garage, expecting to find the bar; instead they found a hole in the upper part of the steel garage door. The bar had missed his beloved Morgan fortunately. "Well we have no way of knowing where it's gone; let's hope it hasn't hit anyone."

"What the hell do we do now? We should continue in increments of one degree," said Rob.

"I won't have a workshop left if we do that."

"Ok let's think, do you have a spare laptop?"

"I could use Marc's I guess."

"Can you get it, Stu, and then I will restore the data. We might be able to extrapolate the angle."

"One thing's for sure, it's all about the angle to the POI… that's progress."

Rob restored the data relatively quickly and extracted the results where there had been an effect. "It looks like an angle of 76 or 77 degrees is about right. The trouble is the accuracy of the launch guide could easily add a degree plus or minus."

"Great, so we have four degrees of tolerance," Stuart hesitated.

So we have to do four more experiments and we can't protect anything. What worries me is that this maybe a perfectly natural phenomenon that your mate Ruthie could explain away, and we are no closer to the floater."

"Only one way to find out," said Rob flatly. They decided to do the lot and started at 78 degrees. Stuart held his breath as he released the bar. There was a bang and this time the bar had disappeared leaving a hole on the opposite wall.

"My hunch is 76," said Rob.

"Me too," and they reset the launch guide, Stuart hesitated and then released the bar, it dropped to the floor but rebounded to about two metres before oscillating between the two extremes. Those extremes of the oscillation reduced until it was stable. They both stepped back; they had found the floater. Stuart's heart was pounding, he held out his hand to Rob who just hugged him with a sort of cowboy yell.

"I know we have lost the videos but I'm getting my phone to see if I can record this." He returned with his phone expecting it to be fried, but it was fine, so he recorded the floating bar and a commentary by Rob on the settings. When they thought they had captured every piece of information they went into the house to celebrate with cold beers.

"That was tense," said Rob. "I still don't know how we got there, much of it was gut feel."

"Yes, but now we know what conditions create the effect but not what stops it, so we have even more questions to answer and after the original oscillation stopped, why didn't it stop for the spanner?"

"We need to figure out who can help us; I think Ruth is back now."

Neither of them could stop talking about it and speculating on its cause, I'm not going to get much sleep tonight, thought Stuart.

CHAPTER 8

A Tangled Web

"Great... so we have no ID, don't know where he came from and don't know whether he will live?" Paul Homer said to no-one in particular. As Police Inspector from the local Halifax department he had picked up the case of this man found on the highway.

"Ok what do we know?" he asked Miriam Wilson a detective constable who had been assigned to him for the last three months.

"It doesn't add up, Paul, this guy has absolutely nothing to identify him... he is wearing clothes that are too big for him and have all the labels cut out. I have sent them off to forensics but by the smell of oil and fish my guess is they were from a fishing boat. I have also spoken to the doctor who says he is in a bad way. As well as various cuts and bruises he has been pumped full of various toxins, mainly sedatives and stimulants. There were a number of bruises on his arms where various injections had been applied."

"You're saying that this man is a victim of something as yet unknown?"

"Absolutely, the drugs are being analysed as we speak."

"You said he is in a bad way?"

"Yes apart from the drugs, he has exposure."

"Life threatening?"

"No. The doctors think he should recover in a couple of days."

"Ok Miriam, keep an eye on him and let me know when we can talk to him, we should have all the results from the path lab and forensics by then. In the meantime see if he is listed on missing persons."

"Will do, as you know I have a big caseload so I will check for locals first and extend it when we have more time." Paul couldn't argue, the amount of admin that they had to do these days meant that time was the first compromise in cases like these.

Stuart didn't wake; it was more of a slow and erratic return to consciousness. At first it was sounds; some sort of hissing, then the haze of fluorescent light, then the two combined with intense nausea. Everything felt so heavy, he couldn't even lift his hand, but he sensed someone nearby even though he couldn't move his head. He tried to say something, but it was more of a gargle, he floated away. So it was, for what seemed like days, but true to forecast, things did become clearer. After they removed the ventilator the hissing stopped although there was still a machine behind him that emitted a ping every few seconds.

He first began to focus on a middle-aged lady, a nurse; she moved efficiently around him, checking a number of monitors that presumably relayed his wellbeing. From time to time other people came into his vision again checking the monitors and talking quietly. He managed a bit of a grunt and they came closer to check him. His eyes were watering badly which made his vision impossible, but they noticed and one of them wiped his eyes. He managed a faint smile.

"Well hello, stranger," the taller of the two images said. "Don't try to talk, we have had tubes down your throat and you will feel a bit bruised." Stuart managed a slight nod. "You may feel sick; it should go soon since we have reduced your medication. The police are keen to talk to you but don't worry they will hold off until we say you are ready."

Stuart still slept most of the time, but he noticed a number of different nurses who cared for him. After two more days he was sitting up and the drip had been removed, without warning, and with no dignity whatsoever the catheter was out too. He returned to eating although it was all soft, mushy and tasteless. The nausea had gone and with a sore throat he mumbled a few words, although it didn't seem like his voice. In the afternoon a man and a woman came into the room accompanied by a doctor.

"Hi, I'm Paul Homer from the Halifax Police and this is my colleague Miriam Wilson," she nodded to Stuart.

"And just in case you didn't know I'm Karen Stone your doctor for the last few days. I'm here to make sure you don't get over-stressed."

"We don't even know your name," Paul said gently, "so we couldn't let your folks know."

What folks? Stuart thought cynically. Well here goes. "It's Stuart Ashley," he said in a dislocated voice. Miriam had to take notes.

"Well Stuart, you have been a bit of a worry to the folk here at the hospital," he continued in a gentle chatty tone. "Where are you from Stuart... I am no good with accents especially the strange voice you have."

"His voice will get back to normal in a while," chipped in Karen.

"The UK, a town called Smythfield," said Stuart weakly.

"Well that's a long way from home," said Paul. "Are you on vacation?"

"I..." Stuart's voice dried.

"Relax Stuart, have a little drink," said Karen.

A few minutes later Stuart started. "I was at a place called Glens Falls in the States, it's a luxury prison for the security folk but they wouldn't say that... and I was kidnapped." Stuart lay back in the bed, the brief conversation had taken its toll.

"I think we should hold it there," said Karen, as she looked at his vital signs on the monitor. "Can we restart tomorrow assuming Stuart is ok?" Stuart gave a vague nod.

"Fine with us, thanks for your time," and they left.

"Shit," said Paul, "if this is for real, we have got a serious situation on our hands."

"That's a bit of an understatement," said Miriam with some irony.

"Look, Miriam, when we get back to the office can you check it out? If it holds water then I will alert the chief!"

"Great, Paul, so what do I do about my caseload?"

"I've got one too remember... but this is top priority, I can get our workload offloaded if the Chief agrees."

Miriam spent the rest of the day on other cases, which she interleaved, with the task of validating Stuart's identity, he was pretty well known, and she kicked herself for not recognising him. What the hell was he doing in Halifax though, and this story about kidnapping?

"Paul, I have done a check and he is definitely Stuart Ashley, the inventor of LeviProp, so this is a pretty important situation, to say the least."

"OK Miriam, get some uniform police over to the hospital ASAP, we need to protect this guy."

Paul was just about to alert the chain of command when the phone rang. "Hi this is Karen Stone from the hospital," Paul readied himself for bad news.

"What can I do for you? Is Mr Ashley ok?"

"Yes, he's fine, it just that we ran routine x-rays on him, just to check if anything was broken and something unusual came up on the image. It's some sort of electronic device on his upper back just under the skin."

"Can you extract it?" asked Paul.

"Sure," said Karen. "I don't think Stuart Ashley knows about it."

"Don't do anything about it yet, this is a very sensitive situation, I think Ashley may be in danger, so I am sending some police over to keep an eye on things. Can I phone you back later, I have your mobile?"

"My mobile won't be on, but you can bleep me," she said.

"Ok, I will be down to the hospital later today or early tomorrow," and he hung up.

Paul decided to see the chief immediately since they were in the same building and he might not get through easily by phone. Chief Morgan's personal assistant came from the Rottweiler school of helpfulness. It was late and despite his pleas, Paul couldn't get to the chief for an hour, and he only managed that since the chief was leaving for another meeting. Paul fell into step with the chief who was already being briefed by another officer. At least Paul had the time to give the chief a précis that would give him the magnitude of the issue.

"We have a major international incident on our hands and I expect it to go ballistic," he interrupted.

"Ok Paul talk to me in the elevator," the small group got into the elevator and Paul went through everything he knew.

The chief had been in his job for five years and had a sixth sense when everyday police life took a nasty turn as with the Moncton shootings a few years back. He knew Paul to be a steady officer who wasn't given to hyperbole. By the time the elevator had reached the underground car park Morgan had decided to back Paul.

"Right Paul, I agree this is not only serious in itself, but the implications are likely to be international." He pressed the fourth-floor button and the small group returned to his office. "Hold all calls and cancel all meetings for the next day," he said to the Rottweiler.

He called in Susan Curtis, his deputy, to make plans. "Paul you keep the case, what do you need?"

"Someone to pick up my caseload and assuming Miriam is with me then she is snowed under as well. I have aligned uniformed cover at the hospital 24 by 7."

"Susan can you pick up the case offload and square the uniform resource?"

"I'll get on it now, Chief."

"Ok but come back as quickly as you can, just in case we need more cover."

"Chief, if Ashley has a transmitter under his skin, it would suggest some foreign secret agency is involved, or maybe our own? Do you have any contacts?"

"I sure do, luckily the CSIS is located in Halifax. I will make contact with them. It's late, go home and get some sleep; get to the hospital first thing tomorrow, assuming Ashley agrees, get that chip removed so we can check it out. Keep me updated Paul... day or night!"

"Sure, Chief." Paul left and arranged meet Miriam at the hospital the following morning.

"I have organised to transfer your caseload," he said as he met Miriam at the hospital reception.

"Thanks Paul, I have already passed some of the work over and agreed to do some briefings here, I can't say the rest of our team are happy about it!"

"Let's see Ashley and get his approval to remove the chip; hopefully he may be able to shed some light on how he turned up here."

They found Karen Stone at the ward. "How is he, Karen? We would like to have a talk with him today?"

"He is in pretty good shape, all things considered. He is still slightly sedated from last night but has had some food and his voice is coming back."

"We will need his approval to remove the chip," Paul continued "how quickly can you do it?"

"It's pretty simple, so we can remove it today if he agrees."

Stuart started to think through his situation. It had obviously been UK people who had extracted him, no-one else could have known of the reference to tennis from Dawson. It seemed like Dawson and his team was in a corner, they had made it clear that some agreement had been made that gave the US control over Stuart. Clearly it was a complex relationship that caused Dawson to resort to back door methods to extract Stuart. He didn't remember being tagged but that meant the US people knew he was in Canada; would they come after him? He vaguely saw uniformed people outside his room, which suggested the Canadian authorities were worried for his safety.

He considered his options; none of which seemed attractive. Firstly he knew Rick Marsh and Bruckner had put out the word that Stuart had more discoveries to unfold as a magnet for countries to restart TANGENT. That meant there could be nations who wanted to get hold of him. When he originally came to the US to support the UN initiative he didn't realise how naive he was to the world of international politics; he now knew that the US agenda was complex and devious and certainly didn't support him. He had lost his trust in Dawson and the UK team; they had been so supportive in developing the research programme, and then inexplicably persuaded him to participate with the US under the UN TANGENT agenda. Perhaps he could stay in Canada, after all he knew Lawrence Banard albeit briefly. The idea appealed to him, Canada was more tolerant and did not have so much to lose as the power interests that he had been caught up in. He decided to be completely open with the Canadian police, and certainly not lie; he was a lousy liar anyway.

Meanwhile Chief Morgan had been in a meeting with the head of the local CSIS, Al Smith. Once Morgan had briefed Smith on the background to Stuart's arrival in Halifax, he called in one of his team to do some research.

"He will give me an early précis of the situation in an hour. Do you want to wait?"

"Sure," said Morgan, he knew that his actions would be reviewed at some time in the future and he wanted to be sure that he had diligently followed through.

"You know that we can't always share things, but I will say we have been aware that a special wing of the CIA has been leading a project to do with Stuart Ashley and his discoveries. We also know that the Brits are actively involved, and that the UN is being used as a cover for their actions." Al decided not to mention that they had been monitoring the activity of a British frigate.

"You should know, Al, that the press is probably on to it… hold fire, Al, not deliberately from my department, but there is always a number of ambulance chasers around and I wouldn't be surprised if they are onto something! It's impossible to keep track of everyone around the hospital for example. Ashley is pretty well known and if the word is out that he is in hospital here we need to be prepared."

Al knew he was right, he needed more information and indeed some guidance on how to handle the situation. Responsibility rested somewhere between his Executive and the Foreign Affairs people. He got the chief placed in a small office with a minder and under the pretext of other issues, immediately briefed his executive who confirmed that they would liaise with the CFA. Al was used to situations when he never had all the facts, wasn't in control, and yet was held accountable. He trusted the chief but assigned Clara, one of his top women, to support him and ensure he was constantly up-to-date, the chief was delighted to agree.

It wasn't long before his executive contacted him. The US CIA had already been onto them, with a request for information as to Ashley's whereabouts. Not surprising he thought, given they had a tracker fixed to Ashley. The executive had confirmed that Ashley was indeed in Canada and they were investigating various irregularities. It was a holding position.

The CFA had notified the British Foreign Office who had expressed surprise that Ashley wasn't still in the USA. They would say that, Al thought, especially if they had been responsible for the extraction. So everyone involved had strong views on what had happened with Ashley but diplomatically they were all in denial. The CFA expected the UK Foreign Office to be back to them in next few hours.

As to action, the executive had asked for full monitoring of the situation but not to engage in any pre-emptive way. Al called in the chief and apologised for keeping him waiting in the office. The chief understood and had been getting an update from Paul; Clara joined them.

"Ashley is in good enough shape to talk; Paul Homer from my Department has the detail. It seems that Ashley was extracted under force from Glens Falls a secure CIA site." Al managed half a smile, which would have upset Rick Marsh, he thought. He remembers he was on a motorcycle to start and then transferred to a coach. He was doped up to the eyeballs and only has flashes of events. He remembers getting onto a boat that stunk of fish and that's it.

"Do you think he is telling you everything?" Clara asked.

"Not sure, it's true he was heavily drugged, the forensic analysis confirms it was pretty sophisticated stuff too."

"He remembers a man and a woman both mid-thirties; the woman he thinks was medically trained. They both spoke English, but he wouldn't confirm they were Brits."

"Wouldn't or couldn't?" said Al.

"Paul suspects wouldn't," replied the chief.

"Paul also said that Ashley is completely untrusting of everyone."

"No surprises there... what does he want to do?" asked Al.

"Get back to the UK, I guess. We certainly don't want him here any longer than is necessary." Al remembered his executive's point about comment. "Actually I retract that; maybe he would like to say in Canada, he would be one hell of an asset."

The telephone rang, "It's a secure call," said Al. "I may ask you to leave." Al explained to the caller the latest information on Ashley and who was in the room. "It's ok, we will have a conference call, but this is specifically for this group." He pressed two buttons on the phone and his executive's voice came from the speaker. The introductions were one-way only and the chief had no idea how many people were at the other end of the call.

"It goes without saying that we are in a sensitive position… not of our choosing. The police need to minimise any press involvement or speculation. There is a view that Ashley may be keen to stay in Canada and Lawrence Banard is on his way to meet with him."

Al was glad he had retracted his comment.

Fuck me, thought the Chief, the ex PM coming here!

"Al, you are handling security and coordinates with the Police. Chief Morgan we have cleared it with your people."

"Fine," said Morgan noting he would get his own confirmation.

"We are unsure what to expect from the US since they have been playing a pretty devious game, but it wouldn't surprise us if the US Vice President gets involved. We do expect the UK FO to request they send someone to ensure Ashley's wellbeing. That's it for now." The phone went dead.

Stuart had genuinely shared everything with Paul Homer and Miriam. They had an open way about them that enabled him to recall as much as he could. He really wouldn't speculate on whether his abductors were Brits, his journey from a trusting soul to a complete cynic had been a tough one. He had agreed to removal of the chip on the understanding that someone would explain its function.

Paul and Miriam stayed on and came to see him throughout the day. Sometime in the afternoon he told Stuart that several people from the press were around and that Chief Morgan would be speaking to them later that day. Paul suggested that it would be wise for Stuart to say nothing and he agreed.

Chief Morgan was angry and frustrated. He had been told that he was to handle the press conference on Ashley; he had also been given strong guidance on what he could and could not say... he was just the mouthpiece for the police and the CSIS. He hated press conferences anyway and always felt that he was seen to the public as the official not telling the whole truth. This was compounded by the restrictions that had to be placed on him from above.

And so it was.

He was surprised at the number of press there and confirmed that Stuart Ashley had been found unconscious on the side of the highway, was recovering in hospital, and that his department was investigating how he got there. Then the barrage started; the chief tried to deflect all the questions but knew his responses were weak. One of the questioners asked if Ashley was escaping from the US... was this speculation or do these people know more about this, he thought? He decided to end the conference abruptly to avoid losing his temper.

The speculation increased on the evening's television news and he was advised that Lawrence Banard wasn't coming to meet Stuart. Instead his office wanted to know when he could be moved. They contacted Paul to check whether Ashley could leave the hospital and be transferred to Ottawa, it was only a two-hour flight.

Karen Stone confirmed to Paul that Stuart could leave the hospital; all his vital signs had recovered well but the trauma of events meant he would need some quiet convalescence. She then announced to Stuart that he could leave but re-stressed the need for a month's convalescence. Stuart didn't know what to say, he thought he would stay in the hospital for another week and hadn't planned what to do next. It reminded Stuart that he didn't have anyone to turn to; ironically the power of his discoveries had isolated him. He thought of Zoe and what might have been. His melancholy cleared however when Paul solved that thought.

"If it's acceptable, we would like you to visit Ottawa and meet up with some of our government people and you could then check in at the British High Commission if you like. Of course you may have other plans?"

"No, nothing special, have you any news of the people who

dumped me on the roadside?"

"Nothing substantial," lied Paul. "But don't worry we will manage your security to Ottawa and your stay there. We will do our best to avoid all the press, but I won't make any promises on that score."

"What about clothes?"

"Assuming you're ok to go, then I will get someone to come in and get the basics, our department doesn't run to Armani though," he said with a smile.

Stuart suddenly realised that he had no phone or laptop for months. "Any chance of a phone or laptop?"

"Now that is an Armani budget," said Paul. "I suggest you get it funded through the British taxpayer! I may not see you again, Stuart."

"Paul, thanks for your support, I guess I have been a bit of a headache to you."

"No problem." Paul had actually been relieved of the monotony of overwork.

"All I read is this LeviProp stuff is going to change the world, so why isn't it happening?"

"Great question, Paul, I wish I knew. No let me revise that; I do know some of the factors that are in play and they are the obviously big ones. What's happening below the waterline is much more subtle and complex and created the motives for me turning up here."

"Surely if this discovery of yours provides 'unlimited power' then something must be happening?"

"If only it was that simple, and I confess that when I first made the discovery I thought that everyone, every country would know about it, so they could all enjoy the benefits. Sadly those with the most to lose economically or politically are controlling it. My idealism was unfounded... what a sad bastard I am."

"Well I am an optimist... I know... it's strange in my job, but I bet you that it will come good... maybe in a way you can't see right now." Paul shook Stuart's hand and for a few seconds there was a strange emotion between them. As Paul left he couldn't help but feel for Stuart, who was a pawn in a very complex game. He decided to go back to the room. "Stuart, don't give up and don't be so trusting... make it happen in a practical way rather than solving the world problems!" He left for the second time.

Stuart lay back in the chair, he thought about Paul's last comment and for some reason that moment with Paul had been an awakening. It had been bloody obvious that he had been manipulated over the last year. Yet how had he allowed it to happen? He wasn't a wimp or a shrinking violet, but he had been misled and misused at every turn whether it was the UK or US government people. He pondered the turning points of the past year. He knew that something had forced the UK to pass control of things to the US but had never got to the bottom of it. The UK people all told him what he wanted to hear and in his passion to make IC a reality he just assumed everyone else was a 'believer'. Indeed he was mesmerised at the power and enthusiasm that the US brought to the table. And now... well now it was all lost, his discoveries were being developed everywhere... well nearly everywhere... mainly covertly at this time.

He knew he didn't have the whole picture in his head; the complexity of the world economies, oil, protectionism and political agendas. He suspected that few organisations did have the whole picture or indeed had the levers to influence things but from now on he would be his own man. He shouldn't have decided to contact the UK government for sponsorship, but it had played to his ego. Anyway his illicit flights had been discovered; he knew that now: he should have just gone down the route of commercial development. Despite the UK government's assertations, he did have all the legal patents sorted internationally and he was sure they could be overruled but it did give him some leverage. He had money, although he couldn't say how much had been made over to him by various interested parties. He also knew that there was further research work that was needed around the spectrum of dark matter forces and Gary Marshall was the only other person who would be thinking around this topic.

That's it then, no more nationalist loyalty, no more 'trying to help the world' all very admirable intentions but completely impractical. Instead, let's make a thriving business that can be the vehicle to achieve the same aims... eventually... and I will certainly keep that ambition to myself in future. Why oh why hadn't these thoughts come to me sooner, he mused, and hell I will rebuild things with Zoe and the kids.

It was late evening when a uniformed officer brought a man with two suitcases into the room. "Mr Ashley, this is Nick; he is from the local store and he has brought some clothes for you. Paul guessed your size so it his fault if nothing fits."

"Hi, Mr Ashley, it's an honour to meet you, sir, I have been following all your discoveries. I am studying part-time for a degree in Natural Science."

Stuart just said, "Good stuff... lots to learn," as Nick opened the suitcases.

Firstly he brought out a heavy overcoat with scarf and gloves. "The basics for this wonderful Canadian weather," he said. Stuart tried them on and although large they were adequate. Nick then brought out several pairs of trousers, shirts, pullovers, some underwear, socks and three pairs of stout shoes. The officer and Nick left Stuart to try them on. When they returned Stuart had selected the clothes that fitted.

Nick put the remaining clothes in the second suitcase. "The other suitcase is for you and there is also a wash bag with all the necessaries." He noted the items that Stuart had taken and got the officer to sign for them. "Make it all happen, sir," Nick said as he left. Stuart felt that he had been reading his earlier thoughts. The officer returned to say that a flight to Ottawa had been arranged for early morning the following day and to be ready by seven.

His leaving was a bit of an event; Karen had obviously got up early to say farewell and Stuart gave her a hug followed by lots of thanks to all of the staff. It felt strange since apart from his room, he hadn't been outside before, and in fact it was his first time in Canada in conscious form. So many people wished him every success with his discoveries; perhaps they had all been reading my mind last night, he thought!

The same officer escorted Stuart out of the hospital. "We have given up on the press," he said, "they have been trying to get into the hospital for days, but we can't stop them from being outside and there are no clever exits, so you will have to run the gauntlet."

It was pure pandemonium at the exit; Stuart was a little nervous but remembered his resolve and went through the big doors. There were perhaps 20 police providing a passageway to a large black SUV. They were already having trouble holding the crowds back when his appearance caused a surge. The officer tried to press him forward, but Stuart stopped, he had a flashback to being kidnapped. In the melee, other officers regrouped to thrust him forward to the waiting car. With a hearty shove Stuart was pressed forward, within seconds he was in the car and moving off. He noticed that there were other police cars escorting him to the airport. On the brief journey he had time to look out of the window at Halifax. It looked like an interesting town that in other circumstances he would have liked to explore. He passed an old fort that must have been part of the hostility between the British and French; they travelled on through lots of natural water surrounded by rocky outcrops and then large forests. He arrived at a secure entrance to Stanfield Airport and was ushered through to a small lounge that was empty apart from one man. He was clearly labelled Air Canada and he introduced himself as their representative, meanwhile the uniformed police had melted away. Stuart helped himself to a bottle of water and a newspaper to settle down for the plane. About 20 minutes later a smart young man in a tight-fitting suit came into the lounge, he couldn't have been more than 30 but was already thinning which accentuated his sharp features, further enhanced with a pencil-thin moustache that must have taken lot of time to maintain. He introduced himself as Pierre, a research assistant from Lawrence Banard's office and was here to accompany him back to Ottawa. The representative advised them that they would be boarding in a few minutes and Stuart took the opportunity to go to the toilet. Florescent lighting never flattered anyone, but Stuart saw the strains of the recent abduction on his face, combined with the ill-fitting clothes he was a real mess; Karen Stone was right. He needs to take time out and recover.

As they boarded the plane two anonymous men joined him, they were Al Smith's people with a robust brief that Stuart was at risk and so they were very diligent in checking everything and everybody who could be a threat to Stuart. A complete section of the plane had been curtained off for Stuart and his retinue. Some of the passengers looked at him with interest but most were irritated that he was delaying their flight. The plane took off within minutes of him settling in and, like most flights the journey was tedious. Stuart spent most of the time reading after he failed to get information on

Lawrence Banard from Pierre.

The arrival at Ottawa was similar to his departure. Stuart and his various people were the first to leave, further pissing off the other passengers. This time however the convoy of vehicles met him at the airport and headed off to the town centre.

CHAPTER 9

Slow Down

Rob had agreed to contact Ruth. Fortunately she was back in the UK and promised to come to Stuart's place mid-afternoon that day. She said she would be bringing some test equipment and was it alright to bring one of her PhD students.

Stuart had contacted Mike Lester and left a message. Mike phoned back within the hour.

"Hi Stuart, you sounded excited, the experiment is going well then?"

"Better than that, Mike, we have recreated the oscillation effect with your bloody bars. I promised to phone if we had news, and we surely do, so if you want to come up and see it?"

"Try and stop me, Stuart. Is tonight ok around six? I am sure Gareth and Steve will want to come."

"Great, see you later on."

Stuart went back to the workshop, nothing had changed; the bar was still floating. He had to buy a new laptop plus a couple of cameras, so he could formally record what was going on. He drove to a tech superstore to buy the equipment and when he returned decided to clean up the workshop. It was all a bit of a mess, in their enthusiasm there were remnants of shattered launch trolley everywhere plus all the damage done by the bars that shot out of the building. The next phase should be a little more exacting he thought... but what is the next phase? He decided to shelve that decision until Ruth and Mike had seen things. He rigged up the new equipment just before Rob arrived. They were busy discussing the computer model when Ruth arrived with an attractive young woman in tow.

"This is Alice Booker; she has been helping me at Uni and has a special interest in material science. I won't bore you with her PhD thesis."

"Hi, pleased to meet you and it's not boring at all," said Alice with lovely mischief in her eyes. "I was around when Ruth came back to the department with her fucked-up kit. So I was keen to see what caused it," she said with a laugh.

"That's right, you laugh… it's my budget remember… and you may want some of it someday!"

Stuart immediately warmed to Alice and the banter between the two of them lifted things. They went into the house, but beforehand Ruth just had to have a peep at the bar quietly floating on its own, Alice was mesmerised by it all. Over a cup of tea Stuart went through the experiment's progress over the last month or so since Ruth had last visited. It was an excited discussion with Rob adding and refining Stuart's comments until they reached that last day when they were down to four potential angles of incidence. They showed the remaining videos that gave an indication of the forces involved. It was clear that Alice and Ruth wanted to get back to the experiment when Mike turned up with Gareth.

"Steve couldn't make it, but he wanted to come," said Mike.

"Let's give you an update," said Stuart. "Ruth, why don't you have a look over the experiment in the meantime and see if there are any obvious answers." Ruth and Alice eagerly left for the workshop.

Stuart and Rob again recounted the experiment history for the benefit of Mike and Gareth. It was a good thing to do since this time they used the opportunity to clarify the documentation as they went through the results. Neither of them could believe the forces at play when they viewed the videos. They all joined Ruth and Alice in the workshop; they had set up some more equipment. This time there were four ball-like sensors that had been carefully positioned on the same plane around the bar linked to a new scope that was positioned in the far end of the workshop. Alongside and linked to the scope was a large black box with some levers on the top.

"We're going back to first principles," said Ruth. "Last time I assumed that it was some kind of electro-magnetic effect and that buggered up the kit. This time we have some robust sensors that are linked to scope that will merely observe the flux around the bar whatever it is. This black box is just a sort of filter that we knocked up, such that the scope won't get overloaded."

They turned on the equipment and nervously moved the filter lever until the scope showed some movement.

"It's a very basic scope," she said, "but it's found something, and we do have the ability to step the device up and down to get a more sensitive view of the flux." Initially she went the wrong way and scope showed nothing but when she stepped the device down some sort of signal appeared. She stepped it down even further and the line on the scope became larger and denser. At the lowest setting the line started to separate.

"It's frustrating, there is a clear signal of some sort of flux, but the filter won't step down enough for us to refine it in detail," said Ruth to Alice.

"There's the other filter in the car that we brought as backup; I could modify it to run in series, in theory that would give a wider span of signal."

"Great idea, good girl, now I remember why I asked you to come," Ruth bantered. "A serious talent, this one," she said to no-one in particular.

"Can I help?" said Gareth, clearly impressed with all aspects of Alice. The two went back to the car and retrieved another piece of equipment.

"It's not been tested," said Alice, "but no matter, since we are going to re-strap the settings anyway."

"At least it's not been destroyed this time, Ruth," chipped in Stuart.

"Well as I said, it's all basic stuff and it shouldn't interfere with whatever is going on here," she replied.

Alice and Gareth worked on the kit as Mike examined the bar. He tried to move it.

"Don't bother Mike, I used a block and tackle on the old spanner and nearly broke the beam in the roof."

"It's as if... well it's like it's in concrete, just floating there... I don't know of anything like it... amazing... bugger, my watch is in melt-down." He rapidly threw his watch to the ground. It was very hot and getting hotter. Stuart picked it up with a cloth and threw it outside the workshop. "Has anyone else got electronic watches or anything electronic on them?" he yelled. They should have thought about it before, but it was obvious that there was a force that didn't like electronics; yet the scope and associated kit was fine.

"We need to figure out what gets impacted by the flux and what doesn't... it may give us some insight as to its nature," said Rob.

"And the distance from the force," added Stuart.

Alice called for quiet since she wanted to continue the measurements. Together with Ruth, they recalibrated the equipment from the finish point to make sure the additional filter was working. Once satisfied, they continued to step down the input from the sensors and a strange representation of the flux started to appear. The thick line separated into many thin lines and as they progressed it became clearer that each line was a sine curve, which was exactly the opposite of each adjacent sine curve almost like they were cancelling each other out.

"It's clear that whatever the force is, there is an established equilibrium," said Ruth, "unfortunately we can't capture this data now, but assuming we can figure out the safe distance for electronics we can easily rig up a cable to a laptop."

"Yes," said Alice hesitantly, "but only if we figure out how to deal with the magnitude of the force."

"How so?" asked Stuart.

"Well there is a lot of latent power here," she replied.

"Latent power, my arse," said Gareth "no-one has ever recorded such a powerful flux, I bet you there is no instrumentation around to deal with it, let alone understand what it is."

"I think Gareth's right," said Ruth, "and where the hell is this power coming from?"

They all agreed it was time for a break and went into the house to discuss the next move.

"I suggest we leave the kit in position, so we can easily attach some recording capability," said Ruth.

"I agree," said Alice, "but I suggest we also need to analyse how far the force behaves... so we need some mobile sensors to get an idea how the force decreases with distance."

"If it decreases with distance," added Gareth.

"Well if it doesn't decrease then my car electronics would be damaged, and they are not," said Stuart. "We have managed to create the effect, but how in hell do we turn it off?"

Can you picture the scene? Six bright people with a wide range of engineering and scientific knowledge all were having an experience of something quite outside all natural phenomena. Their minds were racing off in different directions trying to find answers.

Mike Lester had been very quiet up until now. "You may all think this is fantastic, but I am sure Stuart has stumbled onto something that has never been discovered before."

"A phenomena that hasn't been seen before? Statistically that's pretty remote," queried Rob.

"It's not impossible," said Ruth "I wouldn't be so arrogant to think that mankind has figured out all natural science."

"The reason I say this," said Mike, "is that when we analysed the spanner and recreated the equivalent bars, none of us could find anything similar anywhere, their composition and structure is quite unique."

"I think you're right, Mike, because if you look at the experimental results leading up to the floating bar, the angle, the point of inflection is key to its behaviour. So, if you take a material that is unique, and introduce it into a magnetic field at a very specific angle, it's fair to assume that it's never happened before."

"Don't assume it's a magnetic field Stuart," Ruth corrected.

"OK, I suggest that we all agree not to discuss this with anyone," continues Mike.

"Why Mike, what about Steve? Anyway it's not your call," piped up Gareth, "he has been key to the materials work."

"Of course Steve should be included, but then no-one else. Sorry, Stuart, this is your discovery and we are part players. What do you think?"

"I had not even thought about it, Mike, but since this is my discovery, I should own and control its direction of development."

"So far, 'something' may have been discovered but we don't know what it is, how to control or as Stuart says how to stop it, so it's premature to talk about it with anyone unless there is someone who can add value to our thinking," said Rob.

Stuart agreed. "So what next?"

Ruth suggested that they get more data on the flux itself and that may give a pointer to the control aspect. Everyone agreed, and Alice was tasked with building more kit to further filter the flux readings and get more detailed results. She also agreed with Ruth to build some mobile sensor to analyse the flux in relation to distance. Finally they needed to build some software that could record the signals and start to evaluate them.

"It's going to take a while," said Alice.

"I can help and maybe Steve as well," Gareth said as he looked to Mike for agreement.

"Go for it," said Mike, "but it's not an open-ended resource," he said with a grin. Gareth was really happy, a great thing to work on with a fantastic woman, it just didn't get any better.

At Stuart's direction, they agreed to meet in a week's time such that Alice could give a progress update. It was clear as they all left that the sense of excitement was still there.

"I just hope they don't talk about it in their enthusiasm," said Rob, the last to leave.

"Rob, you have been a really good mate with all of this as well as with Zoe... thanks."

Rob looked embarrassed. "Well, shall we keep at it; or wait until next week?"

"Let's keep going… I thought it could be fun to see if we can stop it."

"Done," said Rob as he left.

Stuart realised he was starving and decided to walk to the nearby pub for some air and a snack before turning in. Anyway his brain was going at a million mile per hour; he wouldn't sleep for a while.

In fact he did sleep very well although his brain started its high speed almost immediately he woke. Equilibrium. That's what the scope showed… it's obvious anyway, the bar was floating quite happily in a state of equilibrium. An upward force from somewhere was balancing gravity but why was it floating at that particular height? Is that where the two forces, gravity plus the other one (I must give it a name, he thought) were the same? He tried to recall what had stopped the spanner and checked his notes. It was as Ruth was trying to record the magnetic forces around the spanner that some sort of surge happened. He remembered feeling something, something in the air. He also recalled that the spanner was oscillating whereas the bar was quite stable. I'm posing more questions than answers, he thought, but suddenly a light came on; he remembered that the sound from the generators pulsed in harmony with the oscillations but this time it was just constant. It was that fucking strimmer… that's it, he thought, it somehow induced a pulse in the generators well before the spanner dropped. It has to be that; it has to be. Stuart had a formalised recording of everything so he added these thoughts to the log. It wasn't a fact but an idea and that may become important in the future.

Since he had some time, Stuart decided to do some basic research on gravity… after all the experiment had somehow interfered with gravity. He spent several hours lost on the internet trying to make sense of all the information. It looked like more had been written on gravity than anything else. Moreover it was clear that whilst Einstein's General Relativity theory still seemed to hold most prominence there were a lot of other alternative theories surrounding it. He stopped when he went into information overload. What concerned him was the fundamental assumption that gravity was singular. All of the research seemed to hold good on this basis but for the sake of argument his experiment showed another force in equilibrium with gravity or, indeed, was it another manifestation of gravity? Even the notion of force might be wrong, he mused, perhaps something has been removed or neutralised from conventional gravity. His mind was spinning but he decided to write down his ideas as options for explaining the experiment.

The phone rang, it was Marc. "Hi, Dad," he said in his usual cheery voice. He had been back from his tour for a while and Stuart had sent him several emails all without response. He did get a note from Zoe saying that she knew he was trying to contact Marc and he was staying with her, she said she would get him to phone. She was probably controlling Lucy and Henry too since they hadn't replied to Stuart's notes either.

"I've missed you, Marc, why didn't you reply to my emails?"

"Sorry Dad, but Mum said you would be angry. Especially when we took all my stuff when you were out. I was worried that you thought I was siding with Mum."

"How could I be angry with you? I thought we were all getting on well and then suddenly I am a pariah. Did you think something was wrong... no, unfair question... forget it... am I able to see you?"

"Dad, even I knew Mum was unhappy. Why didn't you see it?"

Well she disguised it well enough to me, thought Stuart.

"Mum said she would fix a get-together and maybe Lucy and Henry can come too."

Stuart wanted to scream 'fuck you all' but knew he would lose his kids that way; he had to be subservient to Diana and Zoe. "OK, Marc, whatever Diana and your mum decide. Just remember I love you," he hung up.

Ten minutes later Zoe rang. It's a set piece, Stuart thought.

"Hi Stuart, did Marc phone you?"

"You know he did Zoe, you were beside the phone." A long pause. "It's bad enough that you have painted me as the ogre in this sordid affair. How long have you been poisoning the kid's minds about me?"

"You live in a world of your own, Stuart… yes you did the basics, but you never gave them your time!" The phone went dead. Stuart didn't know whether to think less of his kids since it seemed like they had all supported Zoe. Hell maybe I did neglect them, he thought. He was just putting it all back into the mental compartment marked 'unhappiness' when the phone rang again.

"It's me again, look we have to talk."

"About?"

"Sorting the estate, the house, a settlement."

"Zoe, this is the stuff solicitors love, let's give them some fun."

"Cynical as ever, you bastard. OK we'll do it your way, the bloody way."

"I expect you know that the locks have been upgraded and the joint account closed. Anyway you've taken all your stuff so there's no reason to come here."

"Goodbye," she said, it had a sense of finality in it. Stuart was still hurting… still, they say the hurt party is the last to know. It was worse, since he knew he still loved her. He opened the filing box that he had been using to hold the papers on restructuring the assets. He was buggered if Diana was going to get her hands on any of it. He couldn't think clearly, and his thought process had been going so well earlier that day. He wandered into the workshop and just stared at the floating bar. He remembered that he had upgraded all the locks, but not in the workshop buildings, so he went out and bought some serious locks and spent the rest of day fixing them.

It was Friday and Stuart had agreed with Rob that they would have a go at stopping the floating bar. They didn't know where to start but did know that there were some potentially dangerous forces around and therefore CARE was the overriding principle in the steps they took.

"Rob, I've been thinking about the argon bubbles in the bar."

"Then you are one sad bastard," joked Rob.

"Let's just say that the magnetic field from the two generators sort of polarised those bubbles into…"

"Into what?"

"Well… some sort of barrier to gravity," said Stuart.

"What have you been smoking, matey?"

"Come on Rob, what do we know? Firstly the composition of the bar is important. Secondly, that the magnetic field from the generators is a definite contributor. Thirdly, the angle of incidence to the magnetic field is necessary. Anything else?"

"Don't think so," said Rob.

"Well we have to think differently, we have a change to gravity… yes?"

"Yes," he said hesitantly.

"So something new is pushing back on normal gravity, or normal gravity has changed in some way."

"Using your thoughts, Stuart, is it fair to assume gravity as a force anyway?"

"Exactly, Rob, we have changed something which has been viewed as a single force since science began…"

"Or Newton at least," added Rob.

Neither of them knew where the discussion was going but it just felt that they were thinking the right way.

"So the bar should be subject to normal force of gravity and therefore rest on the concrete floor. Instead, it's floating 1,221 millimetres above the concrete floor and not oscillating. By the way I think the reason the spanner oscillated was linked to a fluctuation in the magnetic field."

"Frankly, Stu, you seem to be making some rash and unfounded assumptions, after all they are electromagnets."

"Well, I recall I tested a strimmer that I had repaired earlier that day and it went wild. It was definitely impacted by the magnetics from the two generators. I also remember the generators making a sort of throbbing sound louder and softer, so something excited the electromagnets."

"Now you mention it, I do remember that sound. OK, you may be right, but you excited the generators with the strimmer this time as well. Anyway I thought we were trying to see how we can stop the bar from floating?"

"Exactly, so if I'm right and the polarised bars are some sort of barrier then all we have to do is depolarise it."

"Logical, but how do we depolarise it, reproduce Ruth's equipment?"

"I have two ideas," continued Stuart, "we could move the generators. That would be difficult since they are tight to the workshop walls or we could introduce another field to sort of neutralise them."

"OK, Mr Clever, so how do we going to do that?"

"Well I have the other old generator at the end of the workshop."

"You mean that enormous thing, Stu; we could never move the fucker?"

Stuart had checked out the third generator, which was housed under a tarpaulin, it was in a tube frame with two flat tyres. "I remember it took two of us to get it in so if we pump up the tyres we can have a go. It's rated at 15kW whereas the other two are around 6.5kW, so if the actual power output is related to induced magnetics it might just work."

To be fair, Rob didn't have a better idea and until Ruth's team returned, it was worth a try. They went to the workshop, removed the tarp and pumped up the tyres that seemed to hold after many years of being flat. They both tried to move it, but it wouldn't budge; the transport mechanism was seized as well as the diesel motor. Rob had the idea of using a trolley jack to level the unit and hopefully turn the plant towards the parallel field.

"Should we put some power into it to excite the electromagnets?" Rob queried.

"Well we didn't do anything to the other two, but we should check it's not seized. They turned the shaft, which rotated freely, and very slowly they moved the big cart in line with the other two. As they got close and started overlapping the smaller generators there was a powerful flash and the spanner dropped to the ground.

"Well I don't know what we have done but we are on the right path," yelled Stuart, his ears were still ringing.

"Maybe… maybe," Rob yelled back. "But we need to be careful, Stu, these forces are seriously powerful."

The two of them went through the routine of documenting everything they had done and then stopped for the day. Stuart had insisted on returning the big generator to its original position, so he could try and restart the bar the next day.

He noticed the mail on the mat as he went back to the house. There was a solicitor's letter explaining that he should provide free access to the house for Zoe and also complete a form of all his assets and income; it should go to his solicitor, he thought, but instead it went into the bin.

Stuart decided to have a wet shave that following morning, something he didn't do very often. As he looked at himself in the mirror he could see the wear and tear of his separation in his face. It had always looked 'lived in', he thought, but now it looked 'lived out'; he smiled to himself. After breakfast he refreshed himself from his notes on the exact circumstances to replicate the floating bar. Rob was heavily committed to teach for the next few days and Stuart was sure he could manage on his own.

He ensured that everything was in its place and setup the launch guide in line with the grid. He excited the generators with the strimmer. Although the last experiment had worked, he decided to set the POI at 77 degrees. He dropped a new bar into the guide and it settled in mid-air with ease. It wasn't quite the same size bar and that may explain that its recorded height was 1230 millimetres. This is getting good, Stuart thought, I can start and stop the effect, but I still don't have a clue what's going on. He spoke with Mike Lester who agreed with him that it could be possible to align the argon bubbles and agreed to test it out.

He went back to his original thoughts; either he had changed the force of gravity or uncovered another component force. That force was very powerful, and its stable position might be redirected through changes in the angle of incidence as evidenced by the holes in his workshop. Stuart's mind turned to the scale of things, he had replicated the spanner in similar dimensions but didn't have any idea whether he needed the magnetic influence of the generators, or would simple magnets suffice, and could he use a smaller slither of a bar? He decided that he could modify the bar size quite easily, he had several bars to play with and all the necessary tools to make a thinner section. The magnets however were a different issue, would ordinary magnets work to polarise the argon? Or would he need stronger electromagnets? He knew he couldn't explore the phenomenon with the large generator magnets; it was impossible to move them around. He remembered Ruth had talked about a massive flux ... it could mean that industrial strength magnetics were necessary... only one way to find out. Stuart decided to redefine the experiment; he would assume that reducing the bar size and retaining its shape would be ok and he would need to construct a more general-purpose launch guide to give him the 77 degrees-controlled entrance.

And so the magnets; Stuart knew he was a hoarder, and yet all the stuff he kept was based on the promise that it could be useful one day and time after time that promise had been fulfilled. He was sure he had some old horseshoe magnets and several round electromagnets in various junk boxes on shelves; it was just a question of finding them. After nearly an hour Stuart had some elderly round electromagnets on his bench, having abandoned all the others. He selected two that were 50 millimetre diameter, centrally threaded with a pull of 90 pounds. They would be easy to fit and used a 12-volt supply.

He drew a frame structure that would support the two electromagnets opposite one another on the same plane and were adjustable such that he could vary the distance between them. The frame included a launch guide set at 77 degrees that could be varied around the area between the magnets. He was still unsure if the speed of the bar was important, so he incorporated a simple runner to handle it. He started making the frame having chosen to use wood again to keep consistency. He knew he was making lots of changes and that the whole exercise could be a waste of time, but the scale had to be reduced for practical purposes. As an afterthought he decided to allow the magnet's plane to tilt so that he could test the influence of the field once the bar floated.

Now the fun bit, Stuart loved making things and as he built the framework his attention to detail and accuracy plus several revisions meant that three days later it was finished. The last part was the creation of three smaller and thinner bars that he had machined from one of the spares. He had lived on eggs, pizza, coke and beer and was so absorbed he hadn't shaved or showered for two of those days. He wanted to get it ready to show Rob and get his approval and support.

Rob didn't arrive until mid-morning, which was good since Stuart hadn't thought through where he would conduct 'baby floater' as he termed it. He decided to set it up under the car porch, which he hoped would be far enough away from interference of the big generators.

"I can't believe how much you have done and you've restarted the floater as well," said Rob with some admiration. "I think your decision to create a small-scale trial is great. When do you want to try it out?"

"Right now. Ruth left me a message that the team are coming over tomorrow. It would be good if we have more results."

As before they started by documenting everything and Stuart had already taken lots of photos of the new frame which they positioned on a couple of benches under the car porch, although a cold dry day, the conditions were similar to that inside the workshop. Neither of them had any knowledge of the magnetic flux that the two generators had created; indeed this was in the scope of Ruth's actions. The trouble is that they didn't even know if it was a magnetic force... the smaller trial was all guesswork and assumption... not a good start. It was therefore no surprise that nothing happened on the first drop of the bar. They had to assume the angle was right; they had also correlated the entry point on the new trial with the same entry point of the large one. What were the old generators doing? Their static cores had clearly been excited but there was no power input... perhaps they would have to wait for Ruth's equipment. They repeated the exercise having disconnected the 12-volt batteries; no results. Could it be that the magnets were too strong? Stuart decided to separate them with the widest distance possible on the frame. Was it true? Was there a slight wobble of the bar?

They replayed the video and sure enough the bar gave a little twitch. It was the magnetic force!

Rob suggested some sort of rheostat to reduce the power to the magnets. Stuart didn't have anything in his boxes of tricks and decided to extend the frame to allow more distance between the magnets. He went into the workshop and within half an hour had created two A-frames that bolted onto the main frame after some holes had been drilled. The modification had doubled the distance between the magnets. They agreed to set the distance half way along the new modification and try again. This time the bar held in the air briefly before dropping. At the full extension the bar oscillated before falling.

"It's clear, I overestimated the force needed to polarise the bar," said Stuart. "But we are onto something."

"Let's leave it for now, Stu, perhaps Ruth and the team will have some ideas. Come over for supper, you look wrecked."

It's true, every waking hour Stuart had been submersed in the experiment. Somehow a fish supper with Rob and Sue rejuvenated him. He had promised Rob not to talk about the experiment over supper; a promise he had broken, but only for one second with a withering look from Rob.

Ruth and the team arrived just after nine. This time Gareth took Steve to see the experiment and familiarise him with it all. They joined Ruth and Mike for a coffee as Alice was giving Stuart and Rob an update on her progress.

"So, I'm pretty confident that we have enough filters to cover the flux recording," she said, "the mobile sensors have been tested but whether they will record things in this environment is anyone's guess. As for the software, well its work-in-progress, Gareth and I started on it but frankly we are not sure what we are dealing with yet."

"Let's discuss that," added Ruth, "and Mike thanks for Steve and Gareth's time, we really needed them." Mike had been kept appraised and nodded acknowledgement.

"I've got something to add," said Stuart, "I decided to create a small-scale equivalent of the experiment and I misunderstood that when you were talking about a powerful flux, that you meant a magnetic field, but the baby experiment has shown a fairly minor magnetic field is needed... so what is this powerful flux we are dealing with and where is it coming from?"

"When we were last here it was clear there was a powerful force in the experiment, but it did not fit into anything I know. It was my suspicion that you have uncovered some force from somewhere. I know that sounds weak, but if you have eliminated the scale of magnetic involvement then we have to be looking for a new force."

"Well, let's plan today's work," said Stuart. "I suggest we stop the old experiment and restart it again, so you can record everything. I have run into a problem on the baby test since I have too much of a magnetic field!! Weird, isn't it? So I need help to step down the power on the electromagnets, but I don't have a rheostat."

"How quaint," said Alice. "I haven't heard that term for years. Show me what needs to be done and I will sort it."

"Quaint, I am," Stuart retorted. "Ok let's go to it."

They all went to the baby trial first. Stuart explained the issue with the magnets as he did another demonstration. Alice went back to the car to retrieve some equipment; the rest went to the workshop. They set up the monitors further back than originally and set the scope plus filters in the doorway at the end of the workshop. The link from the scope to the laptop was a long thick shielded cable that enabled the laptop to be positioned on the floor in the garage.

It was good to have more manpower as they manipulated the large generator into place. This time they were pre-warned about the flash and the noise, it still startled them as the bar fell to the floor though.

"It's just amazing," said Steve. "I did believe Gareth, but now I've seen it… it's just unlike anything I know of!"

"As I promised, we did the polarisation experiment on one of the remaining bars at Uni," said Mike. "It was pretty straightforward and didn't need much power; I have brought the data anyway."

"The monitors have held," Alice yelled to Ruth. "What did the scope show?"

"An incredible surge but we have captured it this time," she replied. "Let's move the big one back and drop the bar, I want to record that now."

With some grunts, they heaved the old generator back to position and Stuart went through the drop routine. "I am using 77 degrees, it seemed smoother." He decided to test out another spare bar again. The bar obediently floated in mid-air but this time at 1,215 millimetres.

"Have you labelled the bars with their float height?" asked Mike. "If so we can analyse their size and mass against it to see if there is a relationship."

"Yes we have," said Stuart.

"Great idea, Mike. Gareth and I will handle it."

It was late morning and they all stopped for lunch. Stuart had been living a monastic existence and there was virtually no food and certainly no fresh food. They decided to reconvene at the local pub, Alice and Ruth were in a deep discussion about the results that day and Mike, Gareth and Steve were in some argument about mass, magnetism and polarisation. Stuart and Rob joined them with the sandwiches and drinks.

"There are so many unanswered questions," Ruth said to no-one in particular, "it may make sense to bring in one of the research people from Imperial that I know."

"Hold on, Ruth, I think we have enough horsepower around this table."

"Maybe, Stuart, but I have been in science for more years than I care to remember, and I am happy to admit that I haven't a clue what's going on."

"Unlike you, Ruth," chipped in Rob.

"Fuck off, Rob; I really don't know where to start, my contribution would be speculation at best."

"But Ruth this is so exciting… it's new ground, and current thinking may not help," Alice added.

"Well I for one think that together we can crack this, and I hope I include my departmental resource… within its limits."

Both Gareth and Steve were in total agreement. Before Mike continued, Stuart interrupted him.

"I would like to propose an idea," said Stuart. "As you know, I have been living this thing for a few months now and it's clear to me that we have to resolve one of two solutions." He had their attention. "Firstly, that somehow we have found something, let's call it a new force and it's never been identified before. We all discussed this last time, you remember, when we were debating the statistical chance of it never having happened before. Or…" he paused, "that we have played with gravity or a component of it."

"So, I would like us all to focus on these two ideas and disprove them before we speculate on others."

"Stu, you're right, all good science starts with a hypothesis, but your definition isn't tight enough," said Alice. Stuart was feeling a bit miffed at the criticism but kept quiet. "If we found a force within gravity then it's the same hypothesis, it's just that you have determined the source prematurely." It was well said, Stuart conceded in his mind. He looked around; the team was impressed with her.

"Thanks, Alice, so we have a hypothesis and it strengthens the reasons for not adding to the team Ruth."

"Why?" she said.

"Well, my observation is so much science is developed in a progressive way, building on what has gone before."

"We can debate that," snapped Ruth. She was getting irritated, but he didn't know why. Maybe Alice was outsmarting her?

"Sorry, Ruth, it's just I think we need to approach this without any baggage, any preconceptions."

"So, I'm baggage now am I? Stuart there is a perfect logical solution to this phenomenon, you are not qualified and need support, and your ideas are flights of fancy. I've done all I can, if Alice wants to stay, that's fine but I don't have the time for this. Alice, make sure my equipment is back by the end of the week, you can have all the data although what good it will do you." She got up and left with Rob and Alice following her.

"Good riddance, we don't need her, fat old bag," said Gareth.

"Shut up, Gareth, what do you fucking know?" said Steve.

"Look guys. Let's keep everything in perspective. Ruth might be right, I don't know. For my part, our department will support you, Stuart, but within our skillset of materials." Mike was clearly defining the boundary of his support. "We don't have the resources to get into gravitational stuff."

"I never expected you to, Mike; your departmental support has been fantastic."

Alice and Rob re-joined them.

"Well her temper hasn't changed over the years," said Rob. "Moreover she has painted herself into a corner; she won't come back, you know."

"I'm so sorry," sighed Stuart.

"She was angry in the car," said Alice, "she kept saying we need more expertise. I'm in her bad books now and... I don't know how I'm getting home."

"Don't worry, Alice, I will take you," said Gareth, grabbing the moment.

"Are you going to stay, Alice?" Rob asked.

"God yes, this is just unreal... but I have to figure out what time I can spare without screwing up my studies."

The group was a bit flat on their return to the workshop. Alice had grabbed some kit from the car before Ruth left and was busy putting some circuitry together. She had built a way of varying the magnetic field of the electromagnets. On her instruction the monitoring kit was brought from the workshop to record the baby experiment; when it was all in place it was restarted. They had built a plan of power reduction that they hoped would eventually find the float point. The signs were already promising with some floating activity and after seven trials the miracle happened.

Stuart was ecstatic, not only had they learned to start and stop the float but had replicated it in smaller scale. They all just stood around, saying nothing.

Alice spoke first. "I think we neutralised the excited magnetics of the two generators with the larger one. Now we have a controller, we can switch it off instead."

"Hold it, Alice, remember the surge." But he was too late, the bar had shot across the room so fast that it was invisible except for the noise. The bar was gone. There was a stunned silence.

"That was a hell of a force," said Mike, "it could have killed someone."

Alice was shaking badly. "I'm so sorry," she whispered. Gareth and Steve were quickly there to console her.

"Next time, Alice, let's agree what we are doing and when," Stuart snapped. Gareth and Steve looked angrily at Stuart. I give up, he thought.

They all went inside for coffee and to get over the shock. Rob was thoughtful.

"It's strange, the large experiment did produce that result but only when we were getting close to floating, you saw the various holes in the walls; this time it's different."

"No, not really, the spanner dropped when we neutralised the fields which was a gradual process, I just turned it off... what a dick."

"You weren't to know," Gareth responded sympathetically.

"Don't fucking patronise me," she burst out.

Rob defused everything. "It's been a tense day folks, we have made some great progress, so let's reconvene next week."

Alice said she would pick up the equipment over the weekend and left with Gareth and Steve. Mike left too leaving Rob and Stuart to close off the baby trial. They made sure they had all the readings stored on two laptops and placed all the equipment in the garage.

"Supper again?"

"Do you mind?" said Stuart.

"Sue's out, so it's frozen pizza."

"Good I'm used to that."

"And yes... we can talk about the experiment."

Supper cleared the air, or was it the two bottles of wine? Anyway they had a good discussion, and both agreed that they were on the right track. They needed Mike and his team for their specialist skills but most importantly needed Alice for her science and open thinking; only now, it was obvious that the seven people on the project was unworkable.

It had been an amazing day Stuart reflected as he turned in; He decided that the small group of himself, Rob and Alice was formidable. Moreover he knew Ruth's comments were wrong somehow; this was NOT a phenomenon that could easily be explained away... an open mind is the order of the day... we mustn't force fit this into existing scientific theory.

It was a bright spring morning when Stuart headed to the workshop. He couldn't resist another trial of the baby experiment but decided that he would clear some space at the rear of the large garage, so he could set it up permanently. It was just before lunchtime that he started running the experiment, mentally his fingers were crossed but it wasn't necessary, the bar floated to order and at exactly the same height. Stuart was acutely aware of the surge and gently reduced the power to the electromagnets as he closed off the experiment.

He reflected on the hypotheses; it was clear that there was a force and it had to exist already. He became more convinced that he had somehow altered gravity in its earthly form. He knew that gravity in the cosmos was a more complex topic but if he could figure out what was going on in his workshops then he could see how it fitted in the bigger picture. Since equilibrium existed on the floating bar, it was as if he had varied part of gravity and then reinstated it. If that were true then he had perhaps been influencing a component of gravity. If gravity as a force didn't exist but was perhaps a number of different forces that coalesced such it were perceived as a single force. Surely bigger brains than his would have figured it out but not unless they hadn't been able identify the phenomenon as he had; his mind was spinning.

He decided that the massive surges, the times when the bar shot out of control were indications of this component force as much as the force needed to create a new equilibrium for the floating bar. He went back to his thought that the polarised bar acted as a barrier to some component of gravity and that if could vary the angle of the bar once floating then maybe, just maybe, he could control that force.

CHAPTER 10

A Lightbulb Moment

What if he didn't need to drop the bar into the field? He had done it to replicate the falling spanner but if it were fixed in position at the right angle would it still work? In that instance the exact position in the magnetic field would be important but what would happen since the bar would want to establish equilibrium? He had enough data to work out the relationship of the mass of the bar to the position within the field, and the consequent power needed.

He went indoors and started to draw out a way of holding the bar at the right angle within a frame that also supported the magnets. Again he decided to make this frame from wood since he suspected it wouldn't interfere with anything and given the previous forces it would break easily if things went wrong.

The next four days were spent meticulously constructing the new frame. In fact that's not strictly true since the first two designs were scrapped as impractical. Rob had popped in to see how things were going and was doubtful about Stuart's line of thinking but didn't quell his enthusiasm. He felt he had been pretty accurate in fitting the bar into the frame and then proceeded to align the electromagnets. Finally he attached the magnets to the controller and battery with some long flex.

It was early evening on the fourth day when he slowly powered up the magnets. Nothing happened but then suddenly the whole frame lifted into the air and floated; Stuart noted the power settings. There was a slight cracking coming from the frame and he was worried that it would break up. He approached the frame cautiously since he was nervous of flying splinters. He quickly measured the height of the frame and specifically the embedded bar. In so doing he had to touch the frame and was surprised to find that it moved horizontally. He had expected it to be rigid as with the spanner and previous bars. In fact it was held rigid in a vertical position but could be moved horizontally with ease.

It was difficult to gauge his feelings at that time, his pulse was racing, and yet common sense said he should close off the power gently and stop the experiment, which he did. Shit, he thought, I didn't record anything on the laptop or the camera. He placed the frame on the garage bench to examine it. If there were cracks in the wood, he couldn't see any, however a number of tiny cracks showed up after exploring the frame with a magnifying glass. The cracks mainly surrounded the wood that held the bar in place and Stuart guessed that the bar had not been in the exact position, but the flex in the wood had allowed it to stabilise.

"Rob, I am right... it's amazing."

"Hold on, Stu... what is? What's happened?"

"You have to see it, Rob... I can't explain it... come over now if you can."

Rob arrived in a matter of minutes. "What's so exciting, you daft bugger?"

"Just watch, Rob," and with that he gently powered up the magnets and again, abruptly the frame rose to the identical floating position. There was more cracking noise, but the frame held.

"Let's record everything we can," and together they measured everything as well as filming the whole thing.

"You know, I can't help thinking that this is just magnetic levitation... I'm pretty sure that was in Ruth's head too," said Rob. "Perhaps the bars are some sort of superconductors?"

"I don't know, Rob, we are not pushing much power into the fields and what's giving the frame its lift? Maybe some of those effects are in play here but... well... I simply don't know."

They both reviewed the cracks in the wood and agreed it could be dangerous to run the experiment again. Neither of them could see a design flaw but recognised that the forces involved might be too much stress. Stuart decided to rebuild that part of the frame in a hardwood the next day. He spent the whole day making the bar holder component of the frame as accurate as he could taking account of some of the marks on the old frame. When he tested it, the frame rose perfectly; no sound of cracking. He felt he was getting closer still to the phenomenon, but it was frustrating trying to find clues to the science. He was pleased that his thinking had been logical and produced results despite Rob's misgivings, so he felt sure that he should continue the process step by step. But what the hell is the next step, he thought? It was clear that the horizontal freedom was because the fields were permanently aligned on the bar. It was also clear that the effect was outside of the magnetic field something that had not been proved before and killing off the maglev explanation. The ratio of power to magnetic field to float height was constant or was it?

He decided that the next step was to try and vary the angle of the bar in the frame. He had designed the frame so that most parts could be varied which included the angle. Given the power of previous misaligned angles Stuart was naturally nervous of this step. The angle could be adjusted by means of a screw on the side of the frame. Rob gingerly turned the screw gently a quarter of a turn and as he did so he felt the pull of the frame away from him; he turned the screw to its original position and the frame relaxed.

So the bar suffered violent force if it entered to field at an incorrect angle, but that force could be harnessed once the bar was embedded in the field and presumably the polarisation was in place. He closed the experiment and relooked at the frame to see how he could test out the direction of the force and vary it. The holes in the various garage walls were testament to the forces on the bars but its direction was unknown.

Back at the house he managed to speak to Alice to update her on progress. Although she sounded distracted they discussed his plan for exploring the force arising from differing angles of the bar. Stuart expressed his own concern that the experiment needed more accuracy especially if he was playing around with the geometry. Alice promised to have a chat with her colleagues and see what equipment she could borrow to help out; they agreed to meet up that Monday. He sent an email to the team giving them an update and advising everyone of the plan. He also asked Mike if it would be possible to create some thinner plates with the same composition as the bars. He got a quick response from Gareth who suggested machining the remaining bars into smaller plates. He had various contacts in a local metal shop and would see what they could do. He and Steve would also look at getting another opportunity to recast some more bars.

Stuart felt empty, he had spent all his waking hours getting to this point and now when he thought he was closing in on things, the intensity had gone, and he was drained. Apart from Rob, he had hardly contacted anyone. He was hurt by the reaction from the kids but hoped time might heal things, he continued to send them emails and messages but never a response. He hadn't heard from his older sister for six months but then he never tried to contact her either; they were never close anyway. Zoe had been the centre of his world even if she didn't know it and now... well... he was lonely. It was worse than that, he couldn't be arsed to put any effort into socialising. Stuart always felt that life was pre-determined somehow and you made the best of what you had. In fact he had been dealt pretty good cards for a long time so maybe it was his turn to have a low spot in his life.

Pull yourself together, he thought... this is NOT a low spot, you are on the cusp of something fantastic. Somehow it just didn't resonate, so he decided to go... somewhere... it was early afternoon, he packed a weekend bag, got into the Range Rover and headed west... why?... well why not? It wasn't long before he was stuck in jam on the motorway and wondered what he was doing. Still what was the point in going back? Eventually he aimed for Lyme Regis, he had taken the family there years ago and it had some fond memories. However he then had a problem of finding accommodation, it was the fourth hotel that finally was able to offer a room over the weekend. It was a superior executive suite, whatever that meant, but it was comfortable with some silly amenities like a flask of dry sherry in a twee flask that he consumed in a few minutes.

Stuart spent much of the evening in the bar by a log fire with a novel; he hadn't really settled down to read a book for years and he was amazingly relaxed. He had brought a book on magnetic theory and EMF as well as string theory and gravity for dummies that he had been meaning to read; the novel took priority though.

Although the hotel was busy the staff were attentive, and he didn't feel like 'Norman no mates'. He retired about midnight having consumed a reasonable bottle of red wine... it had been a good decision to take off. The following morning he had overindulged in breakfast before heading into the town. He took a long walk around town and the beaches, remembering happy family days. After a pub lunch he went to the local museum and recalled the extraordinary work of Mary Anning. Part of the museum was dedicated to her exploits and although self-educated she challenged the biblical creation narrative and all the supposed experts in geology. Stuart felt a little of Mary in himself... 'if' and he knew it was a big 'if' his discoveries were new and original then he could expect more challenge and criticism of his work so far. Well he would be like Mary Anning: stoic and committed to the task.

He noticed a woman taking photos of various exhibits; she was being directed by another rather stern-looking woman, probably some sort of promotion he thought. Having left the museum shop with a book on fossil walks he went into a nearby café to plan a walk on the following day. It was a small café and quite crowded, but he managed to sit at a tiny table by the window with his tea and plan the next day's activity.

"Is it ok if I join you?" said a voice from behind.

"Of course," replied Stuart, "but there's not much room I'm afraid."

The woman squeezed her small frame past him into the seat alongside. Stuart took a second look, she was quite stunning but not in an obvious way, it was almost as if she wanted to disguise her good looks. Her long auburn hair was scragged back but still showed hints of blonde highlights. If she wore any makeup it wasn't obvious and yet her she had a healthy bloom with a few wrinkles around her eyes, which made her late forties or early fifties, he thought. She wore a sweatshirt that had seen better days as did her jeans, but she had the sort of figure many women yearned for. If hands can be said to be musical then hers were that of a piano player with long fingers and short nails, just right for playing the camera too.

"How was the photo session?" he asked.

"Oh that... well it was awful. Dreadful," she had an educated voice with a hint of Bristol or West Country.

"Sorry to hear that."

"No, well I had agreed to take some photos for the museum as a favour, but I didn't expect to run into a female Alfred Hitchcock," she said with a chuckle. "I normally do promotion shots but the stuff from today... well... I don't know... she wouldn't give me any freedom to do what I thought best."

"So what are you going to do?"

"Well I pretended to take several shots, but I will go back tomorrow morning when she's not there. It weird, they are all volunteers but some of them are power crazy!"

"Harry, by the way," as she held out her hand.

"Stuart Ashley... sort of tourist... Harry?"

"Yes, Harriet... which I hate and surname Hogan; just like the wrestler."

"You've obviously heard it all before," Stuart smirked. "Anyway Harry suits you." It was her turn to grin. "And a professional photographer?"

"Yup, for years, but sorry no weddings no passports, just commercial stuff." There was a long silence as if they had finished the pleasantries. The truth was that Stuart really fancied Harry but was so out of practice with women that he felt clumsy and awkward; in fact he had never been smooth. Harry was relaxed though and started looking at her phone.

"I hate these things," she said, "they are communication devices that have killed communication. No-one phones you these days, it's all fucking text... I'm sorry that was coarse of me."

Stuart laughed. "It's true, I can't remember the last real telephone conversation I had with my kids." They discussed each other's children and it was clear that Harry's kids had a very bohemian upbringing compared to his three.

It was late afternoon and after a second cup of tea, Harry said she needed to get home.

"Thank you for a great afternoon, I've really enjoyed your company," Stuart said rather formally. "Perhaps we could do it again?"

"Yes let's... how about Sunday lunch at the Anchor pub just down the road. It's great food."

"Fantastic, I will need some good food after the walk."

"Look, Stuart, I know all the local walks, why don't I show you the best of them."

"And lunch afterwards?"

"Yes, I will fix a late lunch with them. If we meet down at the Tourist Information offices on Bridge Street at say ten?"

"What about the museum photos?"

"It can wait."

"Done, I'm looking forward to it," he said as she left. He watched her walk down the road and realised his heart was beating abnormally fast. Relax, Stuart, relax, she is just being friendly, don't read anything into it.

He spent another night at the hotel eating a passably good steak with another bottle of red. His mind kept going back to the meeting with Harry, and even had erotic fantasies about her during his sleep. He had a light breakfast and was at the Tourist Office by 930, so he killed some time by walking around the harbour. She was on time and waved as she saw him. Her smile melted him, and he felt foolish although he did give her a welcome kiss on the cheek, which she accepted. She wore a thick cream jumper with tight sort of ski pants finished off by heavy walking boots. She had a waterproof jacket over her shoulder as well as a small backpack.

"You look like you mean business," he said and wished he had brought his boots. "Will these suffice?" he said pointing to his trainers.

"They will be fine," she said with a laugh. "And I have some refreshments," as she patted her backpack. "OK let's go," and she set off at pace towards the harbour. They climbed the steps to the coastal path and Stuart was breathing heavily when they got to the first view. Harry was certainly fit, no chance of respiratory failure, unlike Stuart. They took in the view and he recovered his breath. Onwards and past an old viaduct and up to Wadley Hall, Harry said they were about halfway through the walk. Stuart was enjoying himself, he hadn't done a walk like this for years and with great company. They chatted as they walked, and he learned more about Harry and her family; her husband had died tragically four years ago, the grieving was done but she would never really be over it... life goes on, she said.

"And what of you?"

"What do you mean?"

"Well you have children, so there must have been a woman in your life? You are very evasive."

Stuart did not know where to start. "I thought we were happily married. We had been together for a long time and then a few months back she left."

"It sounds like you were surprised?"

"I was, I didn't think I was complacent, but I obviously neglected her."

"So you are to blame?"

"Obviously... well a bit, maybe a lot. She is in love with another woman... sorry, Harry, it's a bit raw."

She pulled him to her. "You poor bugger," she said. They stayed like that for a while and Stuart was embarrassed by the stirrings in his body. He sensed Harry knew that and they released. They continued the walk and chatted about everything from politics to music, subjects that he hadn't spoke about with Zoe for years. He told her all about the experiment and she was intrigued.

"Can I come and see it?"

"You would be welcome any time."

They passed a couple of footbridges by the old mill before descending down to the town centre. The walk was over... suddenly Harry gave Stuart a kiss.

"You must think me very forward."

"I've never met anyone like you," he replied.

"You said you were going home tomorrow?"

"I am or rather I was, I could stay on for a few days."

"We both had commitments before we met; I still work for a living, you know."

"Is there any chance that we could spend more time together?"

"Yes, I would like that," she replied. "I have to see some people this afternoon, but we could eat at your hotel tonight?"

"I'll book it, say 730?"

"Perfect, see you then." She gave him another kiss as they parted.

He spent much of the afternoon on or around the beach looking for fossils alongside many other optimistic souls. All he could think about was Harry; she overwhelmed and excited him in a way that he vaguely recalled when he first met Zoe. Back at the hotel he took a shower and watched the TV until seven and then went to the bar. Harry arrived early, she looked stunning in a tight-fitting light blue dress, still no makeup but her hair was piled up which accentuated the beautiful shape of her neck. It was an uninspiring meal but made good by their company.

"I hope alcohol doesn't ruin your libido," she said.

"Pardon?" Stuart stammered.

"Well we are going to bed.. aren't we?"

"I'm a little rusty," he said meekly.

"Stop it, Stuart, live for now."

He found himself shaking with anticipation and decided no more alcohol. Harry smoothly steered the conversation back to her plans to develop a photography school.

The meal was over and he led her to his room, they kissed immediately the door was closed and passionately engaged in sex. Stuart knew he had been too quick and clumsy.

"I know what you are thinking," she said as she laid in his arms.

"Go on…"

"Too quick and not very smooth."

"I know, I did say I was rusty."

"Don't apologise for fuck's sake, I wanted you urgently too."

They engaged again early morning and it was a much more loving time. It was a strange breakfast since they were going separate ways after such a close and intense weekend.

"I must see you again," he said, "next weekend?"

"Sometimes, Stuart, people meet up and part, things don't need to be forever."

"You don't want to meet?"

"No it's not that, it's just that I don't want to be in a permanent relationship right now. I have been independent for a long time now and I like it... I like the freedom. If over time, I want to give up that freedom then fine... can you understand?"

"Sort of... but you have no idea how much you have given me this weekend."

"I think I do," she leered.

"No... much, much more... I'm getting too serious."

"Yes you are... come down to Lyme in a couple of weeks and let's pick things up then," she stood, gave him a loving kiss and left.

Stuart felt deflated, Harry was right; they were both of an age where they had built families, so why was he looking for a permanent long-term relationship. Enjoy her company and her freedom, Stuart; as she says, if it develops into something deeper.

He settled the bill and rebooked for two weeks' time, as he got into the car he realised all he had was her name, no phone number, no addresses nothing, what a fool. He hoped he could find some detail on the net: at least she had his address. He was thinking about the experiment on the way back to Smythfield and found Alice waiting outside in her car. Stuart reviewed his progress with her over a coffee. As promised she had managed to borrow some bits of equipment to help with the accuracy of the angles. She had some laser gauges and electronic levels which would pinpoint the geometry.

"Alice, I have been thinking about this for a while and have an idea forming in my mind. It needs some scientific critique and you are well placed to do that, can I take you through it?"

"Sure."

"OK, well we know that we have found a force that seems unlike any other, the placement of the bar changes the equilibrium of gravity."

"Yup."

"We also know that by varying the angle of the bar we induce some motion."

"With you so far."

"If the bar acts as a block to the force it would explain the creation of a new equilibrium and if that block acted as a sort of mirror on the force it would allow the force to be deflected."

"Logical, but speculation."

"Yes, but let's just say that this force is a component of gravity that's in equilibrium of 76 degrees to the other components."

"Hold on... gravity is made up of a number of forces?"

"I know it's a bit off the wall but if we think of gravity throughout the cosmos... there is no 76 degrees... it only exists on Earth. It's relative to us. We have created a new equilibrium with the bar that doesn't conform to normal gravitational rules. Perhaps it's a component of gravity rather than a separate force, I don't know. The alternative is that somehow gravity is a single force and that we have distorted it in a single space although it remains in equilibrium around that distortion."

Alice was deep in thought. "It goes against all known science."

"I know, but we all agreed that we have created a unique set of conditions... unique... so maybe we have uncovered something that science has not known. You do agree that if we vary the angle then we induce horizontal motion?"

"Yes."

"And that the vertical position of the bar is changed but still subject to vertical gravity, just a new equilibrium?"

"Yes."

"So somehow there are two forces or two components at play?"

"It's hard to agree."

"Stay with me, just let's experiment on this basis for the rest of the day and refine and record activity."

They spent the rest of the day experimenting with different angles and built up results based on horizontal movements. They also experimented with the power input to the magnets, but it was clear that once the effect had been induced, further power made no difference. They also reduced the power and established the point at which the effect took place. It was binary but of course directly linked to the size and shape of the bar.

Towards the end of the day, they tentatively experimented with twisting the bar and getting vertical movement. Both knew the power they were dealing with and kept all variations well within a safe margin. Indeed they had no idea of a safe margin really but avoided any drastic changes of angles and limited the maximum angular change to 1.5 degrees. They both agreed to further scale down the experiment with smaller bars and smaller magnets but decided to hold off until Alice had analysed the data.

Stuart started on the next frame, this time allowing for additional variations on size of bars and the plates that were expected from Southampton. Alice felt that the existing electromagnets could be scaled down to match the smaller plates. Stuart continued his monastic existence, concentrating on the new build. He did track down Harry's firm on the web and sent her a note; he was frustrated that he got no reply. Towards the end of the week Alice phoned.

"Sorry I couldn't do it sooner but I'm sending you the results of our analysis, I have got the algorithms on the variations we performed... it's amazing... they are all interrelated. You were right, some of the force increases exponentially with angle. That explains the early disasters." They agreed on two differing size plates that they could then combine with the first results to figure out the plate size ratio to force. "I'm beginning to think your ideas about gravity are right," she said. They agreed to restart the new experiments that weekend if Stuart could get the new frame completed.

Rob had been absent for some while due to school commitments, but he agreed to help out that weekend. Mike and the team would also be coming with some newly engineered plates, they were also going back to the original foundry to cast some more bars; but this was scheduled for a month's time.

The mood was buoyant that Saturday; there had been a constant dialogue between them by email, and so was all up-to-date on the weekend activity. Stuart hadn't quite finished the frame but with the additional help it was ready by midmorning.

"Just think back," he said, "we were all in the dark on this thing and now... well, in theory, we should be able to predict what's going to happen."

"In theory," piped up Alice.

"We still don't know why though, do we?" chipped in Rob.

"Well Stu has his theory, but it's a bit off the wall."

"You'll have to update me some time, Stu," he replied.

Mike, Gareth and Steve had brought some new plates plus further variations based on Alice's email. They had trouble accommodating the different sized plates into the frame but finally kicked off the experiment. Upon powering up, the fame rose to the predicted height and then moved vertically and horizontally to a predicted position based on its angles. They used the smallest plates, which were only 50 millimetres long with lower magnetic power; the frame again performed as planned.

It was now a tradition that they retired to the pub for supper. Steve and Gareth continued their version of wooing Alice, whilst Mike, Rob and Stuart went over the day's results and the plan for Sunday.

"I know it's not very scientific," said Rob, "but let's see what this bloody thing can do."

"We've seen some of that before Rob... remember," cautioned Stuart.

"Yes, but it looks like we have got a handle on the dangers now," he replied.

"On that point, we haven't tested the horsepower of the force yet," said Mike.

"True, ok let's test it out tomorrow."

They all went their separate ways having agreed to restart around ten on the Sunday.

Firstly they attached a harness to the robust points on the frame. The harness had a platform to accommodate weights. They used some old concrete slabs to act as incremental weights. Every time they powered up the unit, the weights were lifted with ease. They guessed that it was lifting about 200 kilos before they stopped for fear of the harness breaking. It happily lifted Gareth and Steve to everyone's amusement transporting them across the workshop and back.

They were becoming more adventurous and decided to set the unit on a slow circular motion. They mounted the batteries on a concrete slab within the platform so the whole frame was independent. Alice had calculated the angle settings and they started the motion. The frame completed several circles until Mike noticed that it was beginning to rise.

"It's not a circle but a spiral," he said, "we should stop it." Sure enough they all realised that the frame was rising… and accelerating! "It's the bloody angle, we weren't accurate enough." He crossed the workshop to make a grab at disconnecting the batteries. The harness hit him hard and threw against the wall, it was now swinging out like a slingshot; they all ducked.

"Get out, everyone!" yelled Rob as he headed for the doors; they didn't need telling twice. Outside they could hear the swish of the frame and harness accelerating ever upwards, there was simply nothing they could do. It smashed through the roof with an incredible rip and splinter hovering above the roof momentarily before breaking up in every direction. There was silence for a while; everyone kept still… just in case.

"How fucking stupid was that?" Mike was the first to talk. "We have been so careful in all that we've done and then we do something with no fucking scientific merit… just for fun."

"Mike's right, why did we do it?…we know how dangerous the force can be," Alice replied.

"Come on… we were all being a bit daft because of our progress, we have just learned a very big lesson," said Stuart.

There was genuine shock in the team; Rob added, "OK folks let's get this tidied up as best we can. Try to salvage the bars and the plates, frankly the rest is destined for the dump."

"I'm not sure if the plates will be ok now," said Mike getting Gareth and Steve to help him with some of the destroyed roof.

"Stu, did you have a tarp we can put over the roof?"

As ever Stuart always had something, and they all helped remove the broken bits of roof and inserted some temporary supports such that the tarp could be hauled over to protect the building. Once it was finished they all said their farewells leaving Stuart and Rob. Any future actions weren't discussed.

"Stu, I think you should slow this thing down and take stock, we have had a big dose of reality today!" Stuart realised for the first time how obsessed he had become; he felt drained and empty. "You're clearly onto something, and I know how much you enjoy the practical stuff but... give it a rest mate... why not spend some time getting a patent, you never know, you could make some money from it."

Rob talked sense, Stuart had no idea of the patent process and saw it as something they should do: it would be a good diversion and could occupy his mind.

As Rob left he yelled, "And, if you feel the pull of practical things... repair the roof."

Stuart started his new project. To register the patent, he needed to research the process and so he got on the net. His day was revived when Harry phoned.

"I didn't know if you would phone me and I suddenly realised that I didn't have your number." Why was his heart beating faster?

"I was just checking whether you are still on for this weekend?" she said.

"Absolutely, I am so looking forward to seeing you."

"Can you make it a bit earlier, say Friday morning?"

"No problem, what time?"

"Well I have had a new garden shed delivered and I need a hand erecting it."

"I could say the obvious coarse remark."

"One erection at a time please," she giggled.

"Do I need to bring any tools?"

"No, I'm sure I have everything."

I'll bring tools, he thought.

"Say nine thirty?"

"I'll be there... hold... hold... what's your address?" She gave him the address and guidance.

"See you," and she hung up; Stuart returned to the patent, he had a couple of days to get it underway.

After a half-day research Stuart's view was that the patent process was very intensive and bureaucratic, it had all the components of tedium for Stuart and yet he knew it had to be done. He decided that he needed the expertise of a professional and contacted several companies on the phone. He managed to fix three appointments for the following day, all of them in central London. He knew he needed an international patent through a Patent Cooperation Treaty. He would have to present some sort of abstract of his experiment, but that wasn't enough, his findings needed a purpose, an outcome. Of course it was obvious... the outcome was that he had found a way to move things around, both up and down in space through the harnessing of a force. He felt that at this stage, it would be wrong to specify where the force came from although he may need to amplify the source further into the process. For the moment it was a new form of... transport. Indeed the force could be harnessed in all sorts of ways, electricity generation for example. It provided for levitation and propulsion... of course... LeviProp ... what a name, Stuart was on a roll! After lots of searches it was clear that the name LeviProp wasn't being used anywhere. He would get the patent agent to check and confirm the name.

He extracted drawings, diagrams and photographs from his recorded data and wove them into a LeviProp narrative. It was a good start and something that he could present to the various patent agents the following day. The document was still guarded since he needed advice from the chosen agent on how much of his invention he had to share.

He arrived in London around nine in the morning for the first meeting. The office was close to Waterloo station and he was ushered into a bland meeting with a basic table and four chairs, there was a high window that just about allowed light in, and a bookcase running landside one wall; the books looked unused for years, Stuart was looking at some sort of old London print on the other wall when a middle-aged woman entered.

"Hello, I'm Fiona Cardew, you must be Mr Ashley?"

"Yes, Stuart Ashley, thanks for seeing me at short notice."

"Well I only have 40 minutes Mr Ashley, we have a standard process to familiarise you with patent application and get basic information to see if your proposition is worthy of merit. Let's get the confidentiality agreement out of the way first."

This statement put Stuart into a negative frame of mind. They must get lots of tyre-kickers, he thought but it doesn't hurt to recognise that the glass might be half full. Nevertheless he went through their process and learnt a lot more about patents. They only spent ten minutes going through LeviProp and it was clear that Ms Carew didn't believe him.

"There is a lot more work you will need to do, Mr Ashley, before we can make a submission. It's probably going to take you about a month, do you have time?"

"I don't know," Stuart lied, "I will have to think about it." This organisation will fail me, thought Stuart.

"Frankly without that level of commitment, we are unable to take it on."

Stuart said his goodbye and collected all the information and left. One down, he thought, I hope they are not all like that, fortunately they were not. Indeed the next two meetings went well and either organisation could have supported Stuart. In the end he chose a company called Brightons. He had met Paul Brighton who ran the business and liked him immediately. He had a 'can do' attitude and was really interested in LeviProp. Not only did he offer to take some of the bureaucratic work from Stuart, but also offered to setup a company with trademarks such that Stuart had the complete package should he want to exploit LeviProp. It was going to cost between £7,000 and £10,000, but Stuart knew that he had to afford it.

He felt good as he journeyed to see Harry. Inwardly he was cross that the last experiment had gone wrong but he had started the patent process and had confidence that Paul would get it done. It was early, and the traffic was light, the satnav directed him to Harry's place.

It was big, very big, and was a composition of many centuries of additions and changes. The stone walls showed a number of different styles, some beautiful mullion windows alongside some crude infill of doorways. As Stuart was inspecting the architecture Harry appeared. She wore a loose sweatshirt with tight-fitting jeans, industrial boots and garden gloves; her hair was tied back, she wore no makeup, she looked gorgeous. She sort of skipped towards him and kissed him fully; he hugged her, he hadn't felt like this for years.

"I've come to do the erection, guvnor," he said in a mock accent.

She laughed, and they hugged again. "Come and have a coffee," as she led him to the side path.

"The house… is just fantastic."

"Manor, darling; house is just so passé!"

And it was, over coffee Harry gave him a potted history of the manor. Its origins were in the 16th century and the 'family' had acquired it around 1820. She had inherited it through a trust from her grandmother a couple of years back. She rents part of the house to her cousin and also has a lodger in a self-contained wing.

"I didn't know I was dating landed aristocracy," chided Stuart.

"Are you dating me, Stuart? How quaint!"

"So with all this, why do you need a new shed?"

"Well, the old one disintegrated and it's close to the back of the house, it holds gardening stuff."

"The garden looks pretty well cared for, how big is it?"

"A few acres," she threw away, "well actually quite a lot, but most of it is rented out to a local farmer, the rest is woodland, so I only have the formal gardens to deal with. OK, I confess there is a gardener who helps out and he is here to help with the new shed, his name is Ray."

"Right, let's get to it then."

She led him through a number of dark corridors ending up in a sort of scullery that opened onto to the garden. Ray was hovering around and joined them as they walked through a path surrounded to rhododendrons to an area with hard standing and a large pallet containing the new shed.

"This is not a shed," Stuart remarked, "it's nearly as large as one of my workshops."

"Oh and how many workshops do you have then, Stuart?" she said rather cynically.

"A few," he responded.

"I would like to see your place."

"You will, Harry, I want to show you my discovery."

"Is that the mysterious experiment you referred to in the pub?"

"Yup but it's moved on, and I need to take some big decisions about its direction."

"Even more mysterious," she replied.

Together with Ray, they began to construct the new shed, fortunately it was constructed in sections that enabled the three of them to lift it and bolt it together. Ray was clearly very fit, fitter than Stuart certainly. However he didn't have the natural engineering skills of Stuart and soon the building was being constructed in an orderly way with Stuart's direction. They encountered a few problems where another two people would have helped, but Stuart always found a way to overcome things. They stopped for a simple lunch and had the basic structure complete by early evening.

"You know how to work a man," Stuart said with a smile. "Where can I wash up?" Harry led him to a bathroom and gave him fresh towels. "Are you joining me?" he leered.

"You have a one-track mind, Stuart. I need to make sure Ray is around tomorrow to help and confirm the restaurant booking for tonight."

"Where are we going?"

"I will tell you later, shower first and join me in the garden room."

"Where is it?"

"You will find it."

He had confirmed his room at the hotel in town at lunchtime, so he just needed to wash the day's sweat from his body. Once freshened, he went downstairs to find the garden room. It was quite a task exploring various rooms until eventually opening a door onto a beautiful Victorian room that was part house and part conservatory. It was a vast space that had seen better days but was furnished with some elegant chairs and sofas plus an array of tropical plants that invaded the whole room. Harry was at the garden end of the room in a cream dress that displayed her lithe figure to its best.

"You scrub up well," he joked. She offered him a glass of champagne.

"Thanks for your help today Stuart."

"It was fun, working with you, it's the sort of thing I enjoy. I did have some ideas about the shed by the way."

"Go on."

"Well if we re-structured the middle section we could move the double doors to the end of the building which would make better use of the space."

"Are you always like this?"

"Afraid so, Zoe my other half... before... got very bored by it!"

"Well if you think we can do it, let's have a go tomorrow."

Harry had arranged for supper in a local restaurant that seemed to carry every food accreditation possible. Fortunately it wasn't a pompous foodie space and they had great fun just chatting; the banter was sharp and fast. It was unexpected when Harry asked to be taken home; Stuart had hoped she might stay the night at the hotel. After a passionate farewell she went into the house having arranged to have breakfast the following morning. Stuart returned to the hotel in confusion, he knew he shouldn't have expected Harry to stay the night, but they were enjoying each other's company so much. Ah well, he said to himself with a sigh.

It was a workman's breakfast; Ray joined them for toasted bacon sandwich with optional brown sauce washed down with a latte coffee. Stuart explained his plan to Ray and together they dismantled part of the building and reassembled it in a new way that required some adjustments to the wall linkages and roof trusses. Amazingly by midday it was complete, and they just needed to fit the roof in the afternoon, fortunately the weather held. By the evening Stuart felt he had been working hard and just wanted to relax, he hoped that when Harry excused herself around five that she might be cooking something.

She was in the scullery as he entered.

"You look done in," she said.

"Excuse me, I am in my prime," he said rather insincerely.

"Well I have run a bath for you; in the blue bathroom; it's on the second floor."

Stuart grabbed his bag and went in search of the bath. It was a large room, probably Edwardian style with a fantastic decoration of delft tiles around a massive fireplace. The freestanding bath must have been built for a giant, he thought; certainly it wasn't environmentally friendly more tired-man friendly. Harry had positioned several lanterns around the room with various candles some giving off a rose scent. Stuart didn't need prompting, stripping off and submerging himself in less than a minute.

He didn't hear Harry come into the room until he felt her hands on his shoulders. "Thanks for today," she whispered in his ear. He looked up to find that she was nearly naked and removing her remaining underwear.

"I've always wanted to share this bath with someone," she purred.

"So I'm someone, am I?"

"No, don't be prickly, you're my someone," and with that she lowered herself into the other end of the bath.

"Let me massage your back, I could see it was giving your grief this afternoon." He was aroused but twisted round to let her knead his back, which she did with some expertise. Lovemaking was a hilarious affair with water everywhere, ending with them tenderly drying one another. They stayed in that night and dined on pizza whist watching a movie; Stuart didn't go back to the hotel. He awoke with a gentle ache that reminded him of previous exertion, it was a good ache and he was alongside a woman he had only known a while and yet he felt like he had known her all his life. She stirred.

"Make me tea... now," she said petulantly.

"I don't recall a please in that sentence," as he started to tickle her. They romped for a while and eventually Stuart conceded to be tea-boy. Over breakfast they went through the walk that Harry had planned for the day, it took in an old wartime factory that had been derelict for years. Harry was keen to take some photos there; she hoped it would complete an assignment that she had to complete plus it could be valuable to her general portfolio. As they left there was a drizzle that looked set for the day, but undaunted, they dropped by the hotel, so Stuart could checkout and collect his bags. The walk started at a car park beside a traditional pub and in view of the weather they booked a late lunch. After a couple of hours they came to a clearing with a large number of buildings in poor repair.

"It looks like an old MoD site," Stuart said.

"I think it was, although I don't know where the access is, there must be a road somewhere." After some exploring they did find an old pathway that had once been a road. Harry unpacked her kit and went off to take snaps as Stuart cynically called them. It felt like a sad place, Stuart thought. Not because of the state it's in, but rather its cold utility and isolation and wet. He found a building that provided some cover from the rain. It obviously was some sort of factory given the size of the buildings, probably munitions, he speculated. His mind wandered back to his experiment. Over the months it had moved from an inexplicable phenomenon to a form of motion. The patent process had clarified this in his mind. He had two areas of focus for the future; firstly he had ideas about the cause of the power, although it made Alice scoff, he needed to get to the bottom of things, a working hypothesis at least. Secondly, he wanted to develop a real prototype of a vehicle that harnessed the power. He struggled with the hypothesis but knew he could make the prototype. He needed time money and scientific support if he was to move forward. Time was fine, and he had some savings, but he needed someone like Alice to break through the science.

Then there is the biggest conundrum of all, opening his finding to the world.

"Deep in thought?" she said.

"Have you finished?"

"Yes I think so, it was worth coming, I'll share the pictures with you in the pub. What was it that was causing the frown?"

"You know, I mentioned that I think I have made a discovery that may change the shape our world."

"No. You didn't say it like that. You said you had found a way to float things… changing the world? Are you serious?"

"It did sound a little pompous, well maybe influence the world might be better. Was I that vague? I didn't mean to be; well I'd like to share it with you since I have to make some decisions."

"Let's walk and talk," she said holding his arm.

Stuart was more careful with his conversation since he wanted to ensure Harry really understood what was happening back in Smythfield without boring her. Harry just listened as Stuart summarised his next decisions.

"It sounds like you will be up against all the scientific community since your hypothesis doesn't fit conventional thinking, that's going to be a big mountain to climb. On the other hand if you can show the world that you have harnessed something that doesn't fit current thinking then you will force them to support finding the answers. You could still progress your hypothesis but don't get worked up over it."

"Good thinking, Harry, you're right, it's not a priority it's just me wanting answers."

"So get on building a really good prototype that will prove your point. Then see if you can get a sponsor, ideally the government."

"What worries me is that I want to ensure that everyone benefits from the discovery. Call me a cynic but there will be lots of interested parties that will want to squash my findings."

"Nothing wrong with being an idealist but be ready to get screwed!"

"I know, I know… but I will have to trust some people."

"When the time is right you can always go public on the net, even better, you could research all the key international players who would be influential in spreading the word!"

"Thanks, Harry, it's good advice, you're a great sounding board."

"I hope I'm better than that," she laughed, "come on let's get that pub lunch."

It was a traditional pub lunch; the beef was slightly overcooked, but the meal was warming after the rain outside. They continued the discussion about the discovery and put more detail behind the thinking. Harry shared her photos with Stuart and it was clear to him that she had real talent for artistic composition.

It was early evening when they left the pub and Stuart dropped Harry off at her place. She had a lot of preparatory work for the next few weeks ahead and needed to get some of it done that night. After a fond farewell it was agreed that Harry should come to Smythfield as soon as the assignment was over.

As he drove home Stuart realised that he liked his relationship with Harry; it wasn't possessive, neither was it remote and yet there was a warm understanding that they had independent lives and at this time wanted it to remain so. He mulled over the discussion they had over his next steps and found himself excited at the thought of building a working prototype although he was very conscious of the dangers if he failed to harness the forces at play.

At home there was a message on the answer phone from Paul Brighton telling him that the first draft of his patent submission was in the post and that he had started all the business paperwork. Stuart was surprised and pleased at Paul's progress; he had chosen a good guy. Stuart was completely absorbed in the prototype when Rob called round. Together they discussed his plans.

"I am going to build a working prototype of a vehicle that can go in any direction, forward, back, up and down."

"And speed?"

"Yes, within reason, but concentrating on manoeuvrability."

"So you don't know what the force is, but it's powerful and dangerous and you're going to build a vehicle? You're mad!"

"Rob, it's the only way forward, the aim is to get attention and enlist the brains to figure out what it is."

"But you have a theory?"

"Yes but Alice thinks it's a bit farfetched, but I am using it as a working hypothesis until something better turns up."

"Well apart from the last farcical event I'm still game."

"It was a farce, but let's move on. Part of the problem is ensuring a tight accuracy in the engineering; something that I have failed in so far. The problem is that I have been using frames and structures based on wood, which has an inherent weakness in its accuracy with the forces involved. As you know I used wood since I'm pretty good with it and it was fast to fabricate things plus it was inert and didn't interfere with the experiments, well now I'm going for whatever materials make the most sense whether it's steel, an alloy, carbon fibre or plastic."

"Will the vehicle be some sort of frame?"

"I thought about that and I'm going to use an old car from the local breakers. I figured out that we should be able to construct another propulsion unit, but the big issue is building controls for steering and acceleration."

"And brakes," Rob chipped in.

"Yes, Rob… and brakes. By the way I am calling it LeviProp, short for levitation and propulsion based on Inertia Conversion or IC. What do you think?"

"It's a good name. When are you starting?"

"I've already put some preliminary sketches together around the controls. I was going to mock them up in wood before proper fabrication. Hopefully I can run them past you as it develops."

Stuart was very private about Harry, but he shared a little of his new relationship with Rob over a beer. Rob was keen to meet her and made an open offer of supper when she came to Smythfield.

Having decided to focus on the controls he had been staring at some sketches for a while. How to control the angle and the twist of the plate was a real problem and then the idea came. If he had two plates linked by solenoids at both ends he would have the ability to change the angle and gain horizontal movement. He still couldn't figure out how to get the vertical force in control. In total frustration he left it all to get some air.

Indeed it was very smelly and oily air at the local breakers yard. Stuart wandered around the place wishing he had put on some dirty clothes especially some heavy boots. It was a large site with bits of car and lorries everywhere, very often piled three or four high. It frustrated Stuart that a place could be so disorganised. There were two or three caravans grouped together alongside a couple of old wooden shacks. There were only a few cars that were in one piece, all the rest were partially dismantled in one way or another. He was surprised that no-one challenged him or asked him what he was doing there.

He noticed an elderly man working by a bench in one of the shacks. He was Mister Grease himself, with a greasy flat cap covering fluffy white greasy hair and woolly sideburns. His wire spectacles were perched on a pointed greasy nose that sat above a thin greasy moustache that accentuated his soft lips. His hands looked like they could never be clean again and matched the general colour of his overalls.

"'help you?" he said out of the corner of his mouth; the other corner suspending a greasy hand-rolled cigarette that had long been extinguished.

"I'm looking for a small car that's basically sound," Stuart asked.

"None 'ere. Only bits 'ere."

"I just wondered, if cars come in sometimes that still run?"

"What for?"

"Just want something where the basics are sound or repairable."

"Banger racing?"

"Sort of," Stuart was becoming monosyllabic as well.

"Some bastard left a red Ford Fiesta across my gates yesterday. Just over there," he said, pointing with a screwdriver.

Stuart wandered over to the car; its body had definitely seen better days but looked sound. He managed to get the door open; it smelled damp. He tested the brake pedal and was surprised to find that it was firm. He wiggled the steering and apart from a few clunks it seemed to respond although at a glance he could see the tyres were barely legal. He couldn't open the bonnet, it seemed jammed, still he didn't need the engine. It wasn't a thing of beauty, but it would do, he thought.

Back at the shack he asked the man for a price.

"Not mine, dumped here, probably nicked," he said. "Got 'undreds of the buggers all over the place. Don't need it."

"I've got a car transport. Can I pick it up?"

"Gates close at six," was the positive reply.

He went home and coupled up the transport having inflated the tyres. Back at the breakers he used the winch to haul the Fiesta onto the transport and secured the car. "Thanks a lot," he said to the man. "I may need some spares later."

"Told you, got 'undreds of 'em," he said, returning to his bench.

Stuart deposited the Fiesta in the drive and went to clean up. His mind was still focused on the drive unit and he went back to his desk. His sketch of the two-plate idea was there. Of course... if he doubled the unit then it would cover all dimensions. He sketched four identical plates all linked together at their ends by a solenoid. He was completed absorbed and input the idea into his CAD system. It worked; he simulated various changes in horizontal and vertical angles and the design responded positively. Elated he went to bed, it was four in the morning.

Stuart woke early, after a light breakfast he had a better look at the Fiesta. There were no surprises when he finally got the bonnet open. He had planned to remove the engine anyway and install the drive in its stead. It prompted him to think about the overall weight of the car and whether he would need to balance the drive accordingly. Another problem to resolve, he thought, as he returned to his desk. He was trying to figure out how to make this new drive unit and contacted Mike in Southampton.

"Sorry, Stuart, we can't afford the time at the moment. Gareth and Steve have a lot of year-end stuff to finish."

"OK, let me know when you surface, and thanks for the new plates, they are perfect."

"Watch out, Stuart, don't be too cavalier with the experiments, you know it's dangerous," Mike sounded guarded, as he was when they first met. Something's changed, he thought; he was mad as hell when the last trial ripped the roof out. "It's so fucking unprofessional" he kept repeating. He started looking up engineering works locally when he remembered old Froom at the factory. Stuart's ambition was to be as good a technician and engineer as Froom. He had been at the factory years before Stuart joined and knew everything about power generation systems and their fabrication; Stuart had used his expertise continually. It would be fun to pop down to the factory and say hello anyway. There were even fewer cars in the car park than he remembered a few months back, more downsizing, he thought. The security people were fine and let him in; there were several friendly waves as he headed to Froom's work area. He looked through the window to see Froom welding something, so he decided to wait until he finished. He looked around the place and had fond memories of his time; it was only the last four months when the atmosphere had become poisonous. Froom broke his thoughts.

"Hello, Stuart, have they brought you back?" he said with a grin.

"How are you, Froom?" Everyone called him Froom, I suppose he has a first name, but no-one cared.

"Clinging on for retirement," he responded. Stuart didn't know his age but put him in his sixties. He was a wiry man, around six-foot tall with the smartest haircut. In fact Froom reminded Stuart of a sergeant major from the fifties, everything about him was clean, tidy and in its place; not like the man from the breakers, he mused.

"What brings you here? Can't leave the old place?" he continued.

"Actually I need some advice and you are the only man I know who can help."

"Don't try and butter me up, it never worked when you were here so there's no chance now."

Stuart smiled. Froom hadn't changed. "I'm building a new drive unit and really do need some advice."

"Ok things are pretty quiet now so show me what you need."

Stuart opened his laptop and brought up the drawings.

"I've seen similar couplings, what does it do?"

Stuart decided to be vague. "Well it's a sort of induction motor."

"Bollocks it is," Froom laughed.

Stuart explained the whole background to him and Froom listened attentively.

"Fascinating, well if you have stumbled on something as you describe then this design needs refining."

"So you believe me?"

"Listen, Stuart I have always thought that our knowledge of natural science is incomplete. Some of these theories are like the wrong piece in a jigsaw puzzle, only scientists force them into shape."

This was a side of Froom that he didn't know. "Will you help?"

"On one condition; I want to be there when you try it."

"Done," said Stuart. "I have the plates made already; it's a special cast from vanadium."

"If you're happy to leave them with me, I will make your drive."

They discussed all of the angles that the solenoids would produce and agreed a set of standards although Stuart had no idea of the implications.

"It needs a sort of joystick to actuate the solenoids, I will put some ideas together." Stuart couldn't believe his luck.

"I'm working on the assumption that reversing the angles will act as a brake."

"I'll make sure that the controller can do that," he said. "Tell you what, when it's ready I'll come over to you with it. You live in Smythfield don't you?" Stuart gave him his address and they agreed to catch up in a week's time.

What amazing luck, he thought, as he drove home. So I can concentrate on getting the Fiesta sorted. Froom had even agreed that he would make two units since there were enough plates. The factory can't have any work on if Froom had spare time.

Part of that week was spent sorting out solicitor's paper for the divorce; he really missed Zoe; Harry was fun and very different, or was she? Still nothing from the kids, that really hurt. He completed the patent filings and the company creation, which involved him paying Paul Brighton £5,000 for the work so far. The rest of the time he spent on the Fiesta. His head said he wanted to restore the car to its original condition however he really didn't want to spend more money than was necessary, after all he didn't want a working car, just something to house the new drive. He did need the existing steering and brakes and started on them. He had to shell out money on new brake pads, but the steering was fine with some adjustment and replacement bushes, he also removed the engine and gearbox. Fortunately he had lots of sheet metal and tubing and so was able to weld a floor into the engine compartment as well as fabricating a sturdy interior cage to reinforce the body. He also welded some struts into the engine bay ready to mount the drive. He spent a lot of time changing the suspension with minimal damping and no drop on the wheels; after all this entire thing should only be on the ground when stationary.

He was worried that if the Fiesta went at high speed then the body might not hold, so he removed any unnecessary parts and made the front more aerodynamic, closing up all the gaps. The windscreen might be a problem at speed and so he found a tough plastic that he could heat weld over the joints. He decided that the new joystick would fit on the left of the car and so fixed a linkage such that foot brake could be operated from the left seat; the steering wheel remained on the right. He fitted additional catches to secure the bonnet and doors before turning his attention to the interior. He glued and moulded thick plastic sponge to all the interior surfaces including the floor. His final task was to replace the left seat with something stronger together with a proper harness. He returned to the breakers and found an old aircraft seat that had a harness incorporated. It was a bit tatty but once repaired he bolted into the Fiesta. The car was now ready for the drive and controls.

He hadn't heard from Froom, so he phoned him on progress.

"Nearly finished; even if I do say, it's an engineering work of art." Stuart knew he would be impressed. "I can bring it over early next week." They agreed that the following Wednesday was best.

It was Saturday morning and Stuart was putting unnecessary finishing touches to the car. On the Friday, he looked at the Fiesta; it was a mess of weld and brackets, so he decided to spray the whole thing black the next day. He only bothered with basic preparation but by mid-morning he had finished, and the Fiesta was looking pretty good. What shall I call it, he thought; it's not a car anymore. Just then Harry arrived.

They embraced for a long time. "I've really missed you," he said.

"And me you," she laughed. "Come on, let's get a pub lunch. Clean up first, though. Is this my new car, I don't like the colour?"

"It's my new LeviProp vehicle actually, and I didn't have other colours so like Henry Ford it's only in black."

"Is that its name, LeviProp, it's a bit boring?"

"No... in fact I was thinking about a name when you arrived."

"Well allow me to choose a name?"

"OK as long as it's not something daft like rocket!!"

"How did you know I was thinking of rocket?" she teased. "Actually I was thinking of Paradox, since as far as I can tell it's all a bit of a puzzle."

"Paradox it is," cheered Stuart. "It's a great name and reflects everything that's happened recently."

"Excluding me!"

"I'm not sure, Harry, you are a bit of a puzzle to me; but a great puzzle," and he kissed her; she always lifted his spirits. Before leaving he looked around the house and the outbuildings including the workshop with the temporary roof. He had ensured the interior of the house was tidy early that morning. Harry saw all the remains of the various experiments as well as looking at some video footage. She replayed the final video of the spiralling platform.

"This is serious stuff, Stuart."

"Didn't you believe me then?"

"No, it's not that, but frankly you do have to see it to understand what you have discovered, and the powerful force involved."

"I know, but I did take your advice on that point. All I have to do now is find a way to insert the new drive in to the Paradox and I really will be able to show it to people."

"Take care, my love," she said with real affection.

"Let's have that lunch, I'm starving. I want to go to Portsmouth, there's a metal workshop that's open today. Do you mind?"

"No, we can explore Portsmouth afterwards?"

"Done."

They had a quick lunch in the local pub before setting off to Portsmouth. They found the metal fabricator in the industrial estate and got their agreement that Stuart could get a frame made up. Stuart was a bit vague since he hadn't got the drive back from Froom. He also didn't know what material to use yet.

They had both visited Portsmouth a few times but still enjoyed some sightseeing before going to the cinema followed by a pizza in an Italian restaurant nearby. On the way home, Harry mentioned that she was off to the USA for a couple of months. Stuart was surprised, hurt and confused that she hadn't told him before.

"How long has it been in plan?" he asked in a sulky way.

"Look, Stuart, you don't own me, I am a free agent," she snapped.

"So you keep telling me... sorry," he drove on in silence.

They arrived at the house, as Harry was getting out of the car she said, "About nine months, my sister is getting married in Phoenix." Stuart didn't say anything.

"Look, Stuart, it was all organised and I didn't expect or plan to meet you, so I have been racking my brains on how to tell you. I knew you would take it the wrong way."

"I did tell you that I have been on various photo assignments internationally over the years, well I'm combining the wedding with some work if you must know." She was still peevish. "I'd better head home."

Stuart realised that his silence had driven her to this position; he had to say something. "Please don't go, I'm sorry... it's just that..." He was making it worse. "I hate myself for being so puerile. I am behaving like a love-sick sulky kid."

"Yes you are, and.. are you love-sick?"

"I suppose I am... yes I am."

"Well so am I but in a grown-up way, I think." She gave him a smile.

"Our first row?"

"No… it's part of getting to know who we are to each other," she said, "there was no easy way to tell you."

"OK… are there any other plans?"

"Yes, I have a couple of new assignments in the next six to twelve months, what about you?"

"Nothing, well apart from proving my invention to the world," he said with his smile. "Are we an item then?"

"Perhaps, Stuart, time will tell, but my feelings for you are very deep and very special." They went into the house arm in arm. It was a strange night, when they were in bed they just held each other firmly until sleep took them away. The morning was less strange with some passionate sex in the bathroom. Stuart went downstairs first to prepare breakfast, he still had an empty feeling in his stomach following the heated words last night. I'm becoming too intense for her, he thought, but this is me, so how should I behave? He was lost in these thoughts when she came into the kitchen. She looked fantastic in her usual jeans and sweatshirt.

"Where's the coffee, the orange juice, the croissants? What have you been doing?" she teased.

"I am too intense, aren't I? How should I be?"

"Stuart it's not for me to say, you must be yourself. I would hate it if you created a façade for my benefit. You do need to relax into our relationship. It's fine being intense and impatient with your invention but not with me… right?"

Stuart reflected for a moment; maybe that was a contributor to Zoe leaving me. "Absolutely," he said.

They spent the rest of the day walking and talking in the local area ending in a pub that Stuart was fond of. Back at Smythfield they said their farewell, Harry assured him that she would keep contact and looked forward to hearing about his trials of Paradox. That night Stuart felt empty, much like when Zoe had left. He was determined to immerse himself in getting Paradox to work and was thinking about the people he should target for a demonstration.

He spent all his time on the mounting frame. As with his progress so far, he knew he was in uncharted territory and so the best approach was trial and error. He considered making a frame identical to the last experiment but in aluminium. He had a lot of aluminium angle strips in the workshop that had come out of some ceiling partitioning. Stuart vaguely remembered from his physics school lessons that aluminium although non-magnetic could still be influenced by the Lenz effect, which might create another magnetic field that could screw up the drive unit; he abandoned the idea. He knew that carbon fibre was a better choice for the frame but had held off investigating it on the grounds of cost and complexity. He decided to discuss the idea with Froom the following day.

It was a good decision. Froom turned up early on the Wednesday and following the inevitable cups of tea, Stuart updated him on his design idea and the frame composition. He should not have been surprised at Froom's knowledge of material science; after all, power generators used the latest material technologies in various ways. Froom was indeed a goldmine of knowledge. He went through Stuart's design, highlighting various shortcomings and correcting them. He also adapted the frame to ensure the drive would function perfectly when mounted in it. Stuart sat back in awe of this man's practical abilities. Froom did agree with Stuart that the best composition of the frame would be a carbon fibre reinforced polymer and knew of a moulding manufacturer who could do the work.

"You should know of them, Stuart, they have done lots of subcontract work for us at the factory; I'll contact them." Within minutes he had got agreement from them to do the work and had sent the revised design for a costing.

Froom retrieved a large wooden box from the back of his beaten-up Land Rover. Inside the box were two of the drive units that he had made. Stuart took a deep breath, at last, the practical realisation hit him; this was the drive unit, the thing that, if it worked, would change everything. The quality of the workmanship was outstanding which he knew it would be. Froom must have had lots of time on his hands. They spent some time going through the operation when Froom heard back from the subcontractor.

"It's pretty simple and if we are OK using their stock materials then they can knock it up by the end of the week. I agreed the price at 1500 quid which, trust me, is cheap." Stuart was already in deep, so another £1,500 was fine.

"It means that you will have a drive that's a real professional unit and assuming it all works will be easily controllable. Sadly that bloody old Fiesta is not of the same quality. Let's have a look at it."

For the first time in his life Stuart was beginning to think his engineering skill was rubbish when compared to Froom. However after a pretty thorough inspection Froom gave it the thumbs up.

"It's not a thing of beauty but the construction is sound, and I like the way you have given the left hand of the car to the controls. I do hope this thing works, Stuart, it's very exciting." Froom did not exude excitement, but Stuart did believe his enthusiasm. "They will deliver the moulding to the factory this Friday, so we should have it all installed to test for the weekend." Froom had committed himself to the project without being asked! Stuart had a number of tasks to complete on the Fiesta that would absorb his time; the major effort was changing the mountings on the Fiesta to accommodate the redesigned frame.

Friday came quickly and, as agreed, Froom arrived by mid-morning. Rob had agreed to help out and was already helping Stuart fix some final things on the Fiesta.

"It's a fantastic job," he said, "they've used a rigid polymer that should hold the unit firmly although it's a bit thicker than I expected. I've got the day off, so we should be able to sort any problems as we go."

They decided to fit the carbon fibre frame into the Fiesta having confirmed that the drive unit would sit correctly in it. They had some problems since the extra thickness did mean some changes to the support structure in the Fiesta, but by mid-afternoon they had the whole unit installed. The control couplings were more of a problem and it was early evening before it was complete. Good sense suggested that they stop then and restart early the next day, and so they retired to Rob's place for some food since Stuart's kitchen was bare. Sue wasn't surprised to receive them and ordered a takeout pizza that together with some cold beers was a perfect end to a very successful day. Stuart was amused to see another side to Froom as he gently flirted with Sue. Froom stayed over with Stuart after letting Mrs Froom know. I must meet her sometime, he mused, who an earth could live with such a man?

They all met around nine the following day. Rob was at pains to advise Froom of the powers involved, the damaged roof being a testament to distracted concentration. They rechecked all the drive installation and coupling controls as well as ensuring all the angles were in a neutral position; finally they attached the battery. Rob nervously got into the driving seat and attached the harness, only then did he think that he should have worn some sort of helmet in case things went badly wrong… fuck it, he thought. He noticed that Froom and Rob were a long way back in readiness for disaster. He connected the drive switch and immediately felt a strong vibration throughout the car. He gently moved the control lever into the lift position and nothing happened although the vibration increased. Stuart decided to shut the drive down, something wasn't right. He got out of the car and explained the results to the other two. They rechecked everything and couldn't find any problems.

"Try again, Stu," said Rob, "it's not like the last experiments, this is big stuff, maybe we need a bigger drive for the weight."

"You know that's not true Rob, maybe it's me, I'm scared shitless to give it too much power."

"Do you want me to do it?" he offered.

"No, I'll have another go," and he re-entered the car. "You can do it," he said to no-one in particular and he moved the lift control quickly up to halfway. There was a massive vibration and the whole Fiesta hurtled upwards, it was several hundred feet up before Stuart had the sense to bring the lever back to around a quarter. Some sense, the Fiesta plunged towards the earth. He knew that in theory it should level out, but he panicked and lifted the controls up again. He could feel the whole of the Fiesta strained under the forces as he slowly reduced the lift control until it hovered, then step by step he gently drew the car down until it was only about 20 feet off the ground and a final movement of the lift controls brought the car down hard onto the ground, the whole fabric of the vehicle groaned as if in pain. Stuart immediately switched off the drive and staggered out of the car. His heart was racing, and he was breathing heavily mainly from fear. The Paradox has gone straight up and straight down with no wandering or variation, Rob had filmed the whole experiment including the fear on Stuart's face as he got out.

"Well done, matey," Rob said clapping him on the back. "Although it was a bit erratic, and you didn't have to go quite so high."

"It wasn't planned, you weren't inside; I was out of control," said Stuart with a shake in his voice.

"Next time try a soft landing, I think the poor old Fiesta suspension took a beating."

Froom said nothing initially and then, "This is... words fail me... it's just amazing and to think I was here for the very first test, how was it Stuart?"

"Well we have proved it works but we need to rethink the controls," he said with more composure. "We need a phase that just initiates the lift to start with."

"Sure, sure, but have you any idea what's just happened here?"

"This has been a long road, Froom, and that last experience has shaken me."

"We should have some champagne," said Rob.

"I think a nice cuppa and a debrief from Stuart," Froom said.

They went inside for that cuppa and Stuart explained all he had done.

"Well, you were getting used to the controls," said Rob.

"Yes I was, Rob, but they are not sensitive enough and I need a base elevation to start with."

"Easily solved," Froom chipped in. I can change the gearing on all the levers and make the lever itself a little longer, which should increase sensitivity. I'll get onto it." Froom went back to the Paradox.

"He's keen," said Rob.

"He is an unbelievable help," said Stuart. "I couldn't have got here without him... and... I have a second drive unit to experiment with as well! Come and have a look. I wouldn't mind your thoughts on another vehicle, frankly I'm not sure the Fiesta will survive."

"Paradox2 already!" said Rob with a grin.

They spent some time discussing the creation of a vehicle from scratch but agreed to defer things until they had more information.

"What we need, Rob, is a startup mechanism that alters the horizontal angle just slightly, to lift the Paradox to say five feet."

"And the same in reverse, so that when you switch off, it slowly descends from five feet to the ground, no crash landing."

"Exactly, now let's get back to Froom, I don't know what he's doing and then we can look at this startup approach."

Around that time an Air Traffic Controller at NATS Swanwick had identified a strange signal in the Smythfield area. The signal lasted only about 30 seconds and was probably an illegal drone or some other clutter; she recorded it anyway.

Froom had nearly completed the changes to the controls, it had been a simple task since he found most of the parts he needed from adapted equipment that Stuart had hoarded.

"Stuart, you are just like me, you hoard lots of stuff," he really enjoyed scavenging among the shelves in the workshops. "I have put the controls into three phases by slugging the signals to the solenoid."

"How have you done it, Froom?" Rob asked.

"Well I overheard your idea about a startup phase and included a small angle limit which will just cause the Fiesta to hover although I don't know how high, but we can sort that later. Then there is a second phase, which delays the signal to the solenoid and also has an inhibitor, and finally there is the raw power linked directly to the controls. I'm just in the process of putting the switch mechanism in, plus lengthening the joystick."

The three of them reviewed the new controls as well as checking the damage on the vehicle. One of the modified suspension struts had sheared and they had to reweld it back in place, apart from that the Fiesta had taken the stress remarkably well.

Stuart strapped himself into Paradox again; he could feel his heart racing as he nervously switched on the drive. The vibrations restarted as he rose about ten feet into the air and hovered. He debated bringing the vehicle back down to adjust the height but decided to test on the second phase of the controls. Having switched to that phase, he relaxed a little and shifted the joystick gently up, the Paradox responded, and the vibrations seemed to ease. He could see Rob and Froom waving. He moved the stick further up and Paradox rose to around 300 feet. Stuart could see all around him the houses and gardens, the nearby forest, as well as the motorway in the far distance. He stayed at that height for about a minute before bringing Paradox back down to its base hover height and finally to the ground with a gentle bump.

He leaped out and grabbed Froom "You are one hell of an engineer, Froom, that was fantastic."

Froom was slightly embarrassed but said, "OK, so now can we go in it?"

It was a repeat of that time when they hadn't thought seriously about the power involved, nevertheless Stuart said, "OK guys let's do it. But before going up again let's reduce the hover height."

It was a simple exercise for Froom who showed the other two how to adjust the controls. Then they all got into Paradox with Rob in the front and Froom in the rear.

"I don't have a harness for you, guys," said Stuart.

"It's OK, Stu, I have a seat belt."

"I don't have anything," moaned Froom.

"I'm not sure how she will respond to the extra weight, so we will take it easy."

"Yes please," yelled Froom as Stuart started the hover phase. It's true that the vibrations seemed louder but apart from that, the Paradox rose to about four feet from the ground. Stuart switched to the second phase and moved the vehicle up to around 40 feet and hovered.

"Try some forward motion," yelled Rob.

"Will it run in second phase, Froom?" Stuart asked. Froom nodded positively. He eased the controls forward and Paradox moved across his rooftop. Stuart didn't want to be seen so he steered towards the forest and gently cruised for a few minutes. Deer broke cover form the forest and the three of them laughed; it was a mix of adrenalin and euphoria combined.

He brought Paradox to roughly the start point and went to hover phase before landing. He switched the system of and they all got out. "I'm not going to test the raw power on this thing yet; I think it would break up," he said.

Rob nodded agreement. "Well the second phase is probably more than enough power to prove your discovery anyway."

"What we need is to find someone who knows how to build high speed planes with all the associated stress," added Froom. "There are some talented people in the RAF at Farnborough."

The rest of the day was spent refining detail on Paradox. Both Rob and Froom had experience of flying the vehicle - if flying was the right word. One major change to the mountings significantly reduced the vibrations and noise such that hovering at 200 feet became a quiet experience. On one occasion, daredevil Rob went up very high although without an altimeter they didn't know exactly how high.

The NATS controller did know the height though and was taking interest in what she now thought was a drone operator breaking the law.

It was early evening when they stopped, and they did break open a bottle of champagne; even Froom had a glass.

"You've opened Pandora's box, Stuart," he said. "Have you any idea of the impact this discovery of yours will have? It touches just about every facet of human existence."

"You're being melodramatic, Froom," Rob said in a joking way.

"No I'm not," he replied angrily. "Look Stuart, you need to get the government supporting you now... and I do mean right now. Promise me you will get someone onto it... ideally the ear of the government's Chief Scientific Advisor."

"It was in my plan, Froom, but I was going to get more facts together first." He did remember Harry's advice. "But you're right, it may be rough and ready, but the time is now."

The following day Stuart spoke to Paul Brighton who confirmed that the process was going well, and he would have patent protection in the next couple of weeks. All the trademarks had been registered and the LeviProp Company was now ready to trade. He ignored the paperwork from Zoe's solicitors and instead researched the best people to contact in government. He also reviewed his summary of LeviProp and made some changes in the light of his recent experiences. He debated about removing the section on his theory that gravity was made up of several forces and that his discovery had harnessed one in particular. He felt sure that his theory also supported the notion of dark matter.

He decided to target Sir Neil Foster, the government CSA Head, as well as Tessa Primrose-Smith the business CSA and Sir Roger Wall the Defence CSA. He emailed his summary to each of them with an offer of demonstration. He also decided to send a follow up hardcopy with recorded delivery.

The next few days were frustrating since try as he might he couldn't penetrate the barriers that the civil service had erected to prevent him contacting anyone. He got "We will get back to you," through to "It's not our department". In every instance his approaches were thwarted. He contacted his local MP who promised to help but never came back to him and so he decided that the personal approach was best. He knew what Sir Roger Wall looked like from the government website and indeed Sir Roger had a distinguished scientific career at Cambridge. Stuart went to the MoD department in Whitehall and asked to see Sir Roger. The receptionist said that he would be in late morning but couldn't see an appointment for Stuart so regretfully… etc.

He decided to wait outside on the off-chance that he could see Sir Roger, and as luck would have it, he arrived in a black government car around eleven. Stuart approached as he got out the car. He was a small man with a pinched face and deep-set eyes with dark shadows, his pallor was almost ill in colour. He was carrying a heavy bag full of papers.

"Sir Roger?"

"Yes, do I know you?" he said with a frown.

"I'm Stuart Ashley; I sent you a paper on my discovery, LeviProp?"

"Never heard of it," he said, as he made his way up the steps with Stuart following. Stuart was unaware of the two security officers who were regarding him intently.

"I just want a few minutes of your time."

"Sorry I'm late for a meeting," and he looked imploringly at the officers who were moving towards him.

"Is this man bothering you, Sir Roger?" the smaller of two large men said.

"No not really," he sighed. "But I'm late for a meeting."

"Sorry sir, this is a secure office, you can't come in."

Stuart yelled across them, "I only need a few minutes, it will change the world." Sir Roger ignored him and went through the revolving door leaving Stuart with the two men.

"I suggest you move on, sir, you can't hang around outside here."

He was about to protest with something about a free nation but decided to leave it. Sir Roger would regret this, he thought. On the train home he decided that demonstration was the only way to get their attention. The dilemma was that Stuart needed to publicise LeviProp to get government attention and yet he didn't want any attention until he was sure the patents were all solid. Could he pull off something public and yet conceal himself? He decided to do something at Sir Roger's old college at Cambridge. He looked at the map and planned to drive there with Paradox on a trailer.

He found a quiet area near the Downing boathouse where he hoped to park and memorised the short distance across the Cam to the College Quad. The next day was warm and dry and Stuart set off for Cambridge with Paradox. He had already tried to manoeuvre Paradox onto the trailer and decided that it was easier to leave her in hover mode and position the trailer underneath. He was surprised to find a quiet parking spot and lost no time in releasing Paradox from the trailer. He switched on the drive and it seemed to all be OK after the journey. He couldn't see anyone around although he was sure it would all be very public, very quickly. He took Paradox into hover mode and quickly brought her up to a hover at about 60 feet, the route seemed very clear as he flew over the Cam towards Regent Street; he could see lots of people staring at the strange shape. He flew over the main gates and centred Paradox on the grass in the Quad. He was going to land there for a few moments but instead just hovered long enough to surprise people. He dropped the parcel; students were already coming towards him and so he accelerated upwards and back to the waiting trailer. It was still quiet when he returned, and it only took a couple of minutes to settle the vehicle onto the trailer. He strapped it back on, and covered Paradox with a dirty old tarpaulin. As he had planned, the whole exercise had been over in 15 minutes and yet he hoped it had the desired impact. The small parcel was addressed to Sir Roger and inside on a piece of wood was crudely written, "You had your chance."

Stuart was home by late afternoon and found Alice waiting for him. He had sent a note to all the team to let them of his successful first flight and Alice was so keen to see it she set off from Wales that same day. As part of her research project she had been working with a colleague from Swansea Uni, she also found it much easier to scrounge high performance compute time there.

"It has to be you and the Cambridge attack," she said. "It's all over the papers about a mystery UFO attacking Downing College.

It doesn't take long for the truth to get distorted, he thought.

"Don't deny it, Stuart, your face is a dead giveaway," she said with a laugh.

Stuart laughed too. "It's a fair cop, guv," he said.

"But why were you attacking the college?"

"I wasn't," and he went on to explain the background.

Alice just couldn't stop laughing. "It must be one hell of a machine to do that," she added.

"The breakthrough came when an old work colleague called Froom got involved. I had created a new drive unit that can fly in any direction, but it needed an expert engineer to help me make it. We now have a drive that can easily be commercialised.

"OK, show it to me, you bastard," she said impatiently.

Stuart removed the tarpaulin to reveal the UFO, which of course was exactly what it was!

"It sort of looks like a Ford Fiesta on drugs!"

"It is, come on hop in, the least I can do is take you for a spin."

Stuart was getting too cocky for his own good, Alice thought, as she got in. He went to hover mode explaining the need for this first step as a buffer to the raw power. He then soared to a few hundred feet with Alice squealing as they zoomed over the forest towards Portsmouth. He swung Paradox back to his house and landed perfectly.

As he did so, the NATS people were building more data on the phenomenon.

They went down the pub having secured the Paradox. "It's a great name," she said.

Stuart brought her up to speed on everything that happened after the near disaster day and how he was trying to find someone in Government to sponsor the development.

"When I was away I thought a lot about your theory and I'm sorry I dismissed it so quickly. It's becoming clear to me that we have always thought of gravity as a singularity and yet the more it's considered as a number of components that exist together but differently throughout the cosmos, the more it makes sense. The terrestrial manifestation is just that, a local equilibrium. In this view the nature of dark matter may have a clearer fit."

Stuart was intrigued with her comment on dark matter. "Anyway I have completed most of my doctorate, so I can now spend more time helping out, that is if you want me."

"Who would turn down a brain like yours?"

"What about my body?" she laughed.

"Easy, Alice, one bit at a time," he retorted. They got back to his house to discover the whole 'attack' on Downing College had gone viral. Apart from photographs, there were a couple of passable videos as well. It had made headline news but there was no mention of Sir Roger who had explained to the police that he had no knowledge of a grudge against him or indeed anyone who had some sort of helicopter. Meanwhile Stuart's paper sat in a pending file on his assistant's desk.

"I made a mistake," he said after some time. "For some reason, Sir Roger isn't going to help, so it's Plan B."

"Which is?"

"Showing Paradox to Parliament; hopefully someone will take it seriously."

"Careful, Stuart, it could be misconstrued as a terrorist attack and who knows what will happen."

"You're right; of course I will avoid any threatening moves."

"When are you going to do it?"

"It's best that you don't know."

"Look, I have lots of connections at Uni, I am sure one of them knows a CSA somewhere. You go ahead with your plan, but I will try to open discussions my end… deal?"

He thought for a while. "Deal." Alice left, thinking about how she was going to pull this off.

Stuart checked Paradox over the next day he tightened some parts that had vibrated lose but couldn't find any problems. He remembered to order an altimeter on line and then started thinking about Plan B. It needed to be something showy that clearly did not have any threat. Entry and exit via the Thames would be good, plus something that no other vehicle could do, under some bridges, up Whitehall around Trafalgar square and back. This is mad, what the hell am I thinking? The Cambridge venture was a stupid thing to do; it was a frustrated and angry response to a mundane civil servant going about his business. Alice is right, matters will take their course and what's the urgency anyway? The more time I have, the more improvements I can make, as well as developing some experiments to reinforce the theory. I can even start the new vehicle with the second drive.

He had given himself a good talking to and felt so much better. He could also develop his skills at piloting Paradox; after all he hadn't really tested the raw power yet. He immediately sent a note to Alice confirming Plan B was dead and received a 'good' message back straight away. There were many other emails from the team about the Cambridge incident asking if it was true, Stuart decided to send a general to all of them confirming what had happened, Mike Lester was particularly angry with him saying that he was behaving in a cavalier way.

There were two things he needed to sort out anyway, firstly he went to Portsmouth where he bought a helmet from a motorcycle shop and then to Maplin's to get an extended two-way radio with headset. When he got home he decided to get more practice with the Paradox. He knew that eventually he would be identified and linked with the Cambridge affair but in some way that was the outcome he wanted. It was fortunate that he was near the forest so hopefully he wouldn't interfere with any traffic. The acceleration in the second phase was awesome and Stuart couldn't help but think of trying out the raw third phase of the machine. It was around 500 feet when he set the controls on minimum and switched to the third phase and knowing that the controls would be super sensitive, eased the stick upwards. The kick in his back was hard and he found himself accelerating upwards, he immediate switched back to second phase. The vehicle had misted up and it was very cold, moreover Stuart didn't have a clue to where he was except he was very high; he felt dizzy. He started to panic since he couldn't see anything, so he put the controls into reverse and hoped he was descending at the same angle as he lost consciousness. When he came round he was still light-headed, he tried to clear the windscreen and eventually managed to see the coastline. Oh God, where the fuck am I?

Paradox continued to descend, and Stuart recovered, he recognised the Isle of Wight. The only way home was to navigate by roads or places he knew and so finally he reached the forest where he had started and then back home. He landed Paradox and just sat there, still shaking. One thing for sure this is too powerful for me, even if I was a good pilot and I'm not! That was it... he grounded himself.

NATS had now started screening the area for activity when Stuart's last episode was identified.

"It's definitely not a drone," she said to the senior controller who was beside her screens. It climbed from just under 400 feet to nearly 5,000 feet incredibly quickly, faster than a military jet. They continued tracking Stuart's journey back to Smythfield. "Got him!" she said. "I can confirm it's the identical location to the last tracking."

"I'll let the police and the MoD know," said the senior controller. "Meanwhile, ensure that we have a continuous monitor on the area."

CHAPTER 11

Things Become Clearer

The convoy from the airport to Ottawa town centre was quick, largely due to the support of the motorcycle outriders. Stuart couldn't see much through the darkened glass so instead considered his meeting with Lawrence Banard. He liked Lawrence, once he dropped his pretentious bullshit; he felt he was an honest man in as much as any politician was honest. He certainly wasn't going to get conned into anything and wasn't even sure what value he had anymore. His work and the discovery had changed everything; even the most sceptical scientists had changed their minds. His initial theory had been proved and extended by better brains than his, although he still had ideas for further development that he and Gary Marshall had debated when in Farnborough. Part of that thinking concerned the future consumption of the IC power and the knock-on effect on Universe, after all there is no such thing as free power. They passed a modern stone sculpture that was the frontispiece to a sweeping canopy entrance to a hotel.

"This is the Hilton Lac-Leamy, it's a great hotel and Lawrence has a suite here," said Pierre.

"I thought I would be meeting him at parliament," said Stuart.

"This is more discreet… and safer," Pierre said, as they got out of the car and headed through the entrance to a waiting lift. They emerged into a large reception area with wooden panelling and leather armchairs. It was poorly lit and the various table lamps further accentuated the place as a transit station into one of the many discreetly hidden doors.

Two women and a man greeted him, Pierre introduced them as Susan Thomas from the Department of Foreign Affairs and Trade, Giselle Arnaut from Canadian Security and Henri Peint from CMoD. Stuart recited their names to himself to register them in his memory, as he did so he found it hard to reconcile them with their roles. Henri didn't look military at all, he was tall, but he didn't have the posture of a man who had spent a lot of his life in uniform, moreover he had soft and gentle feature with smiling blue eyes. As for Giselle and Susan, well it looked like they had got the jobs the wrong way round. Susan looked unlike a Foreign Office civil servant and more like a security person with her short greying hair and wire spectacles and a poorly-fitting grey trouser suit, whereas Giselle was just an archetype bureaucrat in her mid-fifties, slim with dyed blond hair tied into a bun, and elegant scarf that enhanced her bright pink lipstick topped off with an expensive designer dress and very high heels.

Stuart mentally pinched himself… over the last 18 months I have been shafted by the likes of Henri, Susan and Giselle… ignore their appearance, Stuart. Pierre had excused himself to let Lawrence know that Stuart had arrived and after less than a minute he appeared at one of the doorways booming,

"Stuart, why does trouble follow you everywhere? Even Canada for God's sake, come on in, I see you've met the team."

"Team?"

"Well people who wanted to meet you then," he said cautiously.

It was a very large room with one complete wall given over to a fantastic view across the lake. The glass sliding doors led to a large balcony with numerous reclining chairs. The other walls were panelled but in a light wood. There was a vast desk to the left with a number of carefully disguised filing cabinets and to the right, near the entrance, was a conference table for ten-plus people together with a tray carrying refreshments. In front of the big window were three large sofas in black leather each with a supporting coffee table.

"Let's sit over here," Lawrence said, leading the way to the sofas. Judging by the body language Stuart was sure that the 'team' had not visited before.

"So you've had a rough time recently, Stuart?" he asked.

Stuart recounted everything he remembered of his abduction. "I still don't know who they were, but my guess is that they were Brits... but why? I can't figure it."

"Let's get some ground rules straight," said Lawrence. "I am," he paused, "acting as a go-between on behalf of the Canadian Government. Since we have met before, they asked me to facilitate a meeting with these folk. Before they introduce themselves to you, I must stress this meeting is off the record."

"In my experience, that means everyone here can deny everything what they say; so what's the point?"

"I thought you would say that, so I have asked the British High Commissioner here in Ottawa to join us so that he is a witness to the meeting and your government knows what's going on. I also let Peter Dawson know."

"So what exactly is going on?" said Stuart rather irritably.

"Well unlike our cousins next door I will be straight with you. We want to commercially exploit your LeviProp discovery. Our government has two choices: await another country becoming a leader in the technology and being beholden to them for our infrastructure or; applying our considerable talent to developing a home-grown business in LeviProp. The development as I understand it is still at early stages and as you know the UN meeting a few months ago drew out varying country positions."

"It was an amazing demonstration of complete deviousness by every country, I nearly felt sorry for you," Stuart added.

Lawrence grinned. "Like you, I believe this invention of yours should benefit the whole world and I genuinely did hold out hope that something might come out of the UN meeting, but sadly it's not to be; nothing changes. Our country is vast and needs this infrastructure; the wealth that could be created with this technology will secure our international position and avoid US domination."

"Can I chip in here, Lawrence?" said Giselle. "As you know, I'm from CSIS and was involved in the discussion with Al Smith in Halifax. Al was our local officer who communicated with Chief Morgan to Paul Homer."

"Paul's a very good officer," Stuart added.

"You won't be surprised that like other agencies, your invention and its development had been on our radar for a while. We had a view that the US was playing the UK into this scientific alliance idea just to fuck them over. We had some good feedback from Lawrence about the informal aspects of the UN meeting which confirmed our views and when our sources heard Leo Catani bragging about the quality of his development team, we knew you and the UK were being stitched up."

"Go on," prompted Stuart.

"It put poor old Dawson in a difficult position since he had been driving the alliance and was now in an impossible position. Bruckner wasn't going to give you up, so he only had one choice; to extract you, we knew it was a British exercise since one of your frigates appeared just out of territorial waters on the east coast."

"You are very well informed," said Stuart, it all added up.

"That's our job," she said, "and don't let's understate it; we know of several groups here in Canada who want to get hold of you... hence the security. Sorry, Lawrence, I just want to speak before the UK chap joins us."

"Thanks, Giselle, ok let's get Christopher Ball in." As he entered, Stuart was surprised at his youth; he couldn't be more than mid-thirties. He wore a beige linen suit with a white open neck shirt and loafers... not the career FO civil servant. He had a ruddy complexion, greying mousy hair but a ready smile with a twinkle in his eyes.

"Shall we do the introductions?" said Lawrence. "I guess you know who I am?"

"I certainly do, sir," came the reply, "and Susan and I have met before." She acknowledged him, he then introduced Giselle and Henri. Giselle outlined her role and specifically highlighted their knowledge of the Dawson/Bruckner bust up. Ball just nodded, taking it all in.

Henri followed on from Giselle, he said he was in the meeting because the military application of LeviProp was a game changer and it had to be part of any decision that was made. It was clear that Henri was on the scientific side of the military as he had a good grasp of IC and the workings of LeviProp.

Christopher Ball had been passive throughout the discussion, which finished with Lawrence saying, "Before you came in I said that this meeting is off the record but that our objective, that is the Canadian Government, is keen to see if there is some collaboration to develop LeviProp here."

Ball had his briefcase open and withdrew some papers. "Like you, Lawrence, this meeting never happened unless we can get an agreed outcome. I would like to spend some private time with Stuart afterwards if that's OK?"

Before Lawrence could say anything Stuart chipped in, "Fine by me," he awaited a challenge, but it never came.

"You're in Canada now, Stuart, you're not in our control," he said with heavy irony.

"I must say that your intelligence and analysis is spot on. HMG has got itself in a real pickle," more irony and typical British understatement, Stuart thought.

"Our relationship with the US is strained to say the least. Although they know it, they can't prove that we extracted Stuart," he said calmly. "Indeed we have all been manipulated, including you, Lawrence. The US is playing a complex game and the UN charade, only made it even more complex." Stuart looked at Lawrence, to see his reaction; he knew Ball was right.

Ball continued, "The turning point was when you foolishly put some of your theory on the internet. Pandora's Box was open, and the starting gun had been fired."

"I thought I was doing the right thing," snapped Stuart.

"That's as maybe," retorted Ball. "The fact is every military power knew that all their equipment would rapidly become redundant once LeviProp was exploited. The US Government foresaw it immediately, which is why they pumped so much money and resource into your development programme in Farnborough. We now know that they were sending all the findings to Catani's team on the west coast."

"You now know?" queried Giselle.

"Yes, well maybe we were too trusting to start, but we had a pretty good idea when the whole UN alliance thing kicked off."

"So why didn't you intervene?" said Stuart. "You just left me there."

"It was a Cabinet decision, if we had pulled you back it would look like the UK was out for itself and anyway we wanted to see what other countries' positions were." He said rather lamely, he didn't really know.

"So what happens now?" said Lawrence.

"Well the race is on, and we try to pick up the pieces. It's uncomfortable saying you've screwed up; but we have. We know that Catani's people think you have more knowledge than you have shared. If you add the other countries who want to get hold of you then you are at serious risk, Stuart. I promise you... no more half-truths or bullshit."

"I said the same to Stuart earlier," Giselle added.

"So, Stuart, what do you want to do?" Lawrence asked. "After all, it's your chance to retake control of your life."

"Thanks, Lawrence, I've been thinking exactly the same thing." But I haven't figured out what I want, he thought. I wish there was a chance of reconciliation with Zoe? She seemed more positive to him when they last met. Certainly the kids had mellowed towards him as well. Pick up some time with Harry, and have fun? The trouble is they would always be looking over their shoulder and I can't do that to her... she is a free spirit. Everything I have seen of Canada is appealing, it's a great country and the people are pretty straight. I would love to see LeviProp developed for commercial use... as for the military stuff... well it's beyond my control anyway. I would love to develop my ideas a bit further but probably at home; at home? Isn't that where the government screws you? I would want some real assurance. All these thoughts were spinning around when he noticed that the others had gone over to the coffee tray; he went over to join them.

"A lot to think about?" It was Lawrence. "Take your time, we have a great suite here for you, with lots of facilities, even sailing on the lake... fully protected," he added.

A little while later they restarted the meeting and Susan Thomas took the lead. Essentially the deal was a good one. Stuart would retain his IP and license it to a new Canadian company. The company would include Stuart on the board with a lucrative share deal plus salary. The company would only operate in the commercial arena and any military development would be part of a separate government owned organisation.

"I created a similar company in the UK although it was specifically aimed at the transport sector, perhaps the two could collaborate since I wouldn't want a conflict of interests."

"That sounds reasonable," Susan responded.

They went through more detail over a working lunch and Stuart noted that it was being recorded even though the meeting hadn't happened!! By mid-afternoon Lawrence wound the meeting up with a good summary, Stuart reflected how well he had chaired the UN meeting. They all agreed to meet again in two days' time to give Stuart time to consider his position and also continue his meeting with Christopher Ball.

They reconvened in Stuart's suite and it was even better than Lawrence's description, clearly designed for visiting dignitaries, with several bedrooms, a library, a large sitting room with a bar area, as well as its own gym and small indoor pool. Giselle went with them to explain the security arrangements. There were various people in specific locations outside the suite, which were designed for security purposes. The suite had a series of alarms as well as a safe room just by the entrance. Giselle highlighted the various cameras in the suite.

"So that's it, Stuart, all in the interests of being open with you. However there is a weakness around the balcony area; we don't anticipate anyone taking a shot at you, but it is a possible extract space, so I would prefer if you don't use it."

As she left Stuart looked at Ball and said, "They're a pretty good bunch."

"Still I would prefer that we do talk on the balcony." Stuart got a cold beer from the bar and walked out to the balcony. Ball helped himself and followed. "Do you realise that I haven't spoken to a British person one-to-one for months?"

"We could have treated you worse but it's hard to see how," he replied.

"Is that your view... or that of HMG?"

"As with so many politicians, they cannot accept they are wrong. Frankly there are those that in private admit they were wrong and got screwed, and there are the other animals that despite everything always go on the offensive to defend their decisions."

A profound and cynical observation Stuart thought; he was beginning to like Ball. "And which is Dawson?"

"Well, he's my boss, so in theory I need to be loyal," he began with a grin. "However you would be surprised to know that he is one of the rare breed who accepted responsibility publicly and I know he offered his resignation to the PM, who incidentally, asked him to stay."

Stuart was intrigued. "So how much do you know?"

"Not a lot," he replied, "I do have a pretty good idea around the recent events though."

"Go on."

"Well... about six months ago I was in the UK when President Roper put the UN programme to the PM. The Cabinet was in a bit of a mess as I see it. They had already agreed to the scientific alliance with the US and were concerned that the US was already developing a secret offshoot to apply the LeviProp for military uses; something that they denied, but we had growing intelligence otherwise. We were all worried that your invention would have such a profound impact on the world that it needed to be controlled but no-one knew how, so the UN idea seemed like a good solution."

"That's how I saw it too," said Stuart.

"We now know that part of their agenda was to further their commercial aspects of LeviProp using you as a stimulus to the development programme."

"It's a shame no-one asked me... and... by the way... that's not how Dawson presented it!"

"Frankly, Stuart, the US only needed your name... or so they thought."

"Anyway, as I said, the UK Cabinet grabbed the UN programme as a possible solution to the enabling of LeviProp to the world stage."

"I still don't get it," Stuart replied. "Apart from the commercialisation, what was the US agenda then?"

"That part isn't clear; the UK view is that they wanted to draw out various country positions. They see LeviProp as a threat both militarily and economically. Given the outcome, maybe they got a result, or more likely, that they are planning something else."

"Such as?"

"I don't know, but my guess is they will want to forge some new alliances with countries that have as much to lose as themselves."

Everything Ball had said made sense. He reflected that a chance discovery of his had created such a complexity of tensions throughout the world. "So what should I do?" He didn't know why he would trust a complete stranger like Ball but perhaps he valued his opinion.

Ball thought for a while, sipping his beer. "I would forget about all the military implications. After all, you can't change any of it. Old animosities, envy, military distrust, religious hatred, political egos and more, they are all in play."

"Do you know what? I seriously thought that my discovery could help the whole world," he said shaking his head.

"I had my idealism knocked out of me year ago," Ball responded. "It turned into the worst form of cynicism… but now, well I still believe there is goodness in people even when misdirected." He looked slightly embarrassed. "So start with the things you can change rather than the whole world." He was back to his grin.

"So if I take up Lawrence's offer and integrate with the original plans for the UK business?"

"Stuart I can't give you a UK government position what I can say is that they can't stop you. Indeed by keeping the UK engaged they might see an upside."

"So is Dawson still around?" he said, changing the subject.

"Yes and Rose and Nigel are still there too. He has had his wings clipped a little but the ultimate responsibility for the UN fiasco rests with Linda Ramsay. I think as PM she was in awe of Roper and lost her perspective, she didn't want to damage the 'special relationship' whatever that is."

Stuart suddenly felt tired and excused himself from Ball; Karen Stone had said that it would take a couple of months before he recovered fully. He lay on the bed and thought about the day's events; he had already decided to take up Lawrence's offer and immerse himself in work. Tomorrow he would ask Chris Ball for any information of Zoe and the family and also see if they could track Harry's whereabouts. He ordered a meal and some decent wine from room service and flipped through some old films on a massive TV. I wonder who is paying for all this, he thought, and the security... is it real?

He awoke to the sound of the house telephone; it was Christopher Ball. "Come on down for breakfast, if you're up for it, I will show you some of the town; it's agreed with the security folk."

Stuart showered and dressed quickly and realised he would like to get some decent clothes. As he left his suite, he was conscious of the security people discreetly following; they were not so discreet when he entered the lift. He found the restaurant and saw Ball waving from a table overlooking the lake. He was wearing another casual suit and looked pleased to see him, it really was difficult not to like this man.

"Good sleep?" he enquired.

"Fantastic," Stuart replied, "this is the first time I can relax and think clearly for a long time."

"Who is paying for this, do you know?"

"It's the Canadian Government; they hope you will think positively towards them... plus they don't want an incident, and this place is well covered from a security standpoint."

"I've got some ideas for an exploration of Ottawa over the next few days and as I mentioned, it's all been cleared with Giselle."

"I must get some new clothes, but I don't have any money or cards."

"Let me have your details and I will sort it out."

Stuart gave him the account numbers and sort code for his bank as well two credit card numbers with associated details.

"I don't know how you can remember all that stuff; I can't even remember one of my cards." They went through the plans for the day over breakfast. As they were finishing a man joined them introducing himself as Paul Joplin.

"Giselle asked me to coordinate your security for your stay in Canada. I understand you have a relaxing day planned seeing our great city."

"I was just going through the itinerary with Stuart."

"Great, is it ok for me to join you to check that I have the same plan?"

"Delighted," said Stuart. "Fancy a coffee?"

They spent the next 20 minutes discussing the day and Paul had lots of good advice. As they were talking, a middle-aged couple came over to them; they all tensed.

"I'm sorry to invade your privacy," the lady said, "but my husband wanted to meet you, but thought it too rude to interrupt your breakfast."

"My apologies," the man said, "but I just wanted to say how excited I am by your discovery. I'm Professor John Lane and I head up the natural science faculty here at Ottawa." He offered his card. "I'm sure you are busy, but I would love to spend some time discussing IC with you. Perhaps you could come to the University?"

"I'm Madge by the way, and I recognised you from the newspaper. I do hope you will support John, it would be a real feather in his cap."

A pushy lady, Stuart thought, "May I see the newspaper?"

"Please take it," she replied.

It would be good to get back to discussing IC after all the cloak and dagger stuff he thought, but only if Paul clears it. "What do you think Paul?"

"I will need to check it out but if you have time then it's up to you. Can I have the card? We will get back to you, Professor." They shook hands and the couple left.

Paul's radio beeped, and he excused himself to talk. Both Stuart and Ball suddenly realised that they were attracting the attention of the diners following the Professor's introduction. When Paul returned he looked worried.

"We have a problem," he said, "the press is everywhere; it's just a matter of time before they come in here. My guys are organising a rear exit." Another of Paul's men appeared and led them downstairs to a rear service exit. Somehow the word had got out, since there was already a group of people by the exit. Paul's people expertly manoeuvred him to the waiting Mercedes.

"It's not going to be like this the whole day I hope?"

"Sorry, Stuart, I won't guarantee that we can avoid it," said Paul as the cavalcade set off. In fact it was a good day; they visited the Rideau Falls and then down the canal to the Hill for a visit to parliament. Following the tour of the building, Lawrence had somehow arranged a formal reception with the great and the good of Ottawa. Lillian Maglan, the current PM, hosted it with many political and business leaders present; he was being feted that's for sure.

The PM gave a short speech about the progress of science and technology; she spoke about the occasions where something disruptive came along such as IC. Lawrence then said a few words emphasising the importance of Canada seizing the opportunity that IC offers and presuming that collaboration with Stuart was the way forward.

Stuart felt a little trapped. Had he been set up? Anyway, he was asked to say a few impromptu words. Firstly he thanked the emergency service for their kindness and care when he was at Halifax. He also thanked the police and security services for supporting him. He then went on to say that disruptive technologies need an open political and societal environment if they are to be developed successfully. He emphasised that he felt that Canada had all the right qualifications; Lawrence looked on with a smile, as did Christopher Ball. It was a light lunch, but Stuart did have a little too much wine and became rather too expansive about some countries trying to dominate him and his discoveries. Chris Ball took him away to the Rideau Centre to get him some clothes and sober him up. After a satisfying purchase of clothes they went on to the Bytown Museum and market, returning to the rear of the hotel around six in the evening. Paul and his team ensured that Stuart got past the numerous people and press and back to his suite.

Chris spent some time looking at messages on his phone.

"It's Peter Dawson," he said, "he will be arriving here around seven tonight and would like to meet up?"

"Do I have a choice?" Stuart frostily replied.

"Stuart he is trying to build bridges, at least give him a chance."

"I bet he is worried that I am going to license LeviProp to the Canadians."

"Are you?"

"Probably; are you joining us?"

"I don't know, I would like to, and I will ask him when I meet him at the airport."

"I hope you can... and... you can be a witness," Stuart said with a laugh.

More seriously, Chris said, "If I am there, Stuart, you can trust me that I will not let you get screwed even if it means losing my job. I know there are all sorts of political shenanigans in the FO, but I still have my own integrity. Anyway I'd best get to the airport." And he left Stuart to contemplate the meeting with someone he once trusted as a friend who had become his Brutus.

Stuart took a shower and unpacked his new clothes and organised them in the wardrobe. It was around 730 that the security phone rang announcing Peter Dawson with Chris Ball. As Stuart let them in he could see that Dawson was tired. Maybe the journey, maybe all the recent events, he mused.

"Hello, Peter, how was your journey, you look tired?"

"I've felt better," was the understatement, "anyway I am so pleased that we can talk."

"Excuse me if I am a bit wary."

"I understand."

"Do you? Do you really fucking understand, sorry but I don't think so? It's easy to outwit a trusting mug like me but to be fucking outwitted by the US and probably lots of other nations...well!!"

Dawson looked down for moment. "You're right and all I can say is 'sorry' although it sounds so weak given everything that has happened." There was an uncomfortable silence.

"I've arranged supper in a private dining room overlooking the lake," said Chris, "the security is fine with Paul Joplin." The discomfort continued as they walked down to the dining room. Despite the tension Stuart was impressed with the room. It was very modern with various diffused lighting and muted greys and whites with some impressive large paintings that added colour. The long glass wall was curved and hung out over the lake; it was lit in some way that provided a glow to the evening sunset over the water. There was an oval table laid for four people with the continuing contemporary theme. In the background Stuart could vaguely hear some classical music that he knew he should recognise. To the side were two large modern settees with a shared table. A waiter offered champagne.

"Who is the extra guest?" Stuart said, pointing to the table.

"Rose was to join us but isn't well," said Dawson sipping from his glass.

"Is there any way we can have a truce, or is this going to be a fucking shitty supper?" Chris blurted out.

Stuart laughed. It was so unlike a professional foreign office diplomat, and Dawson grinned and looked at Stuart for a response. "OK... truce... on one condition."

"Which is?" Dawson looked slightly nervous.

"I want to know everything and no more fucking lies."

Dawson looked relieved. "Agreed, but can I sit down, I am knackered." It was strange how the informality of language had changed.

They all sat down with a refill of champagne and some canapés. Chris asked the waiter to leave; he could be recalled by a button that formed part of a console embedded in the table. The console controlled the volume on the background music, which Chris increased a little.

"I'm not sure about the security in the room," he added.

"I wouldn't worry, Chris, it's clear to me that we are among friends who know a lot more about recent events than I wish."

"Where do you want me to start, Stuart?"

"I don't know, I felt that we had a great development and support at Farnborough and then the US added their weight to things which was fantastic, so when did it change?"

"It did start well, I agree, and we suspected that some of your team were filtering information back to the US. They US wanted to take a bigger global role and made their offer, President to PM, to provide more resource - funding and people - they took control of the timetable as well. Frankly we didn't need the funding and probably didn't need the resource either but the political view following the reciprocity with the US over the years meant that they should have special status. Especially as we are so dependent of the support from the DoD, we also felt that it strengthened our control of any commercialisation." He took a large pull at his drink. "The turning point was when it was raised at the UN Security Council by China. They accused us of developing a secret weapon that would destabilise the existing military balance, since it made many conventional weapons obsolete. Many other countries joined their lobby."

Stuart had listened in silence. The first part where the US has suddenly become a major player in things he guessed was down to politics and money, but he didn't know anything about the UN Security Council meeting nor did Chris Ball judging by his expression. It was a good time to pause the discussion; they had more champagne and ordered the supper. The discussion became more relaxed.

Peter Dawson restarted. "It was a bit of an ambush since Russia also joined in and France stayed neutral. The US took the position that they were aware of the UK's programme and offered to find a way forward. I think all the players knew how closely the US was involved but wanted to see the next step."

"Did the US say why they took this approach?"

"No, but it made Bruckner look like the peace broker while the UK was the rogue. You can't imagine the diplomatic discussions that happened over several months; it almost went into meltdown. The president finally came back to the PM with the TANGENT proposal which would open up the IC developments to the whole world and defused the situation."

"Is that when you discussed it with me?"

"Yes, at that time it looked like a good plan and operating under the UN badge it would provide an open position for every country to exploit. You did support it?"

"Of course I did, it's what I wanted all along."

"So the real reason why the TANGENT programme was put together was known by very few people."

"Excluding me," said Chris Ball.

"Chris, you would be amazed at how few people knew; there were only three members of the Cabinet, for example. We had been setup by the US and should have been on our guard from then on, but we weren't."

"So what happened next?"

"The proposition was put to the Security Council who after some changes endorsed it; although Russia abstained. One of the changes was that you had to be a sponsor to it, ensuring all the information on IC was available. The US agreed to continue to lead the programme."

"So the US agenda was different?"

"No, like you, we actually thought the TANGENT programme was real, but the US agenda was all about control. They couldn't stop other countries developing IC programmes or stealing LeviProp ideas, but they could control or influence the timetable and release of information. At the same time they used the programme to spy on other countries an also maintain their own military lead."

It was a lot to take in; even Chris Ball shook his head in disbelief.

"There are also some other agendas that Bruckner had, or has, that we still don't know about. The net is that we folded some of the development team and transferred you to the US to support the TANGENT programme. The next thing we heard was the attempted kidnap. We knew there was another game when they reported that you had gone missing from New York. They made a big thing of looking for you and in truth had transferred you to Glens Falls."

"They said that I was in danger and that there were factions that wanted to disrupt the UN initiative and that they had agreed with you that I go to secure location whilst the TANGENT proposition was put together in coming months. I knew I was a captive when they wouldn't allow me to contact anyone."

"We discovered your whereabouts in Glens Falls about two months later and when we challenged Bruckner, the response was that they had strong suspicion of threats to your welfare and would only release you once the UN meeting was in plan. Despite numerous attempts to try and see you, Bruckner would not budge."

"You didn't try very hard, did you?"

"No, we didn't," he said with a sigh. "But once the UN meeting had broken down there were no more reasons for you to stay and we did put the pressure on, but well you know the rest; we had to resort to other means."

"Some means," Stuart scoffed.

"I said I'm sorry, Stuart; if you want me to eat fucking humble pie.. say it!" It was rare for Dawson to swear. There was a knock on the door as the waiters arrived with supper and broke the tension.

They sat down to eat. "I don't suppose you have any news of Zoe and the kids?"

"Actually I did ask Rose to make sure we had an update. She saw her at your old house. She seems settled and the kids are well, but it's best if you hear it from her tomorrow."

They discussed Stuart's thoughts for collaborating with the Canadian Government and Peter Dawson thought it a good idea. He saw the British company as vital to the UK's interests and wanted to discuss its future and the way it could fit with a Canadian development. Stuart's head said that the British Government didn't deserve anything after the way he had been treated, but his heart said that he couldn't desert the country of his birth; stupid thing this nationalism.

They worked through the details of the proposition for the rest of the meal. It was good for Stuart to clarify what the Canadian operation would look like, as well as the UK setup and how the two could collaborate. Chris Ball made some notes such that Stuart could use them for the meeting tomorrow. In the end, it was agreed that Chris would join him for the meeting since it might need some British Government input. By ten o'clock Peter Dawson really looked exhausted and so the supper ended. He was going to stay around for the next few days to make sure that the UK end of things doesn't get compromised… and gets restarted properly.

As Stuart lay in bed, he considered the day. It had been good; the sightseeing had been fun, even the Parliament lunch went well and then to finish it all with the meeting with Peter Dawson and finally get the truth. He knew that perhaps it wasn't the whole truth but enough to explain things. The egos of the PM and the President together with their various senior people made for a poisonous cocktail. He hadn't felt this well since the creation of the development team in Farnborough. He decided that if things went well tomorrow then he would arrange a visit to the University. He also decided to get this business with the Canadians moving so he could go home and rebuild a life. His new pad and phone was coming tomorrow as well, so he could start to connect with people again. Chris Ball had insisted on supplying both of them since he wanted to ensure the highest level of security.

He felt really fresh as he entered the restaurant for breakfast the next day. Unfortunately the word was out that he was resident and there were many people trying to get to him. He was pressed by two young women to sign a paper that he had put on the net a while ago, another person wanted a photograph with him. Stuart retreated and was saved by Paul and his team. Paul was annoyed that Stuart had got to the restaurant without any protection. In the end he was ushered to another small dining room alongside the restaurant.

"Sorry about that," said Paul, clearly embarrassed that his team had lost Stuart for a few minutes.

Over breakfast, Chris Ball joined Stuart and Paul. "It's approved that I join you today."

"Approved, by whom?"

"Both parties," he said. "Peter had a chat with Lawrence earlier. I also brought the notes I made from last night." Stuart read the notes; it was a good preparation for the meeting with Lawrence.

They all met up at Lawrence's suite around ten. Susan, Giselle and Henri were there with two other people. Lawrence gave the big welcome and specifically introduced Nick Spellman and Fran Archer. Stuart knew of Spellman as a successful entrepreneur mainly in the telecom industry. It was always strange, Stuart thought, but so often people look like the things they do. In Spellman's case, he looked like a cross between a street fighter and a bookie. He was medium height with a strong powerful build that his expensive silver suit couldn't hide. He had a white shirt; open at the neck and revealing a vast mat of hair. He had a square face with a heavy shadow over his thick neck and pugnacious face with the classic broken nose, all topped by a blond crew-cut. However it was his large piercing blue eyes that seemed out of place when enhanced by gold wire half-moon glasses. He greeted Stuart with a big hand and a big smile. Fran on the other hand was a large lady with dyed red hair and too much eye makeup with multiple studs in both ears. Stuart wasn't sure whether the studs carried some meaning, but they certainly were not appealing. She just nodded to Stuart and Chris.

Lawrence kicked the meeting off with a document outlining the proposition. Although a public company was to be formed, the Canadian Government kept a 'golden share' that protected Canada and their taxpayers. Stuart would be part of the Executive Board with Nick as CEO and Fran as CFO; Lawrence was listed on the Board as Chairman and Sue Thomas was listed as a Non-Executive. Stuart had 30 percent of the equity and his role was to provide a LeviProp license as well as direct innovation and development. The commitment of 40 days each year carried a serious 7-figure salary as well as a large long-term bonus.

Lawrence asked Nick Spellman to outline the tasks and timetables to get things going. Stuart and Chris Ball were surprised at the thought and level of detail that had been given in such a short space of time. Stuart went through his notes from the night before with everyone and there were no objections at all, indeed all saw the collaboration with the UK as a positive advantage. There was quite a lot of detail to go through and Lawrence excused himself after lunch. By mid-afternoon they had reached a natural end point. Nick asked Fran to summarise the meeting, which she did in an expert way, she is obviously his right-hand, Stuart thought. It was viewed that an announcement should be made in a weeks' time and that all the contracts needed to be signed before a press conference. They agreed to reconvene in two days' time to finalise the draft work. Nick invited Stuart to his place on the Saturday in order to get to know each other. Stuart returned to his room and after a swim he spent some time in the gym. He had asked Paul Joplin to clear and confirm the University meeting.

Around six that evening Chris Ball had arrived with the new phone and pad which needed about an hour to set up and apprise Stuart of the crypto functions. Stuart didn't want to be on his own that evening and invited Chris to join him for supper. Chris was married, but his wife was in the UK at that time, so he was happy to accept. They decided to go to an Italian restaurant that Chris knew and contacted Paul Joplin to clear it.

"I do hope my life is going to give me freedom to roam without security and crowds of press."

"What was it like in the UK then, Stuart? I mean before the UN fiasco."

"It was OK, apart from the nerd intrusions, not much press and no security issues."

"Well I am sure the security folk were watching over all of you at Farnborough," he added.

"Yes, I'm sure," he agreed. "I am just going to send a few emails to let people know I'm still alive."

"I would be staggered if they didn't know, old son, the press has been full of you since your discovery in Halifax. It all started with the cloak and dagger stuff, how did you get there and so on, now it's all about starting up an operation in Canada."

"How do they get hold of this stuff?"

"I don't know, maybe they are just good at adding two and two," he replied.

He sent notes to all his old mates who had been involved from the start, plus a few old friends. He sent a note to Zoe and the kids saying where he was, and finally a note to Harry saying sorry for not being around.

It was the same routine; Paul's team escorted him to the restaurant where they had a quiet table, although he felt everyone looking at him when the restaurateur, an expansive Canadian Italian wanted his autograph and a photo. Having had a great meal and too much Chianti, Stuart readily agreed. In all the publicity, it was interesting to see Chris deliberately becoming invisible. They headed back to the hotel in convoy and went in by a new entrance that had been established since the back-door approach was no longer possible.

More sightseeing had been arranged for the following day, as well as another afternoon/evening with Peter Dawson for an update. Professor Lane had also confirmed the Friday for a meeting and perhaps a lecture on IC. Stuart agreed and scheduled the Thursday to put something together.

The sightseeing went moderately well, it really was impossible to get away from the crowds of onlookers and press so the day was cut short. Instead Stuart spent more time in the gym and the pool; he was pleased that he was starting to regain his stamina. In the early evening, on checking his email, he found several hundred mail items, lots of which were spam or junk. He had a long update from Rob and a request from Alice to phone her. There were lots of notes from the old team members who had helped him in the early days, plus the team members from the Farnborough operation; even a note from Gary Marshall. There was nothing from Lucy or Henry, which wasn't surprising but there was a note from Marc saying he was glad I was OK and copied Zoe. It was a different email for her, and he suspected that Marc was letting him know, so he sent another note to her.

Rose Hammond joined Peter Dawson and Chris Ball for the working supper that evening. The atmosphere was relaxed but business-like, both Stuart and Chris recounted the commercial meeting with Lawrence and his team, the day before.

"It sounded constructive without too many areas of commercial conflict," said Peter.

"None, from my standpoint," I said.

"Is it OK if our lawyers run their eyes over it for you?"

"For you, you mean Peter," I replied.

"Well for both of us then," he responded with a smile.

"Fine, I will have a draft in two days."

"Thanks, Stuart. Rose can you handle it for us?" Rose smiled and nodded agreement.

"When things are signed, we really want you back in the UK, you know."

"Peter, continuing with our agreement for honesty what's the agenda with me now?" There was a pause, and an exchange of looks between Peter and Rose, Chris just looked quizzical. It was Rose who spoke first.

"Stuart, ever since you turned up in Halifax we have been thinking about you."

"You're too kind," I remarked dryly.

Ignoring my comment she continued, "In many ways, things are clearer now and rather simple."

"Go on," I said.

"Well, when you were transferred to the TANGENT programme, the number of interested parties was about as complex as it could be: not just complex from each individual nation's position, but their protected interests and their military investments and aspirations."

"So no different from the UK then!"

She gave Stuart a glance of irritation. "We asked the UK personnel from Farnborough to work with our Chief Scientific Advisors and other scientific academics to produce the UK positional paper on our strategy for the use of IC." Stuart was surprised that he hadn't been involved. Reading his mind she added, "You couldn't be involved since you would be compromised with the UN agenda." She handed him a numbered copy of the document. "If you could have a read and let us know if you want to be involved."

"Essentially, the paper has a number of work streams with priorities although we expect that some of those work streams will overlap," said Peter.

"The obvious one is transport," he continued, "but the paper examines air, sea, rail, and road separately. We break out space travel since it carries little legacy and we can think afresh about its development. We then look at power generation and how we can apply IC to provide electricity."

"But that's going backwards," Stuart interrupted.

"No not really, Stuart, our whole infrastructure is based on electricity and we can't replace it overnight, so we make it more efficient using IC and migrate it over time. There is a high priority workstream to address new applications of IC to such things as industrial processes and manufacturing for example. Consumer products are seen as a lower priority and will evolve over time." Stuart was intrigued, its sounded like a good piece of thought leadership; he was anxious to read it. "Some things are not covered because we can't do everything," Rose added.

"Such as?"

"Well heating and cooling systems could be a contender but if we can generate electricity with IC it doesn't become a high priority." Stuart didn't agree but said nothing.

"All of this work will be driven by a Strategic Development Council, SDC for short," Peter added. "We have yet to work through the detail but it's something we would like you to be part of."

"You haven't mentioned military stuff?" Stuart said. They all smiled.

"What's so funny?"

"We all know your views, Stuart," Peter started. "Not wanting your discovery to perpetuate military ambitions of the world… but… that's not reality."

"So what are you saying?"

"That we proposed to create a separate Military development team for IC which may use ideas from the SDC but will not, I repeat will not, influence the direction of the SDC."

"Easy to say!"

"Yes it is easy to say, but it's people like you on the SDC that will make it happen."

"What about the wider IC research, you may remember I was starting to work on the terrestrial impact of IC."

"It's not part of the SDC agenda; I think we should setup a pure academic research programme."

"And funding of the SDC?"

"There is an outline budget at the back of the document, but we don't see funding as an issue for two reasons. Firstly, if we are to be in the IC industry, if I can call it that, then we have no choice but to engage fully and that means all necessary funding," Rose said.

"And the second reason?"

"It's linked to the first, Stuart," Rose added. "The number of businesses and individuals who are ready to provide seed funding for IC means that in theory we could draw down billions of pounds should we need it."

"Rose has driven this work hard and it's a solid plan," Peter said.

"But Peter it needs action and speed and that is why we want Stuart back in the UK; it would be a big signal that we mean business," she finished. Stuart had liked Rose when he first met her; she had considerable intellect and seemed on the same wavelength as him. It was a powerful piece of work.

"I will need some time to read this and think on."

"Of course, but if we can get a decision at the same time you go public on the Canadian deal it will strengthen our position at home."

The remainder of the evening was a mix of social discussion that enabled Stuart to catch up on the recent news as well as a few clarification points around his return to the UK. At the end of the evening Peter presented Stuart with an ornate parcel. Peter pressed him to open it and he knew it was a Patek Phillipe wristwatch immediately he saw the presentation case.

"I'm afraid we couldn't track down your old one, but I hope this will go some way to say sorry." The great Peter Dawson was choked. Stuart was silent; he could only remember Zoe giving him the original one.

"Thanks, Peter, maybe the wounds will never go, but they are healing. I look forward to coming back home." Peter reminded him that he was heading back to the UK tomorrow morning but would meet up when he got back.

With that, the meeting ended, and Stuart returned to his room, noting the security people were alert at the various positions; he didn't envy their job. Before sleep he had read Rose's strategic paper on IC and as he expected, it was very good, the feeling of contentment washed over him. I am going to get LeviProp going at last, I am going to do further exciting developments, I am going to pick up my life.

It was breakfast as usual with Chris Ball and Paul Joplin but this time in a private room lakeside. It was a relaxed time; there were no more agendas, at least not ones that Stuart cared about. He had made his decisions to sign the Canadian agreement and then return to the UK and join the SDC.

Paul was looking at some notes. "Professor Lane has asked that you give an hour's address to some of the academic staff and students on Friday after his meeting with you. He hopes that you will also join him for lunch. As I said, I'm OK with the security." Stuart was amused that Madge was behind him, making sure her husband got the most publicity from the day. He agreed, and Paul confirmed he would sort all the logistics.

"Can I join you?" Chris asked. "After all, it would be great to hear more about IC and LeviProp." Stuart smiled and nodded.

When he returned Rose was waiting for him. She wanted to go through the preliminary points on the Canadian deal plus get Stuart's view on the IC strategic paper. There were no major issues and Rose took most of Stuart's points regarding the SDC; she really was a class act and he hoped he could enjoy more time with her. It was strange since he felt she liked him but was almost deliberately cool. Later on Stuart spent the rest of the day putting some ideas together for the University presentation. He had his first quiet evening going through his emails and practicing his speech whilst consuming a pizza and a bottle of red wine. He decided to have breakfast sent to his suite, so he could have an early run through of his presentation. He wasn't nervous but knew that he was at his best when he had prepared well, the topic would be thought provoking to the audience. Chris joined him and was happy to be an audience of one, although he knew better than to comment on Stuart's content. Paul arrived a little later and his team got them into the convoy and away from the hotel with little difficulty; either they were getting better or the press was losing interest. In fact the press had not lost interest as they discovered on arriving at the university.

"Hell, what do we do?" Stuart said when he saw hundreds of people surrounding one of the more modern buildings. As the crowd surged forward Paul radioed the convoy that they exit the campus until they could figure a safe way in. There was a lot of excited radio chatter as they drove alongside the campus. After about five minutes the convoy was directed around to an old building that was manned by a large number of the university security people judging by their uniforms. Gantries connected many of the buildings and some had mutual access through underground service corridors and so it was relatively easy to get to the main lecture hall. They entered a service elevator to the second floor and entered a large room that was pretty full with people.

Professor Lane immediately welcomed Stuart and introduced him to a number of college dignitaries, it was all overwhelming; so many people wanted to introduce them including Madge who was so pleased with her coup. One of the dignitaries announced that the lecture would be starting in an hour and there would be a small meeting with Mr Ashley beforehand.

Stuart was ushered into a side room and given some coffee before sitting at an oval table with a number of academics including Professor Lane and... surprise... Nick Spellman; it turned out that he was a member of the university board. The meeting was really a session on how Stuart discovered IC and what the University could learn. It was good conversation and reinforced Stuart's presentation material. The Dean wanted to explore the idea of an honorary doctorate from the University but Stuart felt he was getting in too deep, too quickly and politely said he would think about it. It was then time to go to the Lecture Hall and as they neared it from the main corridor the noise of hundreds of people made him anxious. However as he entered the noise stopped and there was a brief silence, then spontaneous standing ovation. The small group went down to the podium and sat down. The Dean finally called for quiet and gave a formal welcome to Stuart and invited him to speak. Again there was more applause.

"Thank you but I'm sure you should wait until you hear what I have to say," the audience became quiet. The presentation was based on the need to question the scientific wisdom of the present. "... Newton was right for a time, Einstein was right for a time; IC seems to be right... now... but is it just part of the same scientific process and is there more to challenge? There is always a need to question science especially if the present becomes the bedrock of future thinking. The test is one of purity, if a new theorem is developed that is so complex and has to be forced to fit then it's probably wrong. IC when you think about it is so simple, so pure, and so elegant. Mankind has been struggling to understand 'normal' matter but that perhaps is about 5% of the Universe. IC has just opened a door; is IC one force or many collective forces within dark energy and how many others exist within the fabric of the cosmos?..."

Stuart concluded that his discovery gave him concern since IC was only a part of the picture and until we know more, we may be damaging the balance of the cosmos. He had finished, should he have ended on such a pessimistic note? It didn't matter... then the applause hit him again and the small group was pinned to the podium until the security people managed to get him away and back to one of the academic dining rooms. Over drinks the questions continued, and a small group wanted to get to much deeper discussion on IC and how to find other components of dark energy, but Stuart was moved away to the dining table. He had the Dean on one side and Nick Spellman on the other and faced John Lane and two of his colleagues. The conversation was all about the structure of teaching science and how do you teach the current theories but encourage challenge from the students. They need to know enough to challenge things but where was the balance between learning and exploration? They all agreed that it was worth pursuing the idea of developing an advanced challenge-based learning structure and John Lane suggested that they form a virtual team and work up some approaches. Stuart readily agreed to participate.

Paul and Chris turned up at two o'clock, as agreed, to detach him from the proceedings. They returned to the hotel by the same secure route and left Stuart in his hotel suite. He decided to catch up on his email only to find the system had crashed because of too many transactions. It was absorbing to spend some time filtering and restarting the system. There was still a lot of mail, but he caught one from Zoe at her new address. It was a friendly note saying how pleased she was that Stuart was safe and hoped he was doing well; no mention of getting together. By contrast the one from Harry carried emotion all the way through; she rebuked Stuart for not contacting her before but didn't ask why, she just wanted to see him and make sure he was alright. Stuart replied that he would be back in the UK soon and she would be his first contact.

He was surprised to find himself on the evening news with much speculation about a link with Nick Spellman who was interviewed. He was very professional and kept to the agenda that it had been a major coup for the university and that he had high hopes for future collaboration on IC.

Stuart hadn't had much time for himself and enjoyed a relaxing massage followed by an early night. He had expected someone to take him to Nick Spellman's house, so he was surprised that he turned up with Paul in tow always keeping an eye on security. They took the usual exit route where Nick's car was waiting for use alongside the black Range Rovers. It was a silver Bentley Continental fastback that looked like it had just come from the showroom.

"One of my babies!" he said, "I don't have many weaknesses but Bentleys... well," he sighed.

Stuart knew his cars. "1955?"

Nick looked surprised. "Close, 1956 and it's done 182,000 miles. I was going to get you in the old girl, but Paul wouldn't have it; you had to be in a hard top."

"So what's the old girl?" Stuart said.

"Wait, just wait until we get to my place." He said with an excited grin. There was no doubt Nick was a hard operator, but it was easy to like him. They headed north west on highway 17, after a while they turned northeast onto the 148 and then onto Cotnam Island and over the Ottawa river, they continued through the forest until they arrived at a turning that led back down to the river. The road took a sharp turn to the right and a small security block with heavy gates stood ahead, it reminded Stuart a little of Glens Falls but he put it out of his mind. After about a mile they entered a large area of hard standing with buildings on three sides, the two side buildings were obviously garages and the front building had a large arch that led through to the main house.

"Come on, you must meet Miriam and the kids," as he deserted the Bentley, "I'll show you the rest of my babies later." The arch extended its shape into a long glass corridor that opened out onto modern glass building that curved away, it was difficult to see where the trees in the forest stopped as the glass picked up their refection.

"I hate flat glass buildings; but this caused the architect a bugger of a problem." He laughed. It was a massive structure and must have been about 80 metres long and 20 metres high. The entrance opened onto an atrium as high as the building that went all the way through the house and looked out onto the river. The floor was made of large black and white tiles. There was a large row of glossy black steps that dropped down to a lower white floor and onto a vast walled terrace. It was difficult to see any doors at all; the only way to spot them was the black squares on some of the glass that stopped people walking into them. There were several large modern sculptures, one of which looked like a Henry Moore, and an array of lights that were a sculpture themselves. Scattered around was a mixture of modern and antiques furniture.

"What do you think?" Nick was clearly very proud of his home, perhaps estate would be a better word.

"It's fantastic," Stuart said, "you are obviously a serious modernist."

"I don't know about serious… but yes it's a bit of fun and Miriam and I really enjoy design." Just then Miriam joined us, she was in her forties and quite beautiful but not in a manicured way. She wore old jeans and a black washed tee-shirt all of which accentuated a very athletic figure. Her hair was long, dyed blond with grey growing through, grey blue eyes, which held mischief, as did her smile. She ignored Nick and went to Stuart, gave him a strong hug with a kiss on the cheek and a welcome.

"Ok ignore me then," he laughed.

"Well it's rare to have the foremost scientist of the day as your guest," she turned and gave him a kiss.

It was real love and warmth, Stuart's hesitation about the day dissolved. They showed him around the main part of the house and on the way he met their three children who were all just as warm and open as the parents. Eventually they sat on the veranda for some drinks. On the left of the veranda was a large indoor pool enclosed by sliding doors and on the right an open kitchen area.

"You must have a lot of staff to manage all this," Stuart said.

"We keep it to a minimum, I know it's a bit ostentatious, but it is our home and we want to be a family," he said looking at Miriam.

"Stuart, we do have a few people here but only in the day. Half the problem is keeping all this bloody glass clean," she laughed. "And the security presence is a bit higher than normal."

"Sorry about that," Stuart said.

"Forget it, the last thing we want is any security issues; was it bad?"

Stuart didn't know how much Nick knew. "It was pretty grim; looking back; it was like something from a Bond film. Great wine by the way."

Nick took the hint. "Come on, let's sort lunch." They went over to the kitchen area. "Simple barbeque, if that's OK?" They had steak and salad with the kids and Stuart was welcomed almost as part of the family; he felt pleased that his business future in Canada was going to be with Nick.

Much of the afternoon was spent tinkering with one of Nick's cars over at the garages. He had a fine collection of pre-war cars, in particular a 1930 Blower Bentley; his baby. He was restoring an early Lanchester with a wick carburettor and together they managed to get the engine working for the first time in decades. Nick's workshop had just about every piece of machinery necessary to restore old cars; it was the first time Stuart had experienced workshop-envy.

Time passed quickly and by early evening Stuart had been persuaded to stay over and join them for supper. It was a family gathering, with Miriam's sister and her family joining them as well as Nick's younger brother and his fiancée. The following day he arose with a thick head from too much wine the night before; a swim helped him recover. After breakfast they returned to the Lanchester in the workshop and the conversation turned to the formation of the new company. They were both pleased with its structure and the reservations for the UK operation, agreeing that the meeting the following day was more to do with communications and publicity.

Nick insisted that he took Stuart back to the hotel but this time in his light green Derby Bentley. He drove it very quickly and demonstrated his mastery of the unusual controls of the car. Both knew that future meetings would be of a more formal nature, but the weekend had forged a friendship such that they would talk privately if things got in the way.

Fran and her team had been very busy. There had been a lot of work on the communications and publicity of the announcement and Rose too had been involved in the linkage to cover the UK position. All due diligence had been completed on the contracts and the signing and announcement was planned for the Tuesday afternoon in the hotel.

Stuart joined Lawrence and Nick for a pre-meeting on the publicity and communication from Fran and her team. Rose and Chris were included to handle any UK aspects. They all went into the announcement room for the signing ceremony and press release. The room was packed and very hot, Lawrence and Nick went through the announcement and then concluded with a photo session of the signing of the contract; as agreed, Stuart had been quiet but at the end endorsed the enterprise and giving it his full commitment.

"I am delighted to be part of this venture and working with Nick and his team in making LeviProp a world leader." Nick smiled at this comment. "And just to clarify, there is no conflict with the LeviProp and IC business in the UK; indeed I expect them to complement one another. There is more detailed information on the UK position alongside this announcement in your briefing pack."

Then the questions started, and to be fair the combination of Lawrence and Nick handled every question really well. Things only became sticky when the focus turned to more personal questions about Stuart and the position with development in the US. It had been agreed that these questions should be deflected when they came up, but instead Stuart interjected.

"There is no commercial relationship with the US on any of the IC initiatives that we have discussed today and this agreement with Canada is exclusive to the North American continent. There are robust international patents in place and I would expect all law-abiding nations to respect that position." This attracted a very big grin from Lawrence and Nick; even Rose managed a small knowing smile. There were a few more photo sessions and Stuart declined a personal press interview although Nick agreed and went to another room. The main members of the group met up again at Lawrence's suite for some champagne to 'seal the deal' as he put it.

That evening, Stuart met with Rose and Chris since he wanted to plan his return. Giselle Arnaut had already been in contact with the UK security people and logistics were in place with agreement that

Paul would manage things and accompany Stuart back to the UK. Rose and Chris would be joining him, and Chris would be responsible for coordinating Stuart's return to the UK. He wanted to go back to his old house but they both thought it unwise initially.

"Stuart it may be hard to take this onboard, but it may not be possible to return to the fairly sheltered life you had before; I don't just mean from a security standpoint but like it or not you are now in the public domain."

"It's not a question of like Stuart, it's not your choice," Chris added.

"We need to sit down with the UK comms people and see how we can support and manage your private and public life," she continued.

"So I shouldn't go back to the UK then?"

"Come on, Stuart, you see how it is here in Canada, it's going to be like this everywhere. We will help, it can only work if you have some give and take with the public and the press. We can get you privacy, but it comes at a cost to your personal freedom or you learn to live in the public eye." He knew she was right but the thought of always being unable to be just plain ordinary could be unbearable. He had been living in a goldfish bowl since his discovery first went public and was hoping that it all might just blow over; more naïve thinking.

The following day he said his farewell to Canada, at least for the moment. The convoy took him and his few belongings back to the airport where Paul and his team escorted him into a private lounge where they met Chris and Rose. All travel administration was cleared quickly, and they were ushered out to a small coach that took them to the airplane; it was a Boeing 787 that had been specifically sectioned off at the front. As they were first on, there was a long wait before the passengers were all boarded and, at last they could take off.

Goodbye Canada, he said in his head as he looked out of the window onto the forests below, you have been good to me, and with a glass of champagne he settled down to watch a film.

CHAPTER 12

Matter and Antibodies

Stuart didn't put the tarp over Paradox; he would do it later after he had calmed down. He knew he was still physically shaking after the flight and so he went into the house to pour himself a large scotch. He wanted to tell someone about the near disastrous flight and could only think of Rob... he wasn't contactable, so he could only leave a voicemail to ask him to come round. Paradox was very dangerous, and he occupied his mind with ways to build more controls into the power system using a similar system that Froom had installed.

It was about six in the evening when there was an urgent knock on the door. As Stuart approached the entrance he thought he could see some people in the garden. There were three people at the front door, one was clearly a policeman and a burly one at that, the other two were in their forties and casually dressed. The taller of the two was in charge; he had a long pointed nose, sandy thinning hair and was overweight, time had not been kind to him.

"Mr Ashley?" he said. "Are you Mr Stuart Ashley the owner of this property?" He already knew the answer.

"Yes, and who are you?"

He held out his warrant card. "I'm DCI Alistair Booth and this is Sergeant Hawke."

"And I'm plain old Stephen Wright from Security Service," the third man interrupted.

"May we come in?" resumed Booth. Stuart knew that it was inevitable that they were going to find him, he just hoped that his efforts to engage the authorities had worked, now he was on the defensive; he waved them into the sitting room.

"We have reports that you have been flying an illegal craft from this location and that you are suspected of terrorism under the 2006 Act." Stuart was stunned, this wasn't the way he wanted his discovery to be known; his first thought was to get his solicitor. "We have a warrant to search and secure the premises; this is the legal authorisation to so do." Booth gave him a document. He knew he had broken the law but the terrorism bit ... well that was mad.

"I am not a terrorist, but I do advise you that your people searching the premises need to take care."

"Is that a threat, Ashley?" The Mr had been dropped. "We also believe you to be linked with the threats on Sir Roger Wall, a senior member of the UK Defence community."

"Look this is all wrong, I have some delicate equipment in the workshops and some is setup for experimental work. I am concerned that if you don't understand what it is, then it could hurt someone. Are there any technical people here so I can explain it to them?"

"You'll have plenty of time for that, but in the meantime we would like you to come with us for further questions."

"Why... can't I answer any questions here?"

"That was a voluntary request, Mr Ashley, the alternative is that we make a formal arrest."

"This is all out of control." Stuart was beginning to panic; he couldn't get through to these people. The conversation was interrupted by some noise by the open front door, another policeman entered.

"Sorry to bother you, sir, but we have another man who says he is a colleague of Mr Ashley and we thought it best to bring him in." It was Rob and he looked angry and confused.

"What the fuck is going on, Stu?" Stuart was so relieved to see his old mate.

"Do you know this man, Mr Ashley?"

"He's an old friend and has been helping with my discovery." It all sounded a bit lame.

"And you are?"

"Robert Willard… Stu I will go and get a solicitor right now." He turned to leave.

"We would like you to remain, Mr Willard, until we understand your involvement in Mr Ashley's exploits."

"Exploits...you don't mean the flying?"

DCI Homer continued. "Do you know Sir Roger Wall, sir?"

"He was one the chaps that Stuart tried to get to listen."

"One of the chaps? Please explain?" Stuart didn't know whether Rob would help him out of this mess but decided to keep quiet.

Rob was getting angrier. "This man has made a fantastic discovery that he wanted to share with a number of people, Sir Roger being one of them, but they are all so fucking busy that they wouldn't listen, so he sent him a message."

Steve Wright interrupted. "Ok Mr Willard, show us this discovery."

"No, that's down to Stuart."

"Well, Mr Ashley, this is your chance?" Stuart silently thanked Rob; somehow he had deflected the situation.

"Of course, it's next to the workshop, can I show you?"

"Lead on," said Booth, taking back control.

They went out to the workshop, there were several people around outside, some in uniform and some in overalls, there was yellow police tape strung across the drive and the buildings.

Stuart and Rob took them over to the strange-looking Fiesta.

"Is this it?" Steve Wright looked amused.

Stuart started to give an explanation of Paradox, Booth and Wright seemed disinterested, and didn't stop Rob opening the car door.

"You don't believe him, do you?" Rob said as he got in the left side of the car; Stuart knew what he was going to do. Without closing the door he switched the power on and simultaneously thrust the lift control. Paradox quickly lifted to hover at four feet from the ground.

There was silence, everyone was motionless except Rob who yelled, "Do you fucking get it now?" from the open door.

Booth was the first to speak. "Oh shit, how does it do that?"

Rob had closed the door and soared up to about 30 feet.

Everyone on the site collected together to stare at Paradox. Rob went even higher; Stuart waved for him to descend.

"I just wanted someone to listen. To hear and understand what I have discovered… so what do we do now?" Rob who had descended to about ten feet interrupted him.

"You have a simple choice, get someone here who we can talk to about this discovery with Stuart or I'm out of here. Nothing can catch this craft."

The turn of events had completely thrown Booth and Wright; it was Wright who took the initiative and phoned someone. He walked away, gesticulating into the phone for some time. Booth too decided to make a call and was also busy when Wright returned.

"OK, we are not going anywhere, instead we are getting some technical expertise here in the next hour. We need to make sure this site is all secure."

"Good call," said Booth, "this is beyond my pay grade, my super is coming down now, so she should be here soon as well." He turned to the group of policemen who were mesmerised at the Fiesta floating above them. "Now I don't need to tell you that we have seen something remarkable and I don't expect any of you to talk about it; most importantly I need you to make this site secure with no unauthorised people coming in."

Rob showed no inclination to descend and Stuart yelled that they were going back into the house; Rob grinned, he was enjoying himself. The atmosphere with Booth and Wright had changed completely.

"I just don't know what to say." It was Booth again. "So that's the craft that left the message at Downing College?"

"Yes," Stuart said simply, "not terrorism, just trying to get attention; I'm just glad I didn't try Plan B."

"Which was?" Wright asked.

Stuart explained it.

"My God that would have been seen as terrorism, I'm glad you aborted it."

To support his actions, Stuart found copies of the various letters he had sent to senior CSAs requesting a meeting and the lack of response.

Chief Superintendent Alison Greg was the first to arrive. She was tall, in her late forties with a lined face that contrasted with her bright blue glasses. Her long hair was tied into a bun and, with an athletic poise, she reminded Stuart of a ballerina. Alistair Booth excused himself and they both left the house to talk. A little later Steve Wright got a call to say that some of his people had arrived and he went outside to meet them.

It was bizarre, only a few hours ago Stuart faced a hostile, almost aggressive, police process and now, here he was, left on his own; he knew he couldn't leave of course; moreover Rob was still floating in Paradox. He decided to join them and found a lady and a man busily photographing Rob as he floated at about ten feet. Booth and Alison Greg were talking near one of the buildings there was obviously someone else in the conversation at the end of a phone.

Steve Wright introduced the lady, Sam Hewitt and her colleague Ray Lan. "We are both from SIS Research, based in Farnborough," she said, "how does it work?"

"The answer is a bit complicated," Stuart replied.

"I think we might be qualified to understand," she replied in a patronising tone.

"Well it's something I have termed Inertia Conversion, IC for short, and put simply it harnesses a component of what we thought of as gravity."

"Oh really," the patronising tone continued.

"I didn't expect you to believe it, but let's start with the engineering and then work back to the science." He waved at Rob to bring Paradox down. Rob got out of the vehicle and Stuart gave him a big hug. "Thanks mate, I think you might have saved the day."

"Hope so," and he introduced himself to the two research people. Stuart opened the bonnet and showed them the LeviProp unit, explaining how the unit was able to direct a force in all dimensions through the solenoids that varied the angle of the bars.

"I just don't get it," said Ray Lan, "where is this force coming from?"

"You really need to see all the research that has gone into this; it will take some time."

"Stu and I have got some great records of the research we can share."

"Hold on Rob, the plan was to try and get a whole bunch of scientists with different disciplines, so they can help with the theory... but could I get anyone to listen... their minds were closed, and they couldn't be..."

"Fucked," added Rob with a laugh.

Just then Alison Greg joined them. "Who is in charge here?" she said.

"I am," it was Sam Hewitt.

"Well technically I am, as it's my property." Stuart was ignored.

"I am advised that we jointly agree a plan on managing the situation."

"Agreed," said Sam, "it's late, we should reconvene here midday tomorrow after we have taken more advice.

"Excuse me but this situation happens to be my invention, and no-one is going to take control of it."

"I'm sorry, Stuart, it was bad wording but if your discovery is real then we do need to work with you on it." Better, he thought.

"OK if it's not real, then you won't want to come with me in it." There was a long pause.

"I would like a ride," it was Sam.

"Me too," said Ray.

"Alright, I will join you," Alison said.

They all squeezed into Paradox and Stuart explained what was going to happen. He knew he needed to be as gentle as possible and moved the control to hover. Paradox gently rose to around four feet off the ground, apart for some vibration and the groaning of the old Ford structure, all was silent.

"All OK? We will go to 20 feet." Stuart took Paradox up as gently as he could. It was only then he saw the look of fear on Alison's face. "Do you want me to take you back?" he said as kindly as he could. Alison pulled a determined mask.

"No it's fine," she said gripping the seat. He took Paradox up to about a hundred feet and they steered off towards the forest accelerating quite quickly. They did a figure of eight before returning back to the house. Once they had finally settled on the ground Alison opened her eyes.

"It's impossible, but real," said Sam, unable to conceal her excitement. Ray just nodded his head.

Alison, a little more composed said, "We will need to keep up security at the moment, Stuart; I have assigned some police to watch over things until we meet tomorrow. I would like you and Rob to stay here."

"He doesn't have any food and I have drunk most of his booze," chirped Rob.

"We can fix that." She spoke to someone to arrange it.

They said their goodbyes and within five minutes they were left alone with the exception of a number of police.

"What a day," said Rob.

"Never again," I said.

"No, never again." They covered up Paradox and went into the house.

After the day's events Stuart had a restless night's sleep. If Rob hadn't turned up and got his way in, things could have been very different. Some kind policeman had dropped off some hot coffee and croissants from the local shop in Smythfield. Rob had some school matter to attend to but promised to be back as soon as he could to support him. He contacted Alice who could be there by mid-morning; she could help him put all his experimental results into some sort of structure if he was to explain it to others. He had been quite methodical in keeping data, observations and recording so, although it was a slog, it was easy to catalogue.

Sam Hewitt had taken the lead the evening before and organised two key meetings in the morning. A lot of people had their diaries upset and were fairly grumpy at being called to a meeting for which there was no clear agenda. She had spoken with Sir Neil Foster the Government CSA and explained events. She had taken a big risk with him since she was convinced of Stuart's discovery. Sir Neil said there was a full Cabinet that day with a secure subset meeting beforehand; it was an opportunity to get all interested parties together. He promised to ensure that there was a slot on the agenda around eleven. It was all happening very quickly, much faster than Sam had hoped.

The first meeting started at eight and was in Thames House. It was chaired by Sam's boss who was number two in MI5 and also had two other members of SIS that specialised in research as well; Sir Neil Foster, Sir Roger Wall CSA Defence and Alison Greg were there on time too. As an afterthought, Nigel Jones from Sir Peter Dawson's office was included in case it impacted on the commercial aspects of research as well.

Sam suspected she had a hostile audience especially as she had broken their diaries. She decided to give a brief background of recorded flights by an unknown plane from NATS which she correlated with the episode at Downing College; Roger Wall looked uncomfortable. She then went into the raid by Stephen Wright and Alastair Booth and their findings. She provided a detailed background of Stuart Ashley. Finally she closed with photos of the Paradox as well as a video of the flight both outside and inside of Paradox; the audience listened silently. At the end of the video Alison confirmed that it was a true representation of events.

Neil Foster took the lead. "Views?"

"There has to be a rational explanation," said one of the SIS researchers.

"There is! And… it's real!" said Sam. "Come and see it."

"Sam and Alison, I don't think you have been smoking dope, so we have to back it. I do intend to come and see it for myself this afternoon… Roger?"

"I'm in, Neil, if it's true then I'm the one who should have listened."

"Bollocks, you have a lot to do. If it is real then we need to figure out how we manage this Ashley chap. So does it go on the Cabinet Secure agenda?"

Everyone voted in favour with the exception of Nigel Jones.

"OK, Sam, you and I have about an hour to précis this down to 15 minutes."

Over the years Sam had become an expert in presenting half formed ideas to a senior audience and so this proposition was easy, especially as she really believed in it.

The cabinet secretary apologised for a late item on the agenda and said that it would only be discussed if time allowed. In fact, time did allow since most of the agenda was uncontentious. It was a strange meeting where the attendees were discussing some theoretical issue and so it didn't get the attention it warranted with the exception of Peter Dawson. In the end it was agreed that following further investigation it should be brought back to the Committee next week. Sam continued to own the project with policing support from Alison. She asked Alison to strengthen the security with non-uniform and on advice from Nigel Jones she created an evaluation team from a wide discipline including various professors in particle physics from Oxbridge. Neil Foster agreed to chair the group.

It was just after midday when a number of the evaluation team arrived at Smythfield. Most of the research information had been assembled; Stuart and Alice agreed on how to present it all. Stuart wanted to show it as a story and go through the experiments concluding with a demonstration of Paradox. They both agreed that Stuart should start with his theory on a multi-force structure that used to be gravity. Over time Alice had thought about this, and concluded it was at least a good working hypothesis. As well as Sam and Alison, Neil Foster, Roger Wall and Nigel Jones introduced themselves to Stuart and Alice. There were also four other technical people who were referred to as the support staff; they each had laptops and between them a few other bags of equipment.

The sitting room was crowded and stuffy; Neil Foster took the lead and gave an update on the two previous meetings. The objective of the day was to see if there was any merit in Stuart's work and whether the UK government could support its development. He handed the meeting over to Stuart.

"Thank you for your introduction, it is true that I wanted to share my discovery and findings with you, I strongly believe that I have discovered something that will fundamentally change the way we live. For that reason it needs to be shared with the rest of the world and I have put some of the information about it on the web already. The commercial opportunity is immense, and I have registered international patents on something I call LeviProp, short for Levitation and Propulsion. I should say that I have not thought about asking the UK government's support for such development. I'm sure there will be lots of commercial funding, once it's public." The four people at the back were busy taking notes. "Alice and I thought a lot about how we best present my work to you and to some extent I am doing it the wrong way round. Firstly I would like to spend a few minutes on my theory behind the discovery. Alice was originally very sceptical about it but has grudgingly agreed that is a good working hypothesis." Alice grinned as she sorted through some paperwork. "After that, I would like to show you how the discovery developed as a narrative and we can walk around the various experiments and then finally a demonstration of Paradox, which is the name I gave to the first working vehicle." Alice handed out a few copies of the paper.

"This document is a summary of the theory and I know it's not complete but it's a start and something that I intend to develop. At the back, you will find all the people who have contributed to my work; I am sure they will corroborate the findings." Stuart then proceeded to explain how he had distorted the equilibrium on an object accidentally and caused it to 'float' and how he had identified a force that had caused the incidence and created a new equilibrium without impacting the surrounding equilibrium; he avoided using the term gravity. He then went on to explain the way that the force could be harnessed and controlled. Finally he concluded that he had discovered a component of what we had called gravity and was now thinking of ways to apply the same approach to find other components. It was big stuff, and clearly too much for the audience to accept so maybe Stuart should have started with the narrative but he wanted them to question everything.

It was Roger Wall who spoke first. "Stuart by all accounts, you have stumbled onto something, but I wouldn't dismiss previous science so readily, it may be that your... discovery... does fit into existing theories." There were nods of agreement.

"Sir Roger, you may be right, but equally I suggest that everyone keeps an open mind. OK let's go to see an early experiment in the workshop."

Rob arrived, perfect timing, to help with the various experiments. They progressed through from the original 'floater' through the bar dropping stage and then the frame construction. The questions were thick and fast with Rob and Alice helping out on answers. It was interesting to see the animation of the four support staff; there were even raised voices at one stage. Neil Foster and Roger Wall had their own discussion; Stuart was sure they were trying to retro-fit his findings into existing science. Nigel Jones seemed separate from the rest of the group and kept his own counsel.

Finally they got to Paradox and Stuart found it easier to describe the LeviProp power unit as a progression from the previous experiments. Stuart invited Nigel, Neil and Roger for a flight, and they all got into the little Fiesta. Stuart spent some time explaining the controls. As usual he lifted Paradox onto hover mode; he noticed the support team was using several pieces of equipment as well as a camera. Something inside of him wanted to unleash the real power of Paradox to make them realise the importance of his findings but his last experience had frightened him and so he kept to the second phase on the controls. He did however take the craft up high enough for Sir Neil to ask him to bring it down. He flew across the forest and when a clearing appeared he descended to a hover.

All was silent except for some bird song. "Well what do you think?"

"It's quite... amazing," said Neil.

"How fast can it go?" Roger added.

"Good point, I pushed it a bit and it was frightening. I have no idea as to the limits, but I don't think a human could sustain the forces. I was thinking of testing it with some remote controls but frankly I am in the process of building a new craft from scratch, I'm not sure how long this old Fiesta will hold together."

"As long as it gets us back in one piece," joked Neil.

Nigel Jones still didn't say anything but was lost in thought.

"Whether your science is right or not, you have created a quantum jump in transport," Neil concluded.

The rest of the flight was just fun for them, it was a relaxed mood and they wanted to keep going but knew they had to return. As they got out, Nigel Jones looked at Stuart and said,

"Your introduction was right; your discovery will change mankind."

"I want the others to take a flight if that's alright?" said Neil.

"Of course."

"In the meantime can we go back to the house to discuss next steps? Alison and Sam I need you to come too… and can someone get us some tea?"

"I'm sure Rob will handle the flights. Alice can you join us?" Stuart wanted a witness. The seven of them sat down in the sitting room. Stuart kicked things off. "You need to understand Neil, that I wanted you all to know about the discovery so that the UK could share in the benefits but… not to take it over."

"Understood, Stuart, but have you really thought about the bigger picture?"

"There are countries that would do anything to get this technology for Defence purposes. There are also countries that would do anything to prevent its development," said Roger "so your decisions are not easy."

"I know, but forget IC for the moment, LeviProp could help countries out of poverty, it could stop pollution over time and could slowly create a more equal world economically."

"You're an idealist, Stuart, and I don't mean that in a critical way but if for example you stopped the oil economy? Or if some rogue nation developed it for military uses? You cannot just open it up to a world market."

"I know I'm naïve when it comes to these political issues, but I won't let my discovery just reinforce the status quo."

"Stuart, I do understand your position, but I would ask for some time to do two things. Firstly, to look at how LeviProp can be developed for both the UK and the world. Secondly, to look at developing and extending the science behind IC. I promise we will be open with you at all times. I propose that if we can agree something, we will put a joint paper to the Cabinet next week."

"Peter Dawson will want to be involved," said Nigel.

"Of course," replied Neil.

"OK, I'm happy to see your proposition but don't take that as an agreement."

"Alison and Sam, what do we do about security? The press will be sniffing out all the police activity here shortly, if not already."

"I want to stay here, Neil."

"I am worried about continuing this approach to security," said Alison, "not only is it resource heavy but as you say it's a bit of an advertisement."

Sam pitched in. "The reality is that if someone with a malicious agenda gets to hear of your discovery then you are at risk, as are some of your colleagues who have knowledge of the discovery. I propose that we stand the police down with the exception of a liaison officer, and that my department covers things in the interim. For Stuart's sake we will need to find a long term solution."

Yet another turn of events that Stuart hadn't envisaged, but they were right. Whatever the outcome of this plan he would need to take care.

There was a lot of change in the next few hours, all of the police had gone, and four new faces appeared setting up bases in the house and the grounds with their own comms system. The four support staff had an elated flight thanks to Rob; they would be returning the next day to stay for the week. Stuart wanted to spend more time on his theory and Alice promised to help over coming days. He also spent some more time on designing Paradox2.

The wheels in government were turning much faster than usual. It started in a meeting between Nigel Jones and Sir Peter Dawson; what a contrast, Nigel was grey and invisible whilst Peter was larger than life, flamboyant and given to overstatement, however their relationship was one of mutual respect for the fine intellect that they both possessed.

Peter trusted Nigel, he didn't have to see Paradox to know it was real, and like Nigel, he suspected that Stuart's science might be right despite the naysayers. Peter had many roles over the years, he had been Head of MI5 and then briefly MI6 and was always regarded as politically neutral; he was a trusted advisor to the PM and the Cabinet generally. He was currently the SIS overseer although it was never recorded as such; being highly influential, there was very little that he didn't know about. Most recently he had been tasked with ensuring that the National Infrastructure was secure; a role spanning both government and commercial enterprises.

"These CSA folk are getting out of their box, Peter. You should have heard Neil Foster making plans on Ashley's work... what the fuck does he know?" I am really worried; this stuff is so important and such a game changer, we really do need to control it."

"Yet you say Ashley's an idealist and will resist control."

"Yes, but that's because it's not being presented the right way. This man is important, at least his brain is; we need to woo his ego and show him that we understand his values and fundamentally agree with them."

"Fundamentally, of course!" Peter laughed. "What do you suggest?"

Nigel gave him one page. "It's just an outline, but firstly we fund a development team from the UK. Once in place, we open it up to the world scientists, well, the ones we select."

"Good play!"

"We fund the creation of Ashley's LeviProp company giving us indirect control of IP. We also run a shadow development team for our own interests; I'm not sure whether we tell him about it."

"He will still want to share it with the world?"

"Yes he will, and so we create a not-for-profit charitable world organisation with the sole task of ensuring every country benefits from the discovery. If we can't create a bureaucracy where all parties are against each other, and consequently nothing happens, then nobody can!"

Peter chuckled. "You've got the bases covered, I'll clear it with the PM, informally of course."

"So, who should lead it from our end?"

"I thought Sam would be a good choice, she gets on well with Ashley and really believes in the discovery."

"OK, go to it, assume the PM is fine with it and get a sanitised version for approval at the Cabinet." I will get the CSAs onside.

Nigel left with a grin on his face, how he loved this job, working for someone like Dawson with the power of pulling the strings without the puppets knowing.

Back at Smythfield Stuart was more relaxed, he had wondered when he should make his findings public and when he tried, he had made a complete mess of it. Now, the process was underway, he knew the people he was dealing with might have a different agenda to him and so he needed to keep a close eye on them. He had found Sam a pretty open and sincere person and the CSAs were onside but sceptical on the science, but that Nigel Jones he didn't trust.

In the week ahead, Sam brought the news that she would be heading up the government team to work with him if he agreed with the plan. She also showed him a draft of the proposal that Nigel had composed for approval by the Cabinet the following Monday, and told him in strictest confidence, that the PM had endorsed the proposal. Maybe he had misjudged Nigel. He contacted Froom for assistance on refining the controls and got clearance that he could come later that week.

"Since the authorities have been made aware of things, it's like a bloody fortress here, Froom."

"I'm pleased, Stuart, they had to find out some time."

Stuart and Sam spent some time going through all the people who had helped him and planning how to best update them on progress and any associated implications. Stuart contacted each of them by phone and finally managed to get everyone to agree to meet the coming Saturday at a location in Farnborough.

"Government isn't known for its speed," he said to Sam as they drove over to Farnborough on the Wednesday to look at the facilities.

"Not true where Sir Peter Dawson is concerned," she replied. "I know he wants to meet you. Already one of my people has been looking for a secure location should we get approval from you and the Cabinet to go ahead with the development programme. Frankly managing security at your house isn't a practical proposition in the longer term." She paused. "Farnborough is a great location; there is already a lot of secure work there, easy transport access plus the bonus of an airfield. We have found some separate buildings that were mothballed last year by the MoD that I have been told could be suitable, so this is our chance to give them the once over." Stuart was enjoying Sam's positive approach to everything.

They approached Farnborough and turned off towards the airport and the sites of a number of military suppliers; there was one inconspicuous turning on the left which had an entrance normally barred by heavy gates alongside a small building, presumably for security people. After another hundred metres there was another similar barrier with a man waiting nearby. Sam stopped the car and they both got out.

"Hi Josh, how's it going?"

"Fine," he said opening the barrier, "this is normally all locked, but we can get it working and staffed in a couple of days."

"OK, can you take us around?"

There were several buildings in the complex with a lot of hard standing that Josh explained had been used for military aircraft at some time. Some of the buildings looked like they had been there since the 1920s although there were two three-storey buildings that had their origins in the 1970s. It all looked pretty run down. "Actually is hasn't been occupied for about six years, so it will need a bit of maintenance."

"What about power and communications?" Stuart asked.

"No problem on power, there is a lot of high-tech industry around. I'm still awaiting a view on the comms. The airport people are being a bit slow, I will chase it."

They went in and around the two '70s buildings which were

basically office space that could be configured easily. The other buildings were quite a surprise since although they looked like old offices were large hangar-like spaces.

"Wow," said Stuart, "this is exactly the sort of space we need!"

As they explored, they found a number of houses that presumably were for military personnel.

Josh said, "The final building you must see is the old club house," and he led them to the back of the older buildings. "I think it was of the same era as the two older buildings and it must have been part of a bigger military facility back then. He unlocked the door into a large open area with the remnants of a bar along one side, a corridor led to three large recreation rooms and at the back was a changing area, presumably for sports." They returned to the hard standing.

"What do you think?" said Sam.

"It's perfect, but needs some money spent on it. If we could make one of the hangars waterproof with modern electrics that would be a good start."

Sam laughed. "Stuart, if this is to be a showcase of your developments, we need to do better than that. Josh is from our facilities people and I have asked him to give me an estimate by the end of the week to get this place fully functional." That's why he looks stressed, he thought.

On the way back, Sam said, "Stuart please don't think we have unlimited budgets... we don't, but the place has to be fit for purpose and capable of expansion if it's to include a worldwide community. If we get the green light from the Cabinet, then it's your decision on our proposal. You need to think both research and development, and what skills you need for each. We also need some operational people to manage the site; frankly I bet there will be people beating a path to your door." It was hard for Stuart to hide his excitement; indeed Sam knew he was keen to get going and reported accordingly.

When Froom arrived, he was escorted to meet Stuart. "This is all a bit heavy," he said, "but I can understand why." Stuart explained the near disastrous flight and the need to have a better control system. Froom listened and said, "I agree, but it's not really worth it for that Fiesta."

"Let's just treat it as an experiment that we can use as a design basis for Paradox2."

"So you're going ahead?"

"Yes."

"With the government?"

"Yes, the deal is good, it meets everything I want."

"Excellent news, room for a retired engineer?"

"When are you leaving?"

"Stuart I had more fun with you in those few weeks than I have had in years, so I negotiated early retirement. I thought you would want me."

"Want you Froom?... I bloody need you."

Over the next few days the two of them completely redesigned the control system and the solenoids and started to replace the existing system. It was Saturday and the meeting was becoming quite an affair according to Sam. Nigel Jones was organising it with Peter Dawson as host, Neil Foster and Roger Wall were also asked to attend.

Rob and Stuart got to the hotel in Farnborough for breakfast, only to find Mike, Gareth and Steve already there. They chatted through the progress Stuart had made and the involvement of the various people from government. Froom appeared and after the introductions sat down with a coffee. The last to arrive was Alice with Ruth; there was an uncomfortable silence that was broken by Rob.

"Ruth, glad you could come, I'm not sure what this all about but, at least we can get some free hospitality from the state," everyone laughed. She still looked embarrassed.

Mike Lester chipped in, "Come on Ruth, sit by me and have a coffee."

It wasn't long before Sam found them and said that they were ready to start the meeting. They all trooped into a large soulless conference room arranged in a board-style with about 20 leather seats around a long highly polished table. Nigel Jones introduced Sir Peter Dawson who shook Stuart's hand warmly as if he had known him for years. There was an extended round of introductions and Nigel then called the meeting to order.

Stuart was expecting a dour introduction but Nigel Jones sparkled with humour. He was very self-deprecating and even more so about government; it was a good way to position the government people. It was all about doubt and disbelief until his first flight in Paradox and then how difficult it was to convey the importance of the discovery to other sceptics. The lobbying that he, Sam, Neil and Roger had to do over recent days was significant. Neil was kind enough to add that he had a minor version of the sort of disbelief that Stuart had to face. He handed over to Peter Dawson to go through the proposition that they hoped the Cabinet would approve on Monday; he too confirmed that the PM had already given it her blessing. He then went through the plan and the timescale that was new information to Stuart. It was very aggressive and based on taking over the Farnborough site immediately and then redeveloping it as they went along.

"It was a secure location, so we can restore that pretty quickly and there are a lot of buildings, so we can easily start up the development programme in one of the hangars and use the ground floor of the newer building for research."

"Why the unhealthy speed?" It was Mike Lester.

"Safety and security," Sir Peter replied. "Safety, because I am told that this discovery has released potential forces that need to be understood and controlled. Security, because in the wrong hands, this discovery could be very dangerous politically, economically and militarily."

"And the UK Government's interest," Mike said cynically, "are not political, economic or military?"

"You have seen the plan, Mike, we are going to make it an international development programme over time, and we are going to create some sort of international body that will share the technology across the world and yes, I'm not embarrassed to say we do want the UK to be a leader in this technology and finally; there is no aspect of military involvement in the programme, that will be down to the MoD's own plans. This is all formalised in the proposition that is going to Cabinet and you will all have a copy."

Mike seemed satisfied with the answer, as did the rest of the team.

"I should say," Sir Peter continued, "that this is contingent on Stuart agreeing to the Cabinet Proposition." He looked at Stuart.

"For the record, I'm very comfortable with the whole proposal," Stuart said.

"This brings me to the discussion around your respective roles in supporting Stuart's discovery so far. It seems to me that there are a number of issues, most important of which is your existing knowledge of the discovery. I believe it's fair to say you all know a key part of the discovery relevant to your skills but Stuart apart, no-one has the overall picture."

"True… perhaps with the exception of Alice and Rob," said Stuart.

"Now I haven't discussed this with Stuart and confess that this is in the early stage of thinking and so I need your input. What we want to avoid is uncontrolled application of IC without truly understanding what's going on. I have taken advice from our CSAs as well as two eminent physicists from Oxbridge and their idea is that the research side of things should be classified as 'secret' initially so that we concentrate our efforts to getting a clear position of the theory behind this discovery. At that stage we would then go public through some sort of academic paper. I'm not sure whether we should treat the LeviProp development in the same way?"

"What is the implication of this 'secret' classification?" Rob asked.

"Well, it means that any of your work associated with the research would be protected and you couldn't go public on it."

"I assume that means we can't even talk about it?" Rob again.

"Yes, what's been said in the past is just that, but from now you would be subject to the secrecy act."

"I wouldn't have got to this point in development of IC without all your help and I hope that in some way you will continue to be part of this programme. As an example Mike, Gareth and Steve the material science is going to be fundamental to future development. Regardless of your decision I plan to make each of you shareholders of LeviProp such that there will be some financial recognition of all your support."

The room was strangely quiet as they all thought through their position.

"Let's have a coffee break and get your views afterward," said Nigel.

"Stuart, I know we didn't discuss it with you, but this issue has to be agreed?" said Sir Peter.

"It's fine," Stuart said, "the issue had crossed my mind anyway."

"I think the share option is a good approach," he continued.

"Let's see their reaction."

Stuart decided to take sounding and wasn't surprised that Alice and Froom were up for a full role. Rob too wanted to stay involved but had to think through his teaching options with Sue. Mike, Gareth and Steve had obviously been discussing it and were keen to stay involved but wanted to remain at the university. Ruth merely thanked him for the share consideration.

So it was a simple process when they all reconvened, no strong opposition to signing up for the 'secret' classification with its associated responsibilities. Nigel and Sir Peter were really pleased since it was their biggest area of concern in the whole plan. They finished with lunch and since they were in Farnborough Sam invited them to see the new site. The two CSAs had contributed very little to the day, but Sir Peter was smart enough to keep them onside. They had a planned meeting with the two professors later on the following week and asked Stuart and Alice to join them and discuss his theory. They all agreed to keep their diaries as open as possible pending the Cabinet decision.

It was only five minutes' drive to the new site but Stuart was surprised to find the first main gate already manned; the place had already lost the unoccupied look. Once through the second barrier they all parked next to a number of vans; work was clearly underway. Firstly they toured the new block as he termed it; there were perhaps a dozen workmen getting the place into shape. In one of the older hangars there were more men fixing the roof.

"The Cabinet hasn't met Sam, so how this all being funded?" he said.

"That's Sir Peter for you," she said, "he a bit of a risk taker. He obviously is sure of the decision will be positive and had decided to get things going." Not your usual civil servant, Stuart thought. Everyone in the group was as enthusiastic as Stuart, and he sensed that some of them might want to revise their role. At the end of the trip they all said their farewells and Rob took Stuart home to Smythfield.

There were two voice messages awaiting him, one from Harry asking him to phone the following day, late afternoon; and the other from Zoe, probably about the divorce, he thought. These last weeks had been turbulent to say the least but now Stuart was at ease. The relentless self-imposed pressure had gone, and he had reached a plateau in proving Paradox worked. He felt he could now approach things in a more thoughtful and systemised way; people believed him at last and indeed were going to support him.

He phoned Zoe. "Thanks for phoning back Stuart, we really have to talk."

"I know Zoe, and I'm ok now."

"Why now exactly?"

"No matter, what do you want to talk about, the settlement I guess?"

"Well yes, and the kids."

"Zoe, I have tried to talk to the kids but I'm the Mr Nasty who has hurt you deeply. I once thought that I was close to them but know better now. Fortunately I have started a new life and maybe they will come to know me again in the future."

"It sounds like you have given up on them?"

"No they have given up on me, with a little help from you. Don't worry, I'm not bitter anymore. You won."

"Is this a civilised conversation?"

"Yes it is, I'll get the solicitor to sort things Monday and you can get your share of the spoils. I was putting the house on the market anyway."

"Why? I thought it was part of you?"

"New life, I told you… I'm moving on."

"Well I'm glad you are so… upbeat."

"You started a new life, now it's my turn. There may be a bit of press soon, it's nothing to do with you so please don't comment."

"What do you mean, press?"

"As I say, it doesn't touch you. Bye." That was better, he had always felt defensive and guilty; it's over now and I can move on.

Much of Sunday was spent in tidying up the place. Well, not tidying up exactly, but trying to work out what he would keep and what he would dump. As usual everything was on the 'keep' list but this new research programme wouldn't be based on old used bits of machinery. He would keep all the old car bits and the Morgan, plus all his tools and all the remains of the various experiments he had done as part of the history of his discovery. He actually started shifting all the stuff destined for the dump out of the workshop.

He phoned Harry, it was a bad line, but her plans had changed, and she was coming home this next weekend; he arranged to collect her from the airport.

Zoe phoned back… twice in a day? "I have just heard from a friend that there have been police all over the house… are you alright?"

"I'm fine; things are sorted out now thanks."

"But what's going on… is it to do with your discovery?"

"Zoe, I don't understand where you're coming from? You wanted to end our relationship, so why are you concerned? Just enjoy your new life."

"I still have feelings for you; I can't just forget our time together."

"OK, but don't open old wounds; my new life is just taking off."

"What new life?"

"What's with the inquisition, I haven't dug into your new life." There was silence, so he put the phone down. Something was wrong, but he had enough to worry about.

He phoned for a rubbish skip that Monday morning and was surprised it was delivered by mid-morning and so he started the process of filling it, somehow it was cathartic, nevertheless he still looked at some bits of equipment and thought… maybe… just maybe, I should hang onto it. So it needed all his discipline to really clear things.

At about the same time Sir Peter Dawson was presenting his proposal to the full Cabinet. He had circulated the briefing over the weekend and hoped that most of the politicians would have a chance to read it. The departments with CSAs had already given their input and endorsement to it. Sir Peter was quizzed over LeviProp and IC with some of the questions showing a complete lack of scientific knowledge.

The PM, Linda Ramsay, made a strong case for the project stressing the point that the UK would be in at the very start of this discovery and could really become a world leader in the technology. Sir Peter took the action from the PM that they needed to see a communications plan since the project couldn't be kept secret for long; it would inevitably become public and the government didn't want to be on the back foot. The Secretary for Higher Education stressed the importance of engaging the academic community, everyone agreed, and Sir Peter was tasked with adding this section to the overall programme, the secretary offered his staff to help, and Sir Peter agreed. The Chancellor had more concerns over the proposed budget; his treasury staff had briefed him that there was a history of massive over-runs with development projects in general and there needed to be some phases defined with independent reviews. Sir Peter agreed to work with the treasury on the appropriate controls.

In the end there was enthusiastic endorsement of the project with the request for a Cabinet visit to the new site when something suitable could be demonstrated. Sir Peter left the Cabinet office; he was pleased with the outcome since he had anticipated all the reservations and didn't see any obstructions. He let his team know and to get some urgency behind things. Why the urgency? Well the PM was right; the press would find out soon enough, the Cabinet was known for its leaks. The UK needed to get a technical lead of around six month or more if it was to avoid losing its market advantage. He knew he had to protect it from the US for as long as possible. He also knew he would have a much tougher task keeping it out of China's hands... or the Russian's. The PM knew this too as did the Cabinet, so it was going to be a sensitive time over coming months.

Around lunchtime Stuart went to the pub for a snack and was halfway through a crossword when his phone rang, it was Nigel Jones.

"Sir Peter asked me to let you know that the Cabinet unanimously agreed to the project... congratulations! He wants to move quickly, and Sam is organising a meeting tomorrow at the new site."

"I'll be there by nine. Is that early enough?"

"Excellent, I'll let her know."

"I didn't thank you for all your support," Stuart added.

"That's alright, just remember if there any issues and you need to contact me informally. Enough said?"

"Thanks, I will Nigel," and he hung up. Stuart's heart was racing; this is it, now it's real work. Somehow it was much easier to dispose of things when he got home. He didn't know how the others would be told but he phoned Rob anyway. Rob was over the moon and had decided, with Sue's agreement, to go part- time teaching so he could stay involved; Stuart was delighted. A little later Alice phoned for an update and Stuart let her know the decision in confidence; she could make herself available as soon as possible, Stuart said he would advise her tomorrow.

And so at nine the next day Stuart arrived at the Farnborough entrance to his new office; it was like going back to work again. He guessed that a couple of cars in front of the entrance could be press. He had to check and register his car before being allowed through to the second barrier, where the guard automatically raised it with a wave. It was very busy with cars and vans parked everywhere. He assumed that the meeting would be in the new building and had to check in again with the guard; Sam was there to meet him.

"Sorry Stuart, we have to use guards at present until the new security system is installed, so it's a bit heavy at the moment."

"No problem... better that way."

"Come on in, the place has changed already, I want to go through some things with you."

They both got a coffee from a temporary kitchen and went into a large room with a horrible seventies' lighting system. There was a desk, a sideboard, and a large conference table all in expensive teak; they weren't new and of a previous era, but it all looked a lot more business-like than before.

"I can live with all this, but no bloody communications, it's driving me mad. All I have is my mobile and even then the signal isn't very good."

"How long will it take to fix?"

"It's a big job and even with the pressure I can leverage, we won't get the new cables to the site for a week. It's with the Facilities Manager, Rashid, he's a really good guy and will get this place into shape very quickly. His people are building an office next door for you, so let him know what you want." She looked at her list.

"Security, all in good shape; Felix Weymouth is in charge, he works for me, I'll introduce him later. HR is with Amanda Stone; she will be coming in tomorrow. Operations are with Anne Little, she is in the hangar building; we'll see her later. Finally equipment requisition and maintenance is with a chap called Peter West, he a real terrier."

"It all fantastic, Sam, and so fast."

"Well as you know, I did have a bit of advance support from Sir Peter!"

"So what about the research and development programmes?"

"They stay with you and I plan that we will get you two deputies to help lead the work."

"I will want Alice on the research side and Froom on the development side if that's OK? Rob is keen to join, and I think he would be best as advisor to me."

"No problems, I will get Amanda to put them on the payroll."

"Payroll?"

"Stuart, they can't work for nothing, this has to be run as a proper enterprise."

"Of course, I just hadn't thought."

"Sir Peter is dealing with your salary package though."

"One of the highest priories is getting the right people on the team to support you."

"Such as?"

"Well on the research and the development sides as well as linking into the academic community."

"It's going to be tough, finding the right people who don't have any pre-conceived ideas."

"I agree, I think the development side is going to be easier and I've asked Sir Roger Wall from MoD to suggest some people, especially some aeronautical people who know how to design and build planes."

"That's a great idea, Sam. The old Paradox is not designed for speed!"

"The research side is tougher, and Sir Neil Foster has sent me some names and recommended them for interview. I think you know that two names have been put forward to provide the academic links." She found the note; "They are Professor Hans Smit, from the Particle Physics Faculty in Oxford and Professor David Clarke from Cambridge." Stuart was nervous; these were heavyweight academics that have spent all their life building on current science. How would they respond to his radical ideas?

Sam waved at a young man walking past the office, he came in. "This is Freddie Young; he has just graduated and is our office manager, so he will handle your diary and any other arrangements you need." Freddie was a naturally likeable person, skinny with dark curly hair, a disastrous beard; definitely a party animal, they agreed to get together later that day.

Sam and Stuart planned to use much of the rest of the week interviewing candidates. They didn't have an exact headcount but they both felt that an initial research group of six people including Alice and Stuart would be sufficient. However on the development side they needed a wide expertise covering material science, electrical engineering through aeronautical design and construction. They needed people like Froom who could be multi-disciplinary. They agreed several interview teams to speed things up and decided to offer a trial employment period in case the individuals couldn't cope with the radical nature of the work. Nigel Jones, Neil Foster and Roger Wall had agreed to help out which added a lot more weight to the process. The academic links would be left to later.

There was no catering available yet, so Sam and Stuart went to the local pub for lunch; Anne Little and Peter West joined them, they seemed like good people, but they were poorly briefed, and it was a good opportunity to update them. They all returned back to the hangar area where progress was good; both hangars had been thoroughly cleaned, repainting had started. The roofs had been fixed, the massive sliding doors were being repaired and new lighting and three-phase electrics were being installed. Stuart asked Freddie to organise the transport of key equipment from Smythfield to the hangar, Sam reinforced that it was to be secure transportation.

There was so much to do, and Stuart was impressed with the quality of the team and the way they worked together, helping each other; they had an enthusiasm that only comes from the excitement that you are doing something special and breaking new ground. There was a meeting planned the next day with Sir Peter and Nigel to tie up the legal framework. They needed a name for the whole enterprise and decided on LeviPropIC Systems. It all looked OK and Stuart passed it to his solicitor to check it over. He also got agreement from the Paul Brighton that his patents were secure. His financial package was beyond his expectations. Any research outcome from IC was to be shared equally between Stuart and the UK government although there was no reference to such research being shared with other countries.

The lack of communications meant that everyone concentrated on getting the rest of the infrastructure in place. There would be a high performance computing facility in the other new building but there would also be a 'big pipe' linking it to a network of other HPCs.

The interview process was tougher than expected. In truth the team was not ready; moreover various people associated with the project had selected the candidates. It was difficult, since each individual needed convincing of the worth of the project, without the team devolving too much about it! Towards the end of the week they had four potential candidates for the development side of things but no candidates for the research side; perhaps they shouldn't be surprised. More worrying was that some speculative pieces had started appearing in the press about a new secret airplane; fortunately there was no reference to Stuart.

Nevertheless, they started building plans. Alice and Stuart defined the research plan that was basically to prove Stuart's hypotheses. The development side of things was a bit clearer in that they agreed to create two vehicles, one to test out the power of the IC drive and the other to offer a practical utility vehicle. Stuart felt pleased with the events and activities of the week. Admittedly there had been a lot of admin but it was all necessary to get the enterprise onto a sound footing.

It was Saturday and Stuart was waiting for Harry to arrive. He hated airports; they are soulless transit camps and apart from meeting people, everyone else is in weary resignation, except of course, for the bored staff. Some might say it's the start of a holiday, but the operation is so fragile that most of the time people would rather a transporter from Star-Trek to avoid the misery. So it was no surprise that the plane was late, and Stuart killed time by queuing at one of the coffee chains and setting down among the detritus to read a newspaper. Later on, he queued by the arrivals gate and his heart leapt when he saw Harry waving. If she had a long journey it didn't show, she looked great. He didn't know that she had freshened up in the lounge beforehand.

They hugged each other for a while before going back to the car where they kissed.

"I really missed you."

"And me you," she replied. Her work had finished sooner than expected and so, rather than stay on, she wanted to come home. She went through her time in the US, which had clearly been successful and fun. "And what have you been up to... crashed the Paradox yet?" She laughed.

"It's been quite a time." He went through the last few weeks activities.

"So it worked, you've got sponsorship... big time!"

"Sure, but I have my reservations, I'm not sure I'm in control of things anymore."

"Do you want control of it, Stuart?"

"No, I suppose not, I don't know."

"So what do you want?"

"To prove my theory and get a working vehicle into the world... and I don't want someone misusing it."

"And will you get it?"

"Yes, it looks like it, well the first two anyway... and I am going to make some money too."

"It always helps," she laughed. "I'm not sure how you prevent misuse." They had a relaxing weekend reacquainting themselves with one another. They went to a local concert on the Saturday and had a late lunch after a long walk on the Sunday; the weekend had gone. Before he left home, one security lorry and a transporter had arrived to collect his equipment and Paradox. The crew were a tough-looking bunch and very efficient; they expected to be at Farnborough by mid-morning.

Stuart hadn't felt as relaxed for years as he drove to Farnborough. There was an orderly queue of cars waiting to get through security, how the place had changed in a couple of weeks. There were still a few cars parked alongside the entrance and Stuart felt that he was being watched. He had agreed with Sam that they would lay on a demonstration of Paradox in the afternoon for all the people that had recently joined so they had an idea of the magnitude of the undertaking. Froom wanted a specific demonstration for the development candidates. The recruiting process had stalled for the moment and they agreed that if they could persuade the two academics to see a demonstration then they too might help with advice on resources; the action was left with Amanda Stone.

Stuart's office looked chaotic as Freddie tried to get some order into Stuart's various papers and so he went to the research area to see Alice. She was deep in thought as he entered.

"Sorry to interrupt, Alice, but I wanted to update you on the plan to use academic links to identify new candidates."

"I was in the process of re-reading your hypothesis Stuart... I have to say I was sceptical at first but... well it does seem sound now I re-read it... where did your thoughts come from?"

"I don't know, Alice, maybe it's a lack of science that enabled me to take a different view of things."

"Nonsense, you have a good scientific brain. Admittedly you have limited knowledge and maybe that helped, but it's more than that... somehow you have speculated... made a big leap into something that fits and make sense... without any real evidence."

"I'm not sure if I should tell you where I think it leads," he said cautiously.

"Surprise me."

"Well, just suppose that there are many separate forces that come together to make what we think of as gravity and that their integration produces an equilibrium in our solar system and maybe beyond, but not everywhere in the cosmos, indeed they could create neutral states of existence which we cannot identify, such as dark matter. Black holes could be another distortion of equilibrium. I want to see if we can find more forces, and from that, start to build a better understanding of the composition of the cosmos. Indeed to understand the nature of each of the forces, since I suspect they are all different."

There was silence as Alice considered things. "God I don't know, Stuart, it's difficult enough to understand what you've discovered."

"Alice it has to be understood in context. Somehow I have broken out a component of something that we once thought of as singular, so we need to see how it all fits back together."

"So, what's the plan?"

"Well, we try to figure out what we have and how it fits into the big picture... and... at the same time; we try and look for more forces."

"OK it's a big task, I'll put a plan together but the sooner we get some more serious horsepower the better."

They both wandered over to the hangar to see the arrival of Paradox and the equipment. All the experimental equipment was already being setup in different parts of the hangar. Froom introduced two of the development candidates and wanted Stuart to demonstrate Paradox to them. They checked the vehicle over to ensure no damage in transit and the three of them got in; the large hangar doors were still open. Stuart put Paradox into hover and then gently eased it out of the hangar to navigate around the site at about 50 feet and then back. They wouldn't need the afternoon demonstration since everyone on site stopped to stare at the strange vehicle. The two candidates didn't need any more convincing, they were both from the aeronautical industry and were keen to participate. They knew a lot of folk in the nearby research park who they could recruit plus a couple of test pilots who might be interested.

Over coming weeks, things progressed well, but not as fast as Stuart wished. The communications were established and the supercomputer was installed. They finally had a visit from the two professors; they were an interesting pair of individuals who knew each other well.   David Clarke was in his late forties and quite small and portly, he still had dark curly hair that extended to his wild beard, Stuart thought he could see the remnants of a previous meal in it, in fact he could see evidence of other food on his jacket; not a snappy dresser he thought. He must have bad eyesight judging by the thick lenses of his glasses and had a strange blink every ten seconds or so. He spoke with a gentle Scots accent that was warm, yet precise. In contrast Hans Smit, although about the same height, was slim with a smart brown suit. He too was in his late forties, but his face was heavily lined, which somehow accentuated his piercing blue eyes, his thinning hair was carefully combed back to do its best which wasn't good enough. His English was clipped with a slight accent.

They both viewed the meeting as a formal affair and Stuart responded accordingly. He took the opportunity to explain the history of his discovery and was able to show a floating bar from one of the experiments. If either of them were surprised, they didn't show it; perhaps they had been pre-briefed! There were detailed questions throughout which he and Alice handled. It wasn't hostile, but Stuart had the distinct feeling that they were here to disprove or explain away his findings. They finally got to the demonstration of Paradox. Stuart explained the power drive and the controls; so far he thought it wise not to mention his hypothesis. By now, he was a slightly better pilot and took them on a flight around the site, he explained that he wasn't using the second phase of the power since it was too dangerous, but just for fun he did accelerate rapidly up to about 500 feet just to show off.

They all retired to the research area where Alice was due to give an explanation of Stuart's hypotheses, however they asked for time to have a private discussion between themselves. They had been quite undemonstrative throughout the whole morning and even seemed unimpressed by Paradox, however when Stuart watched their discussion through the glass partition it was very animated. Eventually, they emerged from the room.

David Clarke started. "Hans and I wanted some time to discuss what we have seen today and how it fits in with current scientific thinking. You may know there are lots of emerging theories, some of which could support what we have seen today. We need to spend more time investigating it, however our initial thoughts is that your findings do not fit any current thinking."

"This is important," Hans added, "since it could have endorsed some pretty fantastic theories that are around. David and I are not given to overstatement, but it looks like you have made a breakthrough in fundamental physics that will change all our thinking."

Stuart laughed, "For months I tried to find a rational solution to all this and I couldn't... I do have a fantastic theory myself; would you like to hear it?" They were both eager to hear.

Alice gave the presentation on Stuart's hypotheses and they both listened in silence. At the end Stuart added his bigger plan to see if he could find more components of gravity.

"It's no more fantastic than us believing that gravity was a single force," Hans said. "Look, if David agrees, we need to get a few of our colleagues to come here and see how we can support and extend your work here. I would like to do it in the next few days?"

"Fine," said Stuart, "we are looking to get some additional resources to help out on the research."

"I think I speak for Hans when I say we would like to be involved directly and both have people who would be significant contributors on the programme."

"We will need to clear it with Sir Peter Dawson, but it sounds great."

Two names were selected of those that were put forward, Dr Jerome Housden who was currently doing research at Cambridge and Jonathan Ben who had recent returned from MIT and was looking for a new research project. They both had questioning minds and were enthusiastic to the new ideas coming out of Farnborough. They quickly settled in and Alice was delighted at their contribution. The research became broader as the team worked on the context of the discovery and how it related to and changed existing thinking, they were all pleased that some early work elegantly fitted with past research and indeed explained some of the anomalies that past theories were unable to accommodate. The site was now a hive of industry and many of the houses had been converted into small apartments which were suitable for the research and development people; Stuart had a rather grand apartment that he now used mid-week. The old Clubhouse had been renovated and as well as the recreational facilities now had a good 24-hour canteen.

There was increasing press comment in the newspapers and on the web; it was inevitable with so many people involved in the work. Stuart had been accosted several times as he was leaving Farnborough and the press was now waiting for him when he got home. He sought guidance from Sir Peter's office and it was agreed that a formal statement should be made followed by a press briefing. He had a meeting with Nigel Jones and various people from his office to discuss details of the announcement; Nigel had appointed a press officer to oversee things. Although he only visited Farnborough a couple of times each month he was acutely aware of the current status. Stuart had a robust argument with Nigel since he felt that it was time to allow the wider community to know details of the discovery. Nigel had clear guidance from the Cabinet that it was supportive of making the discovery available but in a timely way, so that other countries would be included once the basic research had been completed.

"There are leaks on the web plus the press, I'm not sure we should be controlling it," I said.

"Stuart, please remember the original agreement that you endorsed. You did say that you wanted more research resource so let's use this opportunity to announce the invitation for the international academic community to participate."

That satisfied Stuart; he knew the UK wanted an early lead and who could blame them? This way they have their lead and the discovery becomes international. Stuart had no knowledge that there was a shadow development team working close by in a MoD location. Meanwhile the development side of the shop had grown rapidly, and the three projects were fully staffed. As well as the utility vehicle and PowerParadox as it became affectionately known; they were also working on a new drive design that offered much more flexibility in all dimensions to better control the power.

Harry and Stuart were spending more time with each other and on a couple of times he had taken her around the site. She had met many of the team over supper when she stayed over. They had discussed the forthcoming press announcement and apart from a couple of speculative news items his life had been fairly private, they both knew it was going to change.

The plan was to hold the announcement at one of the London Institutes, but it quickly became apparent that there was major interest and they had to organise it at the QE11 Centre, there were over 800 people planning to come from across the globe.

Harry had stayed over the night before which gave Stuart the opportunity to practice his part of the announcement with her. He was nervous only because of the scale of things, after all he had presented his discovery many time before. She joined him at the Centre and was surprised at the crowds, presumably press, already there in advance; fortunately they were helped by security folk to get into the building.

Sir Peter, Nigel and their team were already there, and they briefly went through the agenda one last time; Sir Peter would chair the question and answer session at the end. They all sat at the front of the auditorium as the doors were open, Stuart saw that most of the team were there, and nodded to a few of them, Harry held his hand tightly.

It took about five minutes for the audience to quiet and Sir Peter was able to start.

"Ladies and Gentlemen, this press announcement will go down as one of the most important events in history. What we will be talking about today is a discovery... a discovery so profound, that it will touch everyone in the world... and I really do mean everyone." The auditorium was so silent. He went on to talk about the UK government and its support of a man who had made this remarkable discovery. It was a strong plug for Sir Peter and the Cabinet for having courage to back something so 'game changing'. Eventually he introduced Stuart.

Stuart stood at the podium with an apple in his hand and waited for silence. "There once was a great man called Sir Isaac Newton and he made a fantastic discovery about something called gravity," he dropped the apple. "Now, Ladies and Gentlemen that apple no longer has to drop because gravity as we know it no longer exists and I will show you why." He went through the history of his IC discovery making sure all the people who had supported him were acknowledged. Finally he showed a video of Paradox in early flight; throughout the auditorium pads were busy writing and recording.

"In conclusion we are now working on a new drive unit to give us more flexibility and control, but we are making two vehicles, the utility vehicle isn't finished yet but is designed to be configured for people transport, or heavy commercial loads, or agriculture." He put a photo of the vehicle on the large screen behind him. "The second vehicle we call PowerParadox, which is designed to understand the performance and limits of the forces involved and consequently will be both manned and unmanned."

"Today, we can show you the prototype of PowerParadox," and with that, the screen was retracted to show the vehicle hovering about ten feet from the stage. There was a strange sound coming from the audience... perhaps one of disbelief? It was a far cry from original Paradox. "This vehicle had been designed and assembled by people who know about extremes; in speed and materials and stresses. Our pilot will show you there are no tricks, please don't be alarmed." The PowerParadox turned to face the audience, just about everyone was taking photos. It then moved forward and upwards to the balcony before going vertical and up to the roof of the building. It then rolled very slowly back down and reversed towards the stage where it remained in a hover.

The audience all rose to applaud the demonstration with many of them coming forward to get to the stage. Security people appeared from nowhere to control the crowd. Sir Peter Dawson took to the stage to settle people down and once a semblance of order prevailed he restarted. This was the last session of the morning and Sir Peter made it very clear that he was delighted with the research and development happening in the UK, yet the very nature of the discovery meant the government was beholden to open out the discovery to the rest of the world; they would be creating an international forum to design ways for this to happen. At the first phase, he invited academics from around the world to submit applications to be part of the IC and LeviProp teams.

The questions session had to be abandoned since the meeting had become chaotic with a large number of people leaving, presumably to file their news story. The whole team had to be ushered into a private room where they were all briefed not to speculate with the press but channel everything through the press office. If they felt intimidated in any way they were to report it to Nigel Jones.

Harry was right; it was the end of privacy.

CHAPTER 13

Breakdown

From that day on there was always some item, some article, about Stuart in the papers. He had given up on the net; he had begging notes, crank notes, religious notes you name it, but most of all hostile and bullying notes... so he opted out. He created a secure alias for communicating with friends and colleagues that shut out the rest of the world. Not so, alas, his personal life, Zoe had contacted him saying she and the kids were being hounded and to get something done. Nigel Jones said he would try and help out but that hopefully time would help.

It was a nightmare time; everyone on the team was being pursued in some way. It was far worse for Harry, at first she shrugged it off, but their meetings became more clandestine and they continually had to plan ways of avoiding publicity. It came to a head one weekend.

"Sorry Stuart, I can't carry on like this."

"I'm so sorry, Harry, there is nothing I can do, if there was, I would have done it."

"I know, but something special between us is tarnished, so I am going to re-invent my life somewhere away from here."

Stuart knew it was coming. "Will I see you again?"

"Maybe, if this world gives you space. You are paying a big penalty for your discovery."

It was a sad parting and Stuart returned to Farnborough where no-one could get to him. He felt empty, he was empty, he had no friends apart from Rob and except for work everyone he met felt so insincere, as if they had their own agenda. It was the lowest point in his life and his discovery had been the cause. Stuart knew he was given to times of obsessive behaviour, ignoring other around him. Losing Zoe and the kids had created a cancer that was slowly eating into him challenging his ability to build, let alone hold, any close relationships with people. This personal self-doubt in his own worth made him irritable and intolerant of his teammates and it was unsurprising that they communicated with him less and less. He spent too much time trying to analyse himself and his shortcomings, but whichever way his mind spun, he couldn't find any answers.

Stuart shunned any publicity and instead threw himself into work and it did give him a distraction, he became totally focused on finding another component of gravity. He knew that he had recreated a new equilibrium and so there must be other forces in play, moreover the team had done some mathematical analysis that was beginning to point to other such forces within the cosmos. He didn't know whether the force he had discovered had such unique characteristic that using bars with the same composition would work but thought it a good starting point. He had the equipment team build a device that would enable him to test out different angles and amplitudes to a much finer precision than before.

Rob tried to intervene in the crisis. "Come on, Stuart, stop driving yourself, you've hardly slept in the last few days and you look like shit."

"Rob, I'm fine, I think I'm getting close."

"To what, Stu? A fucking breakdown. At least come over for supper, Sue hasn't seen you for a while."

"Come on, Rob, buy me a pint at the clubhouse." So they went over to the club and despite a few curious glances had a couple of pints.

Rob thought he knew what was eating into Stuart but couldn't get him to open up. "You can't go on like this you know that?"

"Like what?"

"The impact you're having on the team, Stu you need counselling."

"Thanks Rob I know you mean well." And he got up and walked out.

That evening, Rob phoned Sam about Stuart's state of mind. "Rob, we all are worried about him; losing Harry was a bigger blow to him than he knows. We have tried to contact her, but she won't return our calls."

"Well we could see if Zoe will help, but it could be explosive?"

"Do you think she would see him and try and help?"

"I don't know, Sam; perhaps we need some advice from a professional counsellor?"

"I will talk with Nigel and see if there is anyone we could use."

Nigel did find someone, Pru Cane; she had extensive experience of dealing with stress disorders and compulsive behaviour. She had a close crop of grey hair that set of her fine features; her lined face showed a history of humour rather than the tension that such a job carried. She was slight with a hint of yoga in her stature.

"I've had a chance to study things, but I really need to meet Stuart now," she said to Sir Peter and Nigel Jones at their offices in Whitehall. They agreed to introduce Pru at Farnborough later on that week. It was a normal regular progress meeting; indeed the development programme seemed to be going well but the research side has stalled mainly due to Stuart.

Pru had been introduced as a psychologist who could help out in future recruiting. At a break in the meeting Pru approached Stuart and asked him to show her around; he was reluctant but finally agreed when Sir Peter requested him to show the early experiments. He completed a demonstration and explanation of one of the early floating frames. "You must be very proud, Stuart, to make such a fantastic discovery."

"I was, and I should be, but funnily enough I'm not, in fact I'm not needed now."

"That's nonsense; you are the leader, the free thinker, the man who makes things happen..."

"Maybe, but that was then."

Pru goaded him. "You're the man Stuart... not a shrinking

violet... what's eating you?"

"What's eating me... I'll tell you what's fucking eating me... I once had a life with a great family... that's gone. So then I started a new life and now that's over... I can't go anywhere without being hounded... so what have I got?... IC and LeviProp...fucking great."

There was a long silence and Pru studied his face... it was tired. And there was a hint of tears, Stuart turned away.

"Stuart, I have seen lots of people under stress of all sorts, please let me help?"

"What can you do for Christ's sake?"

"Honestly? I don't know, but it's got to be worth a try... hasn't it?" He didn't respond. "Would you mind if I saw your wife?"

"Why? Anyway she won't see you... she's thoroughly pissed off by all the press hounding her!"

"I'd like to give it a try if you'll let me. Then perhaps we could chat again... come on, you've nothing to lose." He nodded agreement.

It was hard for Pru to meet Zoe; eventually she confronted her as she was getting into her car. Zoe relented, and they went into her flat. Pru spent some time explaining who she was and why she needed help.

"I don't hate him you know, and I really didn't want to hurt him, but the opportunity came for me to breakaway and start a new life, something I desperately needed."

"I believe you found a new partner?" Pru said carefully.

"Yes Diana... but we're not together anymore... maybe I'm like Stuart... no good with relationships," she said in a mock laugh.

"I'm sorry, I didn't mean to probe; I'm just trying to find out what makes Stuart tick. Right now I would say professionally that he has had some sort of mental breakdown." Zoe sighed. "You don't seem surprised?"

"Stuart is a very rare breed, a person of high intensity in everything he does. In relationships, as a husband, or as a father, he works out what he thinks the highest ideal should be and sticks to it rigidly; if he meets his ideal he can't figure out why things are going wrong, after all the ideal is the highest. He never heard me scream at his obsessions day and night, and as soon as something was achieved, I waited for the next obsession to emerge. Sometimes there were so many obsessions you couldn't get through to him, and yet, he was sure we were all happy because he was meeting his ideal. I know he doesn't understand why I left him… he would say it was Diana… but it was because I needed to escape, and Diana gave me that opportunity. It was the same for the kids, he would do anything for them, but he never really got close to them to understand their emotional wants and needs; somehow it was outside his scope."

"Go on," said Pru.

"And yet he is a kind man, so kind, that he created the highest ideals because he loves us. It's mad, isn't it? He doesn't even know that I wanted a husband, a father who could fail, who was fragile and knew he could never meet all the standards of the best but would try hard and just love us all." She was unable to hold back the tears any longer.

As Pru drove home she reflected on Zoe's words. Stuart was an idealist and he had failed, he had restarted his life with Harry and I bet he was building a new ideal for her, but it collapsed. She had spent enough time with the team at Farnborough to know that Stuart was frustrated; he was a good engineer and problem solver, but the team was probably one of the best in the world and they eclipsed his talent, not deliberately, indeed they all saw him as their leader and yet it caused an insecurity that he had never had before. The research side was no different; Stuart felt overshadowed by their intellectual horsepower.

It was a dangerous complex of pressures that needed resolution urgently. One thing had become apparent very quickly as she talked with team members was that he was very special and had a unique gift of viewing things differently. He had a talent for new ideas and creating a new vision on things. Somehow his mind was able to consider and reconcile dissonance by inventing harmonising solutions. True he wasn't the best engineer, or the best scientist, but everyone recognised his gift and wanted to be associated with the way his thought process worked; it was a magnetic attraction that he didn't know he possessed. This was going to be a tough task. She saw Stuart the following day.

"How is Zoe? Is she OK? Did she say how the kids were?"

"I think she is fine, Stuart, I know she appreciates all the money you have sent her; it's clear she misses you and she would love me to help you."

"I've told you, Pru, I'm fine, just a bit tired that's all, but I would love to see her... preferably without Diana."

"That would be OK; they are no longer an item."

"Really, then can you arrange it?" He was already thinking of a reconciliation.

"No, Stuart, I won't arrange it unless you agree to my terms."

"What terms, Pru?"

"That you agree to a programme of counselling." She decided that the only way to handle Stuart was to be bold. "You are in a mess, Stuart; you think you are worthless and nothing could be further from the truth, all the teams need you and you are letting them down. You need to understand yourself and return to the person you once were... but... with some modifications."

"So, I'm a head case then?"

"If you want to put it like that... yes... you think about personal things too much. Do you want to stay like you are?"

"OK... enough I'll give it a shot."

"Right, it starts tomorrow, I'm going to get Zoe here to talk about you; nothing else, just you, your relationship is on hold... agreed?" He nodded.

"Then I'm going to get other people to give their view of you and after all that feedback we agree a way forward to restoring your self-belief."

"You've got it all worked out, haven't you?"

"Yes, Stuart, you won't believe some of the people I have had to deal with. We just need to put everything back in their proper boxes."

"Sounds easy."

"It won't be, and you'll discover your biggest enemy."

"Which is?"

"Honesty... being able to be honest with yourself... self-discovery is never easy."

Pru had decided that the comfy settee approach would not work with Stuart and that the meetings needed to be semi-formal and so she arranged a round table meeting room. She met Zoe at the Farnborough reception and had a pre-meeting about what she wanted to do and how to approach it. Stuart joined them a little later. It was tense, they both smiled at each other and tears were shared.

"I am managing this meeting, Stuart," Pru started, "and I want to ask Zoe some questions about you. I want you to listen, and not challenge her. Zoe had agreed that she would use examples to support anything she says."

The whole session was emotionally charged, but always with tears, never anger. At the end Zoe agreed to come back in a few months. Pru pulled all Zoe's comments together and presented Stuart with his desire to create 'Ideals' in his relationships; standards that were so high they became clinical and unbending. Over several sessions Stuart started to recognise his behaviour and together they shared ways of changing. It was all about relaxing the boundaries of his ideal behaviour and accepting his ability to fail and dealing with it. The most important discovery he made was that others may not match his ideal profile or indeed want to, and he should recognise and value people accordingly.

Over that same time Pru introduced a series of videos showing individual interviews she had done with a wide group of the team. It was a revelation to Stuart; they all held him in high esteem and most were envious of his gifts. They were all worried about his recent diffidence, and how it was unlike him. Pru followed it through with more analysis of Stuart's ability to see things differently using team discussions.

Alongside his therapy she introduced a fitness programme and a social programme, so he had no space to retreat into himself; it was working. After a couple of months he was practicing the techniques that Pru had taught him to deal with his 'standards' and his confidence in his own ability was returning although it was still fragile. About that time, he went into the research area and encountered Alice and Jerry Housden in a heated argument.

"Hey, you two... what's the problem?"

Alice was flushed with anger. "It's bloody Jerry, he won't listen."

"Alice you just don't get it." Jerry shot back. "I believe that I can show mathematically that the IC force you discovered is variable within the Universe."

"Nonsense," said Alice, "your computation is too isolated. Have a look, Stu." She displayed the calculations on a large screen. This was one of those times Pru had described, where he should trust his talent. Jerry took him through the calculations and Stuart was pleased he could follow the logic. He stared at the screen, it wasn't right somehow; he inverted the logic in his head and it showed there must be a second force somewhere... but where? He grabbed a pad off the desk and wrote down the logic. If there was a second force and it existed in opposition to the known IC but was influenced by differing masses then it could explain the position on earth that we know as gravity and would also explain behaviours in the cosmos as the two forces balanced and rebalanced themselves depending on the nature of nearby masses.

Alice and Jerry showed marginal interest as Stuart extended the inverted formula to balance the second force. After an hour they drifted off for a cup of coffee. When they returned Stuart was still busy scribbling on his pad surrounded by discarded paper. He was sure that the solution could be found if he changed the formula to show two types of mass, but there was no reasoning behind it. Nevertheless he experimented with the formula and eventually found a way to make it work. If it were true then it would explain how such forces had been created individually in the first place.

It was after seven in the evening when Stuart pushed the pad away and dropped his pen; he was exhausted, his brain had been running flat out for hours.

Alice and Jerry came over. "I think I've done it," he said sagging. He stepped back from the pad as Alice and Jerry went through it.

Alice looked stunned, "Where did all that come from, Stu?"

"I don't know, it just looked obvious, if there was a second force then mathematically it works and explains the variable nature, but it wouldn't work without a second type of mass, but that fits too as you can see. Thinking about it, maybe that principle could be extended."

Jerry just sat there going through the working and transposing into the computer. "It fucking works, I don't believe it, it fucking works! You're a fucking genius."

"I'm not sure about all that fucking," joked Stuart. If there was a switch to rebuild his broken ego then this was it. It looked like it could explain the expanding universe as well as phenomenon such as black holes. The neutralised part of the two forces was always the greatest component and could correspond to what is known as dark matter. It became folklore; the time when Stuart solved a part of the fundamental structure of the universe known as the gravitational pairing.

Pru and Stuart continued their counselling, but it was clear to her that he was on the mend. He insisted that they meet regularly anyway, just in case he slipped back to the old routine.

"Is that your new ideal?" Pru joked. They had become close friends and it was going to last.

A few days later Zoe came to call, Pru was still there to see how he behaved. He was full of his discovery and then realised that she had come to see him... not his work.

"Tell me about the kids, will I ever see them again?"

"Well they are all very pleased that they have a famous father and the money you gave them has helped as they were all broke. I think they are ready to see you."

"I'm not sure I'm ready to see them," he said looking at Pru.

"You're ready, Stuart, just remember the techniques."

"I know they would love to see this place."

"Great, I will fix it," and then thought, "and Alice, one of the team can show them around."

Pru smiled, he had remembered.

They went to the club where Stuart introduced Zoe to a few people before taking a separate table. "I can't undo the past, Zoe, I'm just so sorry I was blind to everything," he held her hand very gently. "There were some good bits, weren't there? Good memories and some sharp fun."

"Of course Stu... good memories. I would like to be friends, but just friends."

"I understand, but if we can see each other from time to time so you keep me on the road."

She laughed, "As I have done for years. It would be my pleasure."

Peter Dawson came in with Nigel in tow; their private time was over.

"Stuart, I assume this lovely lady is Zoe? I'm Peter Dawson, a partner of Stuart's." Zoe knew who he was and his powerful position in government. "I hope you don't mind the interruption, but this is the first chance I have had to get to Farnborough and congratulate Stuart." Zoe looked confused. "Don't you know?"

"I know my ex-husband has discovered powerful forces that no-one knew existed." The ex-husband bit still pained Stuart.

"Three days ago this man, this genius, has solved the fundamentals of the cosmos." Dawson was never given to overstatement.

"It's not the whole picture, Peter, in fact it's just a start, there is still a lot more to learn. Anyway it's not public."

"Will you stop being so damn modest? Jerry Housden has told Hans Smit and David Clarke, so the cat's out of the bag." Stuart was a bit miffed that Jerry had spoken to anyone about it. Zoe got up to go.

"Please don't go, Zoe."

"I have to Stuart, but I look forward to seeing you next week?" she said it as if it was a plan.

"Of course, I'll phone to confirm." She gave him a card with her new address and phone number.

"Lovely lady," said Peter, "I do hope you two get together again." Stuart wasn't sure of the sincerity in that comment, so he dismissed it.

"Right, the pressure is on."

"What pressure?" said Stuart looking confused.

"With this new finding we must expand the work here to the rest of the world."

Stuart was delighted; it was what he had wanted all along.

"As you know, we had promised to open things up to the

international academic community, so this is the chance. I have asked Hans and David to put a proposal together that will be peer-reviewed by the Scientific Advisor community. I have given them a month and then we announce it."

"I would like some input, Peter."

"Of course, Stuart; you have the last say. Would it be OK if the PM makes the announcement… it would look very good for her?" Stuart smiled. He would be delighted to be out of the limelight.

CHAPTER 14

Sesame

He did see Zoe that following week; it was still a little formal, but Stuart's minders had at least ensured that it was a private affair in a local pub in Smythfield. Zoe was now doing voluntary work at an arts centre in Portsmouth and was looking at buying a place on the city outskirts. Stuart was pleased that he could pass on some of his growing wealth to let her enjoy her passion for the arts. They discussed his mental state in an open way and as Pru predicted, she helped him think through the various things that were bothering him.

One of which was Jerry Housden telling other people about the mathematic session. Stuart had a nagging feeling that the existence of two forces and just two forces, seemed a bit too easy and that it could be millions of forces all paired, and meeting the same condition. He had tried to apply this idea but had drawn a blank; nevertheless his mind was still open to the idea. At least it lays the foundation for a completely new line of research and analysis, he thought; when he saw Jerry he decided to have it out with him.

"Jerry, I wish you hadn't shared the big sums that I worked on."

"I meant to see you, Stuart, to apologise. I am so embarrassed, in all the excitement... I lost my head." It was clear that he was still excited... just like a young boy catching his first fish.

"Fine, well next time let's chat about it? Anyway I still think there is more to it."

"Stuart, I have spent hours with the HPC, computing and simulating your formula and it just keeps working and resolving itself so if there is more it hasn't become apparent." They agreed to work together with Alice around his ideas, if for no other reason but to put his mind at rest.

He spent some time with Hans and David and agreed the content of the announcement document. The planned visit of the kids was scheduled and although it should have excited Stuart, he was nervous about how it would go. It did surprise him that Zoe had already met Alice and organised the day. Although it was unspoken, many of the team got involved in the visit to support Stuart. After Zoe and the kids' arrival and clearance he met them at the conference area. It was very uncomfortable for all of them and he couldn't think of a way to ease the tension and his apology for letting them down made it worse.

Zoe and Alice took control and escorted them around the site with everyone eager to meet them. It may have been planned, but over the morning each of them held back to chat with Stuart. Lucy was the first to join him.

"Dad, I'm glad this has happened it has been awful for all of us. I hope we can meet up?"

"Of course, just tell me where and when?" He was cautious not to presume anything.

"Well how about supper in town? You could meet me at work, there is a PR reception in the evening, and it would be great to have my famous dad there." Same old Lucy; always an angle.

"Done, just send me the details."

A little later Henry said, "Dad, I'm really sorry, I was torn between you both, but I knew you could take care of yourself and Mum was much more fragile." If only you knew, he thought but just smiled and nodded. "Anyway, I hope we can see each other, I'm really interested in what you're doing here... and I need a job."

"I'm sure you would be useful in LeviProp Henry, we are just getting going, I will get something organised."

It was towards the end of the morning that Marc approached him. "Thanks for the money, it's making college life easier." He was distant.

"How is college, Marc?"

"Fine."

"What are you studying?"

"Geography." All one word answers; of all the kids Stuart thought he was closest to Marc. "See you sometime... and thanks again." He re-joined the group.

He remembered Pru's advice, relax, it would take a while and not to be pre-judgmental. As they were all leaving Zoe turned and gave him a kiss on the cheek; it was a deliberate move in front of them all to say things had been forgiven.

"That was tough," he whispered.

"Stick with it, Stuart, it will never be the same but...well, just look to the future. See you soon..."

The following week there was a normal review of project progress, it was rare for Peter and Nigel to be there; presumably they wanted to announce the international programme. As Stuart entered there was applause and stamping, he looked slightly embarrassed as he took his seat at the conference table.

The first part covered the research work and a discussion on Stuart's proof at a high level; the review then covered the three development projects. The new drive unit had been tested and was functioning well in all dimensions. The plan was to replace the drive in PowerParadox and begin testing the limits of the drive. The utility vehicle was complete and undergoing testing general testing, it would be the first manufactured vehicle from LeviProp. Froom and the team had created half a dozen small one-man personal vehicles for getting around the site as a proof of concept, needless to say there had been a few accidents mainly based on recklessness. It did stimulate a big debate on the need to create flying standards and in the end they agreed that initially there would be three height settings from the ground; basic hover and drive at one metre, normal transport at five metres and possibly high speed at ten metres. Hans and David agreed to incorporate it into their document and that they would put forward ideas on international standards to define virtual flying corridors and flying codes. It was a timely point for Sir Peter to introduce the announcement paper that Hans, David and others had been working on. Nigel passed the paper to each participant. The paper were marked 'Confidential' and numbered; they adjourned for an hour to give everyone time to digest the contents.

In summary following the public announcement the Government had received intense lobbying from so many nations about releasing information, the paper recommended the creation of a worldwide academic community. Every country in the world would be asked to nominate a small scientific team that would share in an open public way all information associated with the current research and development around IC. It laid out a formal process with meetings and checks to ensure the process was not abused.

Sir Peter Dawson went through the paper in more detail than expected.

Rob asked, "What about LeviProp licenses, Peter?"

"That's a normal commercial issue that would be handled through the LeviProp business," he replied.

"The agreement on LeviProp is that the business should focus on making the Drive Units and not the vehicles although we would retain some vehicle specialised manufacturing," added Stuart.

"Such as?" from Alice.

"Space vehicles, I think we can take a lead." It was Hans Smit.

"What about military use?" asked Jerry. "So far we haven't talked about it but just think what this technology will do?"

"I agree," said Stuart. "Sir Peter and I have discussed this and frankly I don't want anything to do with it. Having said that, it would be stupid of me not to recognise the impact it will have."

"Not to mention the massive redundancy of some equipment and arsenals," Rob added.

"Peter, I don't expect you to answer this, but I assume that your military colleagues are already developing IC projects?" If Peter was uncomfortable, he didn't show it.

"I'm not going to duck the point; Stuart and the answer is yes. There is a UK shadow team developing military equipment. I am not prepared to tell you more; we did discuss this area of military use a while ago and you said you did not want to be involved... fair enough?"

"Absolutely, but the military should pay for the licenses if they use LeviProp."

Sir Peter smiled. "Of course, Stuart, the UK Government has a vested interest in LeviProp. We should speak about LeviProp after this meeting. Can I move onto the announcement?" There was general agreement. "It's clear for such an announcement to carry credibility it needs an independent sponsor, not the UK Government." There were wry smiles from most of the audience. "It seems like the United Nations could be the ideal route to carry the work forward and they have a group called International Centre for Theoretic Physics (ICTP). It really fits their remit and Hans Smit knows the people there and has invited them to join us next week. Hopefully we can encourage them to take on this role. We have sent them a confidential briefing paper already. Assuming they agree, the PM will launch the programme when she speaks at the UN next month. It will create a couple of issues for us here."

"Such as?" asked Alice

"Well the first issue is your time and how much you can or want to put into it, and second is security, but I think we have an idea that may work."

"I think the time issue will work itself out, Peter," said Hans, "typically the subject matter and the interest will evolve, and the trick is to make sure things are shared at the appropriate time. This would operate much as international science collaboration works at the moment."

"OK, well you and David will be driving it forward."

"We must have Stuart as Chairman though," Hans added. Stuart nodded his agreement.

"We are fortunate that there is a lot of spare army facilities nearby in Aldershot, so we can setup a secure campus should the nominees want to work nearby."

Following some minor admin details the meeting closed and Stuart, Nigel and Peter reconvened for the LeviProp meeting. Stuart had not really spent much time on the business side of things lately, but Nigel had, and he gave them an update. Funding had not been an issue and a site for manufacturing the drive had been found on the outskirts of Manchester. They were now in a position to start recruiting and building the assembly line for the drive. Nigel handed out the CVs of the proposed executive team; it was very impressive with some very public business names involved; all of them had agreed to be part of the business. Stuart mentioned that he wanted Henry to be included in the business and it was agreed. All the commercial documentation had been signed a while ago.

Progress on all projects continued and the PowerParadox (PP) had produced some astonishing acceleration and speeds. It was now at the stage that it was necessary to test the vehicle in unmanned mode since the stresses on the pilots had been at their limits. The first such test was planned this Friday at the military airfield. It was going to be a vertical test and all air traffic had been restricted from the area. The plan was to accelerate upward for about ten miles and then open the drive to full power for five seconds; no-one knew whether the craft would hold together but there were various recording devices littered around the vehicle and a wide array of radar monitoring devices. The US, Russian and Chinese governments had been specifically advised of a 'test' to avoid any misunderstanding. They had all queried what was happening, and the UK response was that the PM would be announcing something at the UN the following week.

Some of the development team had gone to the test site but Stuart and Rob stayed in the Farnborough office with a whole set of monitors.

The test started, and the vehicle was tracked on its trajectory. It was accelerating so fast that all the monitoring devices had difficulty tracking it. As it approached the full power stage, it just disappeared. There was nothing on the monitors and they waited in hope that the vehicle would reappear. After a few minutes it was clear that PowerParadox had gone. Stuart wanted the data analysis to start immediately and everyone relevant to be around over the weekend to figure out what happened. In his mind, Stuart had an idea that the force was outside of known parameters, was it possible it could accelerate beyond the speed of light? He needed to sit down with the research team and figure it out.

In one of the secret US monitoring sites they had viewed the experiment with vastly more sophisticated instrumentation.

"What happened? It was on the scope and now it's gone, did it explode?" said one of the military staff.

"It definitely didn't explode," said his colleague, "it just disappeared. Although I am recording a faint disturbance which may be its track but whatever it was, it was faster than anything I've seen before."

"What the hell are the Brits doing? We need to get someone talking to them now," said the senior officer on site and he started making some calls.

Similar things were happening in other countries, most of them went to high alert.

Stuart got through to Peter Dawson to update him on the tests; somehow he knew already.

"I can't talk, Stuart, I'm already fending off other countries and I haven't updated the PM and the Cabinet yet. Let's speak later, in fact I'll come down to Farnborough."

Meanwhile the team was collecting data from some of the UK monitoring sites and the same cosmic disturbance had been identified. It was late afternoon when they all met to try and analyse what happened. The first problem they found was that as PP approached full power it was already accelerating so fast that the recordings were useless. Stuart remembered the early experiments and someone's comments about it being more powerful that we understand.

Apart from analytical detail no-one said anything. "OK team, this is a setback," said Stuart, "but actually it shows the power of the IC discovery and how little we understand it. The best we can do is use the data to extrapolate what we think happened and let's get another PP built, the materials composition is crucial. Then let's think through a new test plan to avoid this happening again." The mood of the team changed and became positive again.

"Remember, there are no rules, you must think differently, I for one think it accelerated beyond the speed of light; we are looking at extending our mathematical model." There was silence. He deliberately threw this thought in, knowing it would stimulate ideas.

Sir Peter arrived early evening. "God what a day." He looked tired. "Any news on what happened?"

Stuart gave him an update. "Peter, I know I'm becoming boring, but essentially, we have proved that we have developed a power that is beyond our understanding. I'm not sure we should have been so ambitious with the test, to be honest. I am sorry." He then outlined the future plan and workstreams.

"Don't apologise, Stuart, we all know we are in uncharted territory and now so do a lot of other countries. Who incidentally, are very worried that we have something very powerful." He couldn't resist a smile. "The plan is we hold off giving an explanation until the PM's pitch at the UN. It's just about doable, but the US is really hassling us. They think that we have shared a lot of technology and have been keeping something back. I suspect the PM will cave in to Roper and cut some special deal."

Stuart sat back; this was a long way from his early beginnings in the workshop. There were legions of people working on IC developments in a matter of months; now Prime Ministers and Presidents... it was all out of his control and slowing things down.

In fact, Sir Peter was summoned to number ten early next morning for a meeting. He entered the conference room and met three of the PM's closest advisors as well as the Foreign Secretary and the Secretary of Defence. The PM entered, she looked very fresh, and clearly recent events hadn't disturbed her.

"Ah Peter thanks for coming, we have a scheduled call with President Roper in 30 minutes." He said nothing and waited.

"I've had an informal discussion with some members of the Cabinet and I have decided to include President Roper on the work that you and your team are doing, in advance of the UN announcement."

"Is it just an early briefing, Prime Minister, or is there more behind it?"

"Let's see how it goes Peter; I confess we do have some tradable issues that have been getting in the way of things."

Peter Dawson could guess several of those issues; US defence procurement, technology transfer and security to name just three. They all moved to a secure videoconference room and the meeting was initialised. The introductions were made with some small banter between President Roper and Linda Ramsay. Peter Dawson identified President Roper and Vice President Vincenzo as well as Ed

Bruckner, but he had not met General Martin Stein or Byron Garratt the new Secretary of Defence.

The meeting was cordial but wary with Roper asking what was going on with this missile test and why the UK was not collaborating with the US, as in the past. Ramsay responded in a very matter-of-fact way.

"Over recent months we have uncovered someone who in extraordinary circumstances seemed to have made a world-changing discovery on the nature of gravity. I'm sure your intelligence people have been keeping you advised. We have already made a series of announcements as you know, releasing information on a progressive basis. We have spent a long time investigating this discovery and validating it and part of that validation was based on the tests that you identified. I should say they were absolutely not missile tests."

"Then what the hell were they?" Roper replied rather testily.

"It was simply a vehicle, a space vehicle."

"You've got a spaceship that goes that fast? How fast was it, Byron?"

"Well, Mr President, our best estimate is that it was accelerating towards the speed of light before disappearing… which is impossible."

"I did say it was world-changing, but I'm not a scientist; let me hand over to Peter Dawson."

Peter spent some time explaining the background to Stuart's discovery and a high level summary of IC and LeviProp.

Ramsay took over. "So you see, Mr President, we have a fantastic new source of power and the United Kingdom doesn't plan to keep it to itself."

"Just imagine what it could do to world order, world economics not to mention security of nations." It was Ed Bruckner.

"Just so Mr Bruckner, that why I plan to announce a programme to share our findings at the UN next week."

There was uproar at the US end of the meeting with General Stein saying, "No way, Mr President, we can't allow this."

"I think you underestimated their reaction," said Dawson out of the corner of his mouth.

PM Ramsay interrupted the confusion. "Gentlemen, I don't think you are in a position to allow anything. I know all this is a bit of a surprise and we are keen, in the interests of our relationship, to ensure that the US is positively advantaged."

"What the fuck does that mean?" The President's mask had dropped.

"It means exactly what I said," The PM responded tartly.

VP Vincenzo had said little so far. "I suggest, Mr President, that we adjourn this meeting to consider the implications."

The President nodded agreement. "My apologies, Prime Minister, is there any way we can restart this meeting in say, three hours?"

Ramsay paused before agreeing. "I hope the next meeting will be more constructive." The call closed. "I think we are going to have trouble," she said to no-one in particular.

"If this is the response from an ally, imagine some other countries," piped up the Foreign Secretary.

"Any views on how they will respond?" Ramsay again.

"Our announcement plans may be a touch premature," the Foreign Secretary said.

"We simply cannot keep this to ourselves," said Dawson, "anyway Stuart Ashley wouldn't have it; he had already put some things on the web."

"So I go ahead with the UN pitch?"

"Perhaps, but in a phased way?"

"Go on?"

"Well, you make a vague announcement saying that the discovery is not verifiable yet and that over the coming six months we will be developing the collaboration programme with the UN; continue the progressive approach.

"It gives the US a minimum of six months and the role of influencing the announcement."

From the Defence Minister, "They will want control."

They spent the next few hours restructuring a possible approach to the announcement that could appease the US.

In Washington, it was a very different meeting. For a start it had doubled in size. Ed Bruckner was driving the discussion.

"As you know, they made a press announcement some weeks ago, so we knew something was going on. Since then we have had some indirect information from someone at their Farnborough research site and the feedback on the discovery had been incredible to use their word."

"Pray tell, Ed, why have we only just heard about it?" It was one angry President.

"It was all low key stuff and we had asked to be involved, then there was this latest trial." It was a poor response and Bruckner knew it.

Leo Catani spoke, "Mr President, the most important thing is that we delay the Brits announcing it to the world and we get as much knowledge as we can on this science as fast as possible."

"Thanks, Catani, sense at last. OK, Ed, you and Byron map out a plan for the meeting, give the Brits the trade stuff and the security agreement but I want a nominated team ready to go to the UK in the next few days... do I make myself clear?"

Leo Catani and Rick Marsh were tasked with getting the US team together whilst Ed and Byron planned an offer for the UK Government.

When the meeting restarted the UK attendees were the same, but the US delegation was noticeably larger. The president opened the meeting.

"Thanks for sparing the time, Linda," a conciliatory tone. "We would like to put some ideas forward if that's OK?"

"Of course," said the PM, "we have some ideas too."

"I know we have had some difficulty with the recent trade discussions and I promise you I will clear away the obstacles."

"That's good of you, Mr President."

"I have asked Ambassador Boxford to call at your earliest convenience with a signed document confirming the position. I have also asked him to bring a revised memorandum covering the security immigration and vetting issue that got held up somewhere. I'm sure you will find it acceptable."

Two down, thought Dawson, but what's the deal in return?

"We have worked together on so many scientific and technological developments in the past; we would request that we provide a team of the highest calibre to collaborate on your LeviProp project to our mutual advantage. They would be based in your research location and of course would be fully vetted by your people."

"I know you want us to hold off the UN announcement, Mr President."

"I do, Linda, but we can't hold back the inevitable, so between our respective countries I think we could present a fully worked PowerParadox solution to the world in say, 12 months' time. What do you think?"

Dawson had written on his pad within eyesight of the PM. We never mentioned PowerParadox, their inside information is good!! Go for six months.

"I think we can contain the position for six months but a year?"

"OK Linda, let's go for six months first, followed by a joint review on the timing of the full announcement."

"As long as we don't exceed 12 months, the speculation and pressure will be immense and... frankly uncontainable!" They got their year, Dawson thought, maybe it's not so bad for the UK anyway, but we will have to manage Stuart carefully.

"Agreed. Ed Bruckner will lead from our end and he will have a team list to you in three days; we will obviously expect to joint fund your work. Who is your lead?"

"Sir Peter Dawson will continue to hold responsibility and report directly to me."

"Likewise with Ed, and we should get a shared progress meeting every month."

"Agreed, Mr President."

"Thanks Linda, I'm glad we have resolved things. Does anyone have any other comment?"

Ed Bruckner spoke. "Yes, is it possible that Stuart Ashley could visit the US to brief some of our scientists and help with the UN announcement?"

Peter Dawson replied, "We are happy to extend the invitation; he really wants to share everything with all countries, you know."

Bruckner replied, "We respect that; by being part of the announcement work he can achieve it."

"We will need to agree my communication for next week's speech at the UN. We have to say something since the UN ICTP has been briefed."

"Let's leave it to Ed and Sir Peter to resolve but I'm sure we can phase the release of information."

Peter Dawson nodded. Ed Bruckner added, "I can come over to the UK with some of my people if that helps."

"Good plan, I will free up my diary."

The tension in the meeting had eased and apart from some final diplomatic words it closed.

"You have a lot to do, Peter," it was the PM, "let me know if you need any more resources."

"Watch out for that bastard, Bruckner, I knew him when he was US Secretary of Defence; he is a devious shit," an uncharacteristic comment from the Minister of Defence.

Sir Peter smiled, he knew of Bruckner's ruthless reputation. "I just hope we can manage Stuart Ashley's expectations," he added as he left.

It was two days later that Peter Dawson met Stuart; he had decided to tell him everything about the meeting. "That's it, Stuart, warts and all," he said after giving him a full update, "so, we can expect the US team tomorrow accompanied by Bruckner and his people."

"Frankly Peter, I'm unhappy about the delay in announcement."

"I thought you would be, but they have offered you the option of going there to assist in the announcement process."

"I want to stay here, there is so much to do, but if I can make sure the buggers don't delay things then maybe it's necessary."

"I thought you would be angry."

"Angry no, disappointed yes… but at the moment there are several anomalies that I can't resolve. I think I can understand that we can accelerate beyond the speed of light but what does it mean. Alice, Jerry and I think that it may impact on time itself."

"Sorry Stuart, you've lost me, but perhaps the US horsepower may help?"

"That what I thought too."

"You need to vet them all on skill and suitability; we will have done the background stuff, but we should assume they all have a direct line back to Washington."

It was a very stiff meeting the next day, Stuart saw Peter Dawson with a man who he assumed to be Bruckner and a small group of five rather bewildered people. The two men made a brief introduction of the US team and disappeared into one of the Farnborough offices. Gary Marshall was the first to introduce himself as the team leader.

"This is bizarre, all of us have been working in various areas of physics; we have been pulled from our current jobs at no notice, with the thinnest of briefs but that our role here is of national interest."

"So why did you come?" asked Stuart bluntly.

"I can't answer for the others but the information I was given goes against all the laws of physics, so frankly I thought I could come and have a look and if I've wasted a couple of days… well… what the heck." It was a refreshing honest answer.

The 'others' were Harry Franks currently at Leuven University, Lucy Dubois from Yale, with Nina Lerner from MIT. Lucy openly said she was using this opportunity to see her sister in London whilst the other three had a similar view to Gary.

Stuart, Jerry and Alice had got copies of all their CVs and had yet to discuss them, but they all agreed that the best way to introduce them to the work was a trip around the site. They started by going to the development hangars where they were shown the working utility vehicle as well as the new development of PowerParadox. Stuart left Jerry and Alice to explain everything as well as the recent lost PP event. Initially, the US team was mesmerised but then the detailed questions started, probing and recording. Finally they went to the

Research Centre where, over coffee, Stuart went into his theory together with the current proofs and a summary of future work.

"I don't understand," said Nina, "where did all this stuff come from?"

"It's all Stuart's discovery and thinking; frankly Alice and I haven't a clue how he thought this up, but we were there when he did."

"We should have taken you through the early experiments first, it would help to explain how things grew," added Alice.

Stuart said, "Don't be so modest, these two people have been fantastic contributors. So what do you think?"

"Well I couldn't believe it beforehand and having seen it… well… it must be true but everything I know about says this is false. Or everything I know is false."

"I don't think this is true," said Stuart. "Newton was right in his time as have numerous other discoveries since then, but over the last 50-odd years we haven't challenged the foundation of science. We have accepted that it was all true and built layers on layers of new theories on top. I had the fortune to discover an event that just did not fit and needed fresh thinking. My theories, I am sure will be disproved or enhanced over years to come, that's why I say it's not true. As you saw in my summary, I am sure that there may be more paired forces in varying equilibrium, we just need to find them."

"But the fact is that this discovery alone has opened up massive new sources of energy for mankind," said Jerry.

"I'm still taking it all in," said Nina, "but now I understand why our government wanted us here urgently." Lucy was already engrossed in Stuart's calculations with Alice.

They all adjourned to the club for refreshment and to get to know each other. Although the US team was tired, there was no 'off' switch and the questions kept coming although they were more informed now.

It was mid-morning when they reconvened. In the meantime Jerry, Alice, Ben and Stuart had gone through the CVs; they were all very impressive. It was agreed that they would all strengthen the team but wanted to ensure that each had a role that best met their talents.

The US team had a couple of minders from the embassy whose task was to manage all domestic arrangements including security. They were already engaged with Sam, looking at the Aldershot location facilities to house them. Each person had a very different discipline, but they were all based on historic science and it was agreed that unless they had preferences that they would all work together for a few weeks until they identified their key interest areas.

The next few months were the most special time for everyone at Farnborough, the development of vehicles moved apace with better design and better materials, the LeviProp drive was further refined. The UK/US research team was inspired. Nina and Jonathan developed an understanding with preliminary theories, on what used to be called dark matter and antimatter. Lucy concentrated on the space-time continuum and also supported Gary and Jerry with their work on managing high-level acceleration beyond the SoL. Meanwhile Harry and Alice created a protocol for flight to avoid any collisions. Stuart seemed to be everywhere acting as a catalyst to all the work. When he had spare time he concentrated it on his pet theory that there are multiple pairs of forces in varying forms of equilibrium making up the dark energy of the cosmos. He was also involved in ongoing reviews of the work that Hans and David were doing for the UN. Their brief had been in accordance with the release timetable that Dawson and Bruckner had agreed; in fact they needed the extra time to put a credible piece of work together.

Everyone knew that the work was being relayed back to the US but what wasn't known was that a shadow development team under Leo Catani was tracking behind their work by only a matter of days. The level of camaraderie and bonding made all the work exciting and it wasn't unusual for people to work long into the night and at weekends. Stuart saw Zoe pretty regularly and they re-established their friendship and support although the relationship with the kids never improved.

Meanwhile the pressure from the press continued to build with speculation of the work at Farnborough; the security increased making life more difficult. Far more ominous was the massive pressure on both governments from a number of countries to explain what was going on. Somehow leaks had happened and the level of understanding about the nature of the research was becoming clearer.

At the six-monthly inter-government reviews it was clear that action was needed to deal with these pressures.

There was a US pre-brief and Ed Bruckner was speaking. "So, in summary Ladies and Gentlemen, we have now got all we need from the collaboration with the Brits. In fact there are now a few areas where Leo and his team are ahead of the work in the UK. We will find it hard to contain other countries and so we should start the general announcement programme through the UN; the ICTP have got a project called Tangent that we have been using. I think we can manage Tangent through delaying tactics for six to twelve months after which the US will have a commanding lead in commercial and defence terms.

"It sounds like a good plan and it's what we agreed originally," said the President.

"We may have some legal issue over Intellectual Property but I'm sure our lawyers can sort it out," added Byron Garratt.

VP Vincenzo chuckled. "I was just thinking of the economic power we will have at our fingertips."

"And the Defence capability," added General Stein, "we already have a prototype land machine and fighter vehicle in test."

"One final thing, Mr President, we need Stuart Ashley here and part of the announcement."

"Why... is he really needed?"

"Yes he is; he will add the necessary weight to ensure the likes of China and Russia participate, they won't want to be left out."

"It could be difficult, Ed, I hear he is a bit of an idealist."

"That's true, but we can manage him I'm sure, beside which, our team in the UK report that he is working on something that may have a profound impact on all the work."

"Would he continue his research here?"

"I don't know. I doubt it, Mr President, but we don't want to lose the advantage we have created."

"The Brits may smell a rat, Ed, and I don't want to piss them off."

"Agreed, Mr President." He had got his way.

"OK let's open the meeting."

In fact it was a good meeting; the reported progress was well received. Stuart didn't really want to stop his research but knew he had to be part of the announcement if the whole world was to benefit. He had been thinking about it for a long time and it was now time to do something about it. He had already sent the UN team various papers with the sole objective that no one country would be disadvantaged.

The ICTP had proved to be a good route over recent months as part of the announcement programme. PM Ramsay had initialised the announcement process and a little later President Roper had opened the request for all nations to participate; Roper had won the plaudits for his open sharing approach. The UN team, including Hans and David, developed the consultation programme and an international congress was created to elicit opinions and views. These were consolidated into a number of TANGENT workstreams.

Stuart left Farnborough for the US under arrangements from their embassy; he had forgotten, or got used to, the inconspicuous security presence in his life. It suddenly became more prominent when he was part of a handover briefing to the US security folk at Heathrow. His new minder was called Kevin Angelo who was in his mid-thirties with dark thinning hair and what Stuart would call a 'ferret face'; he was medium height and wiry, wearing expensive casual clothes, not the usual US security image.

Stuart was given exceptional VIP treatment before and during his flight to New York JFK. He was amazed that somehow the press knew of his flight and so he had to be escorted out a side exit by Kevin and his people. Again the press was waiting for him at the Four Seasons hotel in Midtown and so after a brief formal welcome he was quickly ushered to his suite.

It was palatial, God knows who is paying for this, he thought; it was in the serious money bracket, in fact he could afford it himself if he could be bothered to read his bank statements. There was a large L-shaped stateroom with fantastic views of the New York skyline; it had a dining section and bar at one end and a seating area with a massive picture window across the other end. The place was furnished in a modern style with a miscellany of large paintings and sculptures. Although it wasn't his taste, the bedroom was opulent with a very modern en-suite and finally a separate study with all the communication and computing that he might want. There was a knock and Stuart opened the door to find Kevin and one of his people.

"What do you think, Stuart?" Kevin slurred it as one word.

"Quite amazing, what's the security arrangement? Fancy a drink?"

"Love to, but not on duty. Just to say we have checked the suite out and it's clean, we have also got an entry and exit system in place. There will be a few guys around but I'm sure they won't get in your way." Kevin continued, "There are no changes to your itinerary for the first few days but please let me know if anything does get updated. As we discussed on the plane Thomas Huxtable your UK ambassador will be here shortly to give you more detail." It was good timing; Kevin's man opened the door to a man and a woman. The man introduced himself.

"Mr Ashley, good afternoon I am Thomas Huxtable, and this is my wife, Lee." Huxtable was late fifties with a full face and wavy salt-pepper hair. He was mid height but slightly overweight yet impeccably dressed in a blue suit with a white shirt and some sort of club tie. Stuart's eyes were drawn to a large deep scar on his forehead. He was used to people's eyes diverting. "Skiing accident a few years ago; lucky to be alive."

Lee was from Boston and had been married to Thomas for nearly 20 years. Age had been good to her, or maybe Botox had, Stuart thought bitchily. She was petite with long highlighted hair piled up to reveal a slender neck. Somehow a waiter had entered with champagne and canapés, courtesy of the hotel. The three of them sat down with their drinks to check the arrangements for the coming week.

"It's all a bit formal, I'm afraid," said Thomas.

"And stuffy," added Lee, "but we will try and make it fun where we can."

"I hope I can get time to work on the forthcoming announcement," said Stuart.

"I notice you have a meeting with Hans Smit to update you on the UN work," he replied. "Anyway tonight is supper with the Mayor and local dignitaries and tomorrow a meeting with the UN Secretary

General."

"It's all so unreal and a lot of fuss on my account."

"Stuart, I really don't think you understand your importance, I heard that you were a diffident idealist. People want to meet you, be seen with you; like it or not there will be a lot of sycophants as well as one hell of a lot of publicity and I promise that I will help where I can."

Stuart knew it was true, that why he had been dreading the trip.

Lee took his arm. "Don't be so alarmed, it will work out."

Both things were true; there was a lot of sycophancy and Thomas and Lee Huxtable were an enormous help.

The meeting with the UN went very well; the congress had endorsed the various TANGENT workstreams and was in the process of inviting nominations from a number of countries to provide leadership on the impact of IC. This was exactly what Stuart was hoping although the Director General was vague about some countries' participation, notably Russia. He was highly complementary on the contribution from the UK and Stuart was surprised at his breadth of knowledge.

"I have to deal with a lot of problems, but frankly when I look at the impact of your discovery, it makes me very nervous and the TANGENT Programme seems to be the only way to keep some order in the world."

Before he left, Stuart had a chance to chat with Hans and David who were optimistic on their progress; they arranged to meet later on in that week. Next stop was Columbia University for a meeting of academics. In the underground car park he was ushered towards the black limousine that was sandwiched by two other similar cars. Suddenly there was a tremendous crash followed by an explosion. The force knocked Stuart to the ground, his ears were ringing, and his right arm was twisted behind his back, there was thick smoke everywhere and he felt someone pulling at him. He then heard what he assumed to be gunfire and another explosion. There was a cacophony of horns and sirens echoing around him but no more gunfire. The smoke began to clear showing a big fire burning behind one of the cars. Stuart tried to move but as he tried to rise there was a sharp pain across his shoulder. The confusion increased as more people arrived, and a man was talking to him, but he couldn't hear anything but the ringing, the pain made him gasp and he lost consciousness for a moment. He felt people pulling at him and lifting him, he opened his eyes to find himself on a stretcher. The last thing he remembered was being lifted into an ambulance.

He opened his eyes, there was still a ringing in his ears, but it was more muted, his right arm was strapped up and immoveable. He saw Kevin Angelo sitting beside the bed; he looked strained.

"Do you know what happened?"

"It's still being pieced together," he replied.

"Why? Did they want to kill me?"

"It's a possibility, but it looks like they wanted to kidnap you."

"Are all your men OK?"

"Everyone in the rear car were killed," he said in a matter of fact way. "Your driver was wounded but everyone else survived."

"And the attackers?"

"Two killed, the rest escaped."

"I'm so sorry, it's my fault."

"It's our job to protect you and we fucked up. I'll get the doctor."

A middle-aged man in casual clothes came in. "Good to see you awake, how do you feel?"

"Lucky," Stuart replied with a feeble smile, "it's hard to hear, everything is muffled."

"The explosion, sound and pressure does that, it should slowly repair but may take a couple of weeks."

"And my arm?"

"Nothing to worry about, badly dislocated so it will ache for a while plus a few bruises here and there."

"Where am I?"

"In New York; this is a secure wing of a local hospital," he said vaguely.

"We've let all your folk know you are OK and we plan to move you to one of our safe places upstate tomorrow, so you can recover."

Meanwhile over a secure video connection, "Shit, I thought your people were the best." It was Peter Dawson.

"It was a very professional job and they nearly succeeded if the second car had detonated properly… well it could have been another outcome," said Bruckner.

"What next? Do you have a plan?"

"We are moving him to a safe house tomorrow and I think we could keep him there until the UN Taskforce meets in a few weeks' time. Meanwhile we put out a joint communications saying he is fine and will be participating at the taskforce summit. A bit of rest won't harm him anyway."

Dawson thought for a while. "OK let's go with it, but I may come back to you if the PM disagrees. Can we get Henry Huxtable to see him?"

"Of course."

"You know, I'm beginning to have misgivings about this TANGENT thing; I thinks it's too hard trying to get every country to drop their self-interest… your country included."

"UK as well?"

"Yes UK as well." They closed the videoconference.

Stuart was still feeling unwell when the Ambassador came to see him. "If it's any consolation, Stuart, they're pretty sure it was a kidnap plot."

"Great," Stuart said with a thumping headache.

"Actually there is a view that there are forces who would like to end your life, so we have agreed with the US people to keep you in their safe place for a while such that you are ready to pick up your role in the TANGENT Programme."

"How long will that be?"

"A matter of weeks I am told. I have updated all the team in the UK plus your wife."

"Ex-wife." He felt the recent sedatives take effect. "OK see you soon."

That evening an innocuous ambulance left the hospital for Glens Falls.

CHAPTER 15

Springboard

Stuart fell into a light sleep having overdosed on champagne and movies. When the plane landed at Heathrow he felt awful; it was a combination of a hangover and all the physical unpleasantness that that long flights offer. Various officials ushered him into an antiseptic area with bright lights, just to manage the formalities they said. As they waited, Stuart looked out of the smoke glass window onto the runway complex, it was early morning, dull with a gentle drizzle. Somehow he felt home but desperately needed a hearty breakfast. What a journey these last 18 months had been.

Chris and Rose had made all the arrangements for his arrival. They had all agreed that initially a stay in his old apartment in Farnborough made most sense from a privacy and security standpoint. As he arrived, he passed the now permanent group of press at the entrance. During the months away a lot had changed, the site refurbishment had taken great strides and a new glass building was underway and the security seemed more evident. There were a lot more temporary offices at the rear by the hangar area, but Stuart was relieved that his small apartment was intact. It was late morning when he decided to take a quick tour.

At the main building he saw Sam Hewitt through the office window; she was with Felix Weymouth the site security man. She came running from her office and gave Stuart a big hug.

"Glad you're home," she said, "you look OK. Come on in and tell me everything."

"Haven't you been kept posted?" he said with a smile.

"Oh yes, Stuart, classic stuff, just enough information to keep me advised," she said laughing; Felix grimaced a bit in the background.

He was about to tell his story when Rob, Jerry, Alice and Froom came in.

"Just heard you were here," said Rob with a hug. "Glad you're back, matey."

"We've made some interesting developments," said Froom rather formally. "You must come over and have a look."

"I intend to," said Stuart overwhelmed at the reception.

"Thank God you're back," said Jerry. "Let's talk later."

Alice had been holding back; then she clung onto him and cried.

"Well, I was just about to tell Sam what happened so now I can share it," he said as Alice released him and wiped her tears. It took over an hour to go through everything from the early UN meeting then the attempted kidnap and incarceration at Glens Falls to the big UN TANGENT meeting and his re-incarceration. Then there was the real kidnap and the adventure on the ship and finally his safety in Canada. The questions were thick and fast concerning the devious motives of the US people and the incompetence of the UK. In truth some of was speculation since there were many unknowns in the whole narrative.

The meeting broke at lunchtime and Stuart and Rob slipped out for beer at the local; the continued security was very discreet. He was now working full-time at Farnborough, he and Sue had recently moved nearby, citing Smythfield as a changed place with Stuart's old place now an emerging museum for the history of the discovery.

"They have even reproduced the old experiments," he said, "and a copy of the Paradox, but with a new LeviProp drive," he laughed. Sue had seen Zoe recently and she seemed content in her new mansion.

"No women in her life?"

"Not that I know, Stu, she is back doing voluntary work supporting the arts down at Winchester."

They chatted through the past, which had created such a bond and knew that they would easily slip into the old routine of working together. Once back onsite Froom marched him to the main hangar; it too had changed and was unrecognisable. It was a clean high tech area now with many people in blue overalls with LeviProp printed on the back. The hangar was sectioned into about ten areas each with a specific role; Froom would not wear the overalls but instead make a concession to the clean area by wearing a white lab coat. There were several shelves containing an array of identical round cylinders each with an X-shaped bracket on either end.

"LeviProp drives," said Froom, "the new factory has been producing them for a while and we have new factories coming online soon."

"They look very different from the original," said Stuart.

"Not really, we have changed the frame and added a protective casing; otherwise the guts are the same. We have had to add a governor though, to stop anyone being daft enough to try and use all the power. Some are built to operate at a specific height from the ground so there is no need for the vertical controls." He led Stuart to the other side of the hangar where a team was in final assembly of a number of similar vehicles. "These are a sort of tractor, I suppose, they are destined for various farms. Their pulling power is beyond anything they will ever need. We are already franchising a factory in Nigeria." They walked across to another area where Stuart instantly recognised a PowerParadox.

"It's had a lot of changes, so we can better control it remotely. The guys are working on the environmental systems, so we can take it into space. I think Gary Marshall copied a lot of it before returning to the States. Let's go to the old hangar, it's been renovated and is where we have some interesting things to show you." Froom hadn't changed, his passion for excellence was undiminished and he proudly showed Stuart one of the new buses they were assembling.

"It looks like a conventional bus," said Stuart.

"We thought it would be a good idea to keep with a familiar design; when moving, it operates at a fixed height from the ground and with various sensors to activate the drive such that the vehicle will always keep away from any objects in any direction. We've now got one version that serves as a train carriage."

They went over to another area of activity where they were

building a smaller vehicle.

"This is the family flyer," Froom announced. "It operates under driver control like a car when at one metre high. It has the same crash avoidance system that was on the coach. It can also run under highway mode at high speed where the lane management system is in control. The same applies to high speed at altitude but we have yet to figure out the traffic rules."

"Good idea," said Stuart, "I think we're a long way from agreeing a set of traffic rules," remembering back to the UN meeting.

"In the meantime, the government has insisted we develop a LeviProp drive to replace the jet engines on existing planes although Boeing and Lockheed are ahead of us already."

It was all too much; Stuart felt exhausted and skipped supper in the canteen for his bed. He awoke early and after breakfast joined Jerry and Alice in the Research Centre. He noticed Jonathan Ben was there.

"Didn't he go back with rest of the US team?" he asked Jerry.

"He did but asked to come back after a few weeks."

"So he is our resident spy?"

"Felix's security people say not, he is motivated by the team and its work, apparently he dislikes Catani and his standards. He knows he is constantly monitored, anyway he works well with Alice and I think there is some special chemistry there."

"Gary thinks Catani is pretty good." They all sat down to give Stuart an update on their work.

They still hadn't solved the problem with the disappearance of PowerParadox largely due to insufficient data, however they had developed the control system to allow the next PowerParadox to accelerate in very small units that will enable more data to be recorded. Jerry had also made progress on the existence of multiple pairs of forces.

Stuart had been thinking about the same problem for some time, during his interment. "Just suppose that the cosmos comprises many of these structures of paired forces in every dimension and that matter is the result. Where the equilibrium is disaggregated it creates a disturbance that tries to rebalance the equilibrium; this perhaps would explain black holes and wormholes."

"Yes but what causes the disaggregation?

"Good question and I don't know, but it's where I want to focus my thinking. We, for example, are causing the disaggregation by using one particular force on our vehicles."

"True and how did it all start?" said Alice.

"God knows, Alice, but the deeper we go, the more questions it causes. You know I am concerned about cause and effect. If we use this unlimited free power then what happens to the balance in the cosmos, is it an atom in the ocean or something... more... damaging?"

"I'm glad you're back," she said with a grin.

"So am I, for what it's worth, I think we are playing with time as well."

"How so?" it was Jonathan Ben who was listening to the conversation.

"Well Einstein predicted that time ran more slowly in strong gravity. If we know that gravity is not constant but is the product of some temporary equilibrium of forces then it may be possible to control that equilibrium and change time."

"Well, we are controlling that equilibrium now," added Alice.

"No Alice, we are using it but not controlling it."

They all agreed to maintain the existing research workstreams and add Stuart's idea as well.

He was surprised to see Rose later that day; she had come down from London to update him on the Strategic Development work. She was wearing a tight-fitting dress that showed her athletic frame; she sensed him looking at her.

"Yes?" she said, with a hint of annoyance.

"Sorry Rose, it's just a very sexy dress, not like you normally wear." He was digging a hole.

"Actually, Stuart, I have a varied wardrobe and it's none of your business."

"I'm out of line, Rose, it was meant to be a compliment but then my skills with the opposite sex are not good, well you probably know more about me than I do."

"Yes I probably do; and you are a strange one, Stuart. You have a mind capable of incredible originality combined with a compulsive /obsessive disorder and an idealism that is positively naïve."

"Is that all?" he said with a disarming grin.

"No, on top of that, a veneer of authority supported by insecurity and diffidence, you are a wonder to behold." The grin disappeared, and he got up to leave. She held his arm. "What a crazy mix, it makes you very special, and actually... I think you are very special," with that she gave him a gentle kiss on the cheek.

His heart was thumping, and he felt confused and flushed; they held one another, nothing more, they just stayed in an embrace.

"So what happens now?"

"I don't know, Stuart, it's unprofessional of me."

"I don't care about that, but it could make things... complex."

It was her turn to grin. "Let's just take it slowly and see where things lead."

"Agreed, I don't really know anything about you; can we have lunch or supper sometime?"

"Let's go for next Saturday evening, I may not have Peter Dawson demanding something immediately."

"Done, Ill fix something in London; back to business." It was an easy transition.

Rose gave him a document showing the progress of each workstreams, giving her views on the international implications. Stuart was keen to get a broader picture on the post Tangent world. "It's all rather predicable, and happening so fast," said Rose, "the US are claiming they have developed a different IC drive and will not pay any license fees. The LeviProp lawyers are putting a case together but frankly the stakes are too high for the US to give in. All the major car manufacturers have announced new models with IC drives. Boeing and Lockheed are already designing new planes and our intelligence tells us that General Electric and IBM are building new generator sets. So the US thinks it has got what it always wanted, continued control of the world economy."

"But the UK is benefiting isn't it?" he queried.

"Very much so; the arrangement with the EU is commercially very powerful to us. Most countries are keen to engage with LeviProp and that will prevent the US domination since as we agreed LeviProp is only providing the drive units, there is an outstanding deal with South America on the table as we speak. The arrangements with Canada will further support out interests." She was looking at some papers as she continued, "The oil producing countries have reduced their output significantly which has pushed up prices and they are buying even more transport related industries. We think this is just their first shot and things are going to get very nasty. It's what we expected them to do, but sadly increases the pressure on using IC as an alternative to oil even more. Global markets are fragile; we have had some major peaks and troughs in the last two months, it's been pretty bad."

"I knew a bit about it when I surfaced in Canada, but Chris didn't brief me on the detail and how serious it was."

"Not was, but is Stuart, this is going to run for a few years before things stabilise."

"What about China and Russia?"

"Our best intelligence says that they are both investing heavily in IC development, with Russia mainly focusing on military applications. India has already created a prototype as well."

"What a mess, if only TANGENT had worked."

"Don't kid yourself, Stuart; it was flawed from the start."

"Did you know that Rose… truthfully?"

"No, Stuart, we knew there were lots of traps but genuinely thought we could find a way through. There are so many international issues like protocols, standards and transport rules that some remnants of TANGENT will need restarting." They chatted through more detail and the activities of several people who had been involved before his incarceration.

She kissed him on the cheek as she left, leaving Stuart in turmoil. No matter how hard he tried, he just couldn't stop thinking about

Rose. It was strange, he thought, that throughout this escapade I have run into her so many times and yet never recognised her for anything but a serious government official.

He turned the matters over in his head and an idea began to form. He knew he had already accrued a lot of money and decided to create a charity that would ensure that disadvantaged countries would benefit from LeviProp. The universal tractor that Froom had built could be ideal. He had tried to balance the scales and it didn't work. He had learned the lesson the hard way; he now knew the best way was to put his finger on one side of the scales.

There was a lot to do, and a lot to catch up on, so the days were full when suddenly it was Saturday. He had booked a little Italian restaurant around Waterloo at her request and killed time beforehand by walking along the Queen's walk; it was good to see the Thames and people enjoying themselves on the Southbank; nobody seemed to notice him. He still arrived a little early and felt the same old nerves eating into his stomach. It was a small homely place, run by an Italian lady with her family in tow. He had just ordered a drink when she arrived. Her hair was piled up in a messy contrived way, her makeup was barely noticeable, she removed an old fur coat from the fifties, underneath she wore tight black leather trousers with a large fancy brown belt and a sleeveless black top which showed off her shoulders and neck. The torq of white gold set off the honey colour of her skin.

"You look fantastic," he said.

"I told you I had a varied wardrobe," she replied with a laugh.

As they settled at the table Stuart realised how comfortable he felt with Rose. Maybe it was because she knew so much about him; he could just be himself.

"Some ground rules," she started, "it's OK to talk about work especially if things are bugging you."

"Why do you say that?" he asked.

"Because that's who you are, and if you try to adapt and be something else you will just get frustrated." A man on the adjacent table asking for a photo with him interrupted them. Rose nodded gently at Stuart and he relaxed as the man's wife took the photo.

"It's like this all the time; I am sorry."

"Stuart, don't beat yourself up, you can't hide yourself away, just relax and go with the flow. I'm OK with it, you are famous and that's an end to it." She was right; of course, he had relinquished his privacy a long time ago, it just jarred with him sometimes. At least the other people in the restaurant were giving him space.

It was late when they left the restaurant; time had gone so quickly.

"It's been great, Stuart, thanks for a lovely evening. I hope we can do it again." It was a strong signal that their evening had ended. She put her arms around him and he gave her a gentle kiss on the cheek.

"I hope I can see you again. Like this. Away from work."

"I would like it too but let's go slowly." She turned and kissed him fully; his heart was racing, and he knew she sensed it.

"I'm down in Farnborough on Tuesday, let's talk then." She walked off in the direction of Whitehall.

His driver appeared from nowhere, they have a check protocol to ensure all was safe and he got in. On the way home he considered his relationships. Somehow Zoe had now become a friend and he no longer had desires for her, something he couldn't explain. He loved being with Harry, life was so unpredictable, but he couldn't be like that all the time. Rose on the other hand was brilliant, witty and, he thought, very sexy. I could spend the rest of my life with her, he mused, but she has a serious career and has obviously been hurt in some way and doesn't want to rush things.

Rose was thinking very differently. She had been infatuated with Stuart from early on. She had tried to analyse herself. Why was she behaving like an adolescent, it was unbecoming and so she had mentally shut him out until… last week. She thought back to the time when she felt the same about someone; it was Russell, her soulmate for nearly five years; he had committed suicide ten years ago; she never knew why, and she blamed herself for not sensing his distress.

Stuart is a very complex man with an awesome intellect, was she enough for him, she wondered, the emotional self-doubt seem to be resurrecting itself? In spite of all these emotions she held on to the idea that she and Stuart could make a relationship work but only with small assuring steps.

And so it proceeded, in those small steps with both of them savouring the moments. Their relationship quickly became public, with Rob saying something about it being about time. Even Peter Dawson indirectly mentioned how he valued Rose and he watched out for her welfare, Nigel on the other hand gave an uncharacteristic wink when he came into a meeting with them.

They spent much of their spare time in each other's company, with many evenings spent eating together and then reading or listening to music. At Rose's insistence, she always went home although sometimes their parting became so passionate that he hoped she would stay. Then the inevitable happened; it was gentle and loving, finally creating the union that they both wanted.

It was over a year since their relationship has blossomed and it rested on a foundation of emotional security, with every day being a renewal of affection; in their openness they both wondered how long it would last.

Last, it did, and finally they felt safe enough to live together. They planned to find an apartment in London, but it would have to be close to Whitehall and have very secure facilities; it would be a long search.

CHAPTER 16

Bad Timing

The latest GPS Operation Control Systems Centre in the US runs real-time correction between the satellite atomic clocks and the ground clocks. It was early January when one of the scientists at the centre noticed a minor change in synchronising their time with Coordinated Universal Time. There had been a divergence in the past due to the precision of ground receivers and so it was recorded, and an investigation was started. It was all part of the normal process of keeping the system functioning properly.

In Boulder, Colorado, there was one of the largest examples of Foucault's Pendulum in the world. That same January, the university assistant tasked with keeping Pendulum in motion highlighted a minor deviation in its tracking. The information was not really used for anything these days apart from demonstrating the rotation of the earth to students. It had happened once before when one of the staff had inadvertently operated a vacuum cleaner nearby.

THE END...?

Printed in Great Britain
by Amazon